THE MARK

Hugh C. Rae

HUGH C. RAE was born in Glasgow in
1935. For 14 years he was an assistant in the
antiquarian department of a Glasgow
bookshop. He now writes full-time and
lives in a Stirlingshire village with his wife
and daughter.

His first novel, *Skinner*, was published by
Anthony Blond in 1964. THE MARKSMAN
is his sixth book.

The Marksman

HUGH C. RAE

SPHERE BOOKS LIMITED

Sphere Books Ltd
27 Wrights Lane, London W8 5TZ

First published in Great Britain in 1971
by Constable & Company Ltd.
© Hugh C. Rae, 1971
First Sphere Books edition 1973
Reprinted 1987

TRADE
MARK

Printed and bound in Great Britain by
Cox & Wyman Ltd, Reading

'While many biologists consider it a violation of reality to construct mechanical models for the behaviour of living things, mechanistic language does often offer a convenient way of correlating disparate events, which appear to have a casual relation to one another. With this disclaimer one can compare a releaser mechanism to the trigger of a gun. When a marksman presses the trigger of a gun, the only control he can exercise over the subsequent behaviour of the bullet is directional. He can point the barrel here or there. The actual behaviour of the bullet itself, its velocity, is determined by the cartridge that encloses it—the amount of powder and its speed of combustion.'

John Bleibtreu: *The Parable of the Beast*

PART ONE

ONE

The city had altered out of all proportion to the time he had been away. He walked its streets like a stranger now, ringed by unfamiliar vistas. Ranges of high-rise flats, office developments and the buttes of a new components plant rose up from the ridges. The flanks of the low delta of the Wickerburn were scarred with demolition pits and smouldering junk fires purled hanks of oily smoke across the excavated earth. Pubs, picture houses, bookie joints and chapels, monuments whose durability Weaver had never doubted, stood gaunt and shattered as if warring armies had battled savagely back and forth across this quarter of the town. Weaver felt no nostalgia at the devastation which progress had wrought on his former stamping grounds. He was full of a rage sparked by other causes, consciously held it tamped down in his gut as he strode up the Wickerburn and swung into the reach of sandstone tenements which was all that remained of Nimmo Street. The stink came out to meet him like an old hound welcoming the master home; the stink of his youth, ripened by an additional half decade of decay; cat piss and seeping gas, cooking fat and cabbage. He entered the close mouth, climbed quickly to the top landing and braced himself in front of the door; a big man, hard-faced, his skin burned walnut by the Spanish sun, the bespoke overcoat fitting him snugly; not like the shabby runt who had run from this place five years back. The scroll of tarnished brass which his grandfather had screwed into the wood sixty years ago had been replaced by a small tartan-backed brick with a stranger's name picked out of the plastic. Even before his foot hit the door she was screaming at him to go back to hell where he belonged.

He measured the distance and lashed out. His heel stamped the cracked and peeling varnish close to the lock, and her voice dribbled away under the sound of splintering oak. He struck again, and the iron capping embedded in the post gave way with a sound like a pistol shot. His shoulder carried him through into the lobby. The lobby was hardly bigger than a coffin, narrowed down by the coke bunker which his father, a carpenter to trade, had built into the corner. The woman was nowhere in sight. He swung right and stabbed out with his foot once more and the kitchen door flew open. She was crouched in the corner by the stove closet, cowering, the kid cradled against her shoulder and pinned by one hand. In the other hand she held the knife. The knife had a wicked serrated edge and was longer than Muriel's forearm. She waved it at him in posturing defiance as he crossed the room, but the child hampered her. Weaver whipped his cheek back from the blade and reached in from her blind side, caught her wrist and choked off all further movement. Her wrist was no thicker than a twig and he could have snapped it without effort. He broke the knife from her grasp and flung it sidewise across the room. It skidded and vanished under the trailing quilt of the bed in the alcove. Holding her tightly, enveloped in the aura of her hysterical keening and the child's sobbing, he stared at her for the first time in five years. She had the same ravaged look as the streets of Wickerburn, the flesh of her face and body pared away by fatigue and the inroads of fear. Even her fine blonde hair was as coarse as ram's wool. She did not seem like anyone he had ever known.

'Who told you, Weaver?'

'Your old man.'

'The bastard.'

'What happened?'

'Didn't the interfering old blabbermouth tell you that too?'

'Who killed him?' Weaver said.

'Think I know?'

'Why didn't you write?'

'Write where?' she shouted. 'I didn't know where you'd gone. I didn't care either, you and your whore.'

'What about the kid?' Weaver acknowledged the child. He clung to the woman, head across her shoulder, settled now, more coy than scared.

'Mine! Not bloody yours, Weaver. Mine!'

10

Weaver released her. He did not retreat though, holding her penned in the corner, her buttocks against the edge of the stove. 'Tell me about Gordon.'

'Gordon's dead,' she said. 'If you'd been around maybe it wouldn't have happened.'

'How was he killed?'

'Murdered.'

'What did the cops do about it?'

'Bogies!' She grinned viciously. 'Christ, what did the bogies ever do that was right?'

'They searched,' Weaver said, 'so what did they find?'

'Nothing,' she said. 'A big fat nothing. Not that they'd condescend to tell me, anyway. I mean, I was only the mother. The poor wee bastards get themselves chopped every night of the week and it's good bloody riddance as far as the bogies are concerned.'

'I don't believe that.'

'Ach, who cares what you believe, Weaver.'

'Did they enquire about me?'

'Aye, I thought that aspect would worry you,' the woman said. 'I told them you were dead. You *were* dead, Weaver, to me at any rate. Now get t'hell back where you belong and leave me in peace. I don't want you here.'

'My bank sent you money?'

'Sure, it did,' Muriel said. 'You can always trust a bank. It came regular every quarter.'

'The money was for Gordon.'

'What are you goin't'do now, big man: buy him back to life?'

He checked his hand four inches from her throat, the fingers spread out and the thumb hooked to fit her windpipe, then he let it drop. She was still now, watching him, silent. He took breath into his lungs and released it, blowing out his cheeks.

'All right,' he said. 'Gordon's dead; I knew that. I came back to find out who did it and why it happened.'

'Then ask my old man. He found you and he brought you back, so he can fend for you, Weaver. I'm a married woman with a kid of my own, legal and legitimate this time, and I don't want you around spoiling it for me. I don't ever want to see you again, understand?'

Weaver's mouth was as dry as shell-sand and his gut

11

ached; for all that, his explosive rage had diminished. Ever since Doyle's letter had caught up with him he had lived with that rage hot as steam in his belly, lived with it and contained it while he squared his affairs and got out to the airport, flew up to Scotland, drove through the heart of the city then, prudent even in anger, had gone on foot through the neighbourhood of the Wickerburn. Now that the rage had gone, grief would take its place. He would coax the anger to heat again when he needed it, so scald the guilt which was part of it too.

'No more, Weaver,' Muriel said. 'For God's sake, no more.'

She wept, not lowering her head, lifting up her cheeks to show him her tears as if she hoped that they would be token enough of her humanity to appease him.

'Where is your old man?' Weaver said. 'Same place?'

'I suppose so,' she said. 'I haven't seen him.'

The tears streaked her cheeks and freshened them. The child touched the wetness with delicate curiosity but uttered no sound.

Weaver took the wallet from his pocket and slipped out the notes. He folded them across his thumb and held them out to her. She looked at them as if he had offered her dirt.

'For the door,' Weaver said.

Muriel did not move.

He dropped the money at her feet, then turned and walked out.

She did not pursue him, but when he reached the street he sensed that she had taken shelter behind the bedroom drapes and was standing there with the baby in her arms, watching him go. He stepped briskly round the corner into Wickerburn Road and headed south towards the Underground.

TWO

Doyle was drunk. It took him some time to find the proper combination for the simple latch, and drag the door ajar. He peered blearily through the opening, then, with obsequious haste jerked it open all the way. Watching the old man, Weaver moved into the hallway. God knows, Doyle had been old enough when he left Glasgow but at least there had been some evidence of vigour in him. Now all that was left of Vincent Doyle was a desiccated hulk, eerie, tall and lank and almost weightless, like a spectre. Bookshelves, roughly fashioned from bricks and found timber, lined the hall, the planks warped by the weight of the volumes stuffed into them. From the books Doyle borrowed a little of his substance; he was as sallow as calfskin, fragile as rice paper, and the backs of his long hands were brown foxed like spoiled parchment. Shuffling soundlessly over the bare boards, he led Weaver into the parlour. This was the smallest of the flat's four rooms and in it Doyle had built his nest. His armchair, his writing table, his bureau and his cabinets of catalogues and journals were housed here, all clustered round a deep black untidy grate. A half bottle of Black & White whisky was clenched in one of Doyle's fists, two cheap thick glass tumblers fingered in the other.

'You'll take a dram, Weaver?'

'I saw Muriel.'

'Did you now?' Doyle said. 'Then you'll be in sore need of this.'

Weaver took the offered glass and sipped the whisky. It did not comfort him. Doyle downed three mouthfuls in a single swallow and, with seeming embarrassment, waited.

Weaver said, 'The letter only caught up with me last night. I've been out of the country.'

'I reckoned that was the way of it,' Doyle said. He

13

lowered himself carefully into the armchair and gestured to the swivel chair by the bureau. 'Sit down.'

Weaver wheeled the chair closer to the hearth and seated himself. The old man was studying him closely. Some of his animation had returned, a flush of his former vitality.

'I'm glad you saw fit to come, Donald.'

'Did you think I wouldn't?' Weaver said.

'I'd no way of knowing how it was with you,' Doyle said. 'But there was nobody else to turn to.'

'Not even Muriel?'

'She doesn't give a damn now,' Doyle said. 'I'm told she had herself another bairn?'

'You really haven't seen her?'

'No.' Doyle pursed his lips for a moment, then grinned. 'You seem to be in fine fettle, any roads.'

Weaver remembered how alcohol had always rendered Doyle cunning. There was a characteristic deviousness in him which, mated to his introverted nature, protected him.

'I made a couple of good hits,' Weaver said. 'Then the pressure went on and I baled out. I've been in Spain for over a year.'

'What sort of hits?'

'A bank and a payroll.'

'Good company?'

'The best,' Weaver said. 'Not like up here; no hick stuff.'

Doyle glanced at the expensive material of Weaver's suit, and took another mouthful of whisky. 'Gordon was murdered,' he said. 'Did I mention that in the letter?'

'But no details,' Weaver said. 'How was it done?'

'He was roped to the back axle of a truck, then the truck was gunned at considerable velocity back and forward across some waste ground. Gordon didn't survive.' Doyle tipped the bottle and leaked whisky into Weaver's tumbler, then into his own. Weaver swallowed, but the stuff in his throat was like a ball of beeswax which would not dissolve. Doyle said, 'Our friends the bogies made a full investigation but in this instance the best efforts of the law were not sufficient. No arrest was made.'

'All right,' Weaver said. 'Who did it?'

'I don't know.'

'Didn't you try to find out?'

'It's not like that, Donald,' Doyle said. 'It's not like that at all. *Nobody* knows who did it.'

'So you didn't lift a finger, you lousy old sot.'

Doyle's pupils were the colour of laundered denim, creased with a multitude of minute lines, blue on paler blue. 'I could do nothing,' he stammered. 'The bogies were all over. I was hamstrung. Listen, they did try, they tried hard. They thought there was a madman on the prowl, but in the end they found nothing and the case burned out. You know how it is.'

'I know how it is,' Weaver said, coldly. 'What did they lack—evidence for a conviction?'

'It would seem that they didn't even have a suspect worth rubbing,' Doyle said. 'No motive; no suspects; no clues at all.'

'Was Muriel married then?'

'Just.'

'Pregnant?'

'Is it relevant?'

'Was she pregnant?'

'Perhaps; I'm not certain.'

'How well did you know Gordon?'

'He came to the shop occasionally. I suppose you could say I knew him well enough.'

'Better than I did,' Weaver said. 'What sort was he?'

'A quiet lad,' Doyle said. 'Open though. He had no secrets, nothing hidden.'

'Then what was he doing way out on the waste ground of North Grahamshill?'

'Again, nobody knows for sure,' Doyle said. 'Walking, like as not. He was a great one for walking.'

The swivel chair slid away, tilted then crashed back against the wall. 'He was only twelve years old,' Weaver shouted. 'Who kills a twelve-year-old for no reason, for Christ's sake?'

'It happens.'

'Wait,' Weaver gripped the old man by the shoulder. His hand looked incongruously clean against the ragged knit of the cardigan. 'You mean it was one of the packs?'

'Possibly!' Doyle ignored the pain from the bite of the fingers, staring down at the smudge of coal in the centre of the grate. 'But with the packs it's usually something brisk, a blade or a boot. The bogies explored that avenue of the investigation too, but got nowhere with it.'

'The packs don't kill kids?'

'No, they don't *kill* often at all,' Doyle said. 'They kick and they butt and they use the bayonet but somehow they manage not to kill—lucky fellows.'

'Exactly how long since it happened?'

'Fourteen months,' Doyle said. 'On the last night of September, last year Muriel had been married about three weeks.'

'Why did she break with you?'

'We were never close, Donald; you know that.'

'But something happened,' Weaver said. 'Was it the marriage or the killing?'

'I advised her not to marry him. I told her you'd come back; but she married him anyway.'

'I'd no intention of coming back.'

'No,' Doyle said. 'I never expected it. I only wanted her to think again; for the boy's sake as much as anything.'

'Who is the guy, the husband?'

'His name's Brand. He's a steel-worker, forty-odd, fond of his jar. He had nothing to do with it, if that's what you're thinking.'

'And that's the whole story?' Weaver said.

'Aye, that's it all,' Doyle said. 'Except for one thing, one new factor.'

'What's that?'

'You.'

The cab reversed and backed tightly towards the lights of the city, slewed and shot off between the houses, leaving Doyle and Weaver alone on the perimeter of the waste ground. In the middle distance the land lifted steeply to the neglected, ramshackle mansions of the Ridgeway where the gentry had once lived.

'Is this it?'

'That direction.' Doyle shivered and huddled into the folds of the duffle coat which, though threadbare now, still kept out the chill. 'Changed a good deal in the last year. I came only once; just to see, you know.'

To Weaver's left the back gardens of the houses in

Connell Street hedged the road, marking the outer reaches of North Grahamshill. The area did not have the air of a Glasgow suburb, but rather that of a small mining community. Damp November darkness swallowed the far horizons so that Weaver could easily sustain the illusion that nothing lay out there but fallow pastures and the ochre heaps of shale dumps.

The men walked side by side along the pavement. It was cracked and pot-holed and mud-flecked like a newly excavated relic of the Roman period. The open acres adjacent to it were planted with surveyors' stakes and construction dumps, tarns of mud and sour surface ash, foundation pits like mass graves and long bunkers of flung clay, all protected by lattices of close-mesh fencing ten or twelve feet high. One crane, beanstalk tall, sprouted to the sky. A warning light was starred on its topmost strut to steer clear the pilots of the big jets making the run for Renfrew airport.

'Where did it happen; the exact spot?'

'At the third or fourth pole of the fence.'

'How would Gordon come here?' Weaver asked.

'Most likely via Connell Street; or he could have come over the Ridgeway.'

'What would attract him to this dump?'

'No idea,' Doyle said. 'The Ridgeway's dead and Grahamshill's no better.'

'That's something else we'll have to find out.'

'I wonder if it's a chimera worth pursuing,' Doyle said.

They stopped where the pavement ran close to the thrust of tall oxalic-white fencing.

'What do you mean?' asked Weaver.

'Even if we find all the answers, what can we do about it?'

'Kill the bastard.'

'I'm not sure,' Doyle said. 'I'm not sure I could bring myself to do that.'

'I'll do it,' Weaver said.

Doyle nodded. 'Good.'

'Is that the real reason you brought me back here?'

'It was only right you should be told.'

'You want me to track down the killer, don't you?'

'Gordon was maybe more of a grandson to me than he was son to you,' Doyle said, slowly. 'Never mind whether you married Muriel or not; it makes no difference now.

I've considered all this for long enough and I've weighed up the justice of it, and the system.'

'And?'

'I want the bastard killed, too.'

'So you send for me?'

'Are you afraid to do it?'

Weaver laughed. The sound was as dry as a handful of corn-husks tossed on to the ash. It blew softly and dispersed through the moist cold air over the waste ground. 'Old man, you find him and I'll kill him.'

'Good,' Doyle said again.

'But where is he?'

Doyle shifted his head, the gesture gentle and patient but not like that of an old man any longer. 'Out there.'

'All right,' Weaver said. 'We'll find him.'

Doyle smiled. 'I knew you'd come, Donald, and I knew what you'd want to do. It's you I've been waiting for for fourteen bloody months.'

He watched Weaver covertly, but the younger man was no longer listening. He seemed to be searching the skyline, from the outriggers of Wickerburn to the flat, uniform rooftops of North Grahamshill. Whatever thing of value he might have discovered here had long since gone. After a while Doyle touched his sleeve. Weaver turned away and they walked back towards the lighted streets. The cold denuded acres and the close-mesh fence dropped out of sight.

'I couldn't do it myself,' Doyle said, abruptly. 'I couldn't, you know.'

'I know.' Weaver saddled the old man's shoulder with his hand again, but this time the touch was light.

THREE

With cheap striped pyjamas buttoned close around his throat Doyle looked like a whisky priest in a penal settlement. Stubble like a sprinkle of rock salt coated his jowls and his muscles were slack. He lay on his back with his arms by his sides. Weaver squeezed the spectacles on to his nose and held the coffee cup just where he could see it. Doyle's wash-blue eyes were bright, however, and there was no trace of tremor in the tendons of his hand. Maybe, Weaver thought, the nerves have taken too big a beating from a thousand ferocious hangovers and had finally become inured to the effects of excess alcohol. Doyle's lank fingers wrapped themselves around the cup and he scooped it gladly to his mouth. Resting the rim on his lower lip he breathed the scalding liquid back into his throat, hissing.

Weaver perched himself on the bed end.

Daylight had not yet come to beat on the northern drum, but Weaver had fallen into the habit of rising early during his tenure of the villa in Spain. It was cool there in the mornings, a breeze from the sea driving the stink of the town inland, away from the hillside villa. Weaver had breakfasted on the patio, sometimes alone or sometimes with the woman he had had the night before. He could not believe that he was really here in Glasgow. He had imagined that he would never set foot in the city again; the thought had brought no grief with it, only relief, as if a burden he had been obliged to carry since boyhood had been shed once and for all.

'What time is it, then?'

Weaver glanced at the dial on the Rolex on his wrist. 'Almost eight.'

'Jesus!'

'Do you eat?'

'Eat what, breakfast or supper?'

'Take your pick,' Weaver said. 'Have you food in the house?'

'In the larder.'

Weaver found the kitchen and raked through the cupboards like a scavenger. To his surprise the kitchen was clean, not tidy but clean. From a battered ice-box, he finally unearthed a packet of bacon rashers and a couple of eggs. When Doyle joined him, he was already at the stove with a skillet in his hand, fat spitting and the whites of the eggs beginning to congeal.

Doyle wore a war-surplus naval pea-jacket over his pyjamas, and a pair of tennis shoes on his naked feet. In his hand was the day's allocation of Black & White, a sealed half pint. While Weaver flipped the eggs the old man stripped off the goldfoil and thumbed the cork from the bottle. Pouring a dash of the golden liquid into a tooth-glass he took it into his mouth and swilled it round. He swallowed cautiously, sighed, and seated himself at the deal table.

Weaver put the plate in front of him.

As they ate, they talked.

'I'm moving out,' Weaver said. 'I don't want to stay here.'

'Other than the smell, is there a reason?'

'To split the force.'

'Aye, that kind of patter takes me back a bit,' Doyle said. 'The military phraseology. It's anonymity you're after.'

'A commercial hotel will suit the purpose.'

'Wouldn't one of your lady-friends put you up?'

'What lady-friends?'

'Come on, Donald, I'm not daft. You had your share of women before you left this town.'

'Not true.' Weaver said. 'Anyway, women have the habit of blabbing too much.'

'How do we make our start?'

'We need finance and we need a definite lead. I take it you don't make a fortune flogging old books?'

'You're not wrong there, Donald,' Doyle said. 'But I was under the impression that you'd done well with the London jobs.'

'I've been living on the loot for over a year,' Weaver said. 'Besides, most of my stake money's salted in Spain. My account in the Westminster's pretty low.'

'Why do we need money?'

'To oil the right wheels,' Weaver said. 'Who's working these days?'

'Well, I can cite you the price of a set of Scott accurate to the nearest shilling but I'm damned if I can tell you a thing about the scene. I haven't pulled a tickle in twelve years, Donald. The game's closed to me.'

'How about Irwin?'

'Big Jack! Aye, maybe. If anybody'll help you it's Jack Irwin. You and he were always thick.'

'He's still free?'

'Twenty men and a purse-net couldn't catch Irwin,' Doyle said. 'Ask at the Lugger. Ask Pate the barman: he'll put you in touch.'

'I'll do that,' Weaver said.

'In the meantime, what do you want me to do?' Doyle asked.

'Stay sober.'

Irwin lolled in the massive double bed with the indolent authority of a potentate. Soft blankets and crisp sheets were folded across his belly. A couple of years older than Weaver, Irwin was slipping on to the wrong side of forty. His age and his tendency to self-indulgence were reflected in the bulge of his paunch. In manner he was still hale and boyish, big and blond with the high-coloured complexion of a shepherd or a trawlerman. The sable gentleness of his west highland accent was overlaid by the guttural accentuations of Glasgow and sounded as counterfeit and polyglot as a Scots comedian's. Once Weaver had emulated Irwin and envied him his sophistication. Now, after a five-year lapse, Weaver saw him clearly as a provincial hick, professional enough in his field but obsessed with the need to feed his vanity and to show off his success. Pushing away the breakfast tray, Irwin spread his arms akimbo and ostentatiously welcomed the prodigal. In the light of the bedside lamp his chest hair was almost white.

'Weaver!' he hooted. 'It's Weaver risen from the bloody dead!'

Weaver allowed the big man to pump his fist and slap him on the back in rumbling greeting, grinning too to sustain the pretence of unalloyed friendship. It was not wholly sham: Irwin had been good to him, had taught him many useful tricks and had never cheated. Weaver pulled away and Irwin called for the girl to bring another cup of coffee. There was always a girl in residence in Irwin's apartment; always the same type, invariably young and lithe and silent. The current one was no different; eyes flat and unrevealing as burnt-out opals, ash-blonde hair falling straight and long to screen her face. The lean body under the scanty robe suggested that she was very young indeed. Weaver had observed this syndrome in men of Irwin's age and ilk in several parts of Europe. The older Irwin

21

became the younger his companions would have to be.
Finally a balance between need and farce would be struck
and the only antidote to senility would be booze and its
numbing loneliness.

'You haven't met Hazel, have you?' Irwin said. 'A grand
lass. I'd even consider marrying Hazel, if she asked me
nice.'

Hazel blew him a raspberry and went out of the room,
soundless as a squaw, to freshen the coffee in the bowl of
the Cona.

Irwin belched into his fist and reached for the onyx box
on the bedside table. When he shifted his weight the belly
showed puckered creases like the belly of a woman who
has borne too many children. He lit the cigarettes from a
Ronson and handed one to Weaver.

'How did you find me?'

'Enquired at the Lugger.'

'Ah! Pate told you,' Irwin said. 'Without the trusty Pate
half the underworld would collapse. How's it been, then?'

'Can't complain,' Weaver said. 'And you?'

'Plodding gallantly along.'

'Still pulling the little ones?'

'That's me! A man of small ambition.'

It had always been Irwin's style to limit himself to three
or four modest stunts a year. Though he did not specialise
his range was confined and his income was hardly more
than that of a senior executive in a small firm. The man-
agement of his finances was arranged with a lawyer and
an accountant; neither of these gentlemen suffered any
illusions as to its source. Between them they rinsed down
his annual haul and made it respectable for tax inspection.
Irwin continued to plan and execute his quiet tickles as if
each was worth a million in unmarked bills. His caution
and his lack of greed were legendary, yet nobody ever
dared to mock him. He had the incontestable advantage
of a pristine record sheet and only a couple of cops in the
city even remembered his name. From Irwin, Weaver had
learned the meaning of care and the diverse uses of guile.
He had also learned that a little force, properly applied,
can go a long way. On such principles he had based his
own style and founded his solo career: so far the technique
had not failed him.

'You look pretty smart,' Irwin said. 'I take that as a sign that you haven't been entertained by the government.'

Weaver nodded, then briefly and without recourse to detail, filled Irwin in on his successes south of the border. As he spoke he could visibly see Irwin's attitude change to one of awe and admiration. There was no call for Irwin to covet his success: it was only the veneer of casual wealth and the trappings of sophistication which Irwin rated highly, the polish which travel gives to a man. Talking softly and undemonstratively he continued to tell the highlander the scant facts of the situation which had brought him home.

'I'd no idea you were a daddy,' Irwin said, when he had finished. 'I mean, I knew about Muriel Doyle, but the rest of it . . .'

'I'm no longer a daddy.'

'Aye, Jesus, it's a grim business,' Irwin said. 'It's the bloody lack of profit that baffles me. They rampage and strut for no reason at all. What can you hope to do, though?'

'Find him,' Weaver said. 'That's why I came home.'

'I had the suspicion it was no ordinary social visit,' Irwin said. He pulled up his knees and rested his chin against the hillock. 'But it's not me you should be calling on, Donald: this is no inside job, not even the fringe of the rackets. God knows, my contacts inside the hard-core are few enough at the best of times, but it might be a pack killing and the packs are miles out of my province.'

'You could put an ear to the ground.'

'Willingly, willingly,' Irwin said. 'I'll gladly help in any way possible, but you'll not get much joy at all from the establishment. Grassers and pigeons hover where the money is and there's no money in thrill killing.'

'All right,' Weaver said. 'What about the other thing?'

'Work, you mean! Well, that's more in my line. What manner of stunt are you after?'

'I'm not particular,' Weaver said, 'provided it doesn't pull the cops down on my head. I know what it's like here, know how you operate . . .'

'Things have changed a bit, Donald.' Irwin waved his hand. 'Things are harder now.'

'Why?'

'Too many bold young bucks,' Irwin said. 'Too many graduates from the institutions, too many kids willing to take crazy risks for a bob or two. The right kind of job, our sort of job, just doesn't present itself as regularly as it used to do.'

Weaver frowned. 'You've nothing lined up, nothing you could cut me in on?'

Irwin stubbed out his cigarette and immediately lit another. He was making a production of reluctance, too much of a production. Instinctively Weaver felt that Irwin's agile mind had run up a score for him the moment he had entered the bedroom. Why the big highlander was being chary about it, he could not yet fathom. Perhaps Irwin was afraid to offer him too small a tickle, or, for some inexplicable reason, no longer trusted him. Unless things had changed radically Irwin's labour pool never totalled more than half a dozen men of like mind, professional friends who set themselves a little apart from the common ruck of criminals and therefore survived. Waiting for the act to reach a climax, Weaver said nothing.

Finally Irwin said, 'There's one job . . .'

'You sound choked,' Weaver said. 'Is it that bloody hairy?'

Irwin expressed affront, raising his palms. 'God, no, it's not hairy at all,' he declared. 'In fact, it's a peach of a job, a honey, as safe as houses. Hell, I'd take my old mother on this one if she could wheel a car fast enough.'

'Then what's wrong with it?'

'Well, I'm not convinced it's your sort of thing.'

'Anything's my sort of thing,' Weaver said. 'Listen, all I want is a few hundred quid to tide me over while I'm in Scotland. I don't want to hang around this hole any longer than I have to.'

'Nothing wrong with Glasgow,' Irwin said defensively.

'All right,' Weaver said. 'So it's bloody Shangri-la to you, Jack, but personally I don't ever want to see the place again. I've come here to do a job. I'll do it, then clear out, for good.'

'You may have to clear out.'

'Look, if you've got a job in the box you think would suit me, then give me the nod: if not, tell me, and I'll be on my way.'

24

'Things have changed,' said Irwin once more.

'Christ! You're chicken!' Weaver said. 'You've got something in your eye and the sight of it scares you. What the hell sort of job is that?'

'It means weapons,' Irwin said. 'Shooters.'

'So what?'

'You didn't used to be so blasé about guns.'

'Times have changed, remember.'

'You don't object to hefting a shooter?'

'Nope.'

Irwin grinned with his mouth, though his eyes were still perplexed. 'If memory serves me, you were none too happy at the rubber company stunt.'

'We only hauled out six hundred quid.'

'True,' Irwin said. 'At the time, though, it was the violence made you squeamish.'

'Breaking the bird's arm was unnecessary.'

'An accident,' said Irwin. 'Besides, she got compensation.'

Was Irwin hinting tactfully that the new stunt would be similar in structure to the rubber company hold-up? That had been fifteen years ago and he was hardly more than a kid at the time. He could look back on it now without shame or remorse, though, for a while after, he could not quite rid himself of the image of the girl's face grotesquely knotted with terror, and the terror changing to agony as Irwin had thrust up the fat female arm and there had been that crack, like kindling snapped by an axe, and Weaver had dived across the office and stuffed her howling scream back into her throat with the heel of his fist; wetness, arched and gobbling tongue, the pressure of her pain and fear all coming against his hand until Irwin had redeemed himself by clubbing her with the sap and she had slumped into a merciful swoon. Maybe, Weaver thought, Irwin was only trailing this tattered remnant of success to taunt him, remind him that he had almost funked it once.

'I've changed too, Jack,' he said.

Irwin clutched the cigarette in the side of his mouth and clawed himself on the crown of each shoulder, arms folded over his chest. 'I'm sure of it.' He dropped back against the pillow. 'Tell you what, Donald; supposing I sleep on it for a couple of nights. Better yet, I'll sniff around and make sure the job's still tight, then, unless you find an alternative, I'll give you all the facts.'

'If that's how you want to play it,' Weaver said. 'It suits me.'

'Supposing you call again on Friday.'

'When?'

'Nine p.m., right here.'

'All right,' Weaver said. 'Friday.'

He buttoned his overcoat and moved from the chair to the door.

'Hey, Donald!'

With the door already half open and the girl waiting in the hallway like a maid-servant to see him out, he turned.

Irwin winked. 'I'm bloody glad you've come home,' he said. 'I wouldn't dare pull this stunt with anybody but you.'

As he went past the girl and out on to the landing, Weaver thought he glimpsed the trace of a smile beneath the veil of ash-blonde hair, but if he did he could not be sure what it implied.

FOUR

The Pemberton hotel had not existed last time Weaver had walked in the park. It existed now though, an undeniable entity of sugared-grey concrete trimmed with alloy and glass. The entrance was graced with thin sheets of sea-green marble but the finishing did not fool Weaver for a moment; he knew in advance what the rooms, the food and the clientele would be like. Only the view from his seventh-floor bedroom came as a surprise. The city spread before him, south-east and south-west, the river reaches, the squat darts of the bridges bearing their drastic overload of traffic. The room was hardly more than a sleeping closet but it would suit his requirements perfectly. Below and around him he heard the faint stir of other residents, most of them on expense accounts. The hotel was geared to cater for this busy trading; telephones hooded in the baffleboard-studded foyer and corridors so that a line was always to hand. Two small private dining rooms joined the main restaurant and a cocktail bar lay close enough to the conference rooms to allow weary business men to stagger out for quick refreshment during breaks in discussions and presentations. When in need of cover now this was the milieu Weaver chose to give himself protective coloration. He found he could easily pose as an upper-echelon traveller, an industrial or commercial wayfarer. In Leeds, Liverpool, Cardiff, in London too, he could always count on finding a hotel of this calibre. Occasionally he would even convince himself that he was one of them, no better and no worse, but secretly he knew that he was not gregarious enough to succeed in any of their rackets. Some of his fellow residents were bigger crooks than he was, though the rules of their game were different and the dice-cup another shape.

Lunch was worse than he would have been served in London, but better than in Liverpool. He made the simple contrast deliberately, backing Spain out of his system, bringing himself closer by degrees to the reality of Doyle's world, the world which now seemed utterly alien to him, the sort of world in which a boy could be flayed to death and nobody really cared too much. Psychologists and sociologists could rail against the evils of materialism and the predatory society but none of them would ever convince Weaver that the current system, with its boredom and pseudo freedom, was better. If criminologists ever found a way to slice up his brain, set the tissues on slides and project the result on a screen they would no doubt be surprised to find a middle-class aspiration with traces of Protestant conservation and belief in the right of a man to carve his own kind of independence. Though he was a thief to trade, Weaver was no hypocrite. He risked his freedom and his right to justice, pitted his nerve and intelligence against the representatives of an order founded on the very qualities he now typified and which, in popular view, had something of the strain of hero. Part of his anger, the less subjective part, was at the failure of this order to protect him against such futile suffering as that caused by Gordon's death. If he could isolate and examine the causes behind the sadistic act, find a cause, even a weak one, perhaps he could square away his bitterness and

27

guilt and return unimpaired to his own proscribed hunting runs. Doyle too comprehended this need, but the old man hid himself from it behind a fence of Black & White bottles; hiding was no solution. The very nature of the act posed questions: in seeking to discover answers to one set he might, if fortunate, discover other answers too.

Opening his lips, Weaver breathed upon the window glass. River and city clouded over, blurred to a coarse dark stain. Only the sky above the level of the condensation was visible, heavy and porous as limestone.

Weaver pushed himself away from the window ledge. It was time he went down to begin his search in the morgue of the Glasgow newspaper offices.

Arthur Brown wore a double-breasted, pin-stripe suit, part of a jumble sale haul seven years ago. Doyle had never known Brown to wear anything else save once each year, usually in spring, when for a couple of days he would sport a khaki jacket and stained cords, while the brown suit was cleaned and overhauled. The origin of the hat was a mystery; not even Brown could remember where he had acquired it. It too was brown, or had been. The brim was wide and floppy, the silken band lost in the sweat stains which spread up to the furrow of the crown. Brown sweated all the time. Even on the coldest February day a droplet or two managed to seep through the skin above his spectacles, a strange opaque sweat which reminded Doyle of the perspiration on a stick of gelignite when its molecules degenerate into instability. There was nothing explosive or unstable about Brown though. He was fat, suffered a heart condition and watched the world through a pair of wire-framed glasses with lenses like Barr & Stroud prisms.

Brown had entered the secondhand book trade by way of the bric-à-brac business. This instinct for profit had remained unimpaired by the gradual disintegration of his own business. He had flogged off a couple of dozen volumes to Doyle at a price keen enough to suggest that the fat man's acumen might prove an asset. Within a month, Doyle had taken Brown on as a partner. Brown was forty-four. He worked the clackety Royal portable with the patient desperation of a Sparks at the morse-key of a sinking tanker. Dour and contented, Brown had a gift for selling; Doyle a flair for buying. Between them, if they had been younger men and of different background, they might have cornered a local market and capitalised on their combined talents. As it was, each was obliged to fight a losing battle against the other's weaknesses. Doyle was convinced that Brown would one day die on him and leave him in the lurch; Brown that Doyle would run to rummy's ruin and drop the shop from under him. They trod round each other, growling, like toothless dogs.

The shop was a narrow-fronted, single-windowed corridor in the lower end of Bradbury Street, jammed between a dry-goods store and a retail tobacconists. Passing trade was generally thin on intellect and the cash sales were made through the medium of sidelines, the peddling of cheap magazines and comic books and well-thumbed paperbacks. High against the ivory-yellow cornices—the shop had once been part of a dowager's drawing room—the unsaleable deadwood of the booksellers' trade gathered a harsh coating of grime. The second compartment was shelved; the shelves, like those in Doyle's flat, groaned with assorted volumes, the whole structure seemingly balanced on the edge of the dropleaf table which was the extent of Brown's office and domain. Behind the office was a chill storeroom, its filthy window, barred against vandals, staring blankly out on to a yard. Here were boxes and tea-chests full of stock, cartons and wrapping paper, hoarded ends of string, Salters' scales and a butcher's block, scrubbed clean of blood, on which all the packing was done. A couple of doltish schoolboys earned pin-money by occasionally helping out with the heavy labour. In the storeroom, too, was a Calor gas ring, a tea kettle, four chipped cups and a flotilla of old tricorn milk cartons. The latter gave store and shop the sour fecundity of a byre, killing even the prevailing odour of papery damp.

Doyle pushed into the shop. The bell overhead rang like a fairground machine. A couple of hours in advance of his normal hour of arrival he was confronted by the sight of Brown's corpulent face glowering at him round the edge of the office doorway. The face disappeared. The racing staccato of the Royal began again immediately.

29

On his way down the shop, Doyle automatically blocked the ranks of paperbacks and squared the piles of comic books into a semblance of neatness. A single-bar electric radiator was snuggled under Brown's heel's, and sweat shone on his temples. He did not look up from the keyboard.

'You're early,' he said. 'What happened? Did the elephants tramp on your head?'

Doyle fished two issues of the booksellers' weekly journal from his overcoat pocket and dropped them by Brown's energetic elbow. 'Found some titles I think we've got,' he said. 'See if you can find others.'

'Bound to,' Brown said. The rhythm of his typing changed as he laid in a signature block at the end of the quotation. He ripped the sheet from the roller with one hand and fed in a cheap brown envelope with the other. Doyle leaned against the door jamb watching Brown rattle out the address.

'He's come,' Doyle said.

'Who's come,' Brown said. 'The Messiah?'

'Weaver.'

'Weaver!' Brown's tongue slid across the gummed edge of the envelope. 'Ah, yer! *That* Weaver.'

'My . . . my son-in-law.'

'Loosely speaking, you mean.'

'He arrived yesterday.'

'I wondered why you were sober,' Brown said. 'You don't look happy. Thought you wanted him here?'

'I did.'

'Told you you were a silly bugger to send for the likes of him.'

'We'll be working together.'

Behind the rainbow lenses Brown's eyes danced with suspicion. 'In the business?'

'Not this business.'

With the frayed cuffs of his jacket Brown jabbed at the effusions of sweat around his chins. 'The boy, you mean?'

'Yes, the boy,' Doyle said. 'Gordon.'

Thoughtfully Brown pecked out a few letters on the portable. He leaned his elbow on the casing. 'So what?'

'I'm going to be rather busy.'

'You want me to work extra.'

30

The notion of Brown working extra was ludicrous. As it was, he spent twelve hours a day, six days a week, cloistered in the shop. He left it only to purchase the makings of the savoury sandwiches of which he was so fond, or in the evening, to cart back to his desk a wrapping of fish and chips. With a wife and eight children packed into a small council flat, the shop was his haven, his true domicile, work an excuse for exonerating himself from the niggling chores of fatherhood. Though he dearly loved his children and was kind to them, his font of paternal affection was sullied by disenchantment with the woman who had chosen to marry him. If by some miracle he could have rid himself of the harridan who ruled his roost, Brown would have made a perfect widower.

'I suppose you'll want me to handle the sales?' Brown said.

'If you don't mind.'

'I'll be doing the bleedin' wrapping next,' Brown said. 'You know we'll have to shut shop when I'm at the sale rooms, and that means loss of business.'

'I'm sorry.'

The apology startled Brown. He had never had an apology from his partner in all the years he had known him.

'Weaver may want me to do things,' Doyle added.

'Like what?'

'I'm not sure, but I want to keep myself available.'

In the storeroom the kettle chirped. Brown extricated himself from behind the desk, pressing back the bulge of volumes with his shoulder. He waddled into the store. Doyle trailed him and in tandem, well rehearsed, they fashioned two cups of sweet brown coffee. They leaned against the butcher's block, end to end like characters in a grotesque comedy of alienation, each addressing an opposite wall.

'What did he say?' Brown asked.

'He said we must attempt to find the killer.'

'Fat chance!'

'I want to.'

'How long will it take?'

'Weeks, maybe months.'

'The killer, whoever the hell he is, might have shot the

31

crow, left town, emigrated. Could be any bleedin' place in the world by now', Brown said. 'I would be if I was him.'

'That's not good enough,' Doyle said. 'We've got to try.'

'Suppose you have.'

'Brown, if it was one of your kids, would you sit back and do nothing?'

'I'd have seven left to consider.'

Doyle assimilated the answer. He had not discussed the details and the ramifications with anyone other than Brown, and not often or at length even with his partner: yet Brown had given it much thought. The rational compassion of his manner hinted that not only had he analysed the situation but he had experienced it, in part, within himself. The petulant note was missing from his tone now.

Brown's direct involvement in the boy's death began and ended with the visit of the secondary officer investigating the case; there was little enough he could tell the cop. Initially Doyle had been shocked. It took three days of numb sobriety for the effect to wear off and it did so suddenly. Midway between the flat and the shop he had been overwhelmed with anguish, ravaged by it so that he had barely managed to crawl to the cramped security of the inner office where Brown worked. Out of the fog of grief the recollection of Brown's gentleness at that time came to him in fits and starts like the jigsaw memories of an amnesiac. Now he understood that the whole notion of revenge had been put forth only as a cure for his immediate pain; that Brown, failing to pull him round by other means, had roused the hackles of his anger, spurred his purpose as a substitute for despair. But for Brown's shrewdness it was probable that he would have disintegrated entirely, slid swiftly into hapless drunkenness, abandoned the business and the very last of his human contacts, committed a slow and degrading act of self-immolation. Out of necessity then, not conviction, Arthur Brown had planted the germ of the idea of revenge.

The stoicism with which he had faced up to the other major disasters in his life, prior to Gordon's murder, was not strong enough to give him an alternative to Brown's suggestion. Two terms in prison and his wife's desertion were nothing compared to the loss of his grandson. Only the desire to see justice done had tugged him through that period; in large measure it was all Brown's fault. When it became obvious that justice, even in its basic form, had let him down, he had no choice but to devise another method of keeping hope alive. The letter, twelve months too late, had been that means, that method; the summoning of Weaver a last resort. Now, however, he had no wish to wreck the modest stability which he had created for himself, but the origins of the course which Brown had instigated and he had so willingly adopted were undeniable. Could he honestly hold Brown responsible? The ancestral blood of Irish freedom fighters, warriors, bards and romantics, mingled in his veins with alcohol and the red corpuscles of the Scot. That blood, diluted though it was, cried out for a cause. Subtle genetic substances must take the blame then for his present mule-headedness.

As if divining Doyle's thoughts, Brown said curtly, 'If you intend to give up, now's the time.'

'I'm not giving up. What would Weaver say?'

'Ignore him. Let him get on with it.'

'He'll need help.'

'*You* need help, Doyle.'

'I brought him here.'

'Then you've done enough.'

'No,' Doyle said. 'I have to go through with it.'

'Stupid bugger.'

'You encouraged me.'

Brown's memory was all too clear. He was too honest a man to project a flat denial. 'I didn't know about Weaver.'

'And you didn't credit me with sufficient guts to do it on my own.'

'I thought the coppers ...'

'But they didn't, did they?' Doyle said.

Brown pulled away from the block, jerking, spilling coffee down the front of his stained pullover. His jaw line was unusually well defined, thrust out of the dewlap, giving him the momentary appearance of a bulldog ready to snatch at a throat. 'If Weaver does find him, he'll kill him, won't he?'

'I imagine so.'

'Then I hope he fails.'

'Gordon, my grandson . . .'

'Another damned life,' Brown said, 'another damned life altogether.'

'What the law can't do, we're obliged to do for ourselves.'

'For whose good, then, will you build this private gallows?'

'Mine,' Doyle snapped. 'Will you tend the business?'

Brown splashed the dregs of his coffee down the length of the floor, slammed the cup on the block and pushed angrily back into the office. Doyle heard the racket of the roller, then the metallic chatter of the keys flinging letters on to paper. He finished his coffee, rinsed the cups in water from the kettle and emerged from the store.

As he passed, Brown said, 'Yer, I'll do what's necessary here.'

The lenses were not hostile, suggesting rather a pessimistic indulgence.

Doyle nodded.

'You'll never find him now anyway,' Brown called. 'No chance.'

Even as he set out on the first leg of the long search, Doyle was more than inclined to agree. He did not seek retribution now; the relief of hopelessness was all that he asked.

FIVE

Leaving Glasgow behind, Irwin headed the Corsair on to the main boulevard, the trade route west to the highlands, feeder for the offshoots to Dumbarton and the ports of Argyll. Below the car, lee shore lights pricked out the riverline townships. Letting the belt come slack around him, Weaver perched on the edge of the passenger seat, braced a little against the drag, as Irwin poured more power into the Ford engine, opening the throttle.

Weaver said, 'When is the job?'

'Any Friday night,' said Irwin. 'We could do with a

couple of weeks to make sure, but in theory we could pull it any time—even tonight.'

'What's it worth to me?'

'Around three thousand.'

'Bottom price?'

'Not less than two.'

'How many on the kick?'

'Thee and me, Donald, just thee and me.'

'What it is then, a snatch?'

'Armed robbery.'

'You used to be opposed to the heavy stuff.'

'The bloody income tax is killing me.'

'Don't tell me you need the money, Jack?'

'That's about the stretch of it.'

'Tell me.'

'We hit three men, lift the cash and get the hell out of it.'

Weaver shook his head. No longer did he believe in miracles of human stupidity. Opportunities for easy lifts worth four or five thousand were as rare as nightingales in the brickworks of Gartshaws. Even minor firms had been brainwashed into protecting their cash transits with professional security guards.

'I think you should know, Donald, that if you won't play, then the stunt's off. I mean, I'm not putting it up for grabs.'

'We load the guns?'

'Aye.'

'Turning chicken in your old age, Jack?'

'Cheeky bastard!' Irwin said. 'For brass-neck, Weaver, you really take the bloody oatcake.'

'Come off the high horse,' Weaver said. 'You're not buying me, you're buying my situation. This is a dangerous stunt; I want to know just how dangerous, and why?'

'Strong-arm stuff is always rough,' Irwin said. 'Sure, I could rent myself an army, but I can't afford the risk of leaks. It's not the actual job that's risky, it's what could happen after.'

'Cops, you mean?'

'The law's not liable to be summoned.'

The street lamps of a village gave way to undulating fences hazed with frost. Fields swam curtly out of dark-

35

ness but the feeling of the black swathe of the river Clyde broadening to its estuary was still with him.

Irwin said, 'Do you know where we are?'

'Heading west towards Balloch.'

'Right,' said Irwin. 'In ten minutes we'll cut off over the hill, follow the moor track down to the riverside again at Bargowan.'

'I know it.'

'It's this route we'll take afterwards. Chances are we'll be able to pedal home clean and clear, but . . .'

'Still bound by the rudiments of caution.'

'Can't change the spots at my age,' Irwin said. 'Can you still handle a wheel like you used to?'

'Better.'

'Then you'll do the driving.'

'Who do we hit?'

'Remember McFadden?'

'That little fink!'

'Our Joseph is a fink no more,' said Irwin. 'The wee bastard's gone up in the world. He's a bossman now, running a smooth, tight operation in grog shops, clubs and the like.'

'How the hell did he ever wash himself clean enough to find backers, let alone winkle a licence?'

'Grease,' Irwin said. 'It's only a rumour, right enough, but I heard that he had a hand in a big one—the airport stunt. When the others fell our Joe was left holding the boodle.'

'Then he must have an arm in the police.'

'Ten fingers, at least.'

'Christ!' Weaver said. 'I didn't think McFadden had the brains to deal in politics.'

'He's not clean,' Irwin said. 'He's just acting smart about it. He's still up to his ballocks in graft.'

'Protection?'

'After a fashion,' said Irwin. 'Friday night is the night he collects. Most of it, I'm told, is legal cash, but there's enough of the dirty money among it to make it impossible for him to holler cop.'

'Not even to his arm?'

'What could a bent cop do without running the risk of exposure?' Irwin said. 'McFadden gathers the harvest personally. A couple of hard-nose pugs will be with him, but that's the strength.'

'Surprising that nobody's thought of hitting him before.'

'Maybe they have. Maybe they even tried and it didn't come off. Christ, there's plenty would like to ram a shiv into McFadden's tripes, but robbing him—well, it's not the kind of thing that gentlemen do, is it?'

'Gentlemen!' said Weaver. 'That's a laugh!'

'You know what I mean,' said Irwin.

'You've worked out the money route?'

'I have.'

'We take him at the house, not in the city?'

'Smartest way to do it.'

'How does he tote the cash?'

'In a big briefcase.'

'I see why you're showing feathers, Jack. McFadden won't stop looking until he's laid us by the heels.'

'McFadden won't remember me,' Irwin said. 'I'm nothing, a total nonentity in his circles. And you never had much truck with him either, did you?'

'I pulled one team job with him about twenty years ago,' Weaver said. 'Before I even knew you; I couldn't stomach the little rat even then.'

'Personally, I wouldn't dabble in those stinking rackets, not for half the stock of the Royal Bank,' Irwin said. 'If he didn't have himself a solid gold source inside the law he'd have copped it long since. As it is, he'll fly too high one of these fine days and find himself serving a long, long stretch. His big house and his respectable front won't do him much good then.'

'The house at Bargowan?'

'Nothing but the best for our Joe now. It's like a bloody mansion. He stores his wife and daughters there like queens at court, while he does his stuff with a row of pretties up in the city.'

'What *exactly* is my split on this transaction?'

'Forty per cent.'

'Fifty.'

'Greedy bastard,' Irwin said. 'I've spent months surveying.'

'Yeah, but you'll be lucky to find anybody reliable

37

who'd touch it with a forty-foot pole. That's why you've been brooding on it for long enough.'

'Aye, all right, fifty it is—but we divide the cost down the middle.'

'Agreed,' said Weaver. 'How did you gather your news?'

'With caution, of course,' said Irwin. 'And from fifty different sources. Anyway, I question if McFadden will be looking for an outsider. He'll be too busy sniffing out a Judas in his own organisation. He's a paranoiac bugger at the best of times, so I'm told.'

'Can they nail us at the hit?'

'They can, but they won't.'

'Artillery?'

'Blades.'

'Where does he collect?'

'Three places: two pubs and a kind of club for young swingers. You won't know them at all. They're all modern.'

'You're sure he lugs the cash back with him to Bargowan?'

'Positive,' said Irwin. 'He holds it there over Friday, adds Saturday's pile and brings his cashiers down on Sunday. They divide it up and hive it off into various accounts and siphon off the payola. It's too complicated for a simple mind like mine, and of no relevance to us.'

'Why don't we hit him Saturday, or Sunday, and collect a bigger bundle?'

'Friday is the whole week's rake-off. All weekend he keeps guards in the house. Besides, the money's vaulted, and that would make the timing too difficult for a two-man tickle.'

'In theory we could hit him anywhere along the line.'

'In theory, aye; but it's best to do it when he comes out of the car to take the briefcase into the house. He's bound to be sluggish just then, thinking it's been another easy run.'

'In the house?'

'The wife and daughters, probably.'

'And the two pugs?'

'They put the transport away then billet in the house overnight.'

'You have been industrious, Jack,' said Weaver.

38

'I had to be,' said Irwin. 'I didn't know if I'd ever find the right guy to partner me, or if I'd really steel myself to go through with it. But believe me, Donald, it's been like cake in the closet ever since I first thought of it.'

'But *you* didn't think of it, Jack,' Weaver said, quietly.

'What!'

'You heard. It's not your idea. Somebody sold it to you: who?'

Irwin hesitated. He slowed the Corsair, drumming his gloved fingers on the rim of the steering wheel. 'Clever man,' he murmured. 'Aye, you're on the button as usual, Weaver. Somebody did sell me the idea, but I can't tell you who it was.'

'You'd better,' said Weaver, softly. 'Otherwise it's not on.'

'Listen,' Irwin said, testily, 'it's hard cash you're after. I'm not as young as I was and things are tough up here. The game's stacked with amateurs. They skim off the fattest pickings, though they invariably get bagged for it, and . . .'

'Stop bleating, Jack, and tell me the contact's name.'

'I won't.'

'It's an insider,' Weaver said. 'I'll bet it's the bent cop.'

'Look, Weaver . . .'

'Is it?'

Irwin gave in. 'Aye.'

'His name?'

'Greerson.'

'Never heard of him.'

'That's dandy,' said Irwin. 'Just forget you ever did He won't blow on us, if that's what you're thinking. I mean, would you blow if you were skinning fifty or more a week off McFadden.'

'But this bogey is greedy.'

'Everybody's greedy these days.'

'I hate bogies and I hate Judas-types,' Weaver said. 'Put them together and you've got a man I wouldn't trust with a pail of cow-crap.'

'He'll do anything for money.'

'Exactly!' said Weaver. 'McFadden pays him, and the State pays him, and he's selling both of them up the river already. Now *you* pay him, and he might just do the same thing for you.'

'No,' said Irwin emphatically. 'He can't. It has to end with me. If he blew the whistle on me, it would mean he'd go up with me. He won't risk it. You can see the logic in that, Donald, surely?'

'I don't like it.'

'Jesus, man, you can't back off now.'

'Does he know who you're slicing with: does he know about me?'

'No.'

'Then I'm your ace card, Jack.'

'What?'

'Come on, exercise the grey stuff. Don't tell Greerson when we're doing the job and, most important of all, don't even hint at my name. Then he *can't* sell you out.'

Irwin frowned, then nodded. In the underglow of the dashboard light Weaver saw the frown creased out into a grin of understanding. 'Aye, of course, he can't. He wouldn't dare. You've hit it, Donald. You're my ace card, right enough.'

It was pitch dark outside the area of the Corsair. The car was well over the moor road, pitching a little on the poor surface. Weaver had driven this route before, once, and recalled the steepness of the ascent and descent on either side of the high plateau. If there was fog or ice on the night of the job it would make things very tricky. He would need practice to sharpen his ability to handle a car over the twisting track, and he would need a special kind of transport. He must make sure that no matter how talented the driver of a pursuit vehicle might be, he would have the odds on his side.

'I'll do it,' he said. 'But you may as well know I don't like the scene.'

'Because of Greerson?'

'Because,' said Weaver, 'it all looks too smooth.'

'Jesus!' said Irwin. 'You're never happy, Weaver, are you?'

'Never.'

Doyle returned to his armchair by the grate. The velour cushion was heavily indented to the shape of his buttocks.

He slumped into the chair with the sigh of a man who is weary with too much rest. No catalogues or books sat on the wine table, only an almost empty pack of cigarettes, a littered ashtray and a half bottle of Black & White, levelled off to the top of the label. The room was stuffy, fugged with tobacco smoke. Weaver did not know whether the bottle was the first or second of the day. Though Doyle's features sagged dough-like against the bone and his eyes were puffed up, he spoke without the lagging blur of drunkenness.

'I can state categorically that I'm soberer than most judges,' Doyle said. Having pronounced the complex sentence with the smugness of a priest walking a chalk-line in a police tank, Doyle hoisted his glass and celebrated self-denial with a snifter.

'Have you eaten lately?' Weaver asked.

'Had a roll earlier on.'

Weaver fanned the fog, squinting. 'How long have you been sitting there, for God's sake?'

'Quite a while,' said Doyle. 'I've been doing some thinking.'

'About what?'

'I *want* to help you but I don't even know how to begin,' Doyle confessed. 'What can I do: where do I go for information?'

'The kitchen.' Weaver stripped off his overcoat and tossed it across the empty chair. 'You'll think better on a bellyful of hot grub.'

Reluctantly, Doyle trailed the younger man through the hallway into the kitchen. It was cold there, not bitterly so but sufficient to make him shiver and cough as he came out of his laziness. Weaver set about preparing a meal. He found tins on the larder shelf, an odd assortment, but substantial. No culinary wizard, Weaver had long ago learned the rudiments of preparing appetising nourishment and extended the craft now to include the feeding of Doyle. At least food would absorb a little of the nicotine and alcohol which clogged the old man's bloodstream.

Weaver said, 'I've got myself a job.'

Startled, Doyle said shrilly, 'Work?'

'Not that kind of work: a caper, a stunt.'

'With Jack Irwin?'

'Yeah.'

'Is it . . . safe?'

'Safe enough,' Weaver said. 'It has other advantages. Fringe benefits.'

'When's it scheduled for?'

'Couple of weeks or so.'

'In the city?'

'Close enough.'

'Will it take up much time?'

'Some.' Weaver whipped a potato mix into a bowl with milk and a knob of butter. He added seasoning then held the bowl in the crook of his left arm in a style approved by commercial cooks, and whisked the mixture briskly with a wire egg beater. A fleck of cream darted on to his tie but he did not cease his stirring. 'What conclusions did you reach with all that heavy thinking?'

'If Jack Irwin says the grassers can't help you, and you agree with him, Donald, then all we can do is tread the same paths as the bogies and hope we turn up something that they missed.'

Weaver scooped the potato mash into a pot and adjusted the intensity of the gas flame under it. He lifted the fleck of cream from his tie with his pinkie nail and wiped it on a dish towel.

'The cops questioned a hell of a lot of people,' Weaver said. 'Not only that, three weeks after the night of the killing they pulled in a suspect to help with their enquiries—and you know what *that* means?'

'How did you discover that?'

'In the newspapers,' Weaver said. 'Buried in small print. You didn't pay enough attention, Vince.'

'What does it mean?' Doyle said.

'The old euphemism—the cops had a prime target.'

'But couldn't prove it.'

'Right.'

'And you think perhaps we could?'

'Maybe.'

'But how do we find out who this suspect was, and where he is now?'

'We ask and keep on asking,' Weaver said. 'If that fails, then I have another idea.'

'What's that, Donald?'

Critically Weaver inspected the contents of the pots which were beginning to bubble, and warm the chill air of the kitchen with savoury smells. Doyle fended his way along the dresser closer to the stove. 'Don't keep me in the dark, please.'

Weaver pulled back, reached into the pocket of his jacket and took out a sheet of paper. He scanned the neat manuscript briefly then handed it to Doyle.

'Here,' he said. 'If you really want to do something concrete, pad round these places and talk to people. Otherwise go back to your bottle and forget it.'

Perplexed, Doyle nibbled at his underlip as if it was a piece of mutton gristle. He dabbed at his spectacles with his forefinger and glanced from the list in his hand to Weaver, nodding, resigned.

'Know what you're looking for?' Weaver asked.

'Aye, I'm looking for signs as much as answers, signs that somebody knows something but doesn't want to tell.'

'It may have been a year ago, but a lot of our class won't talk to cops.'

'And if we do find someone like that, what then?'

'We push.'

Weaver turned to the stove. Sliding two plates from the rack, he spooned out thick helpings of rich brown mince with a porridge ladle.

Doyle read through the list once more then folded it very carefully. He tucked it into the hip pocket of his corduroys and, still frowning, sat down at the table to eat.

SIX

In the early part of the afternoon Nimmo Street was as quiet as a rustic boneyard. Only the croon and flutter of the pigeons which infested the roofs and ledges at the back of the tenements disturbed the silence. The rumble of traffic from the Wickerburn Road, like a distant thunder, served only to intensify the stillness. When the doorbell rang, sending its vibrations through the house, Muriel's fingers jerked open instantly. The little boy grinned and beat his fists against her forearm, struggling to reach the spoonful of mashed banana from his throne on the kitchen armchair. Colin was as greedy and demanding in his desire for food as his father, but Muriel's whole attention was suddenly withdrawn from her son's wants, fastened limpet-like on the ringing of the bell. Rigid, she pushed her fingertips against her mouth, her lips mumbling a little as if muttering invocations to any god who happened to be around to spirit away the caller from the threshold. The bell rang intermittently then settled into a sustained and nerve-shattering trill.

Spoon and feeding cup clattered to the hearth as she snatched up the howling child and ran, not for the cover of the stove closet, but into the lobby towards the sound.

The bell stopped ringing.

Muriel held her breath. Mystified but hushed too by an instinct of stealth caught from his mother, Colin pursed his lips, snuffling. Muriel knew that the caller was on the landing, listening. When the electric mechanism in the dusty black plastic box above her connected and the shrill peal broke out once more she screamed. 'Go to bloody hell.'

'It's me, Muriel.'

'Go to hell, I'm telling you.'

'Muriel, for God's sake, it's me, your father.'

'I don't want you here.'

'Are you sick, lass?'

'Go away.'

'Muriel, let me in.'

'No.'

The baby fretted jealously in her arms. She drew him close, buffering his arms with her breast. His eyes were turned to the door panel as if he had been attracted by the gentle male voice from outside. Muriel stood with her head cocked, waiting. Even though she recognised the old man's voice, unreasoning fear was still high in her, billowing yellow like the gases burned at the waste spout of a chemical plant, laced with the heavy blackness of despair. It was the child she feared for most. Since the day of his birth her love for him had been flawed by this fear.

44

To Bob Brand, her husband, the baby was an object to be occasionally adored, indoctrinated, even at this early age, into manliness, taught the vitrues of independence, arrogance and male selfishness, but otherwise left exclusively to the care and protection of his mother. Even when she had agreed to marry Brand and had gone through the legal forms of ritual necessary to adopt his name and the status of wife, she had been aware of what he wanted of her. Brand used her as cook, laundry-maid and, when he was sour in drink and full of acid at the injustices of life, as a punchbag. Bob Brand was the epitome of hard-bitten Scottish egotism; one of the "peepul', a working man marinated in savage prejudices and countless generations of penury. Home was the one place where he was undisputed master, and his word was law. Brand had been fortunate to bed her just at the right time; though the timing of the seduction was fortuitous rather than calculated. If she had been a little younger she would still have had too much spunk ever to allow herself to succumb. Partly broken by neglect and loneliness and the chore of rearing her son, Gordon, without a father's help, Muriel had been an ideal prey. Brand had been on the scout for just such a dray-mare. He wanted comfort in his middle years and sons to carry on his name. He put the manacle on Muriel without more ado. In the hazily romantic afterglow of a half dozen glasses of port and lemon he screwed her, knocked her up first go and, being a man of unquestioned honour, married her at the double before she could even contemplate abortion.

If Brand had known that the other boy, Gordon, was going to make himself a victim, call down the coppers, and all the fuss and bother, he would have found himself another bitch and let Muriel Doyle, Muriel Weaver, stew. No whit of grief affected him over Gordon's death, only the inconvenience of his wife's disabling anguish, and the coppers running stupid around the house. It would have taken a hatchet in Brand's skull to waken any respect for the feelings of another person; in the locked volume of his heart women were not recorded as persons. Muriel, therefore, was left to face her mourning and the additional burden of her pregnancy alone. In no sense could she lean on her husband, share his strength. In consequence she became so fiercely protective of her second-born son that her every waking hour was marred by the responsibility and the torment of believing that fate might snatch away Colin as it had snatched away Gordon. Everybody, even her father, was an outrider of that menace.

'Muriel, are you still there?'

'I told you t'go.'

'Come on now, lass, open the door. I just want a word with you.'

'About what?'

'About Gordon.'

'Weaver sent you?'

'What if he did!'

'It's over and done with. Tell the interfering bastard that.'

She wanted no contact with Weaver now, or even with her father. They belonged to a past which had ended with her son's murder. It was no longer possible to recall how happy she had been with Weaver. All feeling for him had long since eroded. Even before he took off for the south, Weaver had abandoned her. She hadn't been good enough to hold him. It was no solace that he sent her money. She turned that gesture of kindness against him too. When he had broken down the door and forced his way in, for an instant only she had experienced a flicker of respect for the power of him and the brief illogical hope that he had come back to take her, and her baby, away from all this. Hope had died as soon as she saw his face. Now her father had come, an emissary of Weaver, bringing the stench of the past, the threat of more violence and disruption. Even as a child she had not been close to her father; she had been her mother's girl, and when her mother died—they had told her she was dead: in fact she had run off with another man—even then Doyle did not come back to her. She was farmed out to an aunt, not blood-kin, one of her father's 'friends', who lived in the village of Whitesides. Her father had visited her as he might have visited an inmate of an institution. For four whole years she put up with that cramped depressing house and the crabbed old woman, then, as soon as she turned sixteen, lit out on her own. Neither her father nor her spurious aunt seemed to care much. A year later, while working tables at a city restaurant, she met up with Donald Weaver and he had taken her to his house to live with him as his wife. It might be a stranger outside now, whispering to her, persuading her to open the door to him. Only when he prodded his finger to the bell again did she surrender. Anything, *anything* to stop that devilish racket. One-handed, she fumbled with the bolts and chains which Brand had secured to the mended frame, and at length yanked the door open.

He looked older, her father; looked gaunt and unfinished, like a putty model on a wire frame she had seen in a store once. His eyes were sly.

Baby Colin stared at the grandfather he had never seen before. The old man flickered his gaze from her to the little boy and gave a purse-mouthed grin and waggled his fingers. The child did not respond, holding to his grave inspection.

'What do you want?' Muriel said. She had just enough pride left to control herself.

'I wanted to talk for a bit.'

'I've nothing to say to you.'

'Can I come in? It's bloody cold out here.'

She could not bring herself to keep him standing on the threshold. 'In the kitchen.'

The kitchen was cluttered with old furniture, most of it Weaver's. Brand had been too practical a man to allow sentiment to interefere with economy. If he could learn to live with another man's woman he could easily learn to live with another man's household goods. A rented TV set looked grossly out of place in the shabby setting. On a drying horse before the fire a flock of diapers roosted. Greasy dishes were piled by the sink and the stale smells of frying fat and urine permeated the room. Muriel was suddenly ashamed of the squalor, twisting it back against the old man, blaming him for it.

'If it's about the money he's been sending, he's had it,' she said. 'It's all gone: I spent it on Colin.'

'It's not the money,' her father said. 'Weaver never even mentioned money.'

'Then what?'

'He . . . he wants to . . . find . . .'

'Holy Jesus!' Muriel said 'Not that.'

'Aye.'

'You encouraged him. You sent for him.'

'I did.'

'Tell him to stop.'

'He wouldn't listen to me,' her father said. 'The truth is that I don't want him to stop.'

'Leave me alone.'

'I will,' the old man promised.

He spoke softly, still standing by the door. It occurred to her that he had no great wish to be here; Weaver had conned him into it. The old goat had even donned his Sunday best, his only bloody suit like as not, a baggy tweed thing which she remembered hazily as part of his wardrobe fifteen years ago or more. The tie was one her grandfather had worn and bore the insignia of some Irish Catholic order, too faded now to be legible. Her father was an old man, and would soon die. For a second she considered allowing him to hold Colin but beat down the impulse, crushing the baby tighter to her bosom.

Her father was saying, 'We need to know some things.'

'What sort of things?'

'About what happened to Gordon.'

'Find out for yourselves.'

'I did not know the lad well enough, Muriel.'

'Weaver should have known him, *should* have known him. It's too bloody late now, though, isn't it?'

Then there was anger in him. Like turning the leaf of a book to an illustration she had never seen before, an aspect of her father's character was revealed to her, a reminder that, whatever had failed between them, they still shared the same blood line.

'Stop it, Muriel,' he told her. 'Weaver didn't need to come back here. But he did. Now tell me what I want to know and you'll never be bothered again by either of us.'

She lifted her head, speaking as if by rote. 'Gordon was discovered about midnight by a beat copper. He was lying on the waste ground in North Grahamshill, still tied to the truck. He had died about an hour before.'

'When did they inform you?'

'About one o'clock.'

'Who told you?'

48

'A copper, a sergeant.'

'Here?'

'Where else would I be?'

'With . . . with your husband?'

'Aye.'

'How did they identify Gordon so quickly?'

'He had his name and address on him.'

'Was he usually out so late?'

'Not often,' the woman said.

'But you weren't worried?'

'I was . . .'

'In bed?'

'Aye.'

'Did Gordon like Brand?'

'I don't know.'

'What was his name written on?' Doyle asked. 'The "identification"?'

'I don't remember now.'

'What was it: a bit of paper, a card . . . ?'

'A membership card,' she said.

'Who identified the body?'

She spat the word out, 'Me!'

Baby Colin whimpered. She touched the sagging diaper then impulsively cast him from her, shifting from the hips, swinging the baby into the pram in the recess adjacent to the bed. The recollection of Gordon's face above the sheet was as vivid as a coloured snapshot—pale face, doctored and made presentable: but dead. The evidence of mutilation, snagged lids, ripped nostrils and black scars, washed and fingered down though they were, was hideous on the small white visage. They had even combed his hair back, his fine fair hair but they had missed a little caked blood around the rim of the ear. She bent over the baby in the pram, her back to her father, fussing with fingers that would not function, remembering that night; how Brand waited and was angry because they would not let him smoke in the waiting room. He should have been with her, by her side, there in the room, but he would not go with her, disclaiming, opting out. Later he had told her that she was very lucky to have him—under the circumstances.

'Nobody to do it for me,' she muttered.

She dipped a rubber soother in sugar and gave it to the baby. He sucked on it, lids faintly blue with afternoon tiredness, and a sticky dribble at the corner of his mouth.

She faced her father once more.

The old man handed her a lighted cigarette. She took it without thinking, seated herself on the edge of the chair by the fire.

'Membership of what?' Doyle gently insisted.

She thought about it, bringing herself up out of the mortuary with its stench of medicines and harsh soaps. 'A youth club.'

'Which youth club, Muriel?'

'Grahamshill,' she said. 'He didn't go there often, I don't think.'

'He didn't have many mates, did he?'

'He had his share, I suppose.'

'Did they hang about this club, too?'

'I don't know,' she said. 'Look, it'll do you no good, Da. The bogies have been that way and they got nothing.'

'They have missed something, lass.'

'Does Weaver intend to kill him if he finds him?' she said.

'He does.'

'He deserves to die,' she said. She was silent for a while, smoking in short grabbing snatches. 'Gordon was a clever boy, Da; did you know that?'

'Aye.'

'A smart one; he could have been something in life, something important and respected. He could have gone to a good school, to college, then to the university. He could have been anything he fancied; a doctor or a lawyer. He had the brains for it. He could, Da, he could have been anything he wanted.'

She caught sight of the gesture, the sly shift of the arm and sensed that he was about to comfort her. She flinched, hatred of him slamming down on her grief like a lid, shutting it in and his comfort out.

She leapt to her feet. 'Get out of here, will you? I don't want any more.'

Doyle stared at her for a long minute. She realised that he was sorry for her, and his pity sickened her. She flew at him, beating him with her hands, the cigarette scattering flakes of ash and burning tobacco shreds about him. He did not duck or seek to avoid her attack but stood there mute in his Sunday-best suit and let her strike him again and again across the head and chest until the pain in her hands made her quit. Her arms fell by her sides.

She could have told him that Gordon's death had not been real murder at all. It was a simple act of the God whom none of them saw fit to worship any more, a pennance imposed upon her for all the sins of omission she had accumulated over the years of her life. Her father would not contradict her, but he would not understand. None of them could be expected to understand. Brand, Weaver, her father, the legion of coppers; they were all men, and men did not feel these things as a woman did. They clung to their facts and answers, to their petty notions of logic and justice.

Outside the window the pigeons crooned and croaked and whirred their stubby blue-grey wings. In the pram Colin whimpered in his sleep.

'Stay out,' she said.

And he went, not turning, backing from her, head lowered so that the long jutting Doyle-type chin rested on his breast-bone. He inched back, drifting away from her through the kitchen door, his eyes down, shielded.

She felt relief that he had chosen to leave meekly and without damage. Bob would not have swallowed another half-baked lie about vandals doing in the door again. That was the trivial thought which occupied her mind as she gently dropped the latches and bolts and secured the door against the empty landing. She was gratified that Brand would not learn of the fresh trouble which had blown out of the November sky. Her predominant fear was that he would desert her too. Weaver, her father, and her sons hardly seemed to matter now. Temporarily purged of guilt, she felt able to set them all in their proper places, past and nebulous future, as the case might be.

She returned to the kitchen, lit another cigarette, and stepped into the stove closet to brew herself a cup of tea.

SEVEN

Outside the gates of the yard, Weaver paused. A raw wind set late autumn leaves scurrying round staves and hoardings like packs of demented rats, fluttered the fall of water over the weir to beard the concrete break. The little river was uncommonly low for the season and wallows of greasy mud caught the flotsam of the upstream factories. In the ramshackle repair shed rafter lamps had already been lighted. In the five years since last he had come this way nothing seemed to have changed. Even the carcases of the vehicles, flensed piecemeal for spares, which cluttered the rear of the hoardings looked the same. A new notice commanded his attention, however; a sign of the times. It stated that a guard dog constantly patrolled the area. Hands in the pockets of his overcoat, Weaver peered cautiously into the yard. Like all men who have engaged in burglary he had no love for dogs. He saw no sign of any animal though and stepped through the gates, towards the shedding where the lamps were lit.

The crippled Mark 10 was jibbed up by the front axle. The moment he identified the svelte shape excitement gnawed in his belly like a mouse chewing at a skirting board. The car was identical to the one he had driven on the Wimbledon job two years ago; same colour, same year of registration, right down to the buckled fender, as if it had been magically transported all the way from the south to this backwoods repair depot in Lanarkshire. The Jaguar Mark 10 had always been his favourite machine, smooth and powerful and sophisticated, an extension in metal of the image he had struggled to build for himself; also associated with success, a good luck talisman. So far as he could tell the model on the jib was not badly damaged. Radiator, fender and wing had taken a beating but the ribbing did not appear to extend back into the engine bed. He leaned against the door of the shed studying the car carefully. It wasn't a Jaguar he had come to buy. In terms of the McFadden job a Jaguar would be useless. He needed a Mini, a Cooper for preference; something with keen acceleration and sureness and manoeuvrability but small enough, a hugger, to sling round the twists of the moorland track with confidence. Definitely not a Jaguar. For all that, he coveted the machine, itched in the palms to have its power at his command, to duck under her, touch, tinker and explore.

Cringle came up behind him from the office across the yard. Though he did not turn Weaver could tell that it was Cringle by the soft shuffle of his footsteps. Cringle was tall too, stooped and dyspeptic. The small Errol Flynn moustache was comically out of kilter with his equine features.

'A bonnie car, sir,' Cringle said.

Weaver came round fast, dropping, brought his left hand into action and, to his gratification, felt the thud of Cringle's fist in the palm of his glove. He dipped again and reached and brushed his knuckles across the bib of the man's overalls.

'You're slowing up, George.'

'Christ, it's Weaver,' Cringle said. 'I'd never have recognised you, not in those natty duds.'

'Getting old, George,' Weaver said. 'Five years back you'd have plastered me all over the floor if I'd jumped you.'

'I've given up hittin' prospective clients.'

'You still go to the fights?'

'It's a dyin' sport here,' Cringle said. 'If you don't wear a spotty loincloth or a buncha Indian feathers and fling your arse about the canvas they just don't want to know.'

Weaver nodded: he knew how it was. He did not share Cringle's passion for boxing but he understood it. They graviated into the shedding out of the wind.

'What brings you here, Donald?' Cringle said.

'Business.'

'Your kind of business, or mine?'

'Mutual.'

'I don't do much of it now,' Cringle said. 'Too many suckers on the right side of the street to make it worth while.'

'Would you do one for me?'

'The Jag?' Cringle said.

'How bad is she?'

'Axle and wheel setting; radiator might be cracked.'

'And the engine?'

'Not a scratch.'

'Jerked?'

'On that beast? You're kidding.'

'How soon will she be roadworthy?'

'Christ, I haven't even bought her yet.'

'But you will,' Weaver said. 'How much?'

'You want it fast?'

'I want her for state occasions,' Weaver said. 'Nice, pretty and reliable.'

'Do it in a week.'

'How much?'

'Well, she's earmarked for a dealer.'

'Don't snow me, George.'

'For you—six hundred.'

'I'll pay cash, five.'

'And fifty.'

'Five.'

'Clean money?'

'Green and sweet.'

'Right.'

'And no bloody woodfiller, understand,' Weaver said. 'You can keep the colour as it is, but re-spray her and I'll shell out that as an extra.'

'Christ, that was quick,' Cringle said. 'Time was, you'd have spent a week beating your gums about the price.'

'Yeah!' Weaver grinned. 'But I didn't come about the Jag. What I want is something rather special, and it won't be so easy.'

Cringle blinked: friendship faded from his eyes like the light dying in a servo warning. 'I told you, I don't do it any more.'

'You'll do it for me, George,' Weaver said. 'I can't trust anyone else in the whole damned country.'

Cringle rubbed his hand over his jaw, as if massaging a bruise, then he turned on his heel, beckoning. 'Come on, then. We'll go on over to the office and talk about it.'

The stump of the Victorian parish schoolhouse had gained

a surrounding complex of prefabricated classrooms. Though numerous, they were still inadequate to deal with the population explosion. Doyle found it hard to believe that so many children and young adults could be packed into such a small space. Unobtrusively leaning against the gate-posts, he searched the faces for signs of those likely to have been Gordon Weaver's contemporaries. Never having had the opportunity, or the inclination, to study the younger generation at close quarters it came as a shock to notice the sheer physical size, not to mention the precociousness, of the thirteen- and fourteen-year-olds. He quailed at the thought of approaching any of them outright, but finally, with the exodus almost complete, screwed up his nerve and broached three hirsute youngsters who had paused at the kerb to light cigarettes.

'Excuse me.'

The three regarded him as if he was a species of perambulating virus, saying nothing, passing the match around in close-pinched fingers.

'Did you know Gordon Weaver?'

'What of it then, mac?' The tallest of the group spoke. He was a brutal-looking young man with a growth of hair over his mouth like the moustache of a bull walrus. His skin was pitted with the purple and yellow of acne as if he had taken a fusilade of buckshot full in the face.

'Do you remember him?' Doyle asked.

'Not me, mac.'

'How about you, son?' The boy was smaller, resembled Gordon in size and weight and had a similar trace of reserve about him. Perhaps this one had not yet quite rejected all respect for the authority of his elders.

'What do y'want t'know for?'

'I'm his grandpa.'

'Sure, an' I am Adolf Hitler alive an' well in Wickerburn,' the hairy one said.

Doyle had already slipped back into the speech patterns of his guttersnipe childhood, glottal and rasping and without trace now of meekness. 'Don't give me the patter, son; you knew him.'

The third boy had red hair and high cheek-bones and, as Doyle whirled to face him, he flushed deeply.

'Tell the bastard nothin', Mick.'

'Mick, is it?' Doyle said. 'Right, Mick, a quid for information.'

'The fuzz have treaded this way, mister.'

'I'm not the bloody fuzz. I'm the boy's grandpa, so how about it, Mick?'

'A quid y'say?'

'That the price.'

'Me an' all?' asked the hairy one.

'Bugger off, son,' Doyle said. 'Mick got his bid in first.'

'Show's the green,' Mick said.

Doyle took his hand from his pocket and held up the pound note, folded long like a taper. He was sensible enough to realise that money would not purchase their attention for more than a few minutes. He selected the salient questions from his stock, and said tersely, 'Grahamshill youth club, did you go there?'

'Yep,' said Mick.

'Did Gordon Weaver?'

'Sometimes.'

'Often?'

'Sometimes.'

'Who's the supervisor?'

'Fleming.'

'Is he still there?'

'Club folded,' Mick said. 'Months ago.'

'Where did this Fleming joker go?'

'Christ knows.'

'Is he local?'

'Yep, I think so. Not certain.'

'When the bogies came to the school, did they quiz you?'

'Not me personal-like,' Mick said. 'Some of the mates, and the teachers.'

'Did they find anything?'

'Doubt it,' Mick said.

'Was there anything in the school to find?'

'Eh?'

'You know what I mean, Mick. Was anybody withholding information?'

'If there was I never heard nothin' about it.'

'Was Gordon one of the boys?'

'Don't know what y'mean.'

56

'Was he popular?'

'He never ran with our crowd.'

'Who's crowd did he run with?'

'Nobody's crowd.'

'One of the packs, maybe?'

'Packs?'

'Gangs,' said Doyle.

'Gangs,' said Mick in mock horror. 'Gangs in Grahams-hill!'

'Did he run with a gang, Mick?'

'Know nothin' about gangs,' Mick said, curtly. 'I reckon you've had your quidsworth, mister.'

'Wait!'

Doyle delved into his pocket to find another note, but Mick had already plucked the pound note from his fingers. Doyle cursed himself for his lack of tact. If he had known that talking to the boys would be like trying to photograph wild animals—one false move and they would either turn on you or scoot off over the horizon—he would have been better prepared. Fists stuck in the pockets of his reefer jacket, Mick was already on his way to the corner. His companions flanked him defensively. Doyle thought of following, of trying to isolate Mick and tempt him with more money but he was wary of them, young though they were. He had no fancy to wind up in the casualty ward of the Western with his teeth stove in. Anyway, he cheered himself, his pound had purchased something of value; fresh information, information which had not appeared in print. He had himself a little lead, just a wee tiny one, but better than no lead at all. He would present it to Weaver to show that he had not been sitting on his hands. It was up to Weaver, really, to sort out this Fleming character.

Coming from the shower, cleansed of make-up, Hazel looked fresh and new-minted, innocent and incredibly young. She wore neatly creased bell-bottom slacks of a shocking pink colour and her nipples showed through the crisp white blouse. Her breasts were high and firm. Combed back, her hair was like a sheet of goldfoil, her features, pert and feline, exposed. She seemed younger than twenty, hardly even adolescent, in spite of the size of her breasts. On occasions like this when she stripped herself of the warpaint and the cultivated penumbra of sex, Irwin experienced little or no physical attraction towards her, a twinge of guilt almost that he had taken her body and helped to corrupt her by teaching her all the perversities of the professional whore. Hazel did not seem to object. She made a ready pupil. Her youthfulness was most obvious at this hour of the day. It never ceased to astonish him that she could bounce up full of the joys and radiant after a night of drink and fornication—love: he must learn to call it love—while he could barely lift his eyelids with a crowbar and his balls were full of lead. He sipped the first cup of black coffee and coughed up the phlegm in his throat into a Kleenex. She lit a cigarette and gave it to him as if she were putting a thermometer into his mouth. He could taste the perfume of the soap on the tip.

'Weaver's here,' she said.

Irwin's eyes watered. He coughed again, rackingly.

'I stuck him in the lounge.'

'God!' Irwin wheezed. 'Oh, God!'

'I'll give him coffee,' Hazel said, 'unless you want him here and now?'

'God, no!' said Irwin.

He hawked again and sucked smoke on the filter, and his mouth tasted like the inside of an exhaust pipe. When Hazel padded from the room, he got shakily to his feet. Bloody Weaver seemed to have developed the most uncivilised manners since his term in London. One facet of the Empire Builders—his term for the bloody English— which made Irwin wince was their unreasonable custom of early rising. He lifted his wrist watch from the leatherette stand on the table and peered blearily at it: ten bloody o'clock. Listening carefully, he heard the shower hissing and, below it, the mutter of Weaver's voice. Chatting up Hazel, was he? A pang of envy went through him at the thought of how Weaver had weathered the storm of the years. After all there were hardly two years between them, yet the term in the south seemed to have rejuvenated Weaver, to have preserved in him the dash of a much younger man without subtracting authority and strength of experience. If only Hazel wasn't so damned bland, Irwin thought, then he might be able to tell if she had the hots for the bastard. He had been lucky to discover such a girl. He knew he would eventually lose her to some younger, richer, smarter punter. She would shuck him off the way a baby butterfly shucks off its birth caul, and he would have to find himself another bird. There were few as good as Hazel on the scene. Thinking of losing her filled him with sadness and despair.

The sound of the girl's laughter drifted into the bedroom from the lounge. Struggling, he trundled into the bathroom with as much speed as he could muster and stuck his arm under the shower. Christ! She always persisted in trying to make him a hard man. His eyes widened and a spasm of shock chittered up his arm into his chest as the freezing water struck. He stifled a bellow and jiggled with the tap at the back of the tiled stall until he had fashioned a compromise in temperature, then he dived under the lukewarm spray, chaffed his body with the bath-glove for a couple of minutes, and dived out again. Dried off with a rough towel, he returned to the bedroom and donned the suit of clean underwear and the terrycloth robe which Hazel had left out for him, then went into the lounge.

Weaver was seated in an armchair, balancing a big breakfast cup on his knee. He had all the aplomb, cut and style too, of a stockbroker holding court in the Central Hotel, secure in his inside knowledge of a bullish trend in the market. The tan had faded slightly over Weaver's face, but his eyes were still piercingly bright against the browned skin. He looked like a male model in an airline ad. Taunted by such analogies, reflections of covetousness, Irwin's greeting was civil but hardly warm.

Weaver grinned. 'Rough night, Jack?'

'Nothing out of the ordinary.'

'I've come about transport.'

'Have you now?'

Irwin lowered himself into the couch and shouted the girl's name. She was instantly at his side to present him with the large red coffee cup.

Not meeting her eye, Irwin growled. 'Go an' put some underwear on.'

'Yes, darling.' She went out of the room.

'She's not in on it, is she?' Weaver said.

'In on what?'

'She doesn't know about the job?'

'She knows something's in the wind, but that's all,' Irwin said. 'I keep my women under control.'

'Glad to hear it,' Weaver said. 'This is how we'll do it.'

'If I agree.'

'Yeah! If you agree, of course,' said Weaver. 'I've rented a Mini Cooper.'

'Rented it! I thought we'd knock one.'

'Not with forty miles of road and a Merc gunning behind us.'

'Bloody Cooper, bloody toy.'

'Stop bitching,' Weaver said. 'A Cooper's best for the track. I need a car I can depend on. I've got it under cover. It'll be tuned and primed and fuelled. We'll run it out on Friday while we check the route and time . . .'

'I've done all that a dozen times, for Jesus' sake.'

'We'll do it again.'

'In the Cooper?'

'Yeah, Friday night the Cooper goes back under cover.'

'Where?'

'Never mind that.'

'Can you trust this garage gink?'

'I'd rather take the risk on him than chance a bum car,' Weaver said. 'He's an old friend, and he doesn't know what I'm on. Besides, McFadden's not as efficient an organisation as the cops or the Mafia. He doesn't have enough manpower to make a thorough search. My motorman isn't even based in the city.'

'I don't care for this arrangement.'

'Hard cheese,' Weaver said. 'This is the best way to do it.'

'Okay,' Irwin grumbled. 'Then what?'

'We do a dry run on Friday, store the Cooper again until the following Friday, pick her up, run her direct to the McFadden house, pull the stunt and beat it back over the moor road. When we reach the Balloch crossroads we take the fork up the east side of the loch, swing out along the Fells and come into Glasgow from Stirling direction.'

'Why the bloody tour?'

'All we need's the edge,' Weaver said. 'If we make the crossroads half a mile before the Merc, then he'll have to take his pick, and he'll pick the straight line to Glasgow. The Cooper will outstrip the Merc on the moor road but not on the straight.'

'In theory.'

'What the hell's wrong with you, Irwin?' Weaver said. 'You taught me caution. You used to set up stunts with so much cover and so many alternatives that a bloody computer couldn't work out your escape plan. Now you want to play it like a young hawk with blood in his eye, and no brains in his head.'

Weaver was right. Irwin inhaled the fragrance of the coffee. Disturbing thoughts of Hazel's departure had thrown him out of gear. It was too early in the day for serious business: he had always been a night-owl. After all, Weaver was a professional, and was doing no more than any competent professional would have done. Irwin said, 'I'm sorry. You're right, of course.'

'Rough night?' Weaver said again.

Irwin grinned, though it cost him effort. 'Aye,' he admitted. 'Rough night.'

At this stage he could not afford to alienate Weaver who, all things considered, was the best partner he was liable to find. Lucky, Irwin thought, that circumstances had conspired to bring him home again at just the right time. He needed Weaver now, the strength and shrewdness which he had had himself once, but recently seemed to have lost in no small measure.

'Go on, Donald,' he said. 'About the Cooper.'

'My mate will strip the plates and respray her after the job,' Weaver said. 'He'll hold her for a month or so then flog her as he would have done in the first place.'

'How much does he charge for this service?'

'A hundred quid.'

'Fair,' said Irwin. He supposed it was fair too, though once he could have bought this sort of deal for twenty and a bottle of cheap Scotch. 'I'll go along with it.'

'All right,' Weaver said. Setting the cup aside he brought himself forward in the chair, hands together. 'What about weapons?'

'I'll get them,' Irwin said. 'I have them already, as a matter of fact.'

'How many?'

'Two, hand-guns, in good nick and with ammo.'

'We'll test them, dummy, next weekend.'

'A shooter's a shooter,' said Irwin. He bit off the protest. 'Sure, we'll test them. 'I'm no great shakes with a gun.'

'That's it,' Weaver said. He unclenched his fists and sat back. Irwin could see him switching off the mechanism which did the calculation, as if all the talk had been a playback from a preprogrammed tape. 'Give your girl a shout, Jack, will you?'

'What for?'

'Another cup of coffee,' Weaver said. 'What else?'

Weaver was smiling, the eyes loaded, not cold now but with something in them which Irwin could only identify as scorn. Suddenly he realised that Weaver was dangerous, and needed ginger handling. Anxious to protect Hazel, keep her out of the radius of that danger which women seemed to find so bloody alluring, Irwin got to his feet and went into the kitchen to fetch the Cona himself.

EIGHT

Hands braced on thighs, belly tugging the inside of his spine, Arthur Brown stooped to peer at the wax crayon scrawl on the side of the carton. Even with the help of a match flame he could not make out the coding. Growling to himself, he groped a knife from the block and hacked at the twine which held the boards shut. Puffing and sweating, he rested momentarily against the tower of cartons behind him then stabbed the knife into the wood and flipped open the lids. The books he brought out were dull theological works. Holding them stacked in the crook of his left arm he ran his eye critically up the titles. Peddling theology of this calibre was almost impossible at the best of times, and this was not the best of times. Two kids at home were down with whooping cough and he had garnered little sleep during the night. His wife was kicking up all kinds of hell about being bored; by which she meant that she wasn't getting out for her twice-weekly sessions at bingo with her sister. For two pins he would have smothered her with the pillow on which her nagging head lay. Typewriter, index cards, journals were his only source of therapy, the making of a little extra bread his excuse for working later than ever. The scapegoat for all his troubles was Vincent Doyle. He removed a scrap of paper from the uppermost volume, read the lot cost on it then, with a pencil stub, began to price the batch according to its lights. The exercise was a chore, boring and unexciting. It irritated him that Doyle was not around to share the task.

Brown was still on the first carton when Doyle slipped into the shop some fifteen minutes later. Brown heard the bell, paused, recognised the sound of the old man's footsteps and returned to his labour with a kind of malicious relief.

From the storeroom door, Doyle enquired, 'Has Weaver been here?'

'Don't know what he looks like.'

'Anybody asking for me?'

'Nope.'

'Something's wrong.'

Brown coded an odd volume of *The Golden Bough* and laid it to one side. 'Been to the bank yet?'

'What bank?' said Doyle.

'Our bank.'

'No.'

'Seven cheques to be deposited.'

'Why don't you do it?'

'You're the banker in this concern.'

'I told you I'd be busy.'

Brown turned: Doyle was outlined against the faint cold glow from the office. He looked like a piece of poor-quality soapstone carved by a dunken Chinaman, frail and fretted and elongated. Brown ignored the stir in his chest which exertion and ire had roused. A globule of sweat trickled down his brow into his eye and with it the temper went out of him. 'Weaver hasn't been here. Can't you locate him?'

'I don't know where he's living.'

'Is it urgent?' Brown said, with quickening interest.

'No, no,' Doyle said. He glanced at the watch on his wrist, a boy's cheap timepiece, plain as a penny and almost as tarnished. 'I just like to keep in touch.'

'Is he making trouble?'

'No.'

'Can I help?'

'No.'

Brown did not press the offer. The invitation to involvement had popped out before he could help himself. He did not closely consider his motive, thinking of it as akin to the impulse which dragged him from bed at night to sit with two hacking children, comforting them with his presence and his own discomfort. Gordon Weaver was little more than a nebulous recollection, just the shadow of a young face, solemn and withdrawn. He had long ago lost the feeling of annoyance which the senselessness of the killing had given him. He had never truly felt grief for the dead boy, only for the old man who was left alive to suffer. Brown chewed his pencil, cocking it in the side of his mouth like a cheroot.

'If Weaver does come here,' Doyle said, 'tell him I have some news.'

'Good or bad?'

'I'm not sure yet.'

To Brown all news was bad. 'I'll tell him.'

Doyle shuffled out of the shop, an old man.

Puzzled, Brown went back to pricing the rubbish of theology.

The caretaker leaned on the handle of the broom and watched dust resettle along the floor. It was almost pitch dark in the corridor. Pushing through the unlocked door from the street, Doyle had heard the old man long before he had seen him, the noise of wheezing lungs and the exhausted hiss of the broom bristles on the rock-hard linoleum. He had called out, loudly too, but the caretaker did not hear him. The caretaker was deaf. A metal hearing-aid, like a tobacco tin, dangled from the rule-pocket of his overall. Doyle bellowed into it, and the caretaker smiled.

'Sure, I remember Mr. Fleming.'

'Where is he now?'

'Not here,' the caretaker declared. 'Gone. Nobody here 'cept me.'

'Where can I find Fleming?'

The old man thumbed a wall switch and a single naked light bulb bloomed. Doyle was able to see clearly for the first time. Deafness had warped the caretaker's neck and shoulders, leaving them permanently tilted, like a hulk in sand. His whole frame seemed to be begging for the consolation of audible sounds. Doyle reckoned that he must be well over seventy.

'Where does Fleming live?'

Grinning, the old man lifted one hand from the broom and crooked his index finger. He shifted backwards, drawing Doyle after him, like a hypnotist. Reaching behind his hip he butted the brush against a door and backed off into total darkness, still grinning and beckoning. The atmosphere of the deserted club rooms and the gnarled old man made Doyle uneasy. Even as he groped his way into the darkness beyond the door, he had the inflamed notion that perhaps the caretaker had Fleming incarcerated in a dungeon or nightmarishly embalmed in a gigantic bottle in some cupboard.

'Television,' the old man moaned. 'Television done it.'

The vaulted roof of the long hall sent back sepulchral echoes. A light clicked on, another single bulb hanging from a long, long flex. A platform at one end of the hall supported a table-tennis table and racks of dusty forms. Doyle could taste the decay in his mouth. At that moment he would have traded a finger for a pint of whisky. The caretaker was extolling the past glories of Grahamshill youth club; a famous local institution in its heyday. Supported by charitable funds and administered by a board of rich and conscientious do-gooders it had kept the apprentice lads off the streets and out of the ways of wickedness. Before the coming of age of television and municipal concern had rendered it obsolete, it had produced a tidy crop of boxers, dancers, lifters and other sportsmen. History of this sort bored Doyle but he listened politely, glad when the tale reached its melancholy end. After prolonged litigation with the trustees the premises had been sold to a carpet manufacturer short of warehouse space. Doyle picked at a gap in the monologue and, for the third time, slipped in his question about Fleming. In the caretaker's view, he learned that Fleming had been the salt of the earth, a paragon, sadly misjudged by those in authority.

'And where did he go?' Doyle asked.

'What d'you want with Mr. Fleming?'

'To talk with him.'

'That all, like?'

'I have some money for him.'

'You one of his . . . friends, like?'

'Not really.'

'One of those?'

'One of what?'

'Them! What they claimed he was.'

'What did they say he was?' Doyle asked.

'Funny,' said the caretaker. 'Not that he were.'

'You mean queer.'

'That's the word.'

'Who said he was queer?'

'I never saw no evidence of it.'

'Did the police come here after Gordon Weaver was killed?'

'Gordon Weaver,' the caretaker said in his flat, ugly, droning voice. 'A bad business.'

'Did they question Fleming?'

'They questioned him: persecution, if y'ask me.'

'What did . . . ?'

'Lost him the job,' the caretaker shouted. 'Questioning everybody.'

'You too?'

'Wasn't here at the time.'

'Where were you?'

'Hospital.'

'For long?'

'Six weeks I was away, an' when I come back it were all beginning to shut up and Mr Fleming were gone.'

'Why?'

'The buggers thought he done it, see.'

66

'So the police never got to you?'

'Nah!'

Bands of tension tightened across Doyle's belly.

'I'm fine now though; champion,' the caretaker said. He paused, brooding, as if to ascertain that the healing of what-ever ailment had laid him low at such a crucial time had indeed occurred. 'Won't have no job left, though, come Christmas.'

Doyle's fingers shook slightly as he offered the packet of cigarettes and went through the procedure of lighting one for the old man and one for himself. The tobacco smoke only served to increase his nausea.

So Fleming was a queer, a homosexual, and the bogies had been on to him. They had missed out on the caretaker, though, and if they had missed out on one they could have missed out on others. Doyle felt sick and excited at the same time.

'Lived in Glencairn Road,' the caretaker was saying, 'but shifted. Might be dead for all I know, dead and buried. Lots of folks are dead and haven't told me.'

Doyle put his mouth close to the metal box on the over-all bib. 'Like Gordon Weaver?'

The old man did not retreat into cunning, merely nodded. 'Aye, like him.'

'You knew him well?'

'Knew them all: only the faces was different.'

'Do you remember *Gordon Weaver?*'

'Not the only one to get himself killed, like,' the old man said. 'Most of them die one way and another—the war, the street, work, accidents. Die all the time now, young men do.'

'Do you remember who his friends were?'

'Weaver was one of his friends.'

'One of Fleming's . . . friends, you mean?'

'Had lots of friends, did Mr Fleming.'

Doyle swore under his breath, forcing his lips back from his teeth to keep the smile in place. Something was choking him, like a tip of slag in the nasal passages. Gordon could not have been one of Fleming's 'friends': even the word had a coy and girlish ring to it and, in the context, increased his disgust.

67

'Was Gordon one of . . . a *special* friend?' he asked.

The caretaker smiled at him out of rheumy eyes, eyes like those of a clapped-out old hen, reddish and alert. 'You got nothing for Mr Fleming. You're another bleedin' copper's nark.'

'I don't look like a copper, do I?'

'You do, now I thinks of it.' The old man raised the broom like a halberd and jabbed it at Doyle's groin. 'Pump me, would you, you bugger?'

'Listen, I'm Gordon's grandfather, I . . .'

The deafness was not now confined to the ears. No bellow would penetrate the thickness of the caretaker's skull. The loneliness of deafness had calcified into something akin to madness. He poked out with the broom handle, backing Doyle swiftly into the corridor. Even Doyle could have easily disarmed him but, weakened by the afternoon's revelations, he could not bring himself to indulge in an episode of farce which would be unlikely to yield anything of further value. Weaver, perhaps, would have sucked more from the man, but he had shot his bolt. Aggression would gain him nothing. He backed, then pivoted and went out quickly into the evening street. The caretaker barked and snapped at him from the doorway like an Airedale straining against its leash.

In the nature of man is a basic dislike of involvement in the complexities of death; or was it, Doyle wondered, that Gordon's murder had certain properties which hurt people so deeply that they could not bear to talk of it rationally? Muriel, Brown, Mick, and now this relic, all rebuffed him to some degree or another. Even Weaver appeared to have abandoned him. How could he tell Weaver that Gordon had been mixed up with a queer? Was this a secret that he should keep to himself, out of kindness to the living and respect for the dead?

Dusk had come down over the tenements and the harsh yellow lamps glowed above him. A raw wind drifted along the pavement, scouring it with ribbons of dust, like ice spume over arctic wastes. Doyle shivered. He stuck his last cigarette in his mouth and, with sudden decision, headed towards the main street and the nearest public bar.

The Cooper skidded to a sudden halt as a bus ploughed across it bow. More nervous than he would admit, Weaver cursed the driver in a filthy monosyllable then eased the small car down the dipping hill of Renfield Street into the heart of the city. It was boom time, Friday night, with half-cut pedestrians spilling heedlessly across the four-lane thoroughfare from pubs and from cinemas and snack bars.

'We should've waited until it was quieter,' said Irwin.

'Tonight's when McFadden makes the run.'

'Aye,' Irwin agreed. He fell again into silent contemplation of the hordes of Glaswegians around him.

Weaver threaded the car across the traffic of Argyle Street and into the less active area of the dockland. A circle of one-way streets brought him at last to the head of Parnell Street within sight of McFadden's pub. The bar was the only one in the whole length of the gloomy warehouse-shored gulch. Bands of neon set under sloping eaves showed its location. Even in the Stygian darkness of a midwinter night, dockers and seamen could not fail to find it, piloted by the luminous blue sign, the exact colour of burning meths. The building had a low-slung look; a veritable tavern. Weaver took the binoculars which Irwin had unpacked from their mock-leather case and focused on the front of the pub. Flaking gilt paint under the neon scroll was clearly visible—The Ratlines.

'I thought it was called the Anchor?'

'Too many Anchors,' said Irwin. 'McFadden changed the name.'

Weaver had no call to ask about its interior style. He could visualise it well enough, a spurious antiquity designed by a couple of art students and executed at cut rate by some of McFadden's contact tradesmen; spit and sawdust and a zinc bar and grids over the windows, but none of it real.

They had arrived just in time.

'There he goes,' Weaver said.

McFadden had changed little. The rig was better, chic and expensive, but he was still the same gnome that Weaver remembered. McFadden paused on the pub's doorstep, flanked by two large men in checkered overcoats, like successful bookies. All three rounded the corner into

Brandon Street. Weaver continued his vigil. The back of a pale lemon-yellow Mercedes 300 showed broadside to Parnell Street then slithered smoothly out of sight along the cobbles of the dockside. Weaver thrust the binoculars into Irwin's lap and set off in the Cooper past the monolithic pillars of the new flyover. Even here there was a fair amount of traffic. A drunk—more cash in McFadden's till—slumped bonelessly against a wall, his cap tossed by his side to beg mutely for its owner. A couple of bloated whores plied their trade in a close mouth, then the Cooper was absorbed into the stream of transpontine traffic and swept into the roads on the south side of the river.

McFadden's second gold mine—The Caspian—was a recently erected structure of glass and concrete. It stood on tiptoe over an off-licence on a sparse half-acre of corner ground in the heart of a new high-density housing development. It catered with equal cunning to brassrail boozers and teenage tipplers, and went in for musical soirées most nights of the week. The worlds of the old gullet and the young purse were divided by a spinal cord of lavatories down the centre of the building, and there were several entrances. Irwin told Weaver where to plant the Cooper. The Mercedes was visible in the car park. Concealment was unnecessary; kerbs were flanked by cars of all shapes and sizes and the Cooper fitted neatly into a small vacant slot. They waited a patient fifteen minutes for another sight of McFadden. Still protected by the heavies, he emerged from a side door and went down an avenue by the gable of the building. His round spectacles glinted like burnished coins and in his right hand he carried a fat pigskin briefcase. However routine the collection might be, Weaver noticed that McFadden was still wary and alert, darting glances this way and that as he waited for the Mercedes to be brought from the car park. The pick-up took no more than five seconds. So far, Irwin had been accurate in his assessment; there was no chance of making a clean hit in the city.

The third and last call was back in the city centre, high on the slopes above Cowcaddens. The rock club was enigmatically dubbed Carbon Atom. It lay in a lane which had the atmosphere of a shebeen or a steel engraving of

70

the Ripper's Whitechapel. Even the traces of fog wisping across the gaslamp at the entranceway seemed like more of McFadden's artificial props. Irwin told Weaver that the Carbon Atom was a popular rendezvous with rich young swingers who found a strange camp appeal in the slum territory and wastes of bombsites, a freakish garden set out specially for their romps. The Carbon Atom was also the headquarters of McFadden's organisation, the upper floor given over to a private club for friends, adjutants, parasites and women. In his intimate circle McFadden could number at least one high-court judge and not less than three acquitted murderers.

Weaver placed the Cooper half a block away and settled down to wait. An hour passed before the Mercedes emerged from the end of the lane and turned west, passing the Cooper closely, accelerating. In the depths of the car's rear seat, Weaver glimpsed the bulk of one of the guards, but he could see nothing of McFadden save a hand on the window glass, almost as if he was graciously waving to them, like royalty.

Irwin clicked his stopwatch, then said, 'Do you want to go after them?'

'No,' said Weaver. 'No point.'

'What about the arrival at Bargowan?'

'Not important,' Weaver said. 'It can be checked to-morrow night, or even at the beginning of the week.'

Irwin was consulting figures in a small black-bound notebook. 'Well, that's how it's been for ten weeks, give or take a few minutes. Just like clockwork, the bloody idiot.'

'His loss is our gain,' said Weaver. The quotation was one of Irwin's hoary maxims. He reached down and started the engine of the Cooper, listening to the thrum of it, then he yawned. 'All right, Jack,' he said. 'I'll drop you off, then I'll drive this baby home to bed.'

'Wait,' Irwin said. 'Tell me what you think of the job. Go on, Donald, flatter me.'

'It looks sweet.'

Irwin chuckled and unlocked the glove compartment. He tugged out a heavy parcel, unfolded layers of brown

71

wrapping paper and exposed two guns. One was a Smith & Wesson police revolver, the other a double-action Luger automatic.

'Well, Donald, what do you say?'

'I'll take the Luger,' Weaver said.

PART TWO

ONE

Weaver lay on the bed in the room in the Pemberton with his arms behind his head. The curtains were closed over the windows but he knew what the weather was like, clear and windless. The smirch of industrial fog which might creep up river later in the evening would not rise as high as the moorland road.

He had spent a lot of time in the past week just lying on this bed staring at the ceiling. The McFadden caper stood between him and the ritual of vengeance. Even now he was not bound to honour his promise to the old man. He felt no warmth for Doyle, not enough of any particular emotion to commit himself out of loyalty to an alien act. No, his loyalty wasn't to the old man but to himself, to the personality he had consciously tailored from the shabby cloth of his former self. He had made himself a hunter, had taken on the mantle of toughness and loneliness which that profession demands and now he was obligated to it, slave to it even. Squeamishness and uncertainty were gone. Only dread remained deep in his gut, nibbling stealthily at him like a tapeworm.

The McFadden caper: he bore down on it again.

The Cooper was parked in the hotel's underground garage; tuned up by Cringle, the tanks filled, tyre pressures to his own specification. The Mark 10 was stowed in the third tier of an all-night parking block close to the city centre. It too was fuelled and ready for a fast take-off. If the job went sour, he could be out of Glasgow down the south-bound motorway within minutes.

In his mind, buried below natural anxiety, was the faint hope that something *would* go sour tonight: nothing too serious or crippling, just a nice bit of ill luck to give him the excuse to blow the country for a while. Perhaps it wasn't Doyle, or Gordon's death which depressed him, but the city itself, ugly in the November fogs; mean

houses and reeking pubs hemmed him in like the amphi-
theatre of an arena or the walls of a prison yard.

If he had known in advance that it was going to be this
bad, somehow he would have contrived to smother the
sense of loss and the rage which the old man's letter had
detonated, would have stayed on in Spain until the wound
of the insult to his pride had healed, or his stake ran out.
A real professional, one of the movie-style fascists, would
not have exposed himself to risk over the death of a boy
to whom he hardly ever gave thought and to whom he
meant nothing. Four years ago, sickened with Glasgow,
he had shucked off that load of responsibility and set out
to recreate himself in the hothouses of London. The
period to which Gordon belonged seemed gone like a
rainbow; but the kicks and cunning triumphs, the months
of indolence and luxury, the girls of class whose bodies
he had entered, the cool and witty men with whom he
had worked, all seemed as insubstantial as a hophead's
dream too, now that he was back in the old city, pulling
a stunt with Irwin. No matter how doggedly he concentrated on recalling the intervening years he could not convince himself that anything had really changed. Physically
he was in better shape; his brain sharper, his nerve taut,
but inside, maybe, he was the same punter who had
hustled off south. The thought irritated him and made
him restless. He turned his wrist and looked at his watch.
It was ten minutes short of eight.

He lifted himself slowly from the bed and crossed to
the dressing table. On its melamine surface the gear was
all laid out: gloves, a stocking, the Luger. He had left
little enough to Irwin, and nothing at all to chance.

Lifting the gloves he peeled them apart and fitted one
over his left hand, tugging the fingers on like a second
skin. After the job the gloves and the stocking would be
destroyed, the Cooper would go back to Cringle's to be
transformed, and nothing at all would remain of all this,
except the Luger and the hand that held it.

At eight-forty Weaver drew the Cooper up around the
corner from Irwin's flat. He locked the car, walked the
distance and climbed the steps to the street door. Now
he experienced no chastening emotions, only a mildly

pleasurable excitement as if he was on his way to a party. On the verge of the caper he could still will himself to regard it as just another piece of business, and Glasgow as just another town. Come to think of it, at root there was no difference between this place and Leeds—or Belfast or Birmingham; Irwin was a man of no worse calibre than the hawks in those other towns and even McFadden was just another sucker too vain to look after his wealth.

As he mounted the stairs he found himself whistling a little jazz riff which had haunted him for years.

Hazel admitted him.

Irwin was in the bathroom off the hall, visible through the open door. He was naked to the waist, his pot-belly drooped over the lucky crocodile-hide belt which he wore on every job. Though his greeting was hearty, Weaver noticed strain in the highlander and watched without smiling as he conducted his welcomes with the blade of a bone-handled cut-throat.

'Man, are you all set?'

'Yeah.'

Weaver did not give up his overcoat to the girl. The pockets were weighted with gear and he did not wholly trust her. Her long hair was swept back and tied with a ribbon. She wore an oatmeal wool sweater and a donkey-brown skirt pinned at the hip by two big stag-horn buttons. Her eyes were very bright when she stared at him, as if Irwin's suppressed excitement infected her too.

'Stacks of time, Donald,' said Irwin. 'We'll hang on the feed-bag before we go. Hazel, m'love, whip up something hot for the lads.'

'I'm not hungry,' Weaver said.

'Bit of the old butterflies, then?'

'I had dinner only an hour ago.'

'The workers must eat,' said Irwin. 'Keep the strength up for the tribulations ahead of us.'

'What shall I cook?' Hazel asked. 'What do you fancy, Mr. Weaver?'

'Anything.'

'Eggs?'

'Fine.'

Hazel padded off in the direction of the kitchen. To his astonishment Weaver found himself admiring the movement of the tight girlish buttocks under the cling of the skirt and feeling, for an instant only, a slow and smoky coil of desire in his groin. When he turned to face the lighted box of the bathroom, Irwin's razor was poised over a swathe of pink skin peeled from the frothy coating of lather.

'I like that girl, y'know,' said Irwin softly.

Weaver held up the face of the Rolex. 'Better hurry.'

'Stacks of time.'

The razor scraped stubble, lifting lather cleanly. The cutthroat was another instrument in Irwin's elaborate preparatory ritual. Only before a stunt did he shave himself with whetted steel; perhaps, Weaver thought, to demonstrate to the auditors of whatever destiny Irwin courted that his hand was steady and his nerve strong.

Though his own belief in fate was not so far developed as Jack Irwin's, Weaver was pleased to notice that the cutting edge did not draw blood from the highlander's sensitive jaw.

'Christ, he's not coming.'

'Give him a chance, Jack. He's only four minutes late.'

An open ivory-white E-type convertible squealed into the lower end of Parnell Street. Travelling well above the legal limit, it came shooting up towards the men waiting in the Cooper. Four young people were crammed into the bucket seats and one tall girl, with the bone structure of an antelope, was perched on the hood cover. A long gauze scarf trailed from her fingertips, whipping and fluttering like a pennant in the cold slipstream. The image jarred with the backcloth of the dockland and the girl's laughter had the fragile artificiality of a mechanical doll's. The forced gaiety loitered in the chasm of warehouse walls long after the E-type had snaked out of sight.

'Maybe McFadden's got sick,' Irwin hissed. 'Maybe he's changed the bloody route. Maybe he'd got wind we're . . .'

'Shut up, Jack.'

'If you ask me, we lost the bastard.'

'Wait.'

Below the Cooper, boozers flocked from the doors of the Ratlines. For a moment Weaver could not quite credit the evidence of his eyes, then puffed out his cheeks in relief as

78

two guards and the gnome-like figure of McFadden separated themselves from the crowd and legged it briskly to the Mercedes on the corner. Why had Irwin failed to notice the glint of the lemon-yellow metal? The Mercedes came round and he was able to identify it positively.

Jubilantly Irwin patted him on the thigh.

'That's it, man.'

'Did he have the briefcase?' Weaver asked.

'Aye.'

'All right,' Weaver said. He threw the Cooper into gear. 'All right, Jack, it seems we're in business.'

Wind from the Firth drenched the trees. It was heavy and fluid and dense enough to absorb all the tell-tale sounds which the men made as they skirted the boundary wall. Bargowan, house and grounds, filched light from the moon, sucking it through a stratum of shifting clouds and a silt of rain. The Cooper was hidden in the shadow of a thorn hedge twenty yards from the wall at the rear of the house. Weaver and Irwin crossed the tongue of shrub-crusted earth with the stealth of foxes. As they reached the wall the wind gusted high then withered and faded into silence.

Irwin tapped Weaver on the shoulder.

Weaver leaned his back against the stonework and cupped his hands, palms uppermost, at the level of his groin. In the basket of his fingers Irwin's rubbers slipped and slithered like guddled trout. The full weight of the highlander momentarily racked him then Irwin was gone, mantel-shelving the wall, rolling over into the garden.

Weaver waited.

A rope whirred over the wall-top and slapped the ground at his feet. He snatched up the stringers and passed them round an ash-tree trunk and knotted them firmly. The soft wash-leather gloves did not hinder his dexterity. Experimentally, Irwin tugged the hidden ends of the rope ladder then drew it taut. With ease Weaver swarmed up and over the wall and dropped to the concrete by Irwin's side.

Not by accident the men found themselves in an avenue between a potting shed and a garage, sheltered from sight of the house. Irwin had assured him that the only dog on the premises was a pampered poodle but Weaver strained his ears for the growling and warning bark; heard nothing. Light showed in two ground-floor windows but the kitchen quarters adjacent to the garages were in darkness. When he slipped forward for a closer inspection, his cheap canvas basketball boots made no whisper of sound on the concrete.

Lawns reflected light from the front of the house, outlining Irwin's bulk in sufficient detail to show the blond hair slicked down and ducktailed over the collar of the black nap reefer jacket. Rich with the scent of salt and oil the wind blundered through the treetops and strummed the ornate TV mast riveted to the chimneyhead. The vibrations were weird against the skin, felt more than heard. Weaver hugged his elbows to his gut, involuntarily shivering as the sounds fled with the gusts across the lawns and into the trees on the eastern perimeter of the grounds.

Lifting his arm, Irwin read the hour.

'No mad rush, Donald,' he said. 'We've fifteen or twenty minutes' grace.'

Pumping his hand; fingers starred, Weaver commanded silence. He inched past the highlander and peered out across driveway and curving gardens to the tall pale gates through which the Mercedes would eventually appear.

To his dismay the headlamps of the car were already sweeping the posts. Even as he jerked back out of sight the throaty roar of the engine reached him.

'Jesus God!' said Irwin.

They had timed the operation to allow a margin for error; even so, the unexpectedly early arrival of the Mercedes caught them in a bad position. Not only were they trapped in the avenue but they had not yet had time to sabotage the transport in the garage and eliminate the possibility of pursuit.

Stunned into immobility, Irwin crouched by the wall's edge as the big beams raked the outbuildings. Clapping his glove over Irwin's mouth, Weaver yanked him back out of sight.

'The stocking,' Weaver murmured. 'The mask: put on the mask.'

He did not wait to check that Irwin obeyed him, but

80

pivoted away, darted back along the avenue and, seemingly without breaking stride, clawed up the side of the boundary wall and balanced himself like a wire-walker on top. The rough track of single bricks was so narrow as to be almost invisible yet Weaver danced unfalteringly along it, past the slates of the garage roof to the point at which the wall veered to the left and the trees stepped politely back from the house to make space for drying greens. Light as a frog, Weaver flopped down to the flagstones of the kitchen yard. The Luger butted his hip and his left hand reached to whisk the stocking from his pocket.

The Mercedes was abreast of the yard now, the driver beginning to manœuvre for the mouth of the garage, reversing. Staring into the car's interior, Weaver glimpsed the silhouettes of the passengers, then the Mercedes, like a skittish animal, sheered out of his range of vision once more and was gone save for sound. Fitting the stocking over his hair he unfurled it, tugged it over his skull and buried the folds under his collar. The material was creased and thickly seamed and he did not have full sight through it. There was no second to spare, though, to rearrange the fabric. Shoving himself to his feet, he brought the Luger ready into his fist.

Cutting to the shelter of the kitchen doorway, he paused under the unlit welcome light, listening to the Mercedes' idling engine, then skulked forward and pasted himself to the roughcast gable of the garage.

A kind of rage simmered in him as if McFadden's early arrival was not just a piece of ill luck but a betrayal. All Irwin's careful plans were bent now and only his own fast reaction to an emergency situation had redeemed some semblance of the original pattern. At least he had gained the flank and made sure that it would still be possible to catch the victims in the fork of the trap. Surely Jack Irwin would be intelligent enough to read his design. The stocking muffled his senses to such a degree that he felt almost as ponderous as a robot, and as invulnerable. The sensation was not without compensations. Counting a slow five, his lips brushed the mesh the way the mouth of a fish lips the undersurface of a stream. At the end of the count he flung himself around the corner and ran out into the open.

Headlamps blazed upon the garage doors. The driver was trapped in the intersection of brilliant circles midway between the Mercedes grill and the shutter handles. In a long overcoat and pork-pie hat his attitude was without menace, startled and humble like that of every other victim of ambuscade whom Weaver had seen. Sheened without dazzle, the ribbed alloy doors perfectly outlined him. Peering through the mask, Weaver boasted the Luger at arm's length. The second guard stopped in the act of hoisting himself from the back of the car. Stooped, he had one boot on the gravel. His trouser leg had ridden up to show the top of a canary yellow stocking. On the edge of the door pillar his knuckles were as white as quartz; left hand hidden. Deep in the shadow of the seat McFadden lurked. Weaver cocked his head for a better sight of the little man.

Abruptly the driver shouted aloud, flung his arms sky-wards and dropped. Weaver dropped too, the snout of the Luger tracing a scything arc in the air. That he did not snatch at the trigger was a signal of his coolness. In the field of light the driver's monkish coat was replaced by the highlander's reefer jacket and bullet-bald, nylon-shrouded skull. The vision of Irwin distracted Weaver only for an instant. Even as Irwin lifted the revolver again, the Mercedes trundled forward.

Weaver wallowed over on the gravel and flung himself from its track, chest then shoulders then chest again in contact with the ground. The bumper and arch of the wheel loomed over him and the tyres carped an inch from the top of his head. Splashes of light on the alloy doors massed and split into two distinct and separate cells, narrowing still in focus until the grill clashed with the metal and the car ground to a halt. The Mercedes had travelled no more than fifteen feet and Weaver, a little dazed, could not initially determine what McFadden hoped to achieve by the move; then he picked up sight of the guard and understood the exact nature of the tactic. The guard had a knife in his fist. Caught on his knees, Weaver studied the swirl of the overcoat and the position-ing of the boots. High above him the broad-nostrilled face was as expressionless as an elm-tree bole. He pointed the Luger at the guard's left calf and shouted a warning, would have fired a single round too but for Irwin. The butt of the highlander's revolver rose and stabbed and rose again and, before the guard could even drop the knife and pitch to the gravel, Weaver was up and running. Through a tear in the nylon mask he had sighted McFadden. The little man was sprinting across the corner of the lawn, hand on his hat, elbow hugging the case, legs pumping like pistons and the coat with the fur collar wrapped snugly around his body as if to contain all his fear and panic and hold it from spilling during his flight.

Weaver went after him.

The main door of the house burst open on impact. McFadden threw himself into the hall. Weaver was a yard behind him, hands hooked out to grab the collar. Through the fox-coloured veils of the mask only minute and scattered impressions of the mansion filtered through to Weaver. Later, thinking about it, he could recall an Indian carpet and antique furniture in the French style, porcelain vases and china flower bowls bursting with roses, an oak door, and a saffron runner pouring like a ornamental waterfall between the fluted railings of the staircase. Hung on the far edges of his sight were images of women, a girl and a girl child. The child was clad in daffodil chiffon, her features puckered in bemusement at her sudden awakening from deep sleep.

Weaver closed his fist on spongy fur and plucked McFadden up like a mastiff scooping a rat from a barn floor. The little man screamed piteously, slack mouth gaping under his moustache, a horror of imminent death making his eyes glabrous, the pupils outlandishly enlarged by his spectacle lenses. Gripped by the throat, McFadden squirmed and contorted and ripped at the mask with his fingernails then, flinging all his weight forward, dragged Weaver with him on to the stairs. Pitchfork fingers scraped at Weaver's eyes. Urgently he rammed down with his forehead; struck bone. Nails tugged, ripped lightly, slackened and fluttered away from his cheeks. On all fours, crouched over the victim like a fighting bull, Weaver butted again then, taking aim through the frayed nylon, smashed the stock of the Luger into McFadden's mouth. Blood flowed like a rose from the region of his ear, and his hat popped off. Minus hat and glasses, McFadden looked like a wounded vole, tiny and defenceless: even the chirping sounds which issued from his throat were rodent-like. The delicate lashes blinked up at Weaver, then became sticky and adhered to the flesh, closed up, until Weaver could see nothing of the pupils but thin coppery slivers.

McFadden quivered and lay still.

Pushing back quickly, Weaver stumbled over the brief-case.

The pighide was blocked and trimmed with brass. He swooped on it and snatched it up, turned and blundered towards the door again even as the child flung herself hysterically against his thighs, raging. His first impulse was to lash out with the Luger, but even though he could not properly make her out the lack of weight in the attack told him that it was the child. Her vixenish ferocity stilled the rage in him. He pushed her gently away, his naked wrist pressing her rubbery little breast. She fell soft and wailing to the carpet.

Weaver ran into the darkness.

A freshet of blood had seeped down the nylon and impaired his sight. Impatiently he tore the stocking from his face and stuffed it into his pocket. Racing towards him, Irwin evolved from out of the paleness of the Mercedes' hull. Four doors gaping, the car snouted the garage doors. The guard was slumped inert on the paving just where the gravel ended, the knife in his hand cushioned in blood. Wriggling reflections of light and darker shadows on the hard surfaces told Weaver that the rain had become more forceful. The grain of the drops driving across his face was like the texture of the stocking mesh. His head was spinning, and he staggered. Irwin caught him.

'*Have you got it, man?*'

'Yeah.'

'*Then let's get t'hell out of here.*'

If at that moment Irwin had tried to wrest the case from him he would have felled the highlander too. Irwin's sole concern, however, was with escape. Hauling Weaver after him he accelerated from a shambling trot into a heel-kicking sprint and entered the avenue between the garage and the potting shed at break-neck speed. Leaping at the boundary wall, Irwin shinned up the ladder, straddled the wall then, turning from the waist, ordered Weaver to give up the case.

Brain clearing, Weaver stared up at the big man on the wall top. He saw only a black shape and featureless visage, a leather hand demandingly spread, like a vision of death come to gouge out his soul. Shaking, Weaver fought against fear and the dregs of violence which swirled in him, holding on to the case.

'Weaver, for Christ's sake.'

He closed his eyes and flung his partner the briefcase then groped for the rope struts and hauled himself up and over the wall. Before they reached the Cooper rain had lashed the last of the fever out of him and he was composed and cold again.

Sliding behind the wheel, he gunned the engine and released the brake, raced the little car out of the track on to the hardtop, flung it left, then left again. Lights pulled the gateposts of Bargowan out of the darkness as the Cooper approached, then passed. Thinking he had made it clear, Weaver let out a single dry rasping sob.

Screwed round in the passenger seat, Irwin peered throug the rain-rivered slot of the rear window. He was sobbing too and coughing, racking and harsh, but with his head held rigid, strained. The gates drifted back into the darkness, and the highlander choked off the spasm and began to shout, 'We made it; we made it; we . . .'

When Irwin's gleeful bellow chopped off, Weaver glanced up into the mirror and saw the sheen and glitter of the Mercedes' powerful lamps. They slithered and straightened and came steadily on as the big car sawed around the gatepost and bore down in their wake.

'Oh, Jesus!' Irwin said. 'Oh Christ!'

Weaver bent forward over the racing wheel.

TWO

Elation came over him immediately. He felt high with it. At last he was engaged with something which he fully understood and which stilled the nagging priggish streak in him. His impressions had the clarity of fine tempera paintings, sharply coloured and lined. He saw Irwin giving him alternately face and shoulder, the swing of the big man's body suggesting both awe and a raw sort of fear. Fingers loose, the variations of road surface were transmitted back to Weaver by the medium of the little black leather steering wheel. Below him in the alcove his feet tramped the pedals with innate skill, the highest form of self-expression he could ever hope to achieve. Hand on the rim, hand cupping the knob of the gearshift, eyes welded to the spears of light ahead, he thrashed the Cooper and hurled it into the gap which it burrowed for itself out of the banks of darkness ahead. By changes in the density and angle of the reflected lights in the wing mirrors, he judged the relative position of his pursuers, simultaneously translating cambers and curves, dips and sudden bucking plunges with all the acumen of experience.

The ride stimulated him beyond reasonable measure and negated all fear of danger. To spin the Cooper off the road would not only bring sudden death; it would mean that he had failed to utilise his fullest talent. That failure would hurt him more than the pains of dying by impact, bullet or fire. He seemed to hear himself breathing in perfect harmony with the fluctuations of the engine's revolutions, as if he had become endowed with the gift of pitching his own bodily functions to the functioning of the machine, was thus controlled by it even as he fought to control it. He reached the first incline with a hundred yards on the Mercedes, lost the lead by fifty yards before the central section but picked up the advantage again on the interlinked S-bends. With no appreciable loss of power he broke her from rounded shoulder to inside track, slipping between scrubby hummocks of blackness and dark overhanging ribs of bramble thorn. He pulled her, leaping, out of the spit of the road-mender's magazine, over the second crest and buttoned her on a straddle of the white line where it draped the centre of the next endless slope. The hill was so steep that the muzzle of the Cooper seemed about to drop back through the screen, the tarmac like a vertical wall. The lights streaked up it like circus spots fingering the roof of the big-top, then there was cloud like

86

a billow of soggy canvas and a glimpse of the moorland, sodden khaki and flat, tapering out to the limits of his vision. Wiping steam from the windshield with his forearm, he gunned the car again.

The Mercedes was back in the hollow. Badly throttled, it dipped like a yawl caught by a sudden gale. Weaver saw it only when he reached the high summit and came bounding out of it on to the plateau. He had two hundred yards on the big car now, but he knew he could not hope to hold it on the straight. He thumbed a switch and wipers twitched across the glass, stripping away the veils of rain. The track ran arrow-straight for four full miles before the next series of bends would restore his advantage. Swiftly he worked the Cooper up to its limit and held it there, watching, panting, as the Mercedes loomed on to the track behind and instantly began to reel in the gap between them, yard by yard.

With a quarter of a mile left to the sweep the German car was seated on his tail. He gave it no chance to hang there, but whipped the Cooper from verge to verge, certain that the driver of the brute would soon seize the advantage of weight and bulk to finish him. If he had been holding the wheel of the powerful Merc he wouldn't have hesitated; he would have swept the giant engine up to its ultimate, then let it go, raked the rear of the Mini and wiped it off the road. The pursuing driver's reluctance to make an end of the chase angered him even more than his own misjudgement. He dared not, however, trim his speed until he felt the pull of the left hand entry to the bend. His furious bewilderment lasted ten seconds, then the tyres were gripping differently and the bend was on him. He fisted the wheel, felt adhesion loosen, tamped the brake pedal and heard Irwin bellowing in his ear. The high-lander's elbow chopped him in the rib-cage as the man cowered and ducked and covered his head with his arms. The Cooper slewed wildly as the tilt of the banking rejected it. Weaver fought against the forces, brought her all the way through the first dog-leg and into the stem of the second, held her course through it too, into the last steep sharp corner—then missed gear and line at once. She mounted the hummock, clung there was an instant and, trailing a sound behind her like millstones grinding iron, thudded back into a central position. She snouted the peak again, stick quivering under Weaver's palm; even so he knew he had her tight. When the grating whine deepened into a roar, only then did he dart a glance in the mirror.

There was no sign of the Mercedes.

Downhill all the way to the tree line, the yards stripped away behind him. Once he reached the forest he could shake off pursuit. What pursuit? Pursuit had vanished.

On his knees, like a man vomiting, Irwin craned over the seatback, yelling, '*Look, look, look.*'

Though form and detail were obscure, the mirror showed him enough light to indicate that he need have no further worry about the hunter. Stern foremost, the Mercedes appeared out of the tail of the bend. It rode high on the heatherbag above the tarmac, not even shifting fast. Weaver braked and nudged the Cooper comfortably on to the crown of the road and risked a fast glance behind him. He saw it all, saw the change from ponderous elegance to an ugly desperate skittering skid as the rear fender bit the blacktop, saw the front spring up into the air like the lid of an exploding box and, in slow waltz tempo, saw the big pale lemon car plough overland on to the moor. All the lights flickered at once, flared, and receded into the carpets of rough scrub. What finally stopped her Weaver did not know; the Cooper was into the pines and the road was wriggling again like a wormcast over sand.

It didn't matter; the Merc was finished.

Dropping speed, he sighed and made himself intent on bringing her safe through the last leg of the forest track and out in one piece at the bottom.

Circling the pillars of Jamestown roundabout, Weaver eased the Cooper sedately on to the loch road, put the restricted zone behind him and let her wind herself up to a steady loping sixty. Only then did he lean back from the seat edge and carefully wipe a grease of sweat and coagulated blood from his eyebrows.

'Did it crash?'

'No,' Weaver said. 'It only ran out on to the moor.'

'Will they still be after us?'

'Not now.'

Irwin was quiet for a minute, then said, 'Did you kill anybody back at the house?'

'Don't be bloody stupid,' Weaver said. 'How about you?'

'I doubt it.'

'Don't you know?'

'Who the bloody hell was shoving those wheels,' Irwin demanded. 'Was it McFadden himself?'

'Couldn't have been,' Weaver answered. 'The guard you knobbled first maybe?'

'No, he was still lying there.'

'Dead?'

'I don't know,' said Irwin, then blurted out, 'Christ, no, he wasn't dead. I only tapped him a bit.'

When Irwin stripped off the mask most of his youthfulness seemed to come with it, peeling away from the visage of a haggard old man. He shook a cigarette from his pack and lit it and placed it between Weaver's lips. The smoke tasted as harsh as a mouthful of washing soda. By the third or fourth drag, however, he could feel it soothing him.

'What did you do to the wee man?' said Irwin.

'Hit him with the gun.'

'Hard, I hope.'

'He'll survive.'

'Christ, you turned out to be a real tiger,' said Irwin. 'Is that what London training does for you?'

'It almost went bust,' said Weaver, shaking his head.

'It wasn't my fault,' Irwin said. His voice was strident still, the words tripping over each other. 'They had real hard nuts, that pair. The driver was bad enough but the joker with the blade, Christ, I thought he'd never drop. Man, it was like hitting a slab of granite. I tell you, Donald, it wasn't *my* fault they showed up early like that. I timed it through a dozen nights.'

'Forget it,' said Weaver. 'We did all right.'

Reaching between his knees, Irwin fished up the case. He propped it on his lap and draped one hand over it like a cabinet minister posing with a portmanteau of state secrets.

'I'm hoping it's not dirty washing,' Irwin said.

'Open it.'

Irwin took a gully knife from his pocket and broke the lock. He tugged open the strap and pulled the jaws of the case apart.

'Well?' Weaver said.

Irwin's preliminary chuckle expanded into a belly-laugh. Out of the case he howked a handful of banknotes bound neatly by a rubber band.

'Man, that's my kind of laundry,' he said. 'I'll do a quick tally.'

'Leave it,' Weaver told him. 'Take the stuff home and total it. I'll collect my slice tomorrow.'

'Trusting bugger.'

'You wouldn't cheat me, Jack.'

'I wouldn't bloody dare.'

Weaver braked at the junction close to the end of the loch road, and swung north to take the long route home.

Irwin did not protest the added caution. It did not matter to him what Weaver did, now that the job was over.

He drove the Cooper through the open gate and into the shedding. Cringle pushed the street gate shut and shot the bolt on it then came across the darkened yard. He said nothing as Weaver collected his gear from the car and stuffed it into his overcoat pocket. Weaver took a last look at the Cooper, patted the bonnet in passing then went out of the shed. Cringle closed and padlocked that door too, then they walked together to the office. Cringle fed him a straight shot of whisky. He drank it slowly, then stripped off the wash-leather gloves and prodded them into the mouth of the coke stove, watched them ignite and burn. He fed the discarded stocking in too and watched it go up in smoke.

As well as the whisky, Cringle had on hand a motorist's first-aid kit and a deep tin tray filled with clean hot water. Weaver washed himself and laved away all traces of blood. He scrubbed at the stains on his clothing and, in a scrap of mirror over the desk, inspected the gash on his forehead. It was neither deep nor long; he taped it with a strip of surgical plaster from the box, and left it at that. He combed his hair down to hide the dressing a little, straightened his tie, turned and winked at the mechanic.

'You came out like a rose?' Cringle said.

'Always do.'

'No trouble?'

'None at all.'

'Right, I'll drive you into the city.'

'Thanks, George.'

Lit from above by a slim neon tube the mirror gave him back the portrait of a stranger; not a stranger, maybe, but an ancestor, an older man. It was as if the scars of the night had been instantly recorded in his flesh, like shadows on a photographic negative. He could not bring himself to think about the job. Only a few hours ago he had lain on that bed in this same room with his mind full of the caper; now it might never have happened. Though his limbs were leaden with weariness he could not coax sleep through the stiff sensitive bristles of his nervous system. Other matters filled his thinking, and his mind was suddenly spinning on a different axis.

The bedroom seemed unbearably cramped and confining, and the city outside was dead. In the wee small hours he could not hope to find himself a quiet pub or a discreet club in which to blunt the edges of his depression. It was night still, though the dairy carts were trolling now slow and soft out of their yards and the newspaper vans zoomed out of the city lanes with bundles of papers, fresh baked and still hot like bread. Four hours until daylight. He filled a glass with water and drank it slowly, pacing slowly up and down the three-yard stretch of carpeting, the distance from wall to wall.

It had been like this only once before, in London. There had always been a girl, Muriel or Edith or the American, always some bird to tap off the unnatural energy which spurted along his nerves like a gasoline fuse. He tried to put thoughts of women out of his head; no matter how he tried though, recollections of the girls he had known, Edith in particular, haunted him. The bloody job had not, after all given him release.

Did Edith still live in the elegant tower, the flat with the view of green hills and forests, and the broad balcony outside the bedroom window where they would stand together in the chill grey morning and watch the sun stipple the boulder fields of the distant ranges? He could lift the phone right now and call Edith; nothing to stop him but fear of the changes which time might have wrought in her, and of the broken promise which lay between them. It was Edith who had encouraged him to try his hand in the markets of London. Before he left he made a pact with her, agreed to send for her as soon as he was established; but the promise, in the end, had carried no weight. He had hidden from Edith, just as he had hidden from Muriel and Gordon, in the crowded streets of the capital. Tall, aggressive, cynical, Edith would never forgive him. She was not an answer, anyway, and the notion of contacting her reeked of prevarication. What he needed to neutralise the poisons of this city was something new, something novel, someone who had not known him in the past.

When he lay down on the bed and closed his eyes the ribbon of the roadway across the moor came up to him. He could still feel the thunder of the engine, the small fatness of the wheel, the rubbery touch of McFadden's daughter's breast against his wrist.

He swung his feet to the floor and kicked off his shoes.

The light above the wash basin burned on, but the mirror was mercifully empty. The faint whirr of the air-conditioning system came to him, and the glottal snoring grunt of the joker in the room below turning over in his sleep. By now Irwin would have counted the take, would be lying with his pretty girl, her legs locked round his flanks, his white-haired chest brushing the tips of her breasts.

How come he had always been blessed with good luck? Sure, he was smart, but smarter punters than he had paid out their length of fortune and got pinched in the long run. How come he had managed to escape not only arrest and conviction but even the stigma of suspicion? He was as guiltless in the eyes of the law as Gordon had been. He had no history of remand homes and borstal institutions, no record of appearances before a magistrate. No lawyer had ever finagled the details of the criminal code to set him free, and no judge had ever gravely pointed out the error of his ways. Only the old grey granny of a city wagged her head and he did not know whether she gave him blessing or mute disapproval. Again and again he had chosen to acknowledge that imagined nod, hating the bitch for the hold she had on him as he might have hated a possessive mother. He was, he knew, a statistical oddity; a middle-aged professional criminal with a slate as clean as the day he was born.

For the first twenty years of his life he had been as honest as the next man, product of a respectable home. All during his schooldays, his curtailed apprenticeship as a clerk in a city shipping office, even in that hotbed of petty crime, the Army, he had committed no dishonest act; then, abruptly, four months after his service discharge, he had dropped into it. He did not know the reason for the decision, the *volte face*: maybe it was nothing more sinister than boredom with routine, the promise of a life as humdrum as his old man's had been. But when the chance came, a discreet hint over coffee in the cavernous basement smoker of Macdonald's store, the merest suggestion that he had something worth the selling other than the years of his life, he had said, plainly, *Yes*. Two weeks later he creamed the safe in the shipping office in the company of such noted experts as Jack Irwin and Curly McKay; because he had furnished them with every scrap of information, the job was a gift. Perhaps he should have been nabbed then, but he wasn't, lied his way lightly through a casual interrogation by a detective constable, hung around for three months, changed to another office, then baled out of clerking for ever. Irwin knew a natural when he saw one.

After a dozen jobs, though, the highlander calculated the odds, told him it could not last, prophesied doom, the stretch, the mandatory record, saying that no run of luck could last forever. But last it did: it lasted for Irwin and it lasted for him until, even on dangerous capers, he developed a kind of pessimistic carelessness born out of the expectation that treachery or misadventure were bound to catch up with him this time out. After a while even that feeling passed and he came out of each new caper happy and secure in the knowledge that it was still going for him. Until now! Now it had finally caught up with him.

He lay on the bed and knew that at last he had been struck by the left hook, understood that recompense did not have to be clad in a blue uniform, that it could be nothing more solid than the hazy memory of a boy. He felt no grief now, not a twinge of sorrow, nothing; in that nothingness was the essence of his commitment, the total of what was due.

The fat little leather wheel under his hand, alive with the vibrations of terrifying speed. The light was in his eyes, blinding him.

He shot bolt upright from the bed.

Under the curtain seeped the first foam of daylight. He knew that he had slept, that Glasgow, the old grey granny, had come awake again and had wakened him too out of his cruel and troubled dream.

THREE

If only Fleming too could have been a drifter, one of those fringe people who slide into the fog and are lost without trace. Unfortunately, Doyle had no difficulty in tracking him down. Doyle was afraid of the answers which Fleming might give him, but the unposed questions themselves were torment to the old man. He had never really thought much about Gordon, and did not subscribe to the belief that the boy was some sort of saint. Muriel's faith in her dead son was mostly fantasy. If the boy had lived and grown to manhood the fantasy would have dissolved with each passing year until nothing was left of it but a wee bit of affection and a curdled disappointment. The halo with which she had endowed the lad was a consolation for her grief. Even the birth of another son granted no amnesty in her personal war against guilt. A better father might have interfered, at least have attempted to help his daughter through the bad time, but it was too late for that now, far too late. What could he have done for her, any-how? Prevailed upon her to seek solace from the Holy Church? She was beyond that sort of redemption; besides, he wasn't hypocritical enough to nudge her towards a saving grace in the ordinances of a religion which he had himself denied. If Muriel had gone to the priests of her own free will, he might even have mocked her, given her his intellectual's sneer at her peasant naivety. Muriel was no concern of his: she never had been. Gordon, though, was another person. Somehow he had taken for granted the lad's innocence of collusion in his own death. A word, the wrong word, from Fleming could radically alter that concept, stain Gordon too; he did not want that to happen. Doyle needed to believe that his motives were pure as sacristy linen, otherwise he would be faced with the guilt of having activated Weaver only for his own satisfaction. By Wednesday the cable strung between the poles of conscience and his accursed intellect had become so tight that he was in danger of throttling on it. He just had to find out for sure.

Fleming's name was still listed in the telephone book: Glencairn Road. That evening, Doyle brushed his suit and made himself presentable and took the bus to the cul-de-sac of semi-detached council houses, found the number, rang the bell and introduced himself to the wife of the present tenant. The woman had no call to suspect his motives, or to disbelieve the little white lies he told her.

Did she know Mr. Fleming's forwarding address?

She did.

Would she be good enough to tell him?

She would.

She wrote it on a scrap of paper and put it into his hand.

Doyle looked down at it as balefully as if it was the Black Spot, abstractedly thanked the housewife and left. Now there could be no backing down.

On Thursday night he took himself to Dropmore, a fashionable neighbourhood in the western suburbs, close to the city boundary.

Fleming's latest home was a bungalow in a curving avenue of bungalows all set in neat squares of garden. The number was painted on a shingle of polished pine hung on hooks on an arbour trellis over the painted wooden gate. It was too late in the season for roses but Doyle was willing to bet that the summer would flower a riot of blooms. He lingered at the gate, peering at the curtained window of the lounge, hesitating, nervous. Four minutes, then five, went by and still he could not bring himself to reach his finger to the trigger latch, push the gate open, walk up that brick path and ring that doorbell.

After ten minutes of neurotic loitering his impulse to seek the truth had waned. He turned on his heel and walked back to the bus stop and caught the first bus to the city and the Underground from the city to Wickerburn, climbed the stairs to his flat, entered, slouched into the parlour, broke out two half-pint bottles of Black & White and a glass, slumped into the armchair and proceeded to drink himself systematically into insensibility.

'Why the hell didn't you go in?' Weaver demanded.

'It's not the sort of thing I'm good at,' said Doyle. He shrugged. 'It's your affair, anyhow.'

'Who is Fleming?'

Reaching out of the armchair Doyle groped for Saturday's ration of Scotch. Covering the cork with his fist, Weaver anchored the bottle to the table.

'I told you already,' Doyle said, plaintively.

'Why did the cops haul him in?'

'Because he's . . . queer.'

'A homosexual?'

'It looks that way.'

'The caretaker told you?'

'Aye.'

Pulling the bottle away, Weaver held it in two fists like a safari canteen. 'What else have you found out?'

'Isn't that enough?'

'Muriel?'

'She said nothing of any consequence.'

'So we're stuck with this fag, this Fleming,' said Weaver. 'How *well* did he know Gordon?'

'That's for you to find out.'

'What does that mean?'

'Nothing,' said Doyle, quickly.

'You assured me that Gordon had no secrets.'

'I don't know what to think any longer,' said Doyle.

'Queers don't normally go around killing their boys,' said Weaver.

Doyle noticed how clumsily the words came from Weaver's lips, as if he had to force himself to be sophisticated about this subject, to remain cold and dispassionate. Some happy memories of his years with Gordon *must* remain. It was impossible to believe that the period had left no mark at all. Opening the cork of the bottle, Weaver sucked a mouthful of whisky into his throat, corked the bottle again and replaced it on the table.

'No use blinking it, Donald,' Doyle said. 'It's your job to find out what was between them.'

'Supposing he *was* Fleming's boy?'

'Does it make any difference?'

'A fag can be as crazy as the next man.'

'Crazier,' Doyle said. 'Like a woman.'

'Give me Fleming's address.'

'If he . . . if Gordon . . . was . . .' Doyle kneaded his fists in his lap 'You will tell me the truth, Donald, won't you?'

'That's what you brought me here for,' Weaver said. 'The truth. Where's the bloody address?'

'Here.'

Weaver took the scrap of paper, glanced at it, tucked it into his waistcoat pocket and went out.

Doyle sighed loudly and reached for the bottle.

A lithe, fair-haired young athlete was making mincemeat of the heavyweight, a flat-footed monster in purple long-johns. The youngster propelled himself repeatedly across the ring, coming off the ropes like a slender arrow, whipping up his muscular hips to catch the monster across the throat with his insteps. Even when he mistimed a tiny bit and lost balance, his delicate agility was too much for the heavyweight and the boy fended off the grappler with a forearm chop so sudden and swift that it came over the screen only as a pinkish blur. The monster gurgled and reeled backwards, hamming it up of course. The boy followed him, gallantly going for the calf. Hauling at it like a young Norse godling uprooting an oak, he drew the bear down into an undeniably erotic position flat on the canvas.

Fleming nibbled at his sherry and lit a fresh cigarlet.

Dismal rain enveloped the bungalow and drowned the dreich remnant of Saturday afternoon. Fleming did not care. The programmes on his new coloured television set would keep him enthralled until it was time to prepare

97

a snack, and primp himself up a bit for his rendezvous in the Greenthorn Tree later that night. Fleming was a great lover of sport. As he was a qualified instructor of physical education, he had spent a major portion of his life involved in it. His enthusiasm was not so comic as some folk imagined; he had produced his share of winning track athletes and star swimmers and was willing to stand on that record of achievement. That phase, like all good phases, was in the past and he had to admit that he occasionally missed the excitement of competition. Generally though he was contented with his lot, and if contentment was a perquisite of middle-age then, he had to confess, he was middle-aged. Not such a bad time after all: passions were cooler, hurts less painful. Though many unkind, even malicious, things had been said about him, nobody could ever justly accuse him of failing to adapt himself to circumstances.

The referee counted out the heavyweight. The blond boy triumphantly preened and paraded himself about the ring and skipped back to his corner to be rubbed down and cosseted as was the winner's right.

Fleming filled out another inch of sherry and turned and twisted the cigarlet as if it was a fat panatella. He was in the act of plumping the cushions behind his neck when the chimes rang in the hallway. He listened; the triple notes sounded again, little mellow gongs. He could chalk up a dozen callers who might drop in on him without invitation and about half of them would be welcome. Without rancour, he hoisted himself from the armchair, tweaked his cravat up to cover the fatty wrinkles on his throat, and strolled through the softly carpeted hall to the front door.

Once, perhaps, the stranger might have looked like the boy in the wrestling ring; fair-haired, clean-cut, tanned too, but he was not so young now, not young enough. If he smiled he would perhaps look younger, but first impressions suggested that he was not the sort of man who smiled often.

'Yes?'

'Fleming?'

'Yes.'

The cigarlet was held out in one hand because he

abhorred the taint of stale tobacco smoke in the fibres of his clothing. The manner in which the stranger flicked his eyes at the hand gave Fleming a clear indication of attitude and an inkling of what might happen next. Months of easy living had not robbed him of all his speed and guile. He blocked the fist, brought his knee up, stepped into the attacker, bumped the turned haunch with his kneecap, then dropped. The man was experienced, well in balance, and too strong for him. He failed to bring him down. When his spine brushed the carpet, Fleming rolled over backwards and sprang to his feet again. Even in the midst of fright and bewilderment, the feat kindled a small spark of pride. He held his arms out, wrists cocked, fingers ridged hard. The stranger on the threshold stopped, surprised.

'Well?' Fleming said. 'What's it to be, sir? Yes or no?'

'No.'

'Excellent,' Fleming said. 'So, do you mind removing that Harlequin before it fires the hallstand.'

The stranger did have some respect for person and property. He bent and picked up the smoking butt and ground it into the china ashtray on the telephone table. Fleming, ignoring the stiffness in his back, kept his hands warily loaded.

'I take it that you imagine that you have business to settle with me?' he said. 'I'd be mortally obliged if you'd tell me what the score is.'

'I'm Gordon Weaver's father.'

Fleming lowered his fists to his sides.

'Are you, indeed?' he said. 'I was led to believe that the father was dead.'

'Did Gordon tell you that?'

'I think he did.'

'How well did you know my son?'

Bracing his left foot, Fleming kept himself on guard just in case the man was winding up another swipe: he thought not. He was already one jump ahead of the fellow. He chose his words with care.

'It seems I knew Gordon a little better than you did, Weaver, or you wouldn't be standing on my doormat behaving with such unpardonable truculence. Just for your information, Gordon was not, repeat *not*, one of that horde of boys with whose moral degeneration I am credited. Now, do you want to hit me again, or would you prefer to parley in comfort?'

'All right.'

Fleming took the gamble: he dropped his defensive stance and with a wave of the hand ushered the stranger down the hallway into the lounge.

The garish colours of the screen dominated the room. The godling was writhing about on the canvas, features contorted and ugly with agony, hugging his tripes. Fleming unplugged the set.

'Will you have sherry or whisky?'

'Neither.'

'Bacardi and coke?'

'Nothing.'

'At least sit down.'

Fleming studied the man guardedly. Yes, there was a distinct resemblance to poor Gordon Weaver; in the length and shape of the face, the moroseness of the mouth, the slightly furtive quality in the eyes.

He said, 'I knew your son fairly well, Weaver. I know what's on your mind, and the answer is that I am what you've been told I am, but that I didn't . . . know Gordon in that sense.'

'But you tried?'

'Tried?'

'Tried it on with him?'

Fleming was motionless, the sherry glass in his hand. He said nothing for a moment, then leaned forward towards the stranger, his expression close to savage, showing teeth. 'When did you last molest a twelve-year-old, Weaver? Tell me that; when did you "try it on" with a girl child?'

The man was not unintelligent; to extend the point would have been futile. 'I am what I am,' Fleming continued. 'That has little or no bearing on what you want from me.'

'Why did the cops haul you in?'

'Come now, Weaver, you know what coppers are. If you must know, I had a misdemeanour listed against me; nothing drastic, but enough to bring me to their attention.

The law has a long memory. Answer me a question: where were you when Gordon was killed?'

'Out of the country.'

'In prison?'

'I said, out of the country.'

'What do you intend to do now that you're back?' Fleming asked. 'I presume you intend to do something, since you've gone to the bother of trailing me here.'

'Tell me about him?'

'Surely that's a job for his mother, your wife.'

'I want *you* to tell me about him.'

'I see,' Fleming said. He laid aside the untouched sherry and leaned an elbow on top of the cocktail cabinet. He was relaxed now, curious about this man and no longer frightened by him. He crossed his wrists and rested them against the jut of his hip. 'Very well. I can draw a little sketch of your son, if that's what you want, but I really didn't know him *that* well.'

'Where did you meet him?'

'I think you know that much already,' said Fleming. 'I was temporary superintendent at Grahamshill Youth Club, appointed by the trustees.'

'Did they know about you?'

'No.'

'But the boys did?'

'Let's say they had their suspicions,' Fleming replied. 'They had no "evidence" against me—I'm not that much of a fool, you know—but they surmised. I imagine that any man who bathed regularly and wore clean clothing would have been judged in the same light.'

'You sound bitter.'

'Good heavens, Weaver, I'm not in the least bitter. In fact, I fell on my feet.'

'How?'

'My sister was a spinster lady and I was her only kin. She died. I inherited; and there we are.'

'That was nice for you.'

'Wasn't it?' said Fleming. 'Mildred was a florist. Not only did she leave me this bungalow and something in the bank but she left me the business too. Now I'm a florist. I can't say I'm mad about flowers, but I'm an excellent manager. Surprising how we discover things about

101

ourselves when circumstances dictate the necessity.'

'About Gordon?'

'He was a loner. He had no special friends and he didn't mingle with any of the cliques. When he played games—table tennis, badminton, that sort of thing—I had to rake up a partner for him, or play myself.'

'Why did they hate him?'

'Oh, no, they didn't hate him. They just didn't care about him. He was content—not quite the word—he was *willing* to stand outside the group. I knew him for eighteen months or so, quite long enough for me to understand him. He desperately needed something which Grahamshill club could not give him and I didn't dare risk offering.'

'What was that?'

Turning on his elbow Fleming looked away from the man, stared briefly through the gap in the curtains at the gathering dusk, then down at the thin-stemmed glass of sweet sherry. He dipped his pinkie into the liquid and touched it to the tip of his tongue.

'I asked . . .'

'Yes, yes,' said Fleming, crossly. 'I heard you. Frankly, Weaver, the fact that you have to ask such a question at all means that you would not understand the answer.'

'Fleming, are you taking the mickey . . . ?'

'About death, about homicide, about the killing of a boy? No, Weaver, my sense of humour isn't that grotesque.'

'What did he want from you?'

'He wanted the assurance that he wasn't a freak.'

'A freak?'

'Gordon didn't relate to his environment,' said Fleming, then erased the explanation from the air as a schoolmaster might wipe chalk from a blackboard. 'No, no, far too pretentious. I've listened to too many social psychologists; my noddle's stuffed with their damned jargon. Gordon walked by himself, like that cat in Kipling.'

Fleming paused once more. The allusion did not register. He tried again. 'Gordon did not understand that he was the sort of boy who was naturally a loner, one of a rare species.'

Weaver nodded.

The cliché had found a chink in the man's armour, had

102

pricked him into understanding. Fleming was gratified. Was the bleakness in Weaver's eyes now an indication that he had tripped backward into private memories? Would those memories bring him to the answer he sought? Fleming would have wagered the bungalow and the shop that Weaver was a cat of exactly the same colour as his son. At thirty-five, or was it forty, such a style was bearable, had become a preferred habit, integrated with the character. At twelve, however, the struggle to reach out of the chasm where the difference begins led only to an anguish of rejection. It was Fleming's own story, and this man's too, if he was not mistaken. He had made his point. Let it stand.

'What was Gordon doing in North Grahamshill?'

'I've no earthly idea,' Fleming answered. 'If you're trying to establish a connection between Gordon and the killers I doubt if you'll succeed. The police tried, and the best they could come up with was me, and I wasn't good enough; I mean, they couldn't contrive a case against me no matter how they tried. We may never know for sure what he was doing there on that night—or who killed him.'

'I'll find them.'

'I see,' said Fleming. 'You're after revenge. Well, I wish you luck. I hate to see life wasted. I liked Gordon. He was highly intelligent, bright, and . . .'

'You mean you wanted him but would't risk losing the job?'

'Oh, God!' Fleming exploded. 'Are we back on that tack again? Listen, Weaver, I do not want to possess people: not boys, or men, or women. I am not by nature possessive. I don't want to lay claim to anybody, I'm not even jealous of my friends. Yes, some of my acquaintances are . . . gay, very gay indeed, but I don't need them, not sexually, not to be bound to me. I've had my day of obsessions, and it's long gone, thank God.'

It was a waste of effort to explain himself to this man; besides, he had no need. He had spoken of emotions which were foreign to this stranger, freely confessed to sentiments which this man had never experienced, not even in relation to his own child.

'Is there anything more you want from me?' Fleming said.

'The cops give you a rough time?'

'No, they didn't beat me, or starve me, and intimidated me only a little. But they just refused to understand. I was, alas, at home when the killing happened. I had no alibi. It took them some time to reckon I was telling the truth. I lost my job. The youth club closed its doors for good. I'm sure too that the shock of finding out that her brother was what she had always suspected him to be was instrumental in hastening my poor sister's death. I'm sorry if that sounds flippant. There may be no connection, yet the fact remains that now I am the owner of a bungalow, a flourishing business and a tidy bank account; every spinster's dream. However, the wind which blew me here was ill, Weaver, very, very ill; I am continually conscious of that fact.'

'So you can't help me?'

For an instant Fleming was tempted to tell Weaver that there was no help for his condition; he checked himself. He was suddenly weary of this grim man, wanted to be rid of him, but he wanted too to give him something, a gesture of help. He ruffled mentally through his store of local knowledge, then said, 'On Sunday afternoons in Gartshaws park the boys meet and play soccer; a knockabout, informal affair. Occasionally Gordon went there, to play or to spectate. I'm not sure which, but he went there. He told me so. It might do no harm to wander down to the park on Sunday, nose about, ask a few tactful questions.'

'Thanks.'

'Actually,' said Fleming, as he opened the lounge door and let Weaver into the hallway, 'it might be more effective if you have someone who could go in your place.'

'Why?'

'I doubt if the boys will talk to you.'

'Why not?'

'You look too much like a policeman.'

Weaver almost grinned. 'It's the suit.'

'No,' said Fleming, 'it isn't the suit.'

'Thanks,' Weaver said again, and was gone.

The glass was half full and the second bottle still corked.

Sleep had overtaken Doyle before drunkenness could fix a hold on him, had carried him away like a lump of flotsam from a sandy beach, gently and effortlessly. The catalogue was crimped between his fingers and the half-shell glasses clung to the fleshy tip of his nose. A single long hair, neglected by the razor, trembled on his upper lip like a fine steel wire.

Cupping his chin, lifting, Weaver wakened him. Doyle snorted, blinked, flung up his forearms, muttering, twisting his head from the grip. Leaning closer to the old man Weaver used his forefinger to push the glasses into place hard against the tussocky brows.

'Gordon was clean,' Weaver said.

Orientation was immediate; though lips and wrists and thighs still twitched, the blue eyes were steady, faded but intent.

'Are you certain, Donald?'

'Certain enough.'

'Thank Christ,' Doyle said. 'What did he tell you?'

'Not much.'

'But you got the truth out of him?'

'Some of it.'

Shifting nothing now but the eyeballs, rolling them up, the old man studied Weaver closely. 'He told you something else?'

'Nothing of importance.'

Doyle nodded, winced, nodded again. 'I'm glad about Gordon,' he said. 'It makes it easier for both of us.'

'Does it?' said Weaver.

FOUR

'What's wrong?' Hazel said. 'Don't you like it?'

The dress was like a child's smock shrunk in the wash, hemline resting just below the protrusion of her pudenda, neckline looped from her collar bones to expose the crown of her breasts. At a guess Weaver supposed she wore no underclothing but for the milky pantie hose.

She was prettier than Weaver had realised, beautiful even, with a fine-boned, aristocratic set of features redeemed from being aloof by a wide mouth and pert nose. The sight of the girl was refreshing after his meeting with Fleming. He grinned at her, and she paraded into the centre of the hallway, arms extended, showing him a view of thighs and breasts. He tossed her his overcoat and she in turn tossed it carelessly through the open door of the bedroom, then flung open the door of the lounge. 'This way to the goodies.'

The skirl of rock made Weaver anticipate a full-scale swinging bash, but the lounge held only Jack Irwin and three young girls. The highlander's skin was flushed and he had shed ten years since last Weaver had seen him, as if fear and the hardships of earning a dishonest living had, after all, left no permanent scars. Jet pencil-line pants showed up his thickening thighs and the overhang of his belly. The flounced shirt was not suited to a man who had travelled so far through life. All in all, Weaver thought, he looked like one of the old-time swashbucklers out of a movie matinée serial, but run badly to seed. The broad corn-grained hand spanned the waist of a girl, like some kind of kinky new clasp.

'It's m'friend Weaver,' Irwin shouted. 'Come on in, man, and share the bounty of my house.'

Rising, he dragged the girl with him and lumbered across the room, staggering a little, to greet Weaver.

'Man, man,' said Irwin. 'You're as dour-looking as a kirk elder.'

'I can't say the same for you.'

'Get the jacket off then,' said Irwin. 'A dram and a hug from one of these fine wee heifers'll soon loosen you up.'

Hazel slipped the tumbler of Scotch into Weaver's hand. When he shook it the ice made a cool, silvery sound. He sipped the drink, smiling without amusement, irritated by the set-up. He had never been much of a one for celebrations, especially celebration hard on the heels of a caper; he and Irwin had argued this out before. In particular, Weaver remembered one of Irwin's shindigs, the loot still stowed in the wardrobe; two cops had shown up at the door to answer a neighbour's complaint about the noise. It had taken all Weaver's tact—he was the only one still sober enough to talk at all—to placate the uniforms and get rid of them. After that he had quit going back to Irwin's after a job. This party wasn't on the same scale as the others: even so, it showed that Irwin had already forgotten McFadden and McFadden's power in the underworld. Any one of these hired dolls might be sharper than she looked, sharp enough to do some simple addition and go chirping to one of McFadden's ears. The study of the underworld communications had always interested Weaver. Many of his partners had wound up inside the big walls just because they suffered the need to brag of their cleverness. Cleverness was a constant. Cleverness was silence. Weaver would not allow whisky or the hands of the girls to blunt the edge of his caution.

Leaning over his shoulder Hazel spilled more whisky into his glass. Her breasts brushed his cheek, lingering long enough to let him be aware of their fullness. For a second he supposed that she was drunk too, glanced round at her, surprised to find her as sober as he was himself. Her provocation was deliberate and calculated. He looked away.

Head thrown back, Irwin was hooting with laughter at his own witticisms. Hazel was too good for the old philistine. He knew it now, knew too that she was offering herself to him as a viable proposition: whether for a night or as a permanent thing he didn't dare guess. Desire kindled in him quickly, with a soft roar like ignited tinder. He drew himself away from her, brought the tumbler to his mouth and let a mouthful of the strong malt trickle slowly into his gullet. If his judgement was right he had to consider all the implications of the girl's proposal before he made his move.

In addition to Muriel, a long time back, and Edith, there had been another special girl in London; Caroline, an American student, all the way from Iowa. She had been lean and wheat blonde and young, with an appetite for perversity so acute that Weaver could barely keep pace with her demands. The American had known what he was but kept her mouth shut; though, by now, half of her home town had probably heard of his 'adventures'. It hardly mattered. When, in a strange mood of tenderness,

107

close to the day when she was due to go home, Caroline had asked him if he loved her, he had told her yes, not knowing in himself if it was true or not. Of the dozen women he had laid in Spain, a couple at least had been good enough to make the cover of *Playboy*. Possessing such beauties helped dilute the sordidness and the poverty of his past. It wasn't really the women though, not even the young and golden-skinned ones, that he wanted, only the images, the new and sterling forms of reality which they created.

He stared into the burning logs under the elegant mantel-shelf long enough to imprint the flames on his retina.

What was it that had made Fleming despise him, and why did it anger him to be looked down on by such a weak little pervert? Maybe even Irwin, the antithesis of the runty queer, despised him too: Irwin, red drunk and as rough as a shaggy-haired bull, with his steady income and his girls and his liquor and his clean silk sheets. Irwin was a prisoner too. Only he was free: over the years it had come to seem as if freedom was the talisman which of itself would bring him all that he wanted. The women went, exciting, one by one—Muriel, Edith, Caroline, the pneumatic blondes—he had felt no pang of regret at their going. They had offered themselves for his use and he had used them. Muriel had smothered whatever loving was in him a long time ago.

He glanced up at Hazel. She was over by the drinks table. What about this one? Would he hurt her too? Maybe he should take her into the other room and strip her and bruise her, knead those resilient breasts until they ached, wrench her thighs apart and take her with all the force that was in him. Would that be a fair statement of intent, the fine print on the contract?

'Relax, man,' Irwin said.

'When do we talk?'

'Talk! Who wants to talk? Ach, we'll talk tomorrow.'

'Let's talk now, before you get too pissed.'

'Okay,' said Irwin. 'We'll have ourselves a bit of a seat and a blether and sweep all that under the carpet. Then we can settle down like gentlemen to a gentleman's pleasures.'

'Peace,' intoned Hazel from behind the couch, and spirited away the bottle.

Two girls were dancing. They gyrated and jerked their hips in time to the rock number which boomed from the stereo; a tribal mating. Both were very young; one scraggy with an avaricious mouth, the other strong with massive breasts and snooker-table legs. The third girl was almost beautiful, oval face, and a lithe body under a cheap tissue-thin dress. Weaver seated himself on the sofa by Irwin's flank. He made a lid with his hand to cover the whisky glass. The swaying stab of Irwin's glass was seeking out his hand and he touched rims: a 'wee toast' as Irwin called it, a token of friendship and good Scottish loyalty, empty as an old crab shell. Sentiment, and liquor, glazed Irwin's eyeballs. He exuded the sourness of sweat, armpit stains showing almost to the ripple of the shirt's flounces. In half an hour or so he would sink like a scuttled punt.

'We did't then, Donal', m'friend.'

'We did it all right,' Weaver said. 'Have you heard how McFadden's taking it?'

'Nary a word. He'll be fine though. If any of the scum had been damaged beyond repair it'd have got int' the papers.'

Though he had combed the newspapers that morning, Weaver had found no trace of any story which could relate to the McFadden stunt. Nobody in the McFadden household had suffered death or serious injury. Even McFadden would not have been able to cover up a killing.

'Take't from Uncle Jack,' said Irwin. 'Our celebrations is not preem-ature.'

'How much did we take?'

'Ach, well now, not as much . . .'

'The figure, Jack.'

'Three thousand an' forty-two pounds,' Irwin looked as if he might burst into tears. Whatever Irwin's failings he would not cheat on a partner, especially if the partner was Weaver.

'And my cut?'

'Call it a roun' thousand.'

'You said half.'

'Greerson's due a thousand too.'

109

'You didn't tell me that.'

'Donal',' said Irwin. 'Y'never asked.'

'Christ, a thousand for a couple of lousy phone calls.'

'That was his price,' said Irwin. 'I've the feelin' we just struck a bad night.'

'When do you pay Greerson?'

'He'll call me.'

'Where's the money?'

'Get't later.'

'Where is it?'

'Locked away in a desk drawer,' said Irwin. 'I'm sorry it's less than I forecast, man, but that's the luck'f the draw these days.'

'A thousand's enough.'

After paying Cringle, Weaver reckoned that he would be left with three hundred, plus the two hundred he still had on hand: enough for what he had to do. The Mark 10 was essential and could be converted into cash at any time.

An arm jutted over the back of the sofa and decanted neat malt into Irwin's glass.

'Thanks, lass.' Irwin bussed the crook of the elbow before it had an opportunity to withdraw. 'A gem, that one.'

'Have you ever met Greerson?' Weaver asked.

'He's too cagey for that,' said Irwin. 'He does all his business by phone, from public call boxes.'

'You can't give him his cut by phone.'

'He'll send instructions.'

'You don't know how to contact him?'

'Why should I want t'do that? He's a bloody copper!'

Irwin cupped the glass and hissed as if it was filled with liquid oxygen. Weaver's estimate of the exact degree of his drunkenness was short of the actual; Irwin was far gone. Drawing in his chin like a parade-ground sergeant, he blinked rapidly and repeatedly to dispel what was probably a double image of the room, then canted slowly over on the cushions, holding himself with one hand like a castaway on a life-raft on a pitching sea.

'Lissen, Donal',' he said. 'Neve' mind all that ballocks right now. Tell me 'bout the women. Which one d'you fancy then?'

'I'm looking.'

'Ginger nob?'

'She's all right.'

'Jesus, man, your in . . . insensate passion is just terrible t'behol'. Take'r: take anyone'f them.'

'Does the offer include Hazel?'

Irwin scowled. 'Not Hazel: she's not inclu . . . included.'

'Sure,' said Weaver. 'I didn't think she would be.'

Once more Weaver surveyed the girls. They knew he was studying them and gave him some lackadaisical attention. There was no sign of Hazel: maybe she'd gone to find more liquor.

The girls knew that they would not be unduly bothered by the highlander: he was already too far gone to do more than maul and fumble for a few minutes while an astute young hooker ladled more whisky into him and made sure that he flaked out before he could perform his rites of ablution over her body. Sex wasn't the Scottish vice, anyway, not when there was alcohol in the offing. The drunk only gave away his last meal and his innermost secrets, nothing important.

Irwin beckoned to the girl in the thin dress, a casual and insolent summons. She darted a meaningful glance at her two companions then fixed on an artificial smile and came over to the sofa. Irwin slid a hand around her thigh and probed it up under the hemline of her dress.

Weaver got to his feet.

'Hey, Donal', where y'goin'?'

'To freshen my drink.'

'Aye, man, have yoursel' a ball,' said Irwin. With that statement he relinquished his role as host and dragged the brunette across him, crushing his nose and mouth into her body. Weaver had had little truck with professional whores but guessed that the girl had the situation well under control. Any minute now Irwin would pass out. He backed away from the sofa and took the olive on the cocktail stick from Hazel's fingers and stuck it into his mouth. She was smaller by a head than he was. Her eyes had the glint of calculated wickedness in them, reminding him of the American. Hazel tilted her head and looked past his shoulder at the antics of the couple on the sofa.

'What's he up to now?' said Weaver.

'He's sinking faster than he can undo his buttons.'

The two remaining girls were at the stereo flicking through the collection of tapes, complete with their own bottle of vodka and a couple of limes.

Hazel drew her shoulders back. Her nipples were clearly visible under the material of her dress. She reached up and kissed him on the mouth. Her breath tasted faintly of peppermint.

'Take me out of here,' she said.

'Where to?'

'Your place.'

'No,' Weaver said. 'Make it the kitchen.'

'The kitchen?'

'Sure.' Weaver placed his hand on her arm and steered her towards the door. 'Out.'

Lit by neon strips, the room was big and bright. Rush matting covered the floor and the cooker was as complex as a computer. Formica topped tables, chairs and a large refrigerator made the place seem cool and empty.

'How would you like me?' the girl said. 'Over the chopping block or backed against the fridge?'

'Make coffee.'

'Before or after?'

'Now.'

'Surely that's not all you want, Mr. Weaver?'

'Don't flatter yourself.'

'I'm the Gartshaws oracle,' she said. 'I can tell that you want me.'

She opened a cupboard and set down the percolator, coffee canister, sugar basin and a carton of cream.

'White or black?'

'Brown.'

'Sheer perversity,' she said. 'You're not a bit like Jack.'

'No?'

'You're no penny-ante hood, are you?'

'Listen,' Weaver said. 'I've a couple of things to do here. When I've done them I'll be on my way and you won't see me again.'

'You're not married, are you?'

'You ask too many questions.'

112

'I can keep my mouth shut when necessary.'

'What do you know about me?'

'Only that you worked with Jack years ago, and that he's deathly afraid of you.'

'What makes you think that?'

'You're harder than he is, and you've changed so much.'

'He didn't tell you all that cock, did he?'

'No,' said Hazel, 'but I've more above the bra than he gives me credit for.'

'Just how much *do* you know?'

'I know you pulled a job; that the take wasn't as high as you'd hoped, and that it wasn't altogether clean.'

'What else?'

'If you want your money tonight,' the girl said, 'you'll find it in the bottom drawer of the desk. The key's in the vase on the bookshelf.'

'You know too damned much.'

'Jack'll be out like a corpse by now,' the girl said. 'Collect your money and blow.'

Weaver walked quietly through the hallway and into the study. He did not touch the switch of the ceiling light but worked by the glow of the little desk lamp. He found the key in the vase where the girl had told him it would be, unlocked the drawer and slid it open.

The notes were wadded into three separate bundles. Weaver pulled out a chair, lowered the side flap of the desk and put one of the bundles on it. He counted the notes carefully: one thousand pounds exactly. He laid them on the carpet by his heel and counted out a second bundle. It too came to a thousand. The last made up the difference, exactly as Irwin had said. Weaver separated a thousand pounds in denominations of five and ten and returned the balance to the drawer. He closed the drawer with his knee and clicked the key. He hesitated, then tried the same key in the bottom drawer opposite and pulled it open too.

The Luger and the Smith & Wesson were hidden by a single sheet of mauve blotting paper. Any cop would have found them within seconds of entering the room. In the magazine of the Luger the ammo clip was still fitted and a cigarette box at the back of the drawer held three more clips of the same calibre. Weaver took the clips and put them in his pocket. He peeled fifty pounds from the roll in his hip and put it into the box, covered up the box and the revolver with the blotting paper sheet once more. He relocked the drawer, tucked the Luger into the waistband of his pants and buttoned his jacket over it. He tossed the key into the vase on the bookshelf, then went back to the kitchen.

The girl poured coffee from the spout of the Russell Hobbs, filling a breakfast cup. She added a dash of milk and a spoonful of sugar and gingerly passed him the cup. Seated at the table Weaver gazed down at the liquid as if it contained hemlock. The feeling should have ebbed by now, but it hadn't. It was flooding through him so fast and heavy that he did not even have to look at her to be aware of it.

'Listen,' he said, 'just who the hell are you?'

'Hazel Ferrier,' the girl said brightly. 'Free, white and twenty-one.'

'Where?'

'Hey, what is this, an interview?'

'It could be.'

'For a position,' she said. 'A horizontal position, maybe?'

'Stop coming on like a short-time tart.'

'I've been Irwin's woman almost five months.'

'And before that?'

'Another man's woman,' she said. 'You could call me a professional mistress and you wouldn't be far wrong. I blow hottest where the money grows.'

The cynicism was practised and smooth-flowing but it did not seem to come right out of the heart of the girl.

'How did you meet Jack?'

'At a party.'

'Like this one?'

'Not quite so one-sided,' she said. 'It was a big little wing-ding in a disco. I think Jack was there on the scout for another dolly. Anyway, he whisked me away from the man I was with, just like you're going to do tonight.'

'What makes me a better proposition than Jack?'

'I wish I knew.'

'The last thing I need right now is a woman.'

'Jack told me,' she said.

'Told you what?'

'Take me out of here, Weaver. I can help you.'

'I don't want trouble with Irwin.'

'He won't give you any bother. I told you he's running scared of you.'

'He could still make trouble.'

'Jack,' the girl said, 'will just sit on his little corner and cry his little red eyes out.'

'And you don't give a tinker's damn?'

'Why should I?' Hazel said. 'The bastard's had his mileage from me. I don't like him any more: he's old, you know what I mean, old. Take me with you, Weaver.'

'Like hell I will.'

They left the flat shortly after midnight. The stereo was crooning vintage Sinatra and the two whores had fallen asleep, lying innocently with their heads together. Irwin slept too: he was ugly in slumber, flopped on his back on the rug by the dying embers of the log fire, the flounced shirt open to the navel, stained with sweat and spilled whisky. Seated on the sofa, her legs drawn up under her, the brunette was contentedly lapping a sticky liqueur from a sundae spoon and nibbling at a sausage on a stick. She had no interest in anyone or anything, sleepy too.

Weaver drew Hazel back. She already had her overcoat across her arm and the suitcase, packed with the best of her clothes, stood waiting by the door. She went out on to the landing ahead of him and he held the coat while she put it on. The old gas mantle above her head purred and showed a halo of golden light. Her eyes were very bright. At this precise moment in their relationship she found him exciting: or maybe it wasn't him at all but the situation which stimulated her. Maybe it was never the man but only the ambience the man gave off. Instinct told her that Weaver would treat her as she wanted to be treated, would teach her many things that she did not already know. She hungered for his strength, and her inside knowledge of his mission to this city added to his mystique. He was probably at his best now, operating at his highest level of ability. She wanted to witness and assist, to draw from him a little of that single-minded determination and forcefulness. She knew that he had

115

already shown a hairfine flaw, a weakness, by letting her insistence ravage his commonsense, but she would not hold that against him.

They walked downstairs to the Jaguar. He held the passenger door open for her.

'I knew it would be a stately pussycat,' she said. 'It's funny how you can tell these things.'

'We'll go to a hotel.'

'You're calling the shots, Mr Weaver.' She fished in her purse and worked her fingers in her lap then held up her left hand to show him the wedding band. 'With that symbol of respectability visibly displayed, no grubby little desk clerk is going to come the acid with us.'

'You've done this before?'

'Yes.'

'Maybe you *are* a tart.'

'Maybe I am. Won't you have fun finding out.'

'What name do you use?'

'Simpkins,' she said.

'Why Simpkins?'

'It's the least sinful name I can think of.'

'All right,' said Weaver. 'Simpkins it is.'

'Drive on,' she told him. 'Quickly.'

'What's the rush?'

'Quickly,' she said. 'I'm wet already.'

FIVE

Hazel had forgotten that in the country, even in winter, birds sang with the coming of dawn. In the stark elms behind the hotel rooks craked and the air was full of the chatter of tits, finches and robins. All she had to do to see them was to throw open the windows. That thing about the birds, she should have remembered it. The light too was nostalgically familiar. She thought for a moment, then it came back to her: the ceiling of the nursery, centuries ago it seemed, in the big house not fifteen miles across the hills from this hotel bedroom.

Childishly she had connected the sound of the birds and the marbled light on the nursery ceiling, imagining hundreds of tiny miners with steel-sharp beaks chipping at it. It was hard for the birds in winter, not free as in the rosebloom of summer or the limegreen spring. Impulsively Hazel slipped out from under the downlet, padded to the window, parted the curtains and looked out.

A rolling lawn ended in a narrow white fence: it fringed the roadway which in turn fringed the loch. In the distance the hill was as huge and stark as an alpine peak; the fraud. A feather of spindrift plumed from its northern ridge and the loch was hard and cold, rejecting the advances of the sunlight. On the polished surface the islands floated like clumps of horsehair. In summer at this hour the lawns would already be thronged with tourists and the car park loud with the roar of revving cars, and no self-respecting little bird would sing its song within a mile of the place. It was not summer now though and the lawns were deserted except for the singing birds, and the sunlight was clear and sharp. The qualities suited her mood, and her new man. For every man, a mood; that was the way of it.

The full-length mirror tabbed to the wardrobe door framed her body. Raising her arms she revolved slowly before the reflection, warming herself with the sight of her nakedness like a tender side of beef on a spit.

If only her parents could see her now. They would be shocked, not just by the nakedness but by her unblemished beauty. It had always been their hopeful philosophy that dark deeds and wickedness ravaged the body as well as the soul. She had never really swallowed their stories, and now she had proved them wrong.

The first man in her life had rescued her from the droll and doom-filled tea-times and congregational Sundays of the town where she lived. It had been an easy ride out; he had tempted her with a Porsche, seduced her in a Bristol and driven her away at last in the back of his rally-trim customised Rover. He was the one for her; the only one—for a while. He had rebuilt her, tinkered with her prudery, souped-up her sexual awareness and had finally exchanged her for another model. The second man was older, executive class, with a mansion house and a

117

city penthouse and a Rolls, no less. She might have risked taking him home to tea with the folks if he hadn't had a face as full of obvious sin as a French whoremaster's, and a wife and three kids stashed away on his farm in the Borders. She flew with him too, and let the elderly couple who had found her under a gooseberry bush eighteen years previously hush up the scandal as best they could and take pills to help them sleep at nights. In their own chintzy way her parents were as tough as she was. They sniffed up their tears of outrage and told her, by telephone never to darken their drawing room again. She never did. After the third affair—or was it the fourth—she lost even her childish inclination to flaunt her waywardness in their faces. When this capacity to hurt them died in her she realised that she was free of their influence forever. She did not want to be owned; in the long run, their pride of ownership was stronger than their love for her. She supposed they would have settled reluctantly for a genteel conflict but she would not submit herself to that. After another year or so she even stopped herself dropping them postcards to let them know that she was thriving.

She lowered herself into the wicker chair with the chilly p.v.c. covering and leaned her chin on her hand and thought not about her past but about her present. Why had she jettisoned Jack Irwin? It hadn't really been in her mind to do so until she saw Weaver. There was no logic behind it, yet she trusted the instinct which impelled her to attach herself like a remora to the drifting and the dangerous. Old Siggie was in there someplace: old goatface, bleating about sexual proclivities. Her father had looked a little like old goatface, but she did not buy that theory: too involved. She glanced over her shoulder at the man in the bed. Why had the ordinary loving seemed so extraordinary last night? Why had she been forced to stuff her knuckles into her mouth in case the sounds of her ecstasy wakened the pantry boy? Her small fist still showed the indentations, red and bruised, though her body was unmarked. Weaver was not the kind of man to get his kicks that way. Shaking out her hair she swept it behind her nape and fastened it loosely with two pins.

'Hazel,' she said to the mirror, 'you're really a bit of a nut.'

Weaver came up fast from the bed, shedding the downlet as if it was water. His eyes were flared wide and his big naked body was tensed like that of a cougar ready to spring from a rock. Only then did she realise that she had spoken aloud.

'I'm sorry,' she said.

Weaver let his breath out. 'What time is it?'

'After nine, I suppose. It's daylight.'

He dug the watch from the pile of clothing on the rug by the bed. His back had long hard straps of muscle and his gut had no trace of fat on it yet. When he was dressed he was fairly refined, could almost have passed himself off as one of her father's friends; but naked he had the coarse-grained animalistic body of an artisan. He was clean, of course, but the scars of youthful acne still pitted his shoulders and the veins of his arms were blue. She liked the combination of brutality without cruelty, of endurance without indifference. She liked the man-sized hardness of him too. Most of all, though, she liked him because he needed her, and had a hunger to complement his strength.

'It's ten after ten,' said Weaver. 'I must go.'

'Go where?'

'Up town again,' he said. 'What do you want to do; stay on here or check into another hotel?'

'You've no place of your own?'

'Nope.'

He lit a cigarette and lay back against the pillow. He did not look in the least like Jack Irwin nor, as did some of her lovers on the morning after, like a fat old tom cat recuperating from a gelding.

'One hotel after another?' she said.

'I can work from here if you want,' he said.

'Let's go back: to Glasgow, I mean.'

Weaver did not ask for reasons. 'All right.'

She seated herself on the side of the bed and touched his chest with the flat of her hand as if to make sure that he was a real live breathing male and not some figment of her imagination. He stretched out the hand with the cigarette in it and, with his pinkie, fish-hooked a strand of her hair up behind her ear.

'What is it now,' she said. 'Your son?'

'Yeah.'

'Do you know?'

'Not yet.'

She opened her mouth, then closed it again. She had hinted that she could help him but he had not asked her to explain how. It wasn't the proper time. She laid her cheek against his chest to hide her indecision. Perhaps he would never ask her for help, did not need it. Though convinced that he was a driving man, a real straight-liner, she wanted proof. She was curious too about his methods.

'May I come too?'

'Why not!' he said.

He did not touch her skin, only her hair.

After a while he pushed her gently to one side and left her sprawled on the quilt and went naked into the bathroom. She took the butt of his cigarette from the ashtray and flopped on to her back, inhaling the smoke all the way from her diaphragm. Her belly rose and fell. Past the thicket of her own body hair, like a little islet on a sunlit surface of satin pink, she could look into the bathroom. Water dripped from his face and down his neck as he stooped over the basin; then, with a towel hammocked between his hands, he came out again and studied her as she lay spreadeagled on the bed.

'Round about now,' he said, carefully, 'Irwin is discovering that you've flown the coop.'

'Irwin?' she said. 'Who is this Irwin?'

'Poor bastard,' said Weaver.

She sat up. 'I'm safe with you, aren't I?'

'No.'

She smiled. 'Thank God for that.'

He caught her by the shoulders and pulled her upright. Her body was soft against his hardness.

'Get dressed,' he said. 'I've got work to do.'

The lowering sun slanted the shadows of the picket fence far across the scrub, picked out the granules of glass which were mixed in to the compound of the pitch and glittered like slivers of ice in a bed of lava. Jackets marked off the goalmouths and corners but the touchline was flexible. Play roved widely across the area, the ball and its horde of captors skidding erratically over the rough surface.

Doyle tucked the scarf around his glands and lit another

120

cigarette. He had been slowly drifting closer and closer to the boundary, eyeing the gathering with growing apprehension. The youngest and weakest boy in each team defended the goal; a typical example of mass psychology, thought Doyle, giving the stalwarts a ready-made scapegoat in case of defeat. Doyle did not have the gall to interrupt the match and broach one of the lads directly, as Weaver had told him to do. Even the keepers, with time on their hands, ignored him.

At first the young men had no very definite identity but after a while he found himself able to pick out an individual here and there, to recognise in a vague sort of way some of the faces in the pack. In particular one youth seemed familiar but he could not finger the name for some time. Then it came to him, popping suddenly into the forefront of his mind: Mowatt. He peered against the angles of sunlight, holding the young man in focus as the attack surged up his way and promptly ebbed again. Yes, it was Mowatt, without a doubt.

Mowatt had done some casual work in the shop a couple of years ago; his stint as a packer and delivery boy lasting only a month or so. Doyle, who would not have admitted to knowing the name of anybody under thirty, was surprised at his ability to pluck the chance out of the blue, but Mowatt's gravy-coloured hair and adenoidal expression were unmistakable, and the months had not matured him much. Doyle debated the ethics of scraping the rust off their relationship and, spurred by his promise to Weaver, stood stock still on the touchline, waiting.

Booted wildly out of the ground, the ball went bounding downhill towards the river. A truce was called while the nearest keeper clambered down the slope to retrieve it. The players gathered by the jackets, smoking, swilling from beer cans or coke bottles.

Doyle sucked in a steadying breath and called out Mowatt's name.

Like a stag catching wind of a stalker, the boy raised his head in startled bewilderment. If Doyle had given him half a chance he would have ignored the call. The old man, however, had made his move and embellished the summons with waving gestures. To save himself embarrassment, the boy shambled over to him, a thin rancid steam

121

rising from his shoulders, as if he had been parboiled.

'And how are you, Mowatt?' said Doyle, feigning heartiness. 'Remember me?'

'Aye.'

'Have a gasper?'

'Naw, naw.'

'Go ahead.'

Reluctantly Mowatt took a cigarette from the packet and even permitted Doyle to light it for him, thus committing himself to hang around until the smoke was part-way done.

'It must be a couple of years since I saw you last. How's it going?'

'Great,' said Mowatt gloomily.

'Long time ago,' said Doyle. 'Before Gordon was killed, wasn't it?'

'Wouldn't know.'

'You remember Gordon Weaver?'

'Naw.'

'The fellow who got killed.'

'Aye, I think I heard somethin' about it.'

'What did you hear, Mowatt?'

'Nothin'.'

'You just said you heard something.'

'Just what I read in the papers, like.'

'You don't mind my asking, Mowatt, do you?' said Doyle. 'The bogies didn't do so well so now I'm having a wee go myself.'

'Go at what, like?'

'Finding out who did for Gordon Weaver.'

'Uh!'

'You know the score, Mowatt,' said Doyle, smiling. 'An eye for an eye, and all that. If you hear anything that might be of use to me why don't you give me a look in at the shop; or use the phone if you prefer it. I'll pay for information.'

'You're round the bloody twist, Mr. Doyle,' Mowatt said. 'Christ, he's been dead for near a year.'

'I held off to let the bogies have their fling,' Doyle said. 'I'm not really looking for copper's evidence, anyway, just some clue to the name of the . . .'

'I keep my nose clean, mister,' said Mowatt suddenly. He

wiped his nostrils with his cuff to prove the point. 'Nothin'
I can tell you.'

'Well, you never know,' said Doyle. 'If you do hear anything . . .'

'Aye, sure,' said Mowatt, sceptically. 'That'll be right.'

'Mowatt!'

But the boy was gone, trotting hard head down back
towards the players who, having sniffed the uncommon in
Doyle's arrival, closed their ranks protectively around their
mate.

Doyle hesitated then turned too and walked briskly out
of the park towards the side-street where Weaver waited in
the big Mark 10. He had nothing to tell Weaver, no scrap
of information to impart. At least he had tried though: he
just hoped the gesture would be enough.

The Omega café presented a curved yellow-plaster façade
to passing motorists. Sited on a corner of the road which
bisected Wickerburn and Grahamshill, it was flanked on
one side by a fried fish shop and on the other by a filling
station. It backed on to a triangular acre of waste ground.
The pavement outside was shored with metallic crash-
barriers, hitching rails for the denizens of the districts
who used the place as a meeting ground; an amorphous
crowd, peppered with hairy hippies and leather-clad cow-
boys, riders of the big cycles, minors, moon-faced skin-
heads and the flocks of female camp-followers. The café
was an open port for the exchange of tepid gossip. No
single group, no pack or gang laid claim to territorial
rights here. It remained a no-man's land, shunned by the
hard-nosed rovers and effete hoodlums from the adjacent
empires. Though no appointed pigeons transported rumour
back into the hinterlands of the schemes and no self-
respecting crook dedicated to profit set much store by
data from that source, a thin smoke of information drifted
out from the Omega like the reek of a dung fire beyond
the city walls. Mowatt, in company, came to refresh himself after the match. Mowatt was nothing but a lout, de-
void of intelligence, guile and aggression. What marked
him as different from his companions that afternoon of
his life was that he had once worked briefly for Vincent

123

Doyle who was the grandfather of Gordon Weaver who was dead.

Hardly any of the tenants of the café knew that Doyle even existed or that he had a connection with them, a tiny blood-knot, as frail and fine but as positive as a suture in a cerebral operation. In all that stretch of terrain, webbing out from the Omega, only five people had bothered to store the information. Two of them were in the café that afternoon, two who had also been in the field of play earlier in the day: one was Mowatt and the other was Leadbetter. Leadbetter was not in the Omega by chance.

Slim, sallow-skinned and with dark fluid eyes, Leadbetter's appearance was marred by an ugly mouth. The flaked lips curled close to deformity and the shortened stem between nose and mouth was as prominent as a scar. With such a mouth his eyes had no need to register his emotions, and seldom did. Five minutes after entering the café, Leadbetter shifted from his place at the counter to a chair at Mowatt's table. He was nervous but did not show it. He settled himself, dabbed at the tin ashtray with the tip of his cigarette and held up the coffee cup in one hand.

'What did the bugger want?'

'Eh?'

'The old guy in the park?'

'I worked for'm once.' Mowatt was wary of Leadbetter, of his reputation for slyness. 'In his shop, like.'

'What did he flog?'

'Books an' that.'

'Doyle's his handle; right?'

'Right enough,' said Mowatt. 'Y'know him?'

'Nup.'

'He . . .'

'He what?' said Leadbetter, keenly.

'He had a relative done last year.'

'Who would that be?'

'Weaver.'

'Can't say's I've heard the name,' said Leadbetter. 'What about't?'

'Doyle was askin' for information about the kid, an' who done him in.'

'He expected you t'know somethin'?'

Mowatt's eyes denied all comprehension. 'He knows me, like.'

'See him often, then?'

'Haven't seen'm for eighteen month'r more.'

'How come he picks on you then?'

'Only 'cause he knew me,' said Mowatt desperately. It was beginning to trickle into his intelligence that Leadbetter had more than a passing interest in Doyle, but whatever that interest was Mowatt just didn't want to know. He waited, visibly tense, while Leadbetter finished the coffee and stuck the cigarette butt into the wrinkle in his upper lip, then pushed himself back from the table.

'See yuh, Mowatt.'

'Aye, sure,' Mowatt answered, adding under his breath, 'but not if I see you first.'

Leadbetter paused in the doorway, his eyes focused on a group of young girls who were flaunting themselves along the railings. He did not really see the girls though, or the gleaming hulks of the cycles beyond, or even the huge orange bulk of a bus swishing past close to the barriers. He was mentally occupied with weighing and sifting the information he had gleaned from that idiot Mowatt. He knew it was important, but he did not yet know if it was more dangerous to tell or not to tell, or what would happen if he kept his mouth shut and let it run unchecked. The fusion of several different fears occurred in him suddenly. He blinked and screwed up his eyes and felt the lip twisting higher over his teeth and the cold air of early evening on his gums. He had recognised Doyle from far off, and the fear had been with him again, instantly, flashing through him like a drug. It was basic to his nature to do nothing, but the open mouth was a symbol of his need to talk. Decision came to him and he stepped out of the doorway and crossed the pavement. Ignoring the girls and the cycles, he vaulted the barrier and struck off north into Grahamshill to relay the latest to a unit of higher power.

SIX

She was seated in the alcove in the darkest corner of the hotel bar. Dressed well and demurely she looked older and more sophisticated, showing off her middle-class breeding. Weaver did not yet know what he would do with her or what part she had planned for herself in the events of the next few days. Sense told him that it would be best to dump her now, but some part of him recoiled from the callousness and finality of that solution. He wanted her; he still wanted her.

'Good evening, Mr. Simpkins.'

'Evening.'

'Fruitful excursion, Mr Simpkins?'

'No,' he said. 'What's that you're drinking?'

'Gin and tonic.'

Weaver signalled the waiter to bring two more of the same, then seated himself on the bench. It was early yet and the hotel was exclusive enough for the bar to be almost deserted. Dim lighting, a comfortable corner, a purr of music and a beautiful girl beside him; his disappointment at the futility of Doyle's visit to Gartshaws Park lessened somewhat. Later he would have to face up to the problem of what to do next; he could think of no better course than to go on asking questions until a lead cropped up or, as might conceivably happen, the law got wind of his curiosity, and prudence gave him an out.

'You look good,' he said.

'Thank you, kind sir.'

'Older.'

'I take that remark as flattery,' Hazel said. 'I got a bit bored with the child-bride role. Jack loved it, you know.'

'I like you the way you are now.'

'I'm glad.'

'Do you want to eat here, or . . . ?'

'I want to eat here, *and*,' she said, smiling.

The waiter put the drinks on the table and Weaver paid

126

him with a note. The man bowed and went off between the empty tables. Weaver sipped the drink. The girl was motionless beside him, sensing perhaps that she had lost his attention but not foolish enough to interrupt his thoughts to drag him back to her.

Weaver was thinking of the cash packed into the bottom of the suitcase and of the confidence it gave him. For a while it might even be possible to forget the purpose of the stake and pretend that it would only be used for this, to entertain the girl, to taste the high life and plush cosseting of the city's best hotel. Under the money, though, snuggled the Luger and its three clips of ammunition. He could not forget the potential of those twenty-four bullets.

'Are you thinking about your son?' the girl asked, softly.

'No.'

'If he hadn't died you wouldn't have come back here, would you?'

'No.'

'Do you really want to find his killer?'

'Jack told you too much.'

'Would you rather not talk about it?'

'I don't mind.'

'What method do you use?' she asked.

'I ask questions.'

'Slow and unrewarding, I should think.'

'Once I get myself a lead the rest will be easier.'

'Then you'll bring that strong arm of yours into use?'

'Yeah.'

'It wasn't a private crime, you know,' she said. 'Presumably the police carried out an investigation.'

'So what!' Weaver said. 'I can't go marching up to the desk in the CID headquarters and demand to be shown their records.'

'Did your son mean a lot to you?' said Hazel. 'I suppose he did or you wouldn't be here at all.'

'I had five years with him,' Weaver said. 'I don't go much for kids, but I remember him. I remember the way he felt more than anything. Later, when he was grown a bit, I remember the way he looked and talked.'

'How did he look?'

'Soft.'

'Not like you?'

'Yeah, like me, only soft. Listen, I didn't really know him at all,' Weaver said. 'At the time I was still around but not living in the house any longer, I used to chat to him sometimes, though neither of us seemed to have much to say. I don't know why. Then I quit Glasgow and went south. That's the big buffer, the leaving bit. A good thing, maybe.'

'A good thing for you,' Hazel said. 'But something must have brought you back, some sort of feeling.'

'He was mine, my child, my son, and some bastard killed him. Isn't that good enough!'

'You're going to kill him, aren't you?'

Weaver looked at her, not answering.

She said, 'I'm not afraid of the word. You are going to kill him?'

'If I find him.'

She leaned forward and caught his wrist. 'Not if,' she said, 'when! When you find him.'

'Not so easy.'

'Yes, easy,' she said. Her fingers laced into his. The gold wedding band rubbed against his knuckle as she tightened her grip. 'The chase is only delay. You're kidding yourself. You're afraid, afraid to run them to earth, aren't you?'

'I'm not sure if it matters,' said Weaver.

'You're not angry any longer.'

'I can do nothing if I can't track the bastard down.'

'The police *might* know.'

'Maybe.'

'Be straight,' she said. 'Answer yes or no.'

'The police *might* know.'

'All right,' Hazel said. She took a long breath, like a pearl diver, filling her lungs before a plunge down into the deepest part of the ocean. 'Jack, presumably, told you all about McFadden and his set-up?'

'What of it?'

'You know about Greerson?'

Weaver nodded. Slowly he disentangled his hand from hers and lifted the glass to his mouth. He turned his head from her, the lids heavy, hooded, brooding. At the bar a portly man in dinner dress was holding an ice-cube between finger and thumb and sucking on it as if it was a sweetmeat. Under the canopy a red jacket shifted position soundlessly, and the mild sweep of strings from the hidden amplifier absorbed the tinkle of glasses. He tried not to listen to her but she was too close now.

She said, 'Go to Greerson; he can give you the information you need.'

'No.'

'But why not?'

'Greerson's as twisted as a corkscrew.'

'Don't you think I don't know,' she said. 'But you can handle him. Look, you're not afraid, are you?'

'No.'

'I can put you in touch with him, with Greerson.'

He whipped round. 'You can?'

'Why do you think Greerson allocated that last caper to Irwin. He didn't know Irwin from Adam.'

'You?'

'Yes.'

She tried to touch his hand again but he pulled it back. Cupping his glass he slid his shoulder on the bench so that he blocked off the room, penning her; a lover's trick, focusing her full attention on him. Weaver did not intend it as such.

'You and Greerson?' he asked.

'Only for a little while.'

'Now what the hell does that mean?'

'I didn't live with him or anything. We saw each other.'

'You screwed together,' Weaver snapped.

'Listen, Don . . .' she said, then gave up. 'Yes.'

She shook her hair and lifted her chin and stared at him defiantly as if to show him that he had no right to expect her to be ashamed of things she had done long before she had known him.

'I wasn't his girl,' she said. 'I slept with him, oh, maybe half a dozen times. I had my own little flat then and he came when he could, which wasn't often. I couldn't be his girl because I didn't care for him all that much. He has a wife and children and a job which takes up a lot of his time. Anyway, he was too afraid to last for long.'

'Greerson was afraid?'

'Yes, of being exposed, implicated. He didn't show it

129

outwardly but the thing was always there with him, chasing him around. He's cunning, too cunning almost.'

'He has to be.'

'I know,' said the girl. 'He wheels and he deals and he trades two ways with some of the biggest sharks in this city but on the outside he's always a copper, all fish-eyes and cold charm.'

'How does he get away with it?'

'I don't know,' she said. 'How can *you* get away with it?'

'I don't cheat on anyone.'

'That's wasn't the question. It's immaterial,' she said. 'What matters is that Greerson worked on your son's case.'

'What is he?'

'Detective Inspector; a floater, I think they call it. He circulates from department to department; sometimes it's the Murder Squad and sometimes the Robbery Detail.'

'Bloody convenient for him.'

'And for McFadden.'

'How long's he been taking payola from McFadden?'

'Years,' said Hazel. 'He's a careful man is Greerson. He does both jobs well, you see. He peddles information, not protection. He'll sell jobs by telephone, public call boxes always, make his collection months afterwards.'

'Some canary should have shopped him by this time.'

'The canaries may not know,' the girl said. 'He only deals with the big men.'

'Like Jack Irwin?'

'That was different,' said Hazel. 'I hadn't seen Greerson for a couple of years, then one afternoon I met up with him in a store in town. He had kept tabs on me: he knew I was living with Irwin and he began pumping me for information. I hadn't any to give him. He wanted a thief, somebody outside the usual circle. We know now that he planned to take McFadden and that's why . . .'

'What happened?' Weaver interrupted.

'I told him the only thief I knew was Irwin, and then we parted again. Another couple of weeks went by, then one morning, early, he called me.'

'Where?'

'At Jack's flat. He guessed that I'd be the one to roll

out of bed and answer the phone—I told you he was shrewd—and I was. Jack didn't really wake up. Greerson wanted to meet me and we set up a rendezvous.'

'Where?'

'A marvellous place, actually,' the girl said. 'One of the mid-morning diesels out to Motherwell. I don't think there was another soul on the whole train.'

'He had decided to risk it with Irwin?'

'Yes. I don't know why. It didn't seem to me like Irwin's sort of stunt, but Greerson asked me all sorts of questions and then said he would contact Jack directly. My name wasn't mentioned. Jack was caught between two stools. He wanted to do the job but he had to find a partner that he could trust.'

'How were the deals made?'

'Always by telephone. So far as I know they've never met face to face.'

'Then I showed up?'

'To Jack you were a gift from the gods.'

'Why did you come away with me?'

'I wanted to,' Hazel said.

'Greerson put you up to it?'

'If you don't know the answer to that,' she said adamantly, 'then there's no hope of a future for us. God, Weaver, I don't operate. I do what I want to do, and right now I want to be with you.'

'To watch me kill a man?'

'To help you.'

'To help me kill, then?'

'Oh God,' the girl said. 'You're obsessed with killing.'

'You think I *want* to go through with this?'

'Yes, otherwise . . .'

'Doyle brought me back from Spain. He knew what would happen. I'm sick of being a bloody instrument.'

'Even for your son?'

'There's nothing I can do for Gordon now.'

'Then take your money and clear out of Glasgow. I mean, why are you sitting here in a hotel bar talking all around it if you don't want to do it at all? You can't blame anyone. You can quit.'

'Want another drink?'

'Damn you, Weaver, don't *withdraw*.'

'Just what do you want with me, Hazel?'

'When you've done this thing you'll leave Glasgow,' she said. 'You have some cash and you have the skill to make more. I want you, and I want to go with you.'

'We can leave now, tonight.'

'No.'

'Is this some sort of bargain?' he asked.

'How can I go with you when a chunk of you will be stuck here forever, like a wasp-sting, dragged out of you, broken off. How can I? You can't leave it, and I won't leave you. Listen, Don, I can have Greerson on the telephone in five minutes. If you offer him money he'll trade with you. It's nothing to him to sell you information. There's no risk for him in this deal. He'll come across, I'm sure of it.'

Weaver sat back, hunched into the corner of the alcove, hands draped over his thighs. More guests had entered the room now, women, elegant in evening dresses making elegant noises, a little louder than the music. The tumble of fresh ice-cubes filling the bucket on the bar top sounded like a landslide. Two red packets owned the space behind the bar. One was slim with a chin and cheekbones like three smooth pebbles; the other was bullnecked.

'Call him,' Weaver said, suddenly.

He tugged a handful of loose coins from his pocket and spilled them on the table, let her pick what she needed for the lobby pay-phone. She clenched the silver and coppers in her hand and stared at him, a last second's uncertainty.

'Go ahead,' Weaver said. 'Call him now.'

The houses of North Grahamshill had no more individuality than barracks blocks. One street was identical with another and the only recognisable landmarks were an occasional row of shops and a couple of prefabricated clinics. There were no churches and no chapels, no bars or cinemas, no sports or community centres, not even a school for the district to call its own. All sources and institutions of learning and diversion stopped short at the highway which marked the Grahamshill boundary as if

132

they feared contamination from the dunning ugliness of the interior.

In the front room of the upper apartment of a four-in-a-block terrace house two young men met for an evening meal.

The younger was a month short of twenty. Though the conversation was serious and accented earnestly enough, the boy could not hide his impish cheerfulness. His head was large and sat on his shoulders as solidly as a stone ball on a mansion house gate-post. His shoulders had bowed and set in a scholar's stoop through bearing the weight of it. Dark haired, dark eyed, unshaven, his frankness and amiability had deceived many men, and some women and brought them grief in the end. This was Bremner. O'Hara was of finer build; lean to the point of emaciation, with hands as slender as plant tendrils. His high-bridged nose was shrunken with congestion and his mouth had been warped a little by the healing of a scar which nipped into the cheek like a lamprey. In twenty-two years his eyes had silted over with an accumulation of cynical wisdom. Bremner wore a flowered shirt and pearl-grey broadcloth pants; O'Hara a black sweater and jeans as sombre and unadorned as the vestments of a priest. They spoke quietly but with obvious lucidity. A stranger might have supposed them to be lower-class intellectuals caught in a discussion of social theory. No passion quickened the steady, almost pedantic, rhythm of the conversation, only an occasional pause as one or other sipped tea from his navvy's billy-can.

The room was heated by an electric stove, the bars disguised by plastic logs. The bulb over the table was crammed into a shade too small for it. The furniture, a three-piece suite and dining set, had been purchased through a discount store. Tallow coloured light made a pool on the newspaper which served as a table covering. The paper was sprinkled with hard crumbs. On it rested a pint carton of milk, a plate of bread rolls and a pile of fruit tarts hygienically sealed in waxed cardboard.

The young men at the table ignored the girl. She had removed her skirt and was crouched by the hearth shaving her legs with a battery shaver. Her stiff blonde hair was pinned so high on her scalp that it showed the mouse-

133

brown roots. Her thighs were heavy, and mottled with fire freckles and her open cardigan allowed one bulbous breast to poke through like the snout of a manatee. This display of female flesh affected neither of the young men but the girl did not seem put out by their indifference and went on with her labour contentedly, making herself even more beautiful just for her own satisfaction.

'A year's a long time,' O'Hara said.

'Still, he was asking,' said Bremner.

'No panic.'

'Leadbetter was scared.'

'Leadbetter was born scared,' O'Hara said. 'Old Doyle can't do a bloody thing t'harm us. Christ, if the coppers couldn't put a nozzle up Leadbetter's arse and make him open his mouth then what chance's the old man got?'

'Maybe he knows already.'

'O'Hara considered the possibility. 'Well, if he does, we can make him forget.'

'I'd skip first,' said Bremner.

'You wantin' to skip?'

'That's the last thing I want,' said Bremner. 'Thing's goin' good for me here.'

'Then sit tight.'

'For how long?'

'The old bugger's only chewin' air. He's after a reaction but he won't get it from us,' said O'Hara.

'How about Leadbetter?'

O'Hara tipped the billy with his forefinger and made it chime dully, repeating the gesture with more rapidity until the can tilted and spilled its dregs. He dabbled his pinkie in the loch then sucked it. When he took his finger from his mouth it was cleaner than the rest of the hand.

'Marilyn, more tea.'

The girl scrubbed at the inside of her thigh. The machine emitted a small sawing sound not quite loud enough to be irritating.

'Marilyn,' O'Hara said again.

The girl flung down the razor and struggled to her feet. As she padded through from the living room to the kitchenette her buttocks flopped under the panties, insolently. Still the men paid her no heed.

134

'I hope it isn't snoops again,' said Bremner. 'I'm gettin' fair sick of snoops.'

'Why should it be snoops?'

'The old man could stir them up again.'

'One old man, an old rummy at that,' said O'Hara. 'He's a freak, like Weaver was.'

'Yer, they're all freaks to you, mate,' Bremner said.

'You're doin' okay.'

'An' I want it to stay that way.'

'Sometimes,' said O'Hara, 'I have doubts about you, Kenny-boy.'

'I don't even know yet how it happened.'

'You went with me all the bloody way.'

'More's the bloody pity.'

'You're not with me now, uh?'

'Leadbetter's got no percentage in this,' Bremner said.

'He just wants to keep his wee head on his shoulders,' said O'Hara. 'He's never talked before, an' he knows better'n to talk now.'

'What if the old guy does go to the cops?'

'I tell you it won't get back to the law.'

'I thought it was all over; Jesus!'

'A thing like that's never really over,' O'Hara said.

'What d'we do?'

'I say leave it; sit on it.'

'Sweat it out?' said Bremner.

'No sweat needed,' O'Hara told him. 'We've got the drop on our side. We can always get rid of him.'

Bremner looked up at him quickly, quizzically, but O'Hara merely grinned.

The girl brought in the tea.

SEVEN

Irwin put the suitcases down in the dust and flexed his fingers. The dead weight of the luggage and his exertions seemed to have had a beneficial effect on him, though; the trembling which had ridden him all day had gone now.

135

The bookstall was shuttered and the lights in the station restaurant were dimmed out; the last diner was being swept out of the door by the impatient buzz of the cleaner's Hoover. Irwin glanced up at the board to check again the departure time of the London train. It was easy to find among the scant night-time information. The automatic clock next to the face of the board skimmed off another minute. All that was left to him now was a bare quarter hour in which to make his decision and execute the manœuvre which had been shaping in his mind throughout the long afternoon.

Wakening that afternoon he had found himself tucked up in his own bed in his own flat with the hangover goading and pricking him like a sadistic rider mounted on a tired pony. He did not even open his eyes, only his mouth, shouting feebly for Hazel. No Hazel! He shouted again as loudly as the rigours of the muscles would allow, and still his girl, his gem, did not appear. The cloud gathered over him and the storm of apprehension broke, drenching his already miserable head with another dread. He gathered all his strength and uprooted himself from the bed, swayed and tottered through the still, stale rooms, crunching over the party debris, calling her name again and again, swearing at her latterly when he knew that she was not there to hear him. At length his wanderings led him to the wardrobe and he pulled it open. Empty spaces among the hangers and on the shoe shelf told him that what he had most feared had come to pass. He could not blink the truth of it now. Closing his eyes he leaned his throbbing temples against the long mirror then, shaking, plastered his naked torso against it too as if to bring himself into contact with a visual residue of his lover which might linger there in the glass. Then he cursed her, a stream of vicious and vindictive curses, and cursed Weaver, then, slipping down the mirror like a wet November leaf, cursed himself for ever having been fool enough to take her on.

Later, in the kitchen, brewing coffee, he dropped the glass cupola of the Cona, watched it bounce once on the rush matting then drop again and shatter. He had moved in a spasm to reach the cloth to mop up the coffee, had trodden on the wicked shards of glass, had cut himself across the instep, had bled. Later still—dusk creeping softly over the patches of winter sunlight—he found himself slumped on the end of the unmade bed with the blood coagulated at last and the foot on a towel and a cup of lukewarm Nescafé in his hand; bitter in his mouth but warm enough in his shivering gut. It was about that time that he gathered enough of himself together to be a man again and to begin to think linearly like a man should. He got up and limped quickly through to the study. Weaver had been good enough to take only his share of the cash, but the Luger was gone too. Big man Weaver had it all now; the holy trinity of the tough guy. Weaver had himself the girl, the money and the gun. How could a man as cold as that bastard ever be a loser.

Weaver might be a stinking bastard but he had in him qualities which Irwin could not help but covet. He sat in the desk chair with the Smith & Wesson in one hand and the wads of notes in the other and wondered just how he could box and padlock the devil that Weaver had become. For his own eternal peace of mind, he, Jack Irwin, had to cook up a sharper piece of ruthless arrogance. He brooded about it, inching closer and closer to the facts, to the inevitability of the choices he now had and the decisions he must make. Even now he could not bring himself to snap the chains of reminiscence; thought, as a drowning man might, of the happiness and security and fun he had had in this apartment, and how he had traded his wit and guile and the wiriness of his nerves to protect his snug and hedonistic life-style. Now hard times had come suddenly upon him and, even by his own modest lights he could see that he was halfway to being all washed up. Listen, Jack, he told himself, if you can plan a little robbery like Napoleon planning the sack of Moscow then, for God's sake, you can come up with a little scheme to salvage your own future. At the back of all his suffering was the knowledge that the girl was lost to him for good. With Hazel Ferrier had gone the last rag of his youth; he stood ballock-naked now against the draughts of middle-age. An old man and a youth cannot be harboured together in the same body. In losing Hazel he had lost the last illusion of immortality.

The thick-pile carpet in the bedroom bore a single

footprint; his own—in blood. He contemplated it like Crusoe then dropped to one knee and swabbed at it with a Kleenex. From that act others grew, the active role giving him determination and the beginnings of clear answers to the questions which had tormented him throughout the whole of the waning afternoon.

Within an hour the house was cleaned; soiled linen stripped from the beds and stuffed into the Ali Baba basket; dishes and glasses washed, dried, racked; carpets Hoovered; bottles corked and stored in the cabinet; all the food in the house flung into a carton. Punctiliously he performed the bachelor chores which usually bored him stupid. They weren't chores now but preliminary moves in his strategy. By seven o'clock the flushing of the flat was finished. It no longer seemed like home.

Hunger had caught up with him; the headache was like a conscious lobotomy. He fed himself a single nip from a brandy bottle, pitched the bottle in with the rubbish and, with a cigarette hanging wetly from his underlip, drove himself into the bedroom to finish packing. He built the banknotes into the bottom of a strong pigskin suitcase, left a space in the middle to fit the Smith & Wesson. Padding up the case with the best of his personal linen, he closed it and locked it and buckled up the straps. With the toilet objects from the bathroom went the old bone-handled razor. He would not part with his talisman; he needed all the luck he could get.

Donning his warmest overcoat, and a hat, and his best black leather gloves, he broached the bureau last of all. He scoured it of all its papers and dropped them into a large plastic bag. Only his account books and a few small mementoes of better days went into the second suitcase before he closed and locked and strapped it too. He made several trips to the midden to dump all the debris, stuffing the papers deep down under the ashes and the mash of tea leaves and foodscraps, then returned to the flat and switched off the electrical systems and the water-keys. Finally he carried the suitcases out on to the landing, locked both the inner and outer doors, plucked up the cases and went down and out of the building.

The Corsair was parked close by. He put the cases in the passenger seat, drove the car a short distance to his

138

garage, removed the cases, haggled terms with the manager and paid a garaging fee for two months in advance; then he walked to a cab rank and told the cabbie to take him to Central Station. Even with it all behind him, with that part of it over, he could not quite believe that he would have the nerve, the cold raw guts to do it. Betrayal had never been his bag.

Down in London town with a couple of thousand quid in good cash money, plus his various safety deposits and his securities, if he needed them, he could stretch himself out in comfort for a year or more. That would give him ample time to study the scene and the situations, make himself a few reliable contacts, sniff up some of that sophistication and let the richer air of the big city rejuvenate him as it had done Weaver. Maybe Weaver *had* pinched his bird, but Weaver had also taught him a valuable object lesson. London was where the girls were, where the best stunts took place, where maturity and experience were still considered qualities worth having. The change would do him a power of good. Really, though, he could not be sure why he was running, or why, like some ceremonial burning of his coracle, he was cheating on Greerson too. Whole-hog Irwin! If Greerson wanted him for welshing on the deal then Greerson could just go to the bother of finding him. He doubted if Greerson would: even the long arm of the bent cop had a limited range of strike and London seemed like a safe distance away. Naturally he could not instantly obliterate his trail. He wasn't Weaver living out of a suitcase in swank hotels and rented villas. The Corsair and the flat remained but, if all went well and it was safe to do so, he could hive them off through the discreet offices of his lawyer and his accountant; professional men could usually be trusted. Stepping out of the cab, he had paid the driver and squinted round for a porter. None were visible at that hour and, with the cases balanced on either side of him, he hobbled up through the arches to the ticket office. He slid his notes under the glass shield.

'London: first class.'

With the ticket in his wallet he lugged the cases up to the main concourse, set them down and consulted the board.

139

He could come no further without making his decision. Easy, Jack! Take it slow.

Would he go up to the train, sit himself down like a laird in one of the empty firsts, eat a couple of ham sandwiches, drink a double Scotch, sleep, waking when the train was across the Border, waken in the big bolt-hole, the city of a million opportunities? Would he? A month ago such a retreat would have been unthinkable: then he had been Irwin, homebody, highlander, a man with a slate as clean as a bride's brassière. From the moment that Weaver had stepped through the bedroom door, sun-tanned, smart as a whip, Irwin had felt the presentiment in his bones that it might some day come to this. Now the bastard had the run of the yard—and Irwin grudged it.

The clock sliced off another minute. A trickle of travellers drifted listlessly up towards the train.

Weaver, the hard-nose, had chased him out of *his* city. Jesus, he couldn't just go, leave the arrogant bastard to it. He jerked the cases from the ground and headed for the bank of telephones by the end platform. He found a vacant booth and leaned the cases against his ankles. He fished out the notebook from his vest pocket and the sixpenny bits from his overcoat. Cradling a coin in the slot, he quickly dialled a number.

To his left were the vast and almost deserted reaches of the rail terminal—Glasgow, his city. Driven out by Weaver and the intuitive sense which told him that Weaver was now a man as dangerous as a loaded gun. A man to steer clear of by four hundred miles and hope that that would be enough. Glasgow Central Station was all around him and already he was homesick for the bloody place.

Down the wire a voice spoke sharply. Irwin pushed the coin home.

When he spoke, his diction was ringing and precise with all trace of highland brogue chipped away. 'I want McFadden.'

He paused.

'You heard correctly,' he said. 'Never mind who I am. Tell McFadden I have information for him, pertinent to matters recently on his mind. Tell him.'

Fidgeting, he watched the oblong clock automatically

shuffling away time over the chill and dusty concourse. The vendors under the distant arches were already hawking tomorrow's news and the last couple of passengers coming singly up the platform looked tired and lonely and unhappy.

The voice was different, high-pitched, the way a pampered terrier would talk if it had the gift of speech. He knew it was McFadden.

He said, 'I'm calling about that spot of bother you found yourself in the other night. Now don't talk, please; just listen, listen very carefully. I will say it once and will not repeat myself.'

As he spoke Irwin discovered that treachery was a whole new series of sensations, much less painful than he had imagined; a release, in fact. When he hung up abruptly, he found that the sadness had gone right out of him. He felt encouraged, cheerful, resilient, more youthful already. Aye, London was for him. The metropolis would shelter him and teach him its latest tricks. Green pastures lay ahead of him; young girls with clever notions and no aversion to a few grey hairs; stunts worthy of his ingenuity and organising skill.

Lifting the suitcases, he strode away from the telephone and joined the stragglers on their way up to the big green south-bound train.

The Coruna snuggled close into an elbow of the river. The view from the window was of cranes and mastheads and the spars of the yards and lading locks. The fretwork jungle was splashed with lights and a lunar silvering which gave it the unearthly stillness of a graveyard, a saragossa of land-locked tankers and cargo boats and big black liners. Weaver turned from the window to the hotel room.

The girl came out of the shower.

For a moment she was unaware of his scrutiny and in that moment he thought he glimpsed the sleek and elusive fear which was in her, too. She was nude—not naked, nude—and her body was smooth and lithe. Her breasts had a firm slippery suppleness which flicked up the memory of the touch of the rubbery bud of McFadden's daughter; that faceless child of ten or eleven still so in love with the image of paternal strength and dignity that she would pit

141

herself furiously against a tall man with a gun in his hand just to defend it. Hazel had done all that she felt impelled to do behind the locked door of the bathroom. She was not one to treat him with disrespectful casualness, the attitude of most women to their men. She would not stand before him all self-absorbed, tarting herself up with creams and sprays to make herself cutely appetising for the act of coition. Hazel understood that mystery is part of the magic of it an that the right kind of man prefers his girl natural or, at most, discreetly garnished. In close-up, he had been forced to watch Muriel's slow disintegration, and the experience had altered his tastes radically. In the heat of youth it didn't seem to matter much what a woman wore or how she made herself up but, later, as Muriel had taught him, a man needs a woman who is not so sure of him that she can present herself for love looking like an unmade bed. Brand would not be the fastidious sort, and Muriel would now never learn what it was that had helped to drive him away from her. Caught in the centre of his appraisal and startled by it, Hazel was as beautiful a woman as he had ever laid eyes on.

'Why are you looking at me like that?'

'Like what?'

'I . . . I can't describe it,' she said.

'I was just thinking.'

'Oh!'

'I was thinking that it's strange Greerson wants to see me as soon as tomorrow.'

'Maybe it's convenient for him,' the girl said. She could not quite disguise her disappointment. Perhaps she had been expecting another compliment, the beginnings of a verbal paperchase which would lead to the bed. The unguarded moment and the quality of her beauty had tempered his hunger for her. For the moment, the needle stood close to zero. He watched as she climbed briskly into bed, still nude, propped her shoulders against the pillow and lifted a paperback novel from the bedside table. The cover of the book was stylishly eye-catching; a man and a girl towered through the titling, both masked with smoked glasses, both with shotguns at the ready. Under the ribbed sweater of the photograph the girl's breasts were outlandish; the male wore a cruel smile.

142

Hazel drew the sheet a little higher. In another frame of mind, Weaver might have teased her about her modesty. She was different to what she had been in Irwin's house, not so blatant or aggressive or so insultingly youthful; more beautiful though. He crossed to the bed and lifted the paperback from her hands. She stared up at him, her pupils clear and full of gravity.

'How did you become what you are?' she asked.

The question was unexpected. Weaver paused, then said haltingly, 'I didn't drop into it by accident, Maybe that's how it's supposed to happen, but not with me. I didn't steal because I had to, not out of . . .'

'Deprivation?'

'Yeah,' he said. 'I stole because I wanted more than I had. What I had would have been enough for most folks. I wanted more though, more than I had hopes of getting.'

'Spirals,' Hazel said. 'Have you *ever* had what you want?'

'Always.'

'Stop it,' she said. 'The truth: have you, ever?'

'Nope.'

'Do you enjoy it?'

'I enjoy what it gives me.'

'No, I meant the doing of the thing itself.'

'Yeah, I enjoy it, but not as often as I used to.'

'Jack got pleasure from it.'

'In his class, Jack's sound.'

'He fretted terribly but he really did enjoy it,' the girl said, 'but I don't believe he was much good at anything, except bullying.'

Weaver lifted the paperback and tapped the cover illustration with his knuckle. 'What about this guy?'

'Hm?'

'What do you think of him?'

'You're much more handsome,' Hazel said. 'It's a crazy question, anyway. Are you just drumming up idle conversation because you don't want to come to bed with me?'

'No,' Weaver said. 'I feel like talking for a while.'

'I didn't think you went in much for conversation.'

'Sometimes.'

'All right,' the girl said. 'Tell me then, what's the most difficult thing you've ever had to do?'

143

Weaver leaned on his elbow, the bed sagging under him, and touched her hair. He thought about her question, then nodded to himself.

'I was hidden out in a boarding house one time,' he said slowly, 'after a caper. It had gone well enough. I was the holder, had all the loot, about eighteen hundred quid in a black plastic bag with a zipper along the top. I was in my room, upstairs in this house, when I heard a car stop and, being a bit edgy, looked out of the window. Two cops were coming out of a prowl wagon, making for the front door.'

'A tricky situation.'

'I didn't know what the hell they had on me, if anything, but I wasn't waiting around to find out. I stuffed some dirty shirts into the top of the money bag and went out and downstairs. It was high summer and the cops were in shirt-sleeves and sweating like pigs: a constable and a sergeant. The constable had a face like a prize boar and foam, little hinges of dried froth, at the corner of his mouth. They really gave me the eagle as I came down the staircase. The sergeant was against the main door, shifting on his heels, sort of poised. My landlady was chewing the fat with the other one. I just kept on coming, smiling at her and looking at the cops and they were all looking at me. The woman introduced me as Mr. Lucas; that was the name I was using and the name on the papers I had on me. The young cop had it straight that I was a wrong 'un. He was dead set on pulling his weight, but the sergeant was not so sure. They asked me for identification. I opened the black bag and took out the papers and gave him up the driver's licence with the name Lucas on it. I left the bag open, the shirts covering the money. I told him, the young one, that I was on my way to the laundromat round the corner and asked him what all this was in aid of. The bag was open right there between us. He kept glancing down at it, holding the papers in his hand. Then the sergeant gave him the prod and they let me go. I went out and the cops came after me and stood on the high step and watched me all the way down the street. I didn't run, but I had to hold the feeling of wanting to run in my legs, hold it like you hold a dog. I walked around the corner and went into the laundromat, went in and sat down and waited. I waited ten minutes but they didn't come and the prowl car didn't pass. The waiting was the hard part, that and the not running.'

'What did they want?'

'I never found out.'

'You went back to the house?'

'I parked the loot with one of the others,' said Weaver, 'and went back to the boarding house with some of his shirts in the bag. The cops had gone. Maybe it wasn't me they were looking for. Maybe it was somebody else they wanted: I don't know. I cleared out that night and hid elsewhere.'

'Did that happen in London?'

'Manchester.'

'You've never been caught?'

'Never,' he said. 'That was the closest.'

'Why?'

'It happens,' Weaver told her. 'Some of us have the breaks.'

'It'll be hard for you to confront Greerson tomorrow, won't it?'

'It'll be hard,' admitted Weaver.

'Can he harm you?'

'If I knew for sure one way or the other, maybe I'd worry less.'

'Is it because he's the law?'

'He can't be trusted. He's bent.'

'I doubt if he can harm you without harming himself,' Hazel said. 'Stop picking at it.'

She pinched the hem of the sheet between her fingers and lifted it down and away from her breasts. The gesture was prim, like an elderly spinster folding away her communion gown.

'Stop thinking,' she said.

Weaved cupped her breast, the nipple stiffening under his palm. He kissed her mouth: she tasted still of peppermint, and her body was warm.

When he took his mouth away, she said, 'You see, you can stop.'

But it was different. Somehow he had fallen out of his isolation, and the only direction was down. Even when he entered her, crushing her carefully under him, he could not

145

stop thinking about tomorrow, and the meeting with Greerson which the girl had arranged. A slow and flooding orgasm brought him no relief.

EIGHT

A cable fed from the telephone in the hall, stapled neatly to the skirting up the side of the staircase to connect with an amplification box outside the bedroom door. The sound, therefore, was quite loud enough to snap Greerson out of the deepest sleep. He wasn't asleep this time, though, having only just rolled himself under the covers. After a prolonged and dull shift with his fellow officers of West Central Division, questioning witnesses of a stabbing incident in a dancehall, Greerson was tired. He had already commenced the process of slackening his limbs and draining his mind and lay as still as a cadaver, eyes closed, hoping to God that the damned phone would stop ringing. It didn't. He switched on the bed light and swung his legs to the carpet. On the pillow he could see Margaret's hair done up in curlers: curlers! He had gifted her three sets of fancy rollers but she was still plebeian enough to persevere with curlers. Taking the karate robe of rough grey canvas from the hook behind the door, he belted it about him, descended to the hall, snatched the receiver from its cradle and laid it to his ear.

'Greerson.'

In the sun-porch off the kitchen, Nero, a Doberman pinscher, growled throatily. It was cold in the hall in spite of the central heating. Greerson fingered a cigarette from the box on the table and lit it with the lighter shaped like a riding boot. Standing square, legs parted, he listened, saying nothing. McFadden chattered at him for a full two minutes; only a trained detective could possibly have picked up the gist.

'You want me to come *now*?' Greerson put in. 'I'm not coming now.'

McFadden raved again.

'Not at this damned hour of the night,' said Greerson. 'Tell me about it. No, the phone's safe enough. Who's going to bug *my* phone?'

Mixing blackmail and threat, promises and demands, McFadden got over the fact that he wanted an immediate audience. He kept shouting into the detective's ear, waspishly, almost hysterically, like a woman. It worried Greerson a little when McFadden became as overwrought as this and his instability showed on the surface. Greerson thought of tomorrow's routines and of how much sleep he could still wrest from the night if he gave in to the wee man without more ado. He did not want to go to the Carbon Atom: it was a principle of his not to consort with his contacts, and he had been inside the precincts of the club only a couple of times in the past. To be spotted there at this hour of the night was the sort of minor indiscretion which could blow back in his face; such small lapses of caution could easily be expanded into lawyer's points. Greerson had brought men to the dock and helped the hangman knot the rope around their necks on points just as slender. He was aware of the warring of interests in him, but was thoroughly adjusted to making instant evaluations.

'All right, McFadden,' he said. 'I'm not using that main entrance though.'

McFadden gave him instructions, and a time limit of thirty minutes—snotty little bastard—then hung up. Greerson nipped the cigarette, caught himself in the old habit of frugality, and destroyed it into the ashtray. He climbed the stairs again, not happy.

Over a wooden valet by the bed-end, his suit and fresh shirt were draped. He dressed quietly. All he could see of his wife was that bunch of idiotic bubble curls wrapped in cheap tin, and a row of fingernails like a casket of miniature stilettoes. Shoes in hand, he stooped dutifully over the curlers.

'The office,' he murmured.

Margaret grunted and opened one eye, obsidian and unseeing. He bussed her on the forehead, tasting the grease of her cleansing cream, then switched out the light and left.

Twenty-five minutes later he parked the Viva a safe

147

distance from the Carbon Atom and was walking back along the exposed pavement towards the club. A prowl car passed him just as he turned into the lane but the lads were concentrating on the activity around the front of the building and probably did not even notice him. The risk irritated him, though, and he pushed on angrily through a railed gate, up the gas-lit staircase to the top landing and rang the bell on the scarred old door.

McFadden opened up, ushered him into a long corridor. The corridor was carpeted wall-to-wall with something which felt like buffalo skin. Even Greerson was impressed by the incredible contrast between the squalid close outside and the opulence within. He was also ruefully amused by the whole concept of false doors and secret corridors and disdainful of the kind of boyish mind which had devised it.

The room was elongated, too narrow, tailored, Greerson assumed by the shapes of the tenement attics. It was furnished with a middle-price brand of soft couches and easy chairs. The desk at the end of the room, however, had the veneer of an expensive antique. The desk excepted, the rest of the décor reminded Greerson of something out of a late-night American movie: probably where McFadden had picked up his inspiration. Somebody really should tell the little swine that, even in a dim light, he in no way resembled Cagney in his vintage years. There was no one else in the room with them.

Greerson said, 'Get on with it.'

'What have you found out?' McFadden asked.

'Not a thing.'

McFadden was geared in a sleek blue suit but he hadn't shaved for half a day and the blue jaw did not match the colour of the material. The robbery had been a brutal blow to McFadden's ego. Greerson had already been through one scene with him this weekend. McFadden seemed to consider that he had been betrayed by him, that he was entitled not only to information but to protection from all the evils of the world in return for the retainer he shelled out. Greerson had done nothing, naturally, to pin down the ringleader of the raid at Bargowan. No point, since he had engineered the thing himself. The wee man's frustrated fury amused him and he

148

hoped the incident might impart a salutory lesson; it didn't do to underestimate the cunning of the creatures in the jungle. McFadden had been warned to tighten his security —Greerson had warned him personally—but McFadden arrogantly considered himself too big a man to be a victim. Watching the boss now, Greerson had the chill feeling that some new development had occurred. Fortunately he was not easily given to the corrosive emotions of fear and anxiety, and seated himself casually on the couch and lit a cigarette while McFadden ranted through the usual overture about how much he paid him and how little he did to deserve it. Greerson watched, impassive, bland, as the boss's swarthy, rodent features hardened gradually into a sly composure rendered comical by the lattice of pink tape across his cheekbone and the bridge of his nose. In spite of his money and his fistful of power, it was difficult for Greerson to take McFadden seriously. With what he knew about the organisation he could close the whole business down in three days or less, but the interplay of calumny was just a bit too complex for him ever to have recourse to that measure.

'I had a phone call,' McFadden said. 'Anonymous.'

'Uh-huh!'

'He told me who did it.'

In spite of his control Greerson felt a certain choking dryness in the base of his throat. 'Did he now?'

'I'm told it was a man named Weaver: Donald Weaver,' McFadden rasped. 'Have you heard of him?'

Greerson's expression was benign. 'No, I can't say I ever have.'

'Then you'd better start, Greerson. I want this Weaver guy found.'

'You only have a grasser's word for it.'

'A grasser's word is better than no word.'

'Where does Weaver hang out?'

'I wasn't told that.'

'Was the grasser a woman?'

'A male—I just told you that.'

'So you did,' said Greerson. 'Did you recognise the voice?'

'No.'

'How do you pay him?'

'He ... he didn't ask for payment.'

Greerson pursed his lips and made round eyes, like an ageing comedian delivering the punch-line of a blue joke. 'It has the odour of a grudge case. I wouldn't put too much faith ...'

'Then what *do* I put my faith in,' McFadden demanded. 'You?'

'I did warn you ...'

'*Warn me!*' McFadden shouted. 'Fat lot of good that did me. Listen, they jumped me at the house, my own private house. You hear me, Greerson, they entered my private home, and ...'

'We've been through all this before,' Greerson said. 'Stop wasting my time.'

'Waste ... waste ...' McFadden, incensed, could not utter the words.

'I've put out feelers,' said Greerson.

'And I have a name.'

'But no address.'

'Christ, Greerson, you're supposed to be a cop: find him.'

'Then what?' Greerson enquired. 'I can't charge him, can I?'

'Then get me somebody who'll get rid of him.'

'Hell, you've got more gorillas on the books than they've got in the Congo,' said Greerson. 'You don't need me to find you a gun.'

'Do as I say.'

'Don't get uppity with me, McFadden.'

'Find me Weaver and somebody to deal with him.'

Greerson slapped his hands against his thighs and got to his feet. 'Are you sure that's all you want from me?'

Ignoring the sarcasm, McFadden nodded. 'That's all.'

'I'll see what I can do.'

'You'd better,' McFadden said.

Greerson drove slowly through the centre of the city, heading south towards home. Before he reached the feeder road to the Kingston Bridge, however, he altered his mind and his direction and swung the Viva round the dockside junction and led it north again towards Wickerburn.

The grasser's call was not coincidental; now was the time to check out his theory. He went up to Irwin's flat and found the locked landing door, fingered the bell for a minute and listened to the desolate and unanswered chiming deep in the hallway. As he suspected, Irwin had flown. From that sure piece of knowledge methodical deductions came thick and computer fast.

Weaver had been Irwin's henchman.

Weaver had wound up with Hazel.

Irwin had lost the wool and squealed to McFadden.

Irwin, with a thousand still owing, had promptly left town.

Just too simple.

Just for a moment, too, up in the club headquarters, he had almost been convinced that Jack Irwin had exploded the entire keg. McFadden was unpredictable: what would he do if he discovered that he, Greerson, the tame policeman, was behind the robbery, was cheating the organisation too? He could hardly rub him out: McFadden was not as powerful, or even as hysterical, as all that, but somehow he would make trouble and Greerson was too devious a man to welcome an outright collision. How would he cope with such a disaster? He did not know; it was immaterial anyway. The situation as it stood was taut enough. The thousand which Irwin had embezzled from joint profits was not a fit subject for wrath; of more concern to him was the mixture of motivations which had driven the highlander from his native stamping ground and soured him enough to don the yellow jacket of the canary. It was quite out of character, Greerson thought, though he only had rumour and Hazel's evaluation of Irwin to go by in making a reckoning. Surely Irwin must realise that in fingering Weaver he had virtually condemned the man to death. The loss of the girl, attractive though she might be, would not of itself turn Irwin inside out. Something else? What?

He pondered the problem from all angles during the drive home. Whatever had made Irwin run was the cornerstone to the whole tottering edifice of lies and deception and mendacity and hatred. Was it some quality in Weaver, perhaps? Maybe Weaver was a nut, a psycho. A minute tremor of apprehension rippled through his colon and he discarded all further surmise along those lines.

Tomorrow would tell.

He glanced at the clock on the fascia.

Ten past one: in eight hours or so he would know for sure by the witness of his own eyes and ears what manner of man this Weaver was and what he wanted that only a copper could give. He would know too by the end of their meeting whether he agreed with McFadden and would be willing to give the nod that would put Weaver down.

NINE

Handsome red sandstone mansions protected the park. Most of them were given over to use as private schools or residential nursing homes. The unfenced park was demure and tidy and even the trash of the autumn fall had been broomed from its pathways and lawns. Weaver left the Mark 10 on the end of the rank of commuters' cars by the railway station, walked over the iron bridge which crossed the deep-sunk tracks of the urban line, and crossed the ring road. The park's central avenue ran like a ribbon of grey silk between stately trees and shrubs. The leaves of the evergreens were sugared with frost and the boating pond had a faint haze of mist over it. Weaver followed the avenue for a hundred yards then branched off to the right along a narrower path which led him to the formal gardens. Over the ridges of the mansions on the hill, the sky was like rough asbestos board, charred a little to the north where the industrial schemes snorted smoke against it. Like the spokes of a cartwheel five identical paths broke the circle of shrubs. The hub was a shallow broadwalk around a circular basin in the middle of which rose a fountain. The bowl was dry and clean, ready for winter. The benches stowed into alcoves in the shrubbery were all deserted. Chiselled from a single granite block the likeness of the landowner, donor of the park land to the public, stood high over the fountain base. The granite figure, a whiskered aristocrat in tweeds and stalking cap with a setter carved to his heel and a shot-gun to his elbow, was the only spectator. Alertly watching exits and

152

entrances, Weaver strolled round the fountain basin.

The first sound he heard was the sawing breathing of the dog, the kind of strangled rasping an animal makes as it strains against a leash. The leash was of a steel chain clipped to a broad leather collar studded with brass. Scenting him now the dog struggled for its freedom, but the man would have none of it. He dragged the beast back, claws scraping the gravel, until he won his victory over it, and it capitulated. The Doberman was sleek and beautiful; its tongue lolled over its sharp white teeth. Without a word of command or a gesure of chastisement the man brought it to a sitting position close to his right shin.

'Nero,' the man said. 'The dog's name.'

Weaver nodded, tense.

From a tarnished silver case the man produced a cigarette, lit it from his lighter. No breath of wind spoiled the perfection of the gas flame and he took his time with it. He was five, maybe even ten, years older than Weaver, compact, stocky, with a clear complexion and smooth features, tending to plumpness under the eyes and jowls. His nose had a slight twist to it just at the bridge as if some unkind relative had tweaked it before the bone was set. The Gannex raincoat and the stalker's cap were top quality. When the cigarette was alight and the lighter and case slipped out of sight into his pocket, he slackened his grip on the loop of the leash and brushed the dog's ruff with it, affectionately. The animal brought itself at once to all fours, the fine elongated snout pointing up and back at its master, its rich brown eyes curious.

'Weaver?'

'I'm Weaver.'

'I must exercise this beast: will you walk?'

'All right.'

The excitement had ebbed out of the Doberman now: it was alert but aloof, showing its pedigree as it sniffed the verge, not tugging on the steel links, trotting.

'Fourteen weeks old,' said Greerson, 'but already learning.'

'What do you use?'

'Kindness and experience,' said Greerson. 'How's Hazel?'

'All right.'

'Still as beautiful as ever?'

'I wouldn't know.'

'Haven't known her long?'

'Couple of weeks.'

'You "rescued" her from Jack Irwin, I take it?'

'Something like that.'

'Uh-huh!' Greerson said. 'And what can I do for you?'

'I need information.'

'Classified?'

'I doubt it,' Weaver said.

'Look, if you're setting up a job . . .'

'I'm not.'

'What's the nature of this information?'

'I want the name of the prime suspect in a murder case, one case your boys didn't bring to court.'

Greerson stopped. They were surrounded by the circle of shrubs, but he glanced up and down the rows, listening, wrinkles at the corners of his eyes, almost frowning with the effort of recall.

'Weaver,' he said. 'Gordon Weaver: North Grahamshill?'

'That's the one.'

'What's your interest?'

'He was my son.'

'So the woman lied?' Greerson nudged the dog forward once more.

'I'm not dead,' Weaver said. 'I never was.'

'A "natural" child?'

'A bastard, if that's what you mean.'

'Where were you when it happened—inside?'

'No.'

'Well, you've got a right to be vague,' said Greerson. 'What do you want with the names of the suspects?'

'I have my reasons.'

Greerson made a small wet sound with his tongue, shaking his head slightly. 'Vengeance is mine, and all that,' he said. 'Taking the law into his own hands?'

'What law?'

'We tried, Weaver, we tried awful hard.'

'But got nowhere; not to court at least.'

'You *know* we got somewhere,' Greerson said. 'Or you wouldn't be here with me now.'

'I'll pay for the names,' Weaver said.

'And what makes you think I can be bought?'

'I heard you like money,' said Weaver. 'Nothing to it for you. Tell me the names; I pay you, and that's it over.'

'Until the corpses start to turn up.'

'Only one,' said Weaver. 'The guilty one.'

'I suppose you've an infallible system for deducing guilt?'

'All I want from you is the lead.'

'I've two sons myself,' said Greerson. 'Not at home, now, though. One's at Oxford; got there under his own steam. The younger one's at Edinburgh University, but he seems more interested in golf than medicine. How long had you been gone before it happened?'

'Years.'

'By all accounts he was a quiet boy.'

'So I heard.'

'He didn't appear to have been involved in any mischief.'

'I gathered that too.'

'He was . . . just a victim.'

'Of what?' said Weaver.

'Your woman remarried, didn't she. I mean she married?'

'Yeah.'

'The boy probably felt uncomfortable in the house.'

'I don't need analysis,' said Weaver. 'I need names.'

'How much can you afford?'

'Two hundred.'

'Each?'

'For the lot.'

'A reasonable sum,' said Greerson.

'You'll do it then?'

Greerson killed the cigarette and tossed the butt into the shrubbery. They were coming around the outside rim of the cartwheel for the second time. 'Not so hasty, Weaver. Have you considered what you're asking me to do?'

'The names can't be important . . .'

'Uh-huh,' said Greerson, 'but if I give them to you and anything happens to one of them, then I'm automatically an accessory before the fact. You can swear that you'll do what you must as quiet as a wee mouse, slip off into the undergrowth again without a sound, but it may not work out that way. You can swear too that if you *are* caught you won't even murmur my name, but I don't know you, Weaver. I've only Hazel's word for your integrity and I don't even know Hazel all that well. Anyway, she's an impressionable and impetuous lassie.'

'Nobody would take my word against yours.'

'True,' said Greerson, 'but even a hint would start an official inquiry. The police guard their reputation jealously and accusations of disloyalty and criminal collusion always send them into a flap. Take my word for it. I have rank and status in the Force now . . .'

'Don't snow me, Greerson; you're in crotch-deep with McFadden.'

Greerson's eyes twinkled. 'Tut-tut!' he said. 'You're imprudent, Weaver. Should've kept me guessing about how much you know of my affairs. It illustrates the point, though, doesn't it? You can make trouble for me, and for McFadden. I don't want to risk falling into the pit you're digging for yourself. No thanks.'

'You run bigger risks for smaller profits.'

'How is Jack Irwin these days?'

'I wouldn't know that either.'

Steering the Doberman towards an opening, Greerson led the way back into the sheltered arena around the fountain basin. 'Hazel told you about McFadden?'

'Two hundred's my offer,' Weaver said.

'McFadden had himself a wee spot of bother t'other night.'

'So what?'

'Gun-play, no less. Two of his employees were wounded; mercifully nothing serious. McFadden's Mercedes, about six thousand pounds' worth of machinery, took a bad beating too. His family were shocked and his face was bashed and, as if all that lot wasn't enough, somebody relieved him of three thousand in hard-earned cash.'

'Is that a fact?'

Greerson smiled. 'He's been asking for it, of course, but it came as a sad blow to the wee swine. He doesn't look on the bright side the way I might do.'

'It has a bright side?'

'Uh-huh; as a demonstration of family loyalty. When

the villains took off, nice quiet Mrs. McFadden—not as ignorant of her husband's profession as he had imagined— jumped into the Mercedes and gave hot pursuit; very hot pursuit. Almost caught them too, but she ran out of road at the wrong moment.'

'Was she injured?'

'Just shaken.'

'McFadden's personal affairs don't concern me.'

'Don't lie to me, Weaver.'

'Our trade doesn't concern McFadden.'

'Aye, but it does,' said Greerson. 'Don't you see, if you go then I go too, and if I go then McFadden's Lilliputian empire could be shaken to its foundations. You're a professional. I am too, and so, in his fashion, is McFadden. None of us are savages, but the persons who killed your son are—savages, I mean.'

'Persons: in the plural?'

'We—you, I, McFadden—we work on the capitalist doctrine of get what you can and hang on to it, but the murderers of Gordon Weaver had no such excuse.'

'You really do know who they are?'

'Now, I'm a tidy sort of fellow,' Greerson went on. 'I've saved conscientiously for the years of my retirement. In a couple of years I'll quit the Force and begin to enjoy myself, in the company of my good lady wife, of course.'

'All right, Greerson, so you're a bloody paragon of virtue. Tell me what you know about my kid's murderers.'

'I am telling you, Weaver, if only you'll listen and be patient,' said Greerson. 'I'm talking about mad dogs.'

'Psychos?'

'Call them what you like: all killers are crazy in my opinion. What's more, they rock the boat. Even so, I wouldn't want innocent blood on my conscience. Cops do have consciences too, Weaver. For example, we pulled in a homosexual by the name of Fleming. He occupied the hot seat for two whole days. But the homo didn't do it. Certainly he was queer, but he wasn't a killer. There are those in authority, though, who would have taken him there and then and cropped his ears and launched him from the top of the Finnieston crane; those who would have installed themselves in the place of judge, jury and executioner. I'm not one of them. Fleming was innocent.'

Tense and cautious, Weaver said nothing. At least Greerson hadn't tried to palm him off with Fleming. It would have been a natural piece of duplicity; Fleming had been a prime suspect and Greerson presumably did not know that Weaver was already aware of the florist's innocence. Maybe Greerson *would* sell him the truth.

'When would you pay me?'

'Now,' Weaver answered.

'Well, I can give you the names now.'

'What's stopping you?'

'Ethical considerations.'

Weaver took an envelope from his overcoat pocket and held it down for Greerson to look at. They had veered towards the shelter of an alcove in the shrubbery. The Doberman, bored perhaps, snuffed at the rustic metal casting of the bench, left a curt watery trademark, then returned to yawning attention by his master's heel.

'It's the height of irony, really,' said Greerson. 'If you kill one of them, there's a chance I'll be called in to assist in the investigation, to perform my duty as a faithful servant of the forces of law and order. You *will* make a point of leaving town, Weaver, won't you?'

'I'll drop you a postcard.'

'No, no, I wouldn't do that.' Still smiling, Greerson held out his hand.

Weaver placed the envelope across it. Using his gloved thumb the detective flicked up the unsealed flap and glanced at the contents. He nodded and slipped the envelope into his inner pocket.

'Spill it,' Weaver said.

'Two young men, Jim Leadbetter and Kenny Bremner.'

'Just how young?'

'Nineteen, twenty now possibly.'

'Still in the city?'

'Almost certainly,' said Greerson. 'North Grahamshill was their home territory and both were regularly employed.'

'And they did it?'

'No, Weaver, *you* must prove that. I'm not committing myself.'

'Are they pack animals? I mean, do they run with a gang?'

'Both ran with one of the younger local mobs, but that appears to have been some years ago. Currently, neither of them has any connection with a gang.'

'Wrong tree?' Weaver asked.

'Definitely.'

'What's Bremner like?'

'Surprisingly human,' said Greerson. 'He's cheerful, not daft, and wasn't in the least intimidated by us, by the police.'

'Leadbetter?'

'A different kettle of fish. Ugly, sly, but anxious, not sure of himself. I thought he would crack, perhaps, but he held out.'

'What did you have on them?'

'Not much,' said Greerson. 'In fact, very little, that's why it wouldn't wash in a law court.'

'But you . . . I mean,' said Weaver choosily, 'they *were* prime suspects?'

'We spent weeks trying to scrape up a case against them, watched them for six months, but it was not to be.'

'No other possibilities?'

'None worth a docken.'

'All right, give me the addresses.'

'I don't have the addresses in my head,' said Greerson. 'Besides, you didn't pay for addresses.'

'You're a greedy bastard, Greerson.'

'I'm a business man, that's all,' Greerson said. 'Look, Weaver, make sure you don't . . .'

'What?'

'Forget it,' said Greerson. 'Who am I to give you advice!'

He jerked the leash a little. The Doberman got obediently to its feet. 'Love to Hazel, and good luck.'

Greerson offered his hand but that sort of hypocrisy was too close to the province of the law to be worthy of reciprocation. Greerson had his money and he had the names. All that remained for him to do now was to trace the boys, and arrange the means of execution. The superfluous feelings which had dogged him all during the week were suddenly gone. He looked down at the hand and then up at the bland smiling face, the head cocked as if to say *Be a gentleman, a sport; be civilised.* Turning on his heel, Weaver cut past the screens of rhododendrons and down the narrow path, walking straight and upright away from the cop and his pedigree Doberman pinscher.

TEN

Taking his fingers from the typewriter keys, Brown dabbed sweat from his brow.

'Don't mind me,' he said. 'Just pretend I'm not here.'

'What does he know?' Weaver asked.

'Enough,' Doyle answered. 'It was all Brown's idea, originally.'

'Enough of that cock,' said Brown. 'I didn't know about *him* then.'

'You want to help?' Weaver asked.

'Not on your bloody life.'

Brown shoved sulkily out of the chair and went into the storeroom. Sandwiches lay in a greaseproof bag on the butcher's block. You're a pig, Brown! he thought, as he pushed the books to one side and flattened out the paper. Picking a bread roll filled with chopped egg and mustard, he bit into it. The shapes of the men in the outer office cut off the light. Brown rammed the plug of the electric kettle into its socket and, chewing furiously, peered at the spout for the first wisp of steam. The bread was dry in his throat and he pumped saliva into his mouth and munched with more concentration. He didn't want any part of what was happening out there: didn't want any part of Weaver.

'I have the names,' Weaver was saying. 'Two names.'

'How?' Doyle made the word sound like a yapp-edged Bible dropped from a high shelf, all flat and floppy.

'I don't know where they live,' Weaver went on. 'I need help in finding out.'

'I'll help,' the old man said.

Brown sighed: the old dolt was hooked again. Only when Weaver was around could he find the guts to commit himself to this bloody venture. At all other times he prevaricated, doubted; a right and proper attitude for a man of his age and persuasion.

'I need somebody else too,' Weaver went on. 'Somebody who won't be recognised.'

Brown came out of the storeroom.

'You mean, if they catch wind of it,' Doyle said, 'they might run?'

Wagging the bread roll like a censer, Brown told Doyle, 'They might run straight at *you*, you bloody old fool.'

'I'll be prepared for that,' said Weaver.

Brown looked up into Weaver's stern and handsome mug; hard to credit that at one time Weaver had been just another cheap Glasgow hood. He wore the kind of well-bred and intelligent arrogance which no Argyle Street cowboy ever really acquired. It occurred to Brown then that Weaver really *was* different; not just successful, but of a whole different breed. Eyes full of wariness; deep ingrained wariness, and showing strain too. In the features were memories of the dead boy, that similar sullen intelligence. Brown had never really cared that much for Gordon Weaver: the boy was too withdrawn for his liking, too hard to reach. But he had known him hardly at all and it was unfair of him to make judgement. If only Weaver did not resemble the boy to quite such an extent, maybe he could summon up the gumption to either kick the bastard out of the shop or, more likely, walk out himself. Even the bread tasted of sweat. He gobbled another mouthful, tearing at it so that greenish-yellow crumbs rained on his cardigan.

'It's not you they'll come for, Weaver,' he said. 'It's the person who'll do the snooping in your stead.'

'I won't let anything happen.'

'All he wants,' Doyle explained, 'is somebody to ask a few questions.'

'The names of the men I want are Bremner and Leadbetter,' said Weaver evenly. 'Aged about nineteen, maybe twenty.'

'Did they . . .?' said Brown, curious in spite of himself.

'They killed Gordon.'

'You saw them do it, I suppose?' said Brown.

'Where do they live?' asked Doyle.

'North Grahamshill.'

'Will you help us, Brown?' Doyle said.

'How the devil can I help?'

'Ask a few questions for us,' said Weaver. 'That's all.'

Brown dropped the rind of the sandwich into the waste basket and stared at the clouds of steam which were billowing from the storeroom. Seven children of his own and he had to let himself become involved in the legend of one dead boy. What had started out as an act of sympathy, therapy, had developed into an argument about moral responsibility. One thoughtless gesture of sympathy to save the sanity of a scabrous old punter who was little more than an educated drunkard, and he, Brown, had got himself trapped. Mummified emotions and icy intelligence, Weaver's attributes, impressed him not at all. Weaver was the instrument of fate and as such, well outside the limits of his comprehension. Books he knew about; dealers he could handle; seven Brown children he could contrive to love; but the supposition that he would step deeper into this quagmire because he could not ethically step out of it was an excuse which stuck in his craw like a crumb of mustard egg.

'I guarantee you'll be in no personal danger,' said Weaver.

'Valid for three months?' said Brown. 'Parts not labour. I always read the small print on bills of promise.'

'They don't even know we're after them, do they, Donald?' Doyle said.

Weaver shook his head.

Brown snorted, faded back into the steam.

A moment later he re-emerged carrying the kettle, and three chipped cups which hung from his fingers like giant rings. He set them down on the desk with care.

'You just want me to help you locate them?' said Brown.

'That's all,' Weaver answered.

162

'And you say they lived in North Grahamshill last year?'
'Yeah.'

Brown jabbed at his spectacles with his forefinger, tipped the brown hat back from his scalp with the heel of his hand. He shucked down his jacket sleeve and gingerly fended the kettle across to one side of the desk. Reaching behind him, fingers splayed to encounter the exact weight and girth of the volume, he pulled a book from the shelf: a mammoth volume, bound in soiled scarlet buckram with cheap gilt lettering stamped on the spine and cover. He put it in the clearing by the typewriter frame and laid his hand flat upon it.

Doyle was chuckling drily. 'Of course, of course: so easy.'

'What is it?' Weaver asked.

'City directory,' said Brown. 'One year out of date.'

He squeezed his belly behind the desk once more, sat down, and opened the book at the section marked *North Grahamshill*.

'Right,' he said, 'what were those names again?'

Looping the thong round the stave where the glass had been kneed out of the frame, Greerson tethered the Doberman outside the booth. The working parts of the telephone appeared to be in order in spite of the coating of filth. A scrimmage of names and obscene suggestions frescoed not only the walls but the coin-box and the parcel rack, ceiling and even the floor. Using the numeral code, Greerson dialled Bargowan direct. At this hour of the morning he was sure to find McFadden at home.

He waited, looking out at the park then, fondly, down at the patient thoroughbred. Once he had owned another Doberman but it had contracted a disease and he had been forced to have it put down. The loss of that fine and handsome dog grieved him. Out of all the heartbreak and pain which had come into his life through the holes in police regulations, only the loss of that beautiful animal had touched him on the raw. If the boys, or Margaret, had to die, he wondered if it would be possible to feel more anguish than he had done that day in the surgery when the vet pulled back with the needle and Caesar jerked his head against the padded binding and blinked at him, and he had told it that everything would be all right, had comforted it with the sound of his voice and the tone that meant affection and approval. The dog had crinkled its brow and blinked again until the drug smote into it and quickly killed it. The rich brown eyes and the trust in them showed how utterly without meaning death was to an animal.

'Nero,' he said. 'Nero, here, Nero.'

The muzzle sniffed and groped through a gap in the frame. Bending, Greerson lovingly stroked the hard plane of hair above the creature's nose. A gasp broke from the dog, like the gasp of a woman at the apex of love-making, but more sustained, a steady rhythmic contented panting.

'Good boy; good dog,' Greerson said. 'Sit, sit.'

He straightened and turned his back on Nero as if he did not want the dog to hear him make this call. A moment later the shrill voice belled in his ear.

'You no longer have to worry about Weaver,' Greerson said.

'Is that you, Greerson?'

'Uh-huh!' Greerson answered. 'Did you hear me? I said, Weaver won't be a problem much longer.'

'What d'you mean?'

'I've earned my biscuits.'

'You've nailed him?'

'He will be nailed, I promise you.'

'And my three thousand?'

'That's the price you paid for carelessness,' Greerson said.

'Listen, what the bloody hell's going on?'

'Be sensible,' said Greerson. 'How can I hope to re-deem the cash without spooking the thief? The money's gone, McFadden. You'll have to be satisfied with vengeance.'

'Greerson, if you . . .'

'Joseph, trust me.'

'Hah!'

'Weaver is dangerous to all of us,' Greerson said. 'He's not quite a total menace yet but he's veering that way. Before he can really make trouble, he'll be dead. So stop farting on about the loot. It's been broken up anyway, and it'll be hell's own job to trace it *before* Weaver's nailed, and too damned risky afterwards.'

'Greerson . . .'

'You wanted him smashed,' said Greerson. 'I've arranged it. All you do is sit tight in your country seat and wait to read about it in the papers.'

'Listen here . . .'

Greerson hung up and left the booth.

The method was regrettable but expedient. After all, there was a slight chance that he would be called upon in his official capacity to tidy up the loose ends. It would have been so easy just to present Weaver with all the names and addresses and let him make a meal of it. But it was necessary to give O'Hara time, time to realise that the day of reckoning was at hand.

Greerson untied the leash, paused to clap and fondle the dog before he released it. It hesitated then bounded off towards the park. When it reached the dark places under the shrubs it settled with pleasure to a stealthy sniffing of trails.

Weaver was a threat to stability: O'Hara a threat to society. It seemed like a pardonable equity to cancel out one with the other. Greerson had no illusions about O'Hara: O'Hara was as mad as a hatter, a born killer who would use death to blot out past guilts and current threats. He had encountered a dozen like O'Hara in his time. Best of all, though, O'Hara only knew him as a cop, a member of the opposition. If it had been within his power, and the power of the courts, he would have taken O'Hara and hanged him by the neck. But he could not do this, could not even rake a case together to bring before the sheriff. Bremner and Leadbetter were nothing compared to O'Hara. It was O'Hara, he knew, who had really killed young Weaver. Out of harm, however, might come some good. Weaver would be silenced, and O'Hara locked away for a lifetime.

Greerson tucked the leash into his pocket. He crossed the pavement and entered the park by the main avenue. Yes, he knew exactly how O'Hara would react to a threat, to Weaver's beating in the bush. The type was familiar; his bias uncommonly sound; a cop, after all, was paid to be a judge of men.

Uh-huh, he thought, a pardonable equity indeed.

O'Hara could be counted on to do the rest.

PART THREE

ONE

At ten minutes to six o'clock Leadbetter, knapsack over
his shoulder, came up Killeter Street. Though he was one
of a crowd of workers who returned home nightly at this
hour, Leadbetter walked alone. His day's labour as an
apprentice fitter had claimed little of his energy, but Mon-
days always bored him; most days of the week bored him.
He walked down the path to the rear of the house, let
himself into the kitchen through the back door, and
walked on through the kitchen as if it was an extension of
the pavement outside. His mother was stirring something
in a pan; his father sprawled like a scarecrow in the
armchair in front of the TV set; a clan of younger sisters
brawled on the floor. For all the attention Leadbetter gave
the occupants the house might have been deserted. In
passing, he tossed the knapsack into a corner and continued through the living room and went upstairs. Leadbetter shared a bedroom with his elder brother, Iain; but
Iain had found himself better quarters with a woman on
the other side of the city and the family hadn't seen him
for a month. Only Leadbetter knew exactly where Iain
had gone but he told nobody and nobody was concerned
enough to ask. If the whole family, father, mother and
eight siblings, had been suddenly and discreetly obliterated,
Leadbetter would only have shrugged and gone on about
his business as usual.

With wages left over from Friday, he could afford to
spend the evening down in the Star Bar in Gartshaws,
jawing with his mates, Cuddy and Jamie and Paul and
Big Kenny. He lay on the bed for a while thinking of
nothing in particular, yet disturbed by the peculiar un-
easiness which had marred his rest ever since that Sunday in the park. The events were quite distinct in his
mind, but somehow he could not isolate them. Eventually
he got to his feet, changed his clothes and accoutred himself with an array of cheap trinkets, wrist chains, rings

and a deathshead tie clip. It was seven before he descended the stairs, trod once more over the thin-shanked girls who lay about the floor like folds in the carpeting, and entered the kitchen.

The kitchen was a swamp of steam and wet underclothing. A drying pulley lagged down longjohns and bunches of cotton knickers like the fronds of a hideous plant. Through the mist, Leadbetter could dimly make out his mother over by the sink in the corner. Taking two plastic bowls from a cupboard he helped himself to thick soup and thin stew from a pair of pans on the stove. He carried both bowls and one spoon to the unsteady table, fitted himself into a chair and, with the heel of a pan loaf from the board, began to stuff himself with soup and stew. Silently, the woman placed a beaker of black coffee in front of her son. He swilled it down, wiped his mouth on the back of his hand, wiped the back of his hand on his rump, pushed back the table and moved down the kitchen to the door. He paused to light a cigarette from the tin he kept in his pocket, then his hand went out to the door-knob.

His mother's voice said, 'Man was askin' for you.'

Leadbetter jerked the cigarette from his mouth. 'Askin' what?'

'Man was askin' for you.'

She stuffed her big hands into the bib of her canvas apron and stared at him vacantly, waiting to be dismissed or activated according to his mood. He assimilated the cryptic data slowly, then put to her two simple and and direct questions, all that she could cope with at any one time. She answered him so directly, and without embellishment, that he was almost tempted to probe for options. Recalling the woman's limitations, however, he let it go at that.

He hurried out of the house, turned left into Killeter Street and struck out across the acres of North Grahamshill towards the tenement where Bremner lived.

Bremner laughed and clapped one arm round Leadbetter's shoulders. He steered him as he might have steered a recalcitrant bullock, goading him gently through the confines of the lobby into the big square room which served as kitchen, lounge and sleeping place.

'Don't fret about it,' Bremner said. 'It's only Doyle doin' his nut again. Remember what O'Hara told you.'

Bremner's bantering tone was soothing. The stoop of the neckless shoulders and the large cranium gave him an air of intelligent solidity. Still hugging the younger man, Bremner laughed outright at the notion of Doyle being equipped to do them harm. Leadbetter relaxed. It was possible to relax with Kenny in a way that he could never do with O'Hara. O'Hara scared him. Bremner was a working man like himself, but bloody O'Hara was a parasite, a drone, who played games with the servants of the municipal council and squeezed money out of State departments for his support and sustenance. Transfusing money from the body of society was practically O'Hara's profession; pulling tricks of law and manipulating the technicalities of citizenship which might have been worth a chuckle if done by anyone but O'Hara.

Bremner worked for the Ousbys, a firm of removers and contractors. The brothers were Jewish, shrewd and generous. In his four years with the firm Bremner had learned a lot about the trade and a little about the values of self-sufficiency and loyalty. The Ousbys took pride in the services they offered their clients, and a modicum of this pride was passed on to their haulers and drivers. Some of the men had been with the brothers since the days when one Ousby drove the battered pantechnicon and the other packed the boxes. As perquisites, Bremner had picked up a smattering of knowledge of the antique trade, the upholstery trade and the rag trade. He could now honestly claim to know a man who knew a man who would buy—or if the case required it, sell—anything under the sun. He was familiar with the insides of transport cafés all up the length of Britain, knew which dosshouses offered the cleanest beds, had learned which pubs in which town harboured his brethren. He had taught himself to judge the relative strength of competition, to drum up business out of hours and earn a slice of the subsequent undeclared profits. He knew too how to treat maiden ladies and how to show his appreciation for generous tips; how to make hard work easier by diligent planning. Experience had shown him when to snap the clip on his temper; how to hurt a man enough to prevent retaliation but not enough to maim.

What Bremner had really learned was the knack of being happy. This characteristic would have surprised most of the girls and some of the men who had only seen him drunk or in black temper. At the back of those spasms lay the thing which had happened a year ago and which had very nearly altered the whole course of his life.

Bremner guided Leadbetter to a comfortable chair by the Sunglow. Leadbetter was still so tense that he had to be forced down into the seat like a stake being driven into the ground. The room was clean but cluttered, the bed recess veiled by a heavy blanket, a Duvet sleeping sack thrown behind it like the cocoon of a giant moth. Most of the stuff in the room was new, the prizes of hard bargains and handouts; cheap lines for the lads. Not one item had the taunt of the re-setter on it, though; Bremner was very wary of the law. He ripped the catch on a can of Harp and handed it to Leadbetter. Leadbetter nodded his thanks and poured a slug of the lager into his mouth.

'Still worried?'

'He came right t'the house,' said Leadbetter.

'Was it Doyle?'

'Aye.'

'See him yourself?'

'Me ma saw him. He was askin' for me.'

'Bold bastard,' said Bremner.

'Maybe he knows it was us.'

'Now don't start snivelling again,' said Bremner. 'Doyle knows absolutely bloody nothin'.'

'What'll I do?'

'Just what you did before; keep your trap shut.'

'He came t'the house, I'm tellin' you.'

'And I'll tell O'Hara.'

'An' what'll O'Hara do?'

'Is that what's buggin' you?' said Bremner. 'O'Hara won't do a bloody thing, believe me.'

'I'm scared of him.'

'Slack off, man, for Christ's sake,' said Bremner.

'It's all right for you, Kenny.'

'Look, I'm in it worse'n you an' I'm not shittin' myself

just because some old rummy comes sniffin' around. You've got nothin' at all to worry about, *provided you don't blab*. Alex'll deal with Doyle if it becomes needful.'

'How?'

'He'll warn him,' said Bremner, soothingly. 'And that'll be an end of it.'

'You said that before.'

'And I'll say it again,' said Bremner. 'Come on.'

'Where?'

'To see Alex.'

'Not me.'

'Yeah, you.'

Bremner tripped the switch of the Sunglow and unplugged the transformer for the swingaway lamps. He prodded Leadbetter out of the darkness and into the close, keeping him calm, leading him to the meeting with O'Hara. He could not quite understand why Leadbetter was still afraid.

The padded benches in the long corner of the Explorer's lounge were thick with girls and young men; some dressed as slovenly as dockers but most were tricked out in what—back in Brown's salad days—were known as Sunday Best, not so conservative, though, running now to flowered shirts and transparent blouses. The girls were noisy, parrot-like, hen-like, full of a hysteric vitality, showing off to the bar in general. A guitar group was strumming on the dais under the spots, but the lounge was so long and low-roofed that the music was almost inaudible. The confusion of sounds, hoarse and strangely menacing, disturbed Brown a little, and made him sweat even more profusely. He eyed the group furtively.

The boys sprawled about with insolent disregard for their neighbours, heels up on the low tables among the glasses, legs stretched out to booby-trap the aisles. It was much the same at the bar-rail; young men, mostly, with the manners of hardened drinkers, pints in hand, elbows tight, throats working rhythmically. Whatever had happened to the good old-fashioned public house? Brown wondered; and to the conscience of publicans. Not more than half the number in the lounge tonight were of a legal age to be served proofed liquor. A few girls, sipping fancy tipples, looked to be younger even than his eldest daughter who was just pushing thirteen. Fortified against excesses of indignation with a pint of heavy beer and two packets of salted nuts, Brown observed the proceedings at the corner tables. He studied the quarry from under the brim of his hat and pondered on the motive which had projected Leadbetter so hurriedly to Bremner's house and thence to this garish bar-room.

Only a few hours ago these boys had only been names in a directory. Doyle had been fortunate, if that was the word, to hit on the right Leadbetter first shot. When he first took up the trail, snug in the big Jaguar, with Weaver behind the wheel and the old man, excited as a child with a new board game, beside him, it had all seemed incredibly unreal. Now, though, watching them, straining his ears to catch whispers of the muted conversation which the three of them were having over there in the security of their own padded corner, it began to dawn on him what the purpose of it all might be. Who were they? Three young men, that's all! One of them with an ugly mouth, another with a head like a suet dumpling and the third with eyes like holes burned in crêpe. Bremner and Leadbetter had sought out this third person. They had been engaged in exclusive chat with him since the moment they entered the room; not even pausing long enough to buy drinks. Brown could make out no word from the table, but the gestures were frightening enough. Then it was with him, the realisation that he, Brown, was intimately involved in plotting the death of a young man. He stared at them, bug-eyed, through the smoke. They moved, they existed, they drank and talked and were alive; yet, because he was here, now, hunched passively over his pint, with his mouth full of salted nuts, one of those boys would surely die. Abruptly he was still, head lifted, the sweat-stained hat pushed back from his brow; then he got up and walked out.

The Jaguar nosed from the back of the car park and softly came abreast of him. He stopped walking, flinging himself round to face the open window of the car.

'What is it, Brown?' Doyle asked. 'What's wrong?'

'I've had enough.'

'What have they done?'

174

'Nothing,' said Brown. 'They're inside with their mates, drinking, talking.'

Weaver leaned across the old man's lap and opened the rear door. 'Get in.'

Vigorously, Brown shook his head. 'If I go now I'll be in time to catch the last subway out of here.'

Weaver said, 'All right. Thanks.'

Brown shifted off, his heart thumping as if he had been chased out of the pub. The Jaguar rolled after him, and he stopped again. 'For Christ's sake, leave me alone.'

'How many are with Bremner and Leadbetter?' Weaver asked.

'A dozen or more: girls and boys.'

'Any of them seem to be particularly interested?'

'One,' Brown said. 'A skinny chap with cold eyes.'

Brown walked on out of the car park. He paused on the pavement, breathing the damp air of Gartshaws, waiting, chin on chest, for the big car to slide after him again. It didn't: it reversed and swung out across the cobbled street and went back the way it had come, passing the lights of the Explorer, travelling slowly up to the junction, then it veered left and vanished behind the buildings.

Brown drew in a long breath then set off towards the Underground. He was surprised at the ease with which Weaver had permitted him to escape from the spiral of events which he, after all, had unwittingly begun.

The little yellow plastic radio on the bed table poured out a fat and brassy fanfare of trumpets. Weaver came into the hotel room, walked across it and turned the radio off. Hazel wrinkled her brow petulantly. A paperback was propped against her knees, and the ashtray was littered with butts. A glass and an almost empty bottle of sweet white wine were on the table too. The girl wore a quilted nylon bed-jacket in pale lilac; the garment made her seem like an invalid.

'I thought you'd abandoned me,' she said.

'Sorry I came back at all?'

'I will treat that remark with the contempt it deserves,' she said. 'Did you see Greerson?'

'Yeah,' Weaver said. He poured the last of the wine

into the glass and drank it swiftly. 'More than that: I've found them.'

'He told you?'

'He told me who but not where.'

'God!'

'Two of them: not boys, but not old.'

'Are they the ones?'

'Greerson says so.'

'But you must be sure. I mean personally; personally you must be absolutely certain.'

'I will be.'

'It'll take time, won't it?'

'That depends.'

'Donald?' she said. 'What is it?'

'I don't have to prove anything,' Weaver said. 'Those bastards will tell me themselves.'

'In one day,' Hazel said, 'you move from nowhere to *this*.'

'It's taken longer than a day,' he said, quietly. 'A whole lot longer.'

'Did Greerson say anything about me?'

'Nope.'

'How much did he demand?'

'A packet.'

'Will it be worth it?'

'It better be.'

He stripped off his jacket and tossed it across the foot of the bed. He massaged his brow with his fingertips as if to stimulate his thoughts. Hazel came out of the bed, shedding the robe, dropping it behind her. With her arms back and the robe sliding from her she showed all the artificial grace of a dancer who has gone through the same routine a thousand times. She pressed herself against him. He laid one hand down her flank. Her skin was warm, hot almost; or was it that his hand was as cold as ice? On tiptoe she leaned against him and brushed her lips over his cheek.

'Soon we'll be able to get away,' she said.

Weaver clicked his tongue. 'I've got to *think* like them,' he said. 'Think exactly the way they will think.'

'Impossible,' the girl said.

He inched himself away from her, breaking the hold of

her arms with his hands as he might have snapped a
coupling of a vacuum cable. 'No,' he said, 'that's the
bloody trouble. It's too easy.'

He crossed to the bathroom door, hesitated, leaning
against, slapping the plyboard with the flat of his fist.
'Too easy,' he said. 'All I've got to do now is wait and
watch.'

'For what?' Hazel said.

'For them to make the first move.'

He went into the bathroom and closed the door.

TWO

Thrashed by a dozen casual drivers and frequently bur-
dened beyond its capacity, the mini-van was so badly racked
that only the rope looped around the door-handle seemed
to hold the vehicle together. Even O'Hara was chary of it.
He held his elbow well back from the rope as if the hemp
was a live wire. Over a soiled black tee-shirt, O'Hara wore
a canvas jacket. Bremner, the driver, had disguised his
working rig with a calf-length overall the colour of cow
dung.

'Mind, I only got an hour,' Bremner said.

'An hour's plenty,' O'Hara told him. 'D'you bring the
supplies?'

'In the back.'

'Okay.'

Bremner fiddled with the ignition and toyed with the
throttle and eventually managed to coax the van away
from the kerb in front of O'Hara's house in Radstock
Road.

A strange satin twilight embraced the city at this hour
of the day. The sun would not rise over the spires and
earthworks of the east ridge for another hour or more.
In the morning light, such as it was, O'Hara's face was
colourless, and only the ashen circles around his eye
sockets gave definition to his features. He coughed spas-
modically, hard and dry, like a consumptive; the sound

made Bremner wince. Bremner did not like this time, a
dead time, a time associated with the draggled end of long
overnight hauls and greasy breakfasts in doss-houses, with
the bitter beginning of journeys to the far south with the
pantechnicon light and empty and unwieldy and the high-
ways icy and blanketed with mist. His depression and his
nervousness showed up in his driving. Normally his style
was brisk and taut but at the moment he could not stop
himself giving an excess of attention to the mirror and
the screen and the kick of the wheel. The van jerked
from one set of traffic lights to the next, and its progress
mimicked Bremner's state of mind. He had no real wish
to be on this mission with O'Hara. Though he did not
consider it vital to their freedom and survival he was
temperamentally the kind of person who must tackle prob-
lems head on, a characteristic which O'Hara had attacked
with the forceful skill of a burglar with a jemmy, to
break open Bremner's passivity and reluctance to take
part. O'Hara promised a simple little job, a bit of muscle,
a restrained warning. Doyle would get the message; Doyle
would back down, return to his bottle and his obscurity
and that would, this time, be an end to it all.

Bremner carried no personal weapon. In the van's glove
compartment, however, was a short, stout club, oak wood
carved in the likeness to a posy bound with a thread of
fern. The club had once been the leg of an antique table
but the castor had been replaced by a leather thong, a
piece of handicraft carried out by Bremner in the bedroom of his father's house when he was still living with
his father, three years ago, and ran with the Gartshaws
gang. The club had never been more than a toy. He had
swung it round his head and yelled as loudly as the next
boy but he had never struck a blow with it, even in jest.
His inclinations to violence were not compulsive. When he
had taken the weapon from its hiding place last night to
blow the dust off it, he had felt only a meek sort of
revulsion. He could not understand what impulse had
ever driven him to spend time making it; saw it,
perhaps in the sort of light as a teenage whore
suddenly sees the battered doll which has made her
childish nights less lonely, with irony but no whit of

sentiment. Though he strove to recapture the excitement which such a caper would have engendered a little while ago, he was left only with tasteless apprehension and the worry that he would be late for his first job of the day. Four removals were slated for Tuesday, a crowded schedule, and a prompt start at eight o'clock was essential. Anyway, he bore no animosity towards the old man. A year ago he had been too drunk to fight the contagion of O'Hara's innate malice and motiveless rage. Bremner had not been drunk since then, nor would he ever be drunk again. The swelter of his own bloodlust had frightened him almost as much as the possible consequences of the act. He could not look back on the incident without sorrow and sincere contrition. It was such a small skeleton to have in his cupboard; shame etched the guilt all the more deeply into his conscience. An occasional qualm of horror burst in his brain, cerebral flatulence, at the memory of what he had done, but as the months passed and season gave way to season, the spasms were becoming less frequent and disturbing. Soon, he hoped, he would be rid of them forever. If only the old man had kept his nose out of it.

From the corner of his eye Bremner watched O'Hara screw up his face and hack into his fist. He didn't look dangerous now: nobody in the throes of morning cough could really look menacing. Bremner concentrated on the road ahead, stopped at the tenth set of traffic lights, drummed his fingers on the wheel. If only bloody Leadbetter had been less sharp. If only bloody Leadbetter had kept that twisted gob of his tight shut. Now, though, he had to agree with O'Hara; there was *some* danger of a kick-back, a leak. Now he had to go through with it, warn Doyle to back off or suffer the consequences. It was just one of those things that had to be done. He glanced across at O'Hara again and saw him wipe a spray of mucus from his lip with a rag. Instinct told him that to Alex this latest development was nothing but part of the game, the stuff of life, on which he thrived. After today, Bremner promised himself, he would see O'Hara as little as possible. It was time to go his own route, even if that route led him to the same hell in the end.

O'Hara wiped his mouth on the rag. The morning cough annoyed the shit out of Marilyn. She had even threatened to turn him out of her bed because of it. The bitch was within her legal rights, which was the unhappy thing about it. The bed was her property; the house was her property. He had been obliged to placate her at the time, though later, in another context, he had taken it out of her hide. The council house was listed in the Collins name: Collins was Marilyn's grandma, an old woman, dying by slow degrees in a hospital bed. What the Letting Department of the Council would do when the old biddy snuffed it was unpredictable. Marilyn's only other kin, her father, was busy serving time for breaking and entering. With fifteen previous convictions on the shelf he would not be on the streets again for another three years. O'Hara had never met the stupid old bastard and could willingly wait a lifetime for the privilege. All around him, it sometimes seemed, were rings of old folk just waiting to do him down—Grandma Collins, Marilyn's Da, State officials, CID dicks, and now a clapped-out rummy by the name of Doyle.

It counted not with O'Hara that Doyle was the grandfather of the boy he had killed. He experienced no involvement with the old man, and the sensations of that night were buried so deeply in him that reflective thinking could not sweat them out. Only trauma, an impossible occurrence in a man so inured to the horror of living, was liable to draw them to the surface of his awareness. He no longer felt culpable for what had happened to Gordon Weaver; a little freak, rosy with innocence, in whom O'Hara had glimpsed the quality which he had been born without. His bitterness was a compound of the experiences of his past, a past that had no security and no love in it, marked by the cobbler's knife on his cheek, the weight of his father's boot on his arse, the prick of the shiv of the middle-aged cow who had dragged him out of the gutter and let him, sixteen at the time, share her bed and board for a while until she had found another more potent male to do for her in the night. It was not then lack of prudence or failure which drove O'Hara through clouds of alcohol into murder. Sight of the figure of that boy, armoured by self-sufficiency, had fermented

O'Hara's own sufferings and distilled them into fury. Only death could put that suffering back where it belonged.

Now Doyle had stepped from the shadows, and he, O'Hara, was not drunk and the accusation of guilt, or even of liability, which the old man had flung down like a gauntlet could not be ignored. He remembered how it was with the boy; the ropes, the boy wriggling like a gaffed fish, fish-mute, silvered by the truck's lamps.

The van neared Walton Street.

In the tin interior, cans and carboys rattled and jarred as the tyres splayed out over the cobbles. O'Hara fingered the tip of the split stick in his jacket pocket. Into the cleft he had fitted a razor blade, lashed it tight with gardener's twine. The weapon was swaddled in protective tissue like a valuable gift. It felt functional but delicate too, almost too fragile to lay open a cheek or slit a nostril. With it O'Hara intended to write a message of warning on the living flesh of the father of the mother of the child who had challenged him. He did not intend to kill.

Bremner glanced at him, big head swivelled on the socket buried under the hunched shoulders. Like Leadbetter, though, Kenny-boy knew it was advisable to hold his tongue.

The van came up to the close mouth and he read the faded painted numeral of Doyle's house; then Bremner took the van on past it and parked discreetly between a Triumph and a Rapier.

Shivering, O'Hara got out.

It was still dark, before dawn.

Doyle stirred. Pain flowed thick and honey-sweet through his body. Pain nourished his brain which in turn fed strength down into that part of him where his will lay crushed but not inert. If the attack had been clean and functional he would have been denied this last personal gesture of absolution. How odd, he thought, that the jargon of the church should flush up into his mind now, after it had been so long gone that he could not recall the colour or the smell of it or the sound of the voices in matins or evensong. It was as if his intellect had developed little muscular fists with which to grip the rag-

181

man's bundle of flesh and lug it willy-nilly through the door between life and death.

Just this very morning he had wakened sober enough to contemplate again the futility and the irreconcilable weariness of dying inch by inch. Before Weaver's return he had damned his stamina as a plague and a hazard, reckoned that it would take him five or six years of steady alcoholism to undermine his physique and bring himself gradually to a permissible state of death. Before Brown's speech on vengeance, before the letter, before Weaver's return, he had been willing to accept that fact; surely now he could find the patience to hold himself this side of Hades for just a few more minutes.

Wait for Weaver, he told himself.

Blood from his broken jaw clotted in his throat. He let it trickle over his chin, seeing the track of it beneath him like the trail of a slug. After that first blow he had felt so little pain that he had bowed to the arch of the club and let the man strike him, almost appealing to him to hit him again, offering his neck and the back of his head. He had heard the other one shouting, voices raised, one like a gong and the other a drum, preaching against each other. He had barely glimpsed his attacker, seeing only dark clothing and lean shanks and the bulge of genital organs under tight trousers. The second was only a voice, a shuffling shape in the background, a shouting sound as he sank beneath the rain of blows.

Thinking that it was Weaver he had risen from bed and opened the door, turned casually away, yawning, then turned again. Even without his glasses he had had no opportunity to recognise them. Now, how could he tell Weaver what he did not know? But he did know; he had heard the voices shouting, seen the priest-black clothes on the gaunt frame.

He occupied his mind with the problem as he dragged himself across ten interminable feet of carpeting to the wreckage of the wine table. Raising himself on his shoulder he balanced his shattered arm on the under ledge. The table collapsed. He went down with it. Pain honeycombed his reason once more. If the damned bottle was not on the high mantel he might have been able to reach it and found an excuse to disconnect himself by drinking yesterday's ration from his wee half pint. The Black & White was high overhead, however, out of reach, and even the chipped crucifix was buried under debris in the bottom of the bureau drawer. Neither bottle nor cross really held more than a passing interest. With the ebbing of the pain he clamped his attention back to the real objects of his journey—a white writing tablet and a bullet-shaped pen. Weakness did not sap his determination. The will to failure, that homely stratagem of all Doyles, had finally let him down.

Using the table as a crutch, he stretched out his hand, crept his fingers up to the pen, possessed it. Wriggling, he palmed the little white memo pad too. Complacency forced him to rest. Holding the pen cocked between the broken stump of his index finger and the swollen knuckle of his thumb, he steadied the pad with his brow and began to print out the message, shielding himself from the temptation to be eloquent. His intellect though was closing up; he wrote a little faster, letter by letter.

When it was done he pushed the pad away from him, kept his head where it was, cheek against the carpet, pen clenched in his fist. Softly and easily, like a careful drunk, he released all sense of duty and, at length, of reality.

Book smell, damp in the unventilated morning; the ashes dead in the grate; he was waiting for Weaver, that was all. Waiting for Weaver to correct the mistake. Waiting for Weaver, for Gordon; the boy's unsmiling face, smiling now.

To tell him.

On the landing an old woman, talcum dusted, clad in foam slippers and a house-robe, inclined towards the inch-gap in Doyle's door. The slippers were rooted on her own welcome mat, as if it was a pentagram which she did not dare forsake even to appease her curiosity.

'Are you one of his?'

Already stepping towards the door, Weaver nodded. 'Yeah.'

'Is he sick?'

'Why?'

'I thought I heard noises.'

'When?'

'Earlier.'

Weaver put his hand on the knob, and apparently by accident, let the inch of space close up. 'Did you see anyone?'

'Who would I see?'

'The old man.'

'Never see him, if I can help it,' the old woman said.

'I expect he's drunk,' Weaver said. 'You know what he's like.'

The neighbour trumpeted scornfully through her nose, then abruptly retired, shutting herself up safe from the pernicious influence of Doyle and his relatives.

Weaver pushed into the flat and closed the door behind him. Debris reached out like sprayed shrapnel from each of the rooms. A litter of books bulked over the hall floor. Sprinkled with shards of crockery and the innards of a clock, broken furniture and ripped clothes were strewn about. Chessmen rolled on heads and bases as if imbued with a life of their own. The reek of acid and the pale stench of paint mingled with the earthier aroma of pitch. Black frescoes, larded with heavy cream paint, stained shelves, walls and ceilings. The books had been dressed with the stuff, and the whole mess seasoned with acid. Even as he watched Weaver could see the chemical sinking into bindings and white pages. No slogans daubed the walls, no signatures; the destruction was skilful, complete, anonymous. The mainstays of Doyle's life had been torn down in a hurricane of wanton violence. When he stepped into the parlour, however, Weaver knew that it did not matter.

The old man was crumpled on the carpet. He did not look drunk. The body had withered, shrivelled, as if Doyle had been compelled to drain the very tissues of his flesh to find the strength to live long enough to reach the little table and the writing pad.

Weaver straddled him, holding down the nausea which rose in his throat. He stooped, inserted his hand into the pyjama top and lifted the vest, the woollen garment which had kept the old man warm when the whisky cooled in his blood. The skin was still warm, but only where the crimping of the armpit had retained it. Across the chest it was icy. There was no heartbeat; no flutter of the vein

184

behind the ear. Supporting himself on his hand, Weaver reached over the old man's head and picked up the memo pad. He pushed back from the body and stood up straight, legs braced, his back to the old man on the floor. Squinting in the feeble light, he read what Doyle had written. He read it through twice, his lips moving over the words. He ripped off the top sheet and the next, as far down as the ballpoint had impressed. He went into the bathroom across the wreckage of the hall and bent, open mouthed, over the pedestal; nothing came.

Though the bathroom was undamaged, it had the emptiness of a trust property. The small objects which had had the intimate essence of the old man—shaving soap, razor, tin of tooth powder, laxatives, aspirin—were as dead as ancient artifacts. Quietly, Weaver closed the door, and seated himself on the toilet seat. He read the words on the paper once more, without moving his lips this time, then curled them up and dropped them between his thighs into the bowl. He flushed them away, watching the swirl of water, the bob of the little paper balls, tugging on the chain again and again until every last scrap had gone. He dropped the lid and sat on it and put his head in his hands. For almost an hour he remained in that position, immobile, slack, brooding, then he got up and returned to the parlour to do what he could with Doyle.

THREE

When Weaver came across the empty dining room Hazel sensed immediately that something was seriously wrong. She had seen a similar expression once on the face of her first lover when, in a forest track in Newtonmore, close to a rally check-point, his Porsche had swerved into the tree: he had stalked out of the thick black billow of smoke and the hellish belch of orange flame and walked up the ditch with his hands hanging by his sides and the same look on his face as Weaver now wore coming across the dining room. He seated himself and signalled for a whisky. It was late, close to three, and the lunch menu was off. The whisky arrived. He took it and swallowed it and looked at her as if she hadn't opened her mouth; when she touched him it was as if she touched stone. He took air into his lungs and held it, then let it out so silently that only the dip of his shoulders told her that he had breathed at all. His clothing showed no marks, but the strap of his wristwatch had soaked up something heavy and sticky. She knew at once what the substance was.

'Who is it?' she said. 'Who is it? For God's sake tell me what you've done.'

He seemed to be seeing her now. The lid of his left eye crinkled, made him sly. He caught her wrist and lifted her arm and swung it over the silver coffee pot and the fluted flower-vase and the water jug, the empty slender dark brown bottle which had held wine, swung it and held tightly to her wrist, so that when he rose she came with him and was hauled, embarrassed, from the dining room, leaving her coffee cup half full and a cigarette burning in the ashtray and her gloves on the table behind her.

The Mark 10 was meter-parked close to the side entrance of the hotel. He unlocked it and held the door until she got in, then he got in too and ignited the engine. The interior of the car held the stench of paint and turpentine and other smells which she could not identify.

'Where are we going?' she asked. 'Won't you at least tell me that?'

'The Wickerburn.'

'Have you . . . ?'

'I wish to Christ I had,' he said. 'Wait; don't talk.'

He drove to a street which she did not know, though she felt that the neighbourhood lay not far distant from Jack Irwin's apartment. Weaver parked the car in a street with trees and lozenges of beaten earth down the middle. He let her out, again took her by the wrist, not even the hand but the wrist. She hardly had time to feel the cold air upon her through her dress before they rounded two corners and mounted the steps to a close mouth. He dragged her along as he might have dragged a child. Panic rose in her, the guilt of the guiltless. She tried to imagine what she could have done to anger him, what betrayal she could unwittingly have committed. If she had experienced strength in men before, this demonstration was novel to her, frighteningly primitive. She knew she dared not lag or protest, that he would take her wherever it was he wanted to take her in any manner he must, unconscious across his shoulder if he had to. She felt as a ravished virgin must feel, sucked and drained of dignity and will, yet not wholly lacking in recompense from contact with such demanding power.

He fitted a key to the door of one of the two flats on the third landing, swung the door open and pushed her in ahead of him. She did not even have time to see the name plate before the stillness and the overwhelming effluvia of chemicals clenched at her senses. The hallway had a quality of eccentricity, like a stage set, composed and carefully arranged. Even the books on the shelves seemed to have been patiently set up and the rug on the faded lino had not quite settled. Connecting doors, four or five of them, were closed. On them she could read the source of the stink, a ghost of thinners, thick ribbons of black and white paint along the inner hinges. Now Weaver had released her she had no impulse to move. It seemed as if the bite of his fingers on her flesh had leeched her of all volition. She did not even look behind her when she heard the click of the lock.

'Doyle's house,' Weaver said. 'Doyle; the old man; Gordon's grandfather.'

'Yes.'

'Doyle is in there.'

'Oh!'

'He's dead,' Weaver said. 'Look.'

'No.'

'I said *look*.'

'No, I don't want to.'

'You'll look, Hazel.'

She flung herself to one side. He caught her quickly, pinning her. She couldn't resist him.

'Why?' she said. 'Why?'

'It's what it really looks like,' Weaver said. 'You've been curious: now's the time to find out. Anyway, it's important that you know where and how.'

'Please, no.'

187

Holding her, he stretched and pushed open one of the doors. Light made the room as coldly impersonal as a hospital cubicle. The door jarred against the rim of some hard object.

'No,' she said. 'No, no.'

A passionate dance, long and slow and gliding, shifted her around him. He halted her with his fists on her shoulders, pressing down, the whole length of his body firm against her back.

'Look at him, Hazel.'

She closed her eyes. He inched her forward; the pinch of his fingers leapt up to the nape of her neck.

She opened her eyes.

What she saw was more horrifying than anything she could have imagined; the centres of predictable sanity had prepared her for dismemberment, grotesqueness, blood; but there was no blood. The old man lay in the bathtub, legs stretched out, hands by his sides. Because of the length of him, his upper torso, neck and head were propped against the taps. She found herself looking not down at him then but directly into his face. The face was no face, had no features, was nothing but a pale-grey, flaccid, jellied mass.

She tried to scream aloud but the sound choked in her throat. She tried to tear herself back from the thing but Weaver held her firm. The entire length of the cadaver was the same, like something cocooned in hideous fungus, preserved in the ripening of its own juices.

'Plastic!' She spat the word out. '*Plastic!*'

Where the inner layer was tucked over the chin and stretched with scotch tape a blob of coloured fluid clung like apple conserve.

The scream was now a whimper in the cavities of her brain. Her head dropped and Weaver took her out, cheek pressed against his chest and his arm protectively around her.

'All right,' he said gently. 'All right now. It's gone.'

She drank alternately from cup and glass, mingling whisky and coffee in her mouth, smoking at the same time from the cigarette which Weaver had put into her fingers. She could not believe that she was doing these things, enjoying the tastes even, but she was a sensible girl, she told herself, not callous or irreverent, and the dead, after all, were dead. Only the quivering in the muscles of her thighs and at the roots of her fingers would not be soothed by youthful stoicism, and the nerves at the base of her skull were knotted up into tiny nut-hard balls. She swallowed once more from each container and dragged on the tobacco smoke. Seated at the opposite end of the table from her, the fading afternoon light was full on Weaver's face. It struck her then as ironic that the shock and exhaustion, guilt too perhaps, which ravaged him had contrived to make his rock-hard handsomeness less perfect but more human.

'You didn't have to bring me here, you know,' she said. 'It was a bloody sadistic thing to do.'

'I had to.'

'Why?' she said. 'To share it with you?'

'No,' he said. 'I had to show you because you had to see for yourself. You didn't know him and it wouldn't have been enough just to tell you. Now you know enough: more than you can stomach, maybe?'

'Is that a question?'

'Yeah.'

'They didn't do that to him?'

'They came early,' said Weaver, 'before I got here. The old man let them in, expecting me, perhaps.'

'Did you anticipate this?' she said. 'Did you try ...?'

'Maybe they didn't even mean to kill him.'

'Why did they wreck the house?'

'I don't think they knew he was dead until they were halfway through,' said Weaver. 'Maybe they got scared.'

'And that ... that plastic?'

'Nobody must know he's dead.'

'Oh God!'

'I want to leave the old man here for a while. It doesn't matter to him any more.'

'Filthy,' the girl said. 'Filthy.'

'Listen, I didn't kill him,' said Weaver. 'I've never killed anyone.'

'You can't just leave him.'

'He'll be decently buried,' said Weaver, 'eventually.'

'You mean, you actually went out of here and bought

189

that plastic sheeting knowing you would . . . because you didn't want his body to . . .'

'I cleaned up the hall,' said Weaver. 'He has no personal friends. Nobody will come here looking for him. Just in case somebody does get curious, though, I had to clean up the hall. If they look through the letter hatch now they won't see anything to make them suspicious.'

'You know who killed him?'

'I know now,' said Weaver. 'Greerson lied.'

'Are you sure?'

'That bastard kept back the truth.'

'You're going to take them all out now, aren't you?'

'Do you blame me?'

Hazel shook her head.

'Doyle brought me back,' said Weaver. 'He brought me back to kill them; but he didn't really believe I would come. When I came he saw that it might be possible after all to have the kind of revenge he had dreamed about, had sustained himself with, and he lost the cutting edge, began to have doubts, to waver. It was getting to me, too, Hazel. Sure, I wouldn't have gone through with it, except for you.'

'Me?' she said. 'Yes, me!'

'And that old man in there. He was always the marksman: I was nothing but the weapon, the bullet. He started it and now he's managed to finish it.'

'But why?' the girl said. 'Was it for you, or the boy, or himself?'

'Does it matter?'

'Yes, it does,' she said. 'He invented you, don't you see.' Weaver shook his head. He did not disagree with her or lack understanding but he was indifferent now to such subtle reasoning. He needed no more excuses.

He said, 'If anything happens to me, tell Greerson about the old man. Don't tell just any cop; tell Greerson.'

'If he cheated you, why do you protect him?'

'It's the only way I can do it,' said Weaver. 'I've no time to waste on Greerson. Make sure the old man gets a decent burial. Burial, you hear; he's a Catholic.'

'Yes,' Hazel said. 'A decent Christian burial.'

'That's not all,' Weaver said. 'I need you for other things.'

'As a witness?' she said, sitting up. The nerves at the

back of her neck were as hard as marbles embedded in her spine. 'Look elsewhere for your damned witness.'

'You wanted to share it,' Weaver said. '*This* is what you have to share.'

'You bastard!'

The old man, loathsome in death, had meant nothing to her. Until that hour, she had viewed Weaver as a man in a vacuum, quite hygienic, safe to touch. Now he was out of the vacuum and she could no longer hope to touch him without becoming contaminated by the essences which made him what he was. She would not ever have strapped herself into the passenger seat of the thundering rally Porsche, or planted herself in her executive's lap while he pushed through a deal for a hundred thousand dollars: they had touched her and she them, and had gained nothing. Now he wanted her to be part of him, a thread in the fabric of the myth that was Weaver. It frightened her to realise how close she had come now to the fulfilment of her own ideal of love.

Weaver was saying, 'They would've been caught this time, anyway. They bungled it: they blundered into it and they took away too many clues with them. The forensic boys would have cooked up a case against them and a smart lawyer would have stuck them away for five or ten years. Maybe they're lucky that they have me, only me, after them.'

Hazel frowned: she could not follow the rationale. Was it death that was so horrible, or just death as it sat in the body of that filthy old man?

Weaver said, 'Drink your coffee and let's go.'

'I don't want it,' she said.

'What?'

'The coffee,' she said.

'Then wash the cups,' Weaver said. 'And let's get out of here.'

Bremner applied the handbrake but kept the motor running. After a prolonged pause he touched his palm to the horn, forming a low pattern of sound, a code. Now that it was full dark the streets of North Grahamshill lay in the lull between the end of the working day and the beginning of the nightly exodus. The door on the side of the house opened, casting a wedge of light along the pathway. Out of the light came O'Hara, tugging a sweater over his tee-shirt. He walked down the path, hurdled the gate, crossed the pavement and stooped down to look into the van.

'What the bloody hell's wrong with you, Kenny?' he said. 'Come on up.'

'Nuh!' said Bremner.

'Jesus!' said O'Hara. 'Come on, then.'

'I'm not comin' up,' said Bremner emphatically.

'Suit your bloody self,' said O'Hara. 'Did y'get rid of the stuff?'

'I put it with the cast-offs in a builder's yard.'

'Anybody see you?'

'Nuh!'

'Listen,' said O'Hara. 'If the old bugger had been dead it stands t'reason the news would have been on the box, an' it hasn't been on the box. I've been watchin' particular. Stop muckin' about an' come on. Marilyn'll cook your supper.'

'I'm busy: got thinks t'do.'

'What things?'

'Things.'

'It's him, i'n't it? The old guy's got y'bugged. I only tapped him.'

'You snatched the friggin' club out my hand and battered him half t'death. He could still be lyin' there.'

'If he'd been lyin' there, he'd have been found: an' he hasn't,' said O'Hara.

'See you.'

'Listen, Kenny . . .'

'I don't think we should be seen t'gether for a while,' Bremner said. He stared at the dashboard. 'A long time, Alex.'

'What're you mad at me for?'

'It's not me that's mad.'

'Here, now wait . . .' said O'Hara.

Bremner reached over the edge of the seat and brought up a bundle from the well. He pushed it through the window; a swaddle of brown blanket expertly bound with string. 'You keep it,' said Bremner. 'I won't need it again.'

'Kenny!'

'See you around.'

The car jerked into motion. Supporting the bundle across his arms as if it was a babe, O'Hara stepped back. Through the blanket he could feel the carved roses on the oak. He watched the van hove out of sight, then turned and hopped over the gate and went slowly up into the house again to find a place to hide the weapon.

FOUR

An alloy shield rattled over the doorway and Leadbetter found himself on the pavement. Pubs had long since closed and publicans, having counted the takings and stowed them away in their big well-lighted safes, were now in process of shuttering their premises. Leadbetter had forsaken the public house doorway for the fragrant harbour of a fried fish and chip shop, but it too was closing for the night. He gazed through the window at the tiled interior. Even as he did so the strip above the fryer flickered off and the tiles and brushed metal lost their gleam. In his hand the brown paper was damp with the seepings of vinegar and grease. It took him a moment to grub up the few curled crisp fragments buried in the corner of the bag. He put them on his tongue one by one and crunched them with his front teeth, then all he had left of his supper was the limp paper and the stench on his hands. He rolled the paper into a ball and punted it high, missing the pawnbroker's sign as usual, then, following the line of the kick, set off disconsolately on the long and dreary road home.

Leadbetter knew this road like the back of his hand. It did not unfold before him in visual terms but in a series of half-recorded textures and a changing density of lights, a spectrum of feelings too, low coloured but discernible. If he had been a blind man, still he could have followed the route without faltering. Weary, lonely, cold, he trudged north. His hands dug deep into the pockets of his jacket. The wind weaseled through a hole in his pullover. He walked steadily out of the Wickerburn into the long half-mile of tenements. Though the wind whisked snell there was no frost, only a kind of icy dusk which the huge lunar bulbs of the standards dropped in lieu of light, like a sterile and colourless pollen. The character of the wind changed again and without lifting his gaze from the pavement he knew exactly where he was; knew that the wind was scouring off the monuments along the ridge of the cemetery, like brine from a granite sea. Having shaken the cavernous closes and mile-high boardings which might give ambush shelter to one of the wolf packs from the Wickerburn, or a prowl car with two bored snoops in it waiting to butt and bully him just for practice, he imagined he was safe enough here. Just here—some nights—the dim recollection of the kid came to him; the solitary figure coming out of the waste ground, looking a bit like the way he felt, as if the kid had been a reflection, smaller, younger, less substantial, less astute too, but kin-folk to him; then he walked faster and usually succeeded in leaving the evil thought behind him, hanging like a rag on the spears of the railings of the boneyard where it ended and the first of the houses began. He did not think of Gordon Weaver tonight and had no apprehension in him, no thought of anything at all.

The car caught up with him.

Rubber hissed on the tarred surface. A cell or two in Leadbetter's brain recorded the smoothness of the gear change; then he heard the lurch, the suspension socking down and wheeled around at once. Head and shoulder and arm went out, blocked like a full-back's to fend away the broad nose of the Jaguar as it leapt towards him. He did not even try for the railings. They were smeared with light like a washboard, and if he went for them he would be rubbed against them like an old pair of denims or frayed overalls. He shouted aloud as the metal sliced past his thighs. With a shuddering jerk the Jaguar stopped.

For all the suddenness of the happening Leadbetter was not dazed or stunned. His legs were already opening and his hips pivoting to take off like an electric hare from the trap, when the rear door of the car flew open. He ran fulltilt into it, rebounded violently into the void where the front door should have been but wasn't. An arm wrapped itself around his throat and he took off backwards, kicking

194

and clawing, to land with his shoulders across the passenger seat. He hacked furiously at the door to stop it closing, groped behind him to find the eyepits of the man who pinned him, then the gun-muzzle bumped coldly against the flesh of his neck and he lay utterly motionless, limp. Something soft brushed his knees and the door slammed. He realised with sudden horror that at least one of his attackers was a girl.

'Leadbetter, don't move.' It was a man's voice, cool but somehow casual, almost mocking.

The car slanted into motion, tyres thumped off the kerb. Another car, going Wickerburn way, went swishing past without even slowing. He was still turtled in the seat, the arm locked around his throat and his head drawn back against an overcoat. Only the angle at which the hole in the metal barrel of the gun pressed against his skin had changed. He could not remember it happening. The girl must have it now, the girl in the back seat. There were only two of them, he thought. When the arm went away from his gullet, he still did not try to sit up. The car was rolling on not fast and not slow. In the mirror he could just discern a spill of hair, the colour of a brewer's bottlecap, and one eye and the brow above it, a brow painted dark, raised in enquiry. North Grahamshill was sweeping past outside; all clotted in the corner of his vision. For a fleeting instant the whole scene fermented over the lip of his sanity and his jaws opened and he sucked in air to jettison his terror.

The man said, 'Close it.'

He closed it, holding the bellow down in him, pungent with the vinegar which had come floating in like a sponge with the mouthful of oxygen. He thought he might drown on stifled dread.

'That's better,' the man told him.

Leadbetter forced himself not to stare in the mirror but he could not prevent his innate knowledge of the headwaters of the Wickerburn-Grahamshill boulevard from bringing him information. When it became obvious that this was no ride home, his dread turned molten. He could feel it surging in his guts. The caked ribs of old neuroses broke and crumbled into it, adding to it, making it bubble. Long before the houses thinned and the speckled blackness of the Ridgeway came into sight he knew just where they were taking him. The knowledge gave him no comfort at all. It was worse then; he felt as if his whole body had become as incandescent as the pencil of flame on the end of a welder's torch. Right at the heart of his fear, like a boulder which has such mass that it will not liquify, he was conscious of his extreme youth. An excuse? Grounds for mercy? That was the core of his self-pity and the whole of his strategy. When he thought of the waste of the life of one so young, he wept.

'Stop blubbering,' the man said. 'For Christ's sake, cut it out.'

Leadbetter touched the backs of his hands to his cheeks and felt the wetness on them. He was beyond shame. He covered his face with his fingers, and lay there, balled, snivelling, until the car came to a halt.

Even without looking he knew where they had brought him.

Beyond the range of the lights the waste ground was pitch-black. A scattering of lamps and house lights delineated the further shore, like a fisherman's village under a cliff. The sky overhead had a gritty texture but no colour; it was only a faint pallid emptiness like a vast cupola of weathered sackcloth pinned across infinity. But for the girl in the back seat he might have imagined that this joker was only a wayward snoop doing a bit of overtime, but the girl was there and he had never in his life heard of a snoop with a hand-gun. He knew it was no cop and that considerations of law would not protect him. Pity was all that would save him now. The muzzle of the gun tickled his earlobe with a lightness which was almost playful, except that the girl's hand was perfectly steady and it was his own head that was shaking. Nothing, not even a plea for mercy, came to his lips.

'Leadbetter,' the man said. The tone was tight with resignation. 'So you're Leadbetter.'

The gun was in the man's hand again, huge and ugly, the sort of weapon with which quislings were shot in most of the war movies he had seen. The man held it low in the lap of the heavy tweed overcoat, left forearm making a protective strut for it. Leadbetter had no intention of making a break.

'I can shoot you,' the man said. 'If you want to know how, I'll put the barrel up against your ribs, ram it in and pull the trigger. The weight of your tripes will muffle the sound and nobody round here who happens to hear it will even realise that it was a shot. Anyway, it won't matter to you whether they do or not, because you'll have no heart left.'

'Mister, I . . .'

'Now listen, you don't have to die, Leadbetter. If you do exactly what I tell you to do then I won't bump you: understand?'

'Yuh!'

'I'm going to ask you questions and you're going to give me straight, truthful answers. If you do that, I'll drive you back to your house and let you out. That's a risk I'll take, Leadbetter, letting you go. But I'll only let you go if you tell me the truth.'

Leadbetter could not manage an affirmative syllable, only a porcine grunting sound and a frantic nod of agreement. He had given up weeping. His attitude now was eager, almost sycophantic.

'If I let you go,' the man went on, 'you'll stay home. Say you're sick. Stay home for a couple of days, then just go on about your business. Naturally, you won't tell anybody about all this.'

'Nuh.'

'If you do tell somebody, anybody, I'll find out about it and I'll kill you—unless O'Hara kills you first. Why O'Hara? Because the first few things you're going to tell me are all about O'Hara.'

'I . . . I . . . I don't . . .'

The man ignored his ineffectual protests There was no increase in the pressure of his threat, no scowl or shifting of the gun; he just ignored the making of the denials as if they had never been uttered.

'Go ahead,' he said. 'Tell me about O'Hara.'

'I . . . I . . . know . . . him.' Leadbetter was obliged to swallow between each word; his mouth was not dry but full of water brash. 'He . . . he . . . lives . . .'

'Where?'

'Ra . . . Radstock . . . Radstock Road: Eighteen.'

197

'Calm down and speak clearly. Did O'Hara kill Gordon Weaver?'

Leadbetter nodded frantically.

'Let's be clear on this point,' the man said. 'Did O'Hara tie Gordon Weaver under a truck, out there on the waste lot?'

'Yes.' The word squirted out of him like soda from a siphon. 'O'Hara and Kenny Bremner.'

'And you too?'

'I . . . I . . . was there,' stammered Leadbetter. 'I mean, I saw it. I watched it, but I didn't do nothin'. Ah, Jesus Christ, mister, I never done nothin'.'

'You didn't even go for help?'

'O'Hara would've stopped me.'

'O'Hara *knew* you were in the vicinity?'

'Aye.'

'And he let you go?'

'Couldn't do nothin' to me: we'd been together that night an' . . .'

'And?'

'When it was . . . was clear what they was doin' to Weaver, I ran.'

'But O'Hara came to see you?'

'Next day.'

'And warned you not to talk?'

'Yeah: then the fuzz came and picked me up, but they got nothin' on me. I wouldn't even admit I was there. They couldn't prove otherwise.'

'Who else did the cops pick up?'

'Bremner.'

'And O'Hara?'

'Aye,' said Leadbetter. 'But they couldn't pin anythin' on them neither.'

'You could have given the cops a case.'

'Mister, O'Hara would've killed me for sure.'

'All right. So the cops pulled O'Hara in, too. Which cop was it? Was it Greerson?'

'I think so.'

'Think harder,' the man told him. 'Was Inspector Greerson there at the time?'

'Aye, he was.'

'Why did O'Hara kill Gordon?'

'I ... I ... wouldn't know.'

'*Was* there a reason?'

'They was drunk: not Weaver, the other pair. I wasn't drunk, though, an' I wasn't really with them. I was too ... too *young*, mister. All I done was tag on behind. They were steamin' drunk. They found the truck, an' started up the engine, kiddin' around.'

'Then Weaver came?'

'Aye, he just came out of nowhere an' put the shits up them. He just *came*, just kept walkin' right on and would've gone right on past them if they hadn't fixed on him and took him.'

'How did they take him, Leadbetter?'

'With a rope.'

'Around the neck?'

'I think so.'

'From which direction did Gordon come?'

'Out of the darkness, out of the middle of the ground, walkin'.'

'Alone?'

'Oh, aye.'

'He came from the Ridgeway alone?'

'He did.'

'And O'Hara and Bremner tied him under the truck?'

'He never even struggled,' said Leadbetter. 'I think they wanted a fight, like. I mean, if he'd fought them, they'd maybe have booted him a few times but they'd have let him go. Mind, they didn't give him too much chance.'

'If he didn't run and he didn't fight,' the man said, 'what did he do? How did he react?'

'Just stopped and stood and looked't them.'

'Even when they put the rope ...'

'Yeah!' said Leadbetter. The worst of his fear was gone. For a moment he did not look at the man at all but past him, out across the expanse of the waste ground as if he could see again the figure of the boy, and was full of puzzlement, wonderment almost, at such complaisance.

'He did *nothing*?' the man asked again.

Leadbetter rubbed his upper lip with his forefinger, thinking. 'He shouted.'

'What did he shout?'

'Didn't hear it clear.'

'Where we you at this time?'

Leadbetter pointed through the windscreen. 'Over yonder: where the fence is now.'

'How far from them?'

'Maybe thirty yards.'

'Was the motor of the truck running?'

'Aye, I think so.'

'When did you run away?'

'Soon's they started to tie him under the truck wheels.'

'You actually saw this?'

'Not proper, like: they was workin' at the back.'

'Then you ran away?'

'When O'Hara came down to climb into the truck's cabin, that'll be when I took off.'

'When the truck moved, you mean?'

'I never saw it move 'til I got back to the street here.'

'How did it move, Leadbetter?'

'Eh?'

'In a straight line, in a circle, or what?'

'I was runnin' like hell, mister; I never stopped t'look.'

'You're sure that O'Hara was driving, though?'

'Aye, I'm sure of that.'

'What was Bremner doing?'

'Just hanging around.'

'Watching?'

'Suppose he must've been.'

Fear had definitely dwindled to uncertainty now, an apprehension no stronger than that which he had experienced after the crime. In a way, a strange way, he felt relieved at having unburdened himself to this stranger. He did not think that the man meant to kill him after all. The girl's presence in the car would not stop him, of course: men killed more easily with birds around. It wasn't the presence of the girl so much as her type. No tart this, no Marilyn Collins; she had polished blonde hair and fine eyebrows and a faint rich sexy perfume and her coat was worth a fortune. Leadbetter did not believe that he was about to be shot in the guts and his release from the urgency of panic carried him close to intelligent cooperation, to a link with the man.

'Where were you this morning, Leadbetter?'

'At work.'

'Before work?'

'I start't eight.'

'Before eight?'

'I never got out my bed 'til near half-seven.'

'All right,' the man said.

Behind him the girl stirred, coughed, a feminine sound. In the mirror he caught the flutter of a little bit of hanky as she dabbed her lips with it. It occurred to him that the cough and the appearance of the handkerchief might be scouting signals; he turned his head, peering back at the corner where the gables of the houses were lit by street lamps and fringed by rough evergreens. The gun muzzle spotted the side of his chin and steered his head around again.

'Have you heard of a man called Doyle?'

Leadbetter paused. 'I don't think so, mister.'

'I'll ask you again. Have you heard of a man called Doyle?'

'Aye, he was Weaver's gran'da.'

'Doyle visited your house, didn't he?'

Now Leadbetter began to understand the purpose behind his abduction. Doyle had not been in it alone. O'Hara had wrong guessed; this punter was a marksman for the old man. Not knowing how much the man had planned, Leadbetter was committed to telling the whole truth.

'Aye, he came; Monday it was.'

'When you found out Doyle had called on you, what did you do?'

Intuition told Leadbetter that the stranger could answer this question perfectly well.

'Went to Kenny Bremner's house an' told him. Kenny took me off t'meet with O'Hara.'

'What did O'Hara do?'

'The old bloke had been askin' questions before. O'Hara'd got wind of it. He was cheesed off because the old man was still at it. He was . . . worried an' all 'cause Doyle had come to me. O'Hara thought I might blab.'

'But you wouldn't blab, would you?'

'Not me!'

The man said, 'How old is O'Hara?'

'Twenty: maybe twenty-one.'

'What does he look like?'

The question put Leadbetter at a loss. He was not articulate or observant enough to frame O'Hara's appearance in simple verbal terms. He twisted his hands, thinking, then grinned. The mouth was hideous. He sniggered nervously. 'O'Hara's nothin' but a weed. A bloody wee weed. He wears black clothes and he coughs a lot.'

Since the stranger did not ask him where O'Hara could be found, Leadbetter realised that every jot and scrap of the information he had imparted was already stored in the man's memory. No longer blinkered by shock he saw the transfer of the automatic, looked round full into the girl's face and was startled by the prettiness. Under less strained circumstances he might have experienced sexual hunger, not just the desire to enter her but the obscene urge to humiliate her and bring her low. As it was he felt only remorse, shame that she should have seen him torn up by cowardice and babbling like a loon.

Switching on the ignition, the man deftly reversed the Jaguar away from the dark tarn of nothingness, away from the isolated place where death had come riding on the sound of a truck engine or could have come burning with equal facility from the snout of the burly big gun. Leadbetter said nothing as the car negotiated the streets and interconnecting roads of North Grahamshill and arrived at length at the shadowed patch by the mouth of the clinic's cul-de-sac across from his home. Then he put his hand on the door handle. The kiss of the gun on his nape held him in that pose.

The man rested his forearms across the steering wheel and studied him, not speaking. It was the first time that Leadbetter had been able to see the stranger clearly. He saw a strong, savage, cold, arrogant sort of face, but with a quality etched into it that O'Hara's face would never have, not if O'Hara lived for a century. There was something else in the man's expression which rubbed up tension in him, creakingly tuned his dread as a fiddler tightens the strings of his violin. For a moment he thought he recognised the man. Then the feeling passed, and the man was talking to him again.

'Go on home, Leadbetter, and tell nobody. Don't talk to O'Hara, or to Bremner. If you do, I'll kill you. And

202

if I don't get to kill you then O'Hara surely will. He'll kill you because you talked to me. Understand?'

'I won't say anythin', mister,' Leadbetter vowed. 'Christ, I won't even leave the bloody house for the rest of the week.'

'If you do, Leadbetter, you're as good as dead.'

The man nodded. Leadbetter fumbled open the door and stepped shakily to the pavement. Across the way, the light in the living room of his house was lit in welcome. He ran towards it, not daring to look back, running faster and faster as the thought of the bullet boring into his spine became hideously real. He skidded at the kerb, pivoted briefly, saw the shape of the car waiting like some sleek jungle animal, waiting for him to break cover, then he vaulted the gate and sprinted round the rear of the house and lurched through the back door, through the kitchen and the living room and, still running, flew upstairs. He flung himself into his bedroom, slammed and bolted the door and leaned against it. Rancid sweat was spiced by the lingering pungency of vinegar and grease adhering to the fibres of his clothes as fear and guilt infiltrated the fibres of his thinking. Toppling, he pitched forward across the bed.

For three days Leadbetter remained in bed in his room. For another three days he skulked about the house and peeped through the curtains but did not dare cross the threshold. The discipline, the obedience to his promise was one of the sanest things he had ever done. It saved him from Bremner, from O'Hara and from the threat of the strange man with the gun in his lap and the ghost in his face.

Before Leadbetter found the courage to return to the outside world it was all over and nothing he could have said or done would have changed it. The man, the stranger, had given him luck, had absolved him and, in the long run, had probably saved his life.

FIVE

A recurring dream of childhood wakened her from sleep.
In a sweat of incomprehensible alarm she wakened with
the dream still in her head, seeing the high and stark
white tower embedded in darkness, feeling herself falling
and falling and falling, the child in her following no
plummet-line to earth but tracing the spiral of the wall,
coiling down through the air like a hollow tube in a
vacuum pipe; then she came spinning out of sleep, sick
and sweating, and tumbled into the back seat of the car.

She had no way of knowing how long she had been
caught in that endless spiral. The leather seats whinnied
faintly under her as she moved and her nostrils were choked
with the stuffy atmosphere. Outside no tint of dawn
showed yet. It seemed to her that she was in the same
place she had been when she closed her eyes, hours and
hours ago; still here in the back of a Jaguar lost in the
desolation of Grahamshill.

She lifted her wrist and read the position of the tiny
hands of her watch, almost seven-fifteen. She had been in
the car all night long. Why had Weaver driven all night;
where had he taken her; what had she missed? She seemed
to recall the luminous pumps of a service station, the tired
eyes of the attendant squinting at her.

'Don?'

'What?'

'Where are we now?'

'Quiet.'

She stretched her limbs and rubbed her eyes and looked
at him. All she could see was the back of his head and a
slice of profile, like a head on a Roman coin eaten away
by earth acids and by time. Light from the lamps between
which the Mark 10 was parked did not penetrate the rear
seat of the car. She lifted her nose above the level of the
window, saw pedestrians, some traffic, heard the spluttering
of cold engines and the coughing of passers-by. Weaver
reeked of stale tobacco. The glow of a cigarette reddened

the underside of his palm. She reached out abruptly and clutched his shoulder.

'Where, Don?'

'Radstock Road.'

'Where . . . *he* lives?'

'Quiet, Hazel.'

'Oh, God!' she murmured. 'Not now; not at this time.'

'Yeah,' Weaver said. 'It's as good a time as any.'

She leaned her forehead against the glass. His method was not brilliant after all. It was careless, risky and ham-handed. What else had she a right to expect: a masterly stratagem geared to the putting down of rats? Even so, she could see the possible effectiveness of it, the cold-bloodedness. Weaver was like the window glass, taking on the temperature of the air; cold.

'Where?' she asked. 'Which house?'

'That house: eighteen.'

The curtains on the house diagonally across the roadway were closed. Daylight was coming now, stirred up like sediment by a small stiff wind which broomed the pavements then, abruptly, snuffed out the street lamps, leaving the district in an arctic darkness. Weaver killed the Jaguar's sidelights.

Hazel did not want to be with him now, did not want to have to watch him fulfil his order of execution. She had no pity for the victim; she just didn't want to be tainted by the seediness of it all. Death, she felt, should come in a blaze like Greek Fire, bursting over young men, not a bullet out of nowhere, bringing nothingness.

'We might have to wait quite . . .'

'He's already out.'

'Out. But why?'

Weaver shrugged. 'Maybe he can't sleep. Yesterday he beat up an old man. I suspect, though, he's gone out for the early editions of the newspapers.'

'I don't understand.'

'O'Hara,' said Weaver, 'will be searching the press for a report of the discovery of the body. No report at all means that he didn't kill the old man.'

'But he wanted to, didn't he? He tried.'

'I don't know.'

'Where will he go for the newspapers?'

205

'The shops are about a mile down the road.'

'It is him, Don? It is *really* this O'Hara?'

'It's him: you heard Leadbetter.'

'Are you sure he hasn't gone to work?'

'I'm sure.'

'How long since he . . .?'

'Fifteen minutes,' said Weaver. 'He'll be back at any moment.'

It did not occur to her to ask how he would kill the man.

The factories' hour had come and almost gone. A first flush of clerks, typists and early rising housewives peopled the streets now, the older women wrapped against the morning mist, anchored by shopping baskets, dark and solid seeming as boulders in a stream. It wasn't complicity which made Hazel such a silent accomplice, only the conviction that something so unsophisticated as this could not succeed. What lay beyond the wall of the man's impending death she did not dare imagine. How Weaver hoped to assassinate them, and escape undetected, had no weight for her then. Perhaps O'Hara's death would be enough to appease his sense of personal justice, to avenge the deaths of the old man and the boy. The lost night, the hours of her sleep, perhaps held the threads of his future plotting. Out of the padded luxury of the big Jaguar Weaver would pronounce sentence and, in the same split second, carry out the execution of it.

'Don?'

'Shut up.'

She saw him coming, the figure framed in the right of the windscreen, a figure as small and undernourished as a child's, yet with the face of a man and a man's swagger. Under one armpit snuggled a thick fold of newspapers. He held one paper in his hands, batting it down against the wind licks, loitering, skimming through its pages, drawing closer in a series of erratic steps, jostling up through the waning trickle of pedestrians until he emerged alone. He had the kind of face, now that she could see it more clearly, which she associated with dead poets, all fine-drawn and pale, but the expression bore no mark of innocence or sensitivity, not even of sensuality: the cut across his cheek made the mouth vexatious. Dark hair and dark clothing blustered in the breeze.

'Is that him?'

'Keep back and down.'

The engine puttered, sparked to life, purred, transmitting the vibrations of its pistons through her. The sound of the motor would swallow some of the sound of the shot. Yes, it would be a shot; the Luger, Irwin's gun, was already in Weaver's right hand and he was checking the clip and the other working parts of it. How many bullets would he need to hit his target? Was he that much of a marksman, after all? The light, she supposed, would not be good and the pulse of the car engine would not help his aim. Blank incredulity came upon her. She studied the technique as a disciple will study the intimate workings of an artist, engrossed.

Weaver did not rest his forearm on the window rim. He did not expose the gun at all. He sat back in the leather seat, his hip tilted and jammed against the passenger rest, knees drawn up and braced against the lower crescent of the steering-wheel. Supporting his right wrist with his left hand, he lowered his elbows against his belly. Vision and the direction of the bullet's travel were not impaired by the glass, the open oblong of the side window exactly containing the gate and path of the house. Though Weaver's torso was as tense as steel, somehow he managed to hold shoulders, neck, arms in total relaxation. His fingers slackened on the gun butt, wriggling, flexing, kneading the air, then returning to the grip so lightly that he might have been handling a tasteless model in black spun glass.

Through the wedge of daylight, Weaver maintained general aim, kept it until O'Hara's back blotted out the gate. Under the thin cotton garment, she could see O'Hara's shoulder-blades standing out like blunt malformed wings. He fumbled with the latch.

Weaver's forefinger covered the curve of the trigger. The unadjusted sight wavered a little, then fell still. Very rapidly now, yet with unrealistic sluggishness, he let breath whisper from his lips and took fine focus on the gaunt black-clad back. O'Hara straightened, lifting his head, cocking it as if instinct warned him of mortal danger. He pushed open the gate with his knee. Without sound, lips parted, Hazel shouted, *Now, now, now*.

O'Hara strolled through the gate, kicked it behind him

with his heel and went on up the path. The gable end of the house covered him.

Sweat ran in oily rivulets down Weaver's cheekbones. Slowly he lowered his arms until the Luger was cradled in the lap of his coat. Hazel threw herself forward, caught him by the shoulders and snatched his face round with an unexpected viciousness.

'*What happened to you, Weaver, damn you,*' she screamed. '*What happened, you palsied bastard?*'

He jerked and wrenched himself from her grasp. With the knuckles of the fist which held the gun, he stripped sweat from his temples. Dropping the lid of the glove compartment he pushed the Luger inside and snapped the lid shut. He released the handbrake and took the car smoothly away from the kerb. Hazel craned round and stared behind her at the house, number eighteen, at drawn blinds of cracked brown paper with a naked light behind them.

'It's not the way,' Weaver said.

'God, you picked a fine time to find out,' she said. She was crying softly, a sign of fatigue and released tension. 'What now?'

'They must *know*,' said Weaver. 'They must *know* it's me.'

Her mouth hung open. She could feel the skin of her face crimp and crease and go smooth as an expression of total incredulity flushed into the tissues.

'They must . . .' she said, then flung herself back, pealing out laughter, light, vindictive, hysterical laugher. 'Oh, God!' she gasped. 'Oh, God! What vanity, Weaver. What utterly fantastic vanity!'

She doubted if he heard her. Her lunatic laughter gave way at once to tears. He was gnawing his lip. His eyes were clouded, hardly seeming to see the road ahead.

Even then, she thought later, he already knew just how he would shape his vengeance to make it whole and complete, to make it, as it must be, personal and more devious. She would have her stratagem now but she no longer wanted it; she only wanted out.

'You don't expect me to believe all that cock?' Brown said.

'I don't care whether you believe it or not,' said Weaver.

'You must have a reason for taking him away.'

'I told you, he needs rest.'

'Rest! God, we could all do with some of that,' Brown said. 'I just wish some angel of mercy would come and whisk *me* off for a holiday. I suppose you'll want me to look after this place?'

'The old man says you can close up for a while if you want to.'

'Close up!' said Brown. 'Can't do that. Once you close up you never regain the flow of trade. Doyle should know better. Old bugger, offering me a *fait accompli* like this. Is he sick?'

'No, he's not sick,' said Weaver. 'I took him down on Sunday.'

'Down where?' said Brown. 'Best give me the address, just in case I have to contact him.'

'I don't want him disturbed.'

'What are you, Weaver, his bleedin' doctor?' Brown closed one eyelid, squinting up from the desk at the height of the man. 'Something's happened.'

'Nothing's happened.'

'Weaver, fat and ugly I may be but I'm not a ruddy turnip,' Brown said. 'Now square with me; what's happened to make you whip the old man off the scene?'

'Nothing, I tell you.'

'Am I in hazard?'

'Hazard?'

'Am I liable to get chopped?'

'Don't be bloody stupid,' Weaver retorted.

'Doyle's more or less kin to you, Weaver, so I assume you feel some responsibility towards him, to look out for his safety and his welfare, but I'm nothing to you. I doubt if you give a damn what happens to me.'

'You're in no danger.'

'Guarantees again?'

'I've taken Doyle out of the city because he's ill,' said Weaver: he paused. 'All right, Brown, I'll admit that there's the faint, very bloody faint, chance that he is in a little danger. It's nothing to worry about, but I prefer to play it safe. *You're* not involved, though.'

'He'll spend all his time propping up the bar.'

'Not when I'm with him.'

'So I can't get in touch with him?'

'I'll call you from time to time,' Weaver said.

'That's jolly decent of you,' Brown said. 'What if I decide I want a holiday too?'

'Then take it.'

'No thanks,' Brown said. '*I* can't afford it.'

Brown plucked off his hat and swabbed his brow with a Kleenex. His bald dome shone in the light of the bulb, but he had no pride left as far as Weaver was concerned. He might bluster and protest for a bit yet, but secretly he was glad that Weaver had seen fit to take the old man out of the city. Brown knew that though his own involvement was minimal, Doyle had somehow strayed into the firing line. As a citizen of long standing, Brown was only too familiar with the quirks and crazy intricacies of Glasgow violence. It could grab at a man as suddenly as an eagle swoops on a mouse. Doyle was better out of it.

'Can you run the shop without his help?'

Brown was tempted to tell another lie, but he changed his mind. 'I do already,' he said.

'All right.'

'Hoi, are you off, just like that?'

'Yeah.'

'Well,' Brown said, 'give the old sot my regards. Tell him not to worry, and not to drink too much.'

'Right.'

'And, Weaver, look after him.'

'Sure,' Weaver said. 'I'll look after him.'

It was beginning to flow cleanly again, like a gangrenous wound drawn and purified by strong ointments. He could not be sure yet that his reluctance to kill O'Hara was genuine. Sudden death was no punishment. Back in the days when the law was strong enough to claim an eye for an eye, the ritual had included a lengthy period of waiting; that waiting was part of the punishment, a most forceful part of society's argument. A convicted killer in his cell knew that he was beyond repentance, could do nothing to take away the arrival of that cold morning when a scale of simple ritualistic actions would lead him out to the gallows and an end of everything. Perhaps by telling

O'Hara and Bremner the reasons for his hatred of them
he would redeem for himself some of his lost identity.
Greerson had hinted that he might steer towards this point,
but he did not consider Greerson now. Even as he had
waited for O'Hara's shoulders to step into the Luger
sights, he had been thinking of other forms, other means,
other methods; he was not committed to the bullet.

The girl said, 'You must sleep.'

'Not yet.'

'You can't just keep going.'

'I need something from you.'

She bit her lip. 'What?'

'I need a place out of the city: some place secluded,
like a croft or a cottage.'

'A hide-out?'

'Something like that,' he said. 'Do you know how I
could find one fast?'

Hazel stirred coffee in the thick glass cup. She looked
from the café window at the town's busy main street. She
did not even know the name of the town, nor was she
even sure what county they had strayed into. It was a
town with a café, and that was all that mattered. Weaver's
stomach ached with emptiness and he drank the coffee
and ate the eggburger only to be rid of the distraction of
the pain. Across the narrow table the girl's pretty face was
pinched with lack of sleep and the strain of the incidents
of the morning's work in Grahamshill. He felt sorry for
her; sorry to have dragged her into it, even though she
had asked, begged, him to do so. In the beginning was
hunger and now that had turned to pity; beyond pity lay
a feeling which he could not bring himself to contemplate.
What would become of Hazel Ferrier? If she did not
crack, would she become callous and hard-bitten like the
cheap bitches of the gunmen he had met in London?

'A cottage,' she said.

'Anywhere isolated,' Weaver said. 'It doesn't have to
be up to much.'

The girl's fingers folded the silverfoil of the biscuit
wrapper into a taper and tapped the cup with it. 'Can't
you advertise?'

'It would take too long.'

211

'Yes,' she said. 'I did know a guy who had a cottage once.'

'Who is he?'

'His name's McAllister,' she said. 'He was a painter, or thought he was a painter, but the gilt wore off the gingerbread and he went into his father-in-law's business. Doing very well for himself.'

'What about the cottage?'

'God!' said Hazel, smiling at the recollection. 'It really was primitive: straight out of the annals of popular romance. I think that's why McAllister fancied it. He lived there for about a year, stuck it out throughout one bleak winter, painting like mad. His wife got sickened off and walked out on him, but still he clung to his ideals and his cottage, until things got really too much, and he baled out. I modelled for him once or twice.'

'And slept with him?'

'No,' Hazel said. 'No, funnily enough, I never did sleep with him. He had scruples. I wasn't alone in the cottage with him either: there were four or five of us, slumming it. I went there with . . . Never mind, it's not important.'

'And this cottage was his property?'

'Oh yes!' said Hazel. 'Poor McAllister, he spent every penny of his savings on buying it. He was very neo-platonic then, anti-materialistic. He had his cottage and his new bride and intended to live like Blake.'

'Who?'

'It's in Ayrshire, North Ayrshire, right on the sea coast,' said Hazel. 'But Mac may have got rid of it by this time. Last time I saw him he had moved out to a split-level in Whitecraigs and had given up painting in favour of golf. He still had the cottage then, kept it the way some other men keep their school cricket team photo framed above their desks—a memento to lost youth or something.'

'How long since you last saw him?'

'Six months.'

'Can you contact him?' Weaver said. 'Ask him about it?'

'I suppose I could,' said Hazel. 'It's a hovel, you know. It must be really indescribable by this time.'

'That doesn't matter,' Weaver said. 'Ask him if you can have the use of it for a while. Rent it.'

'I need a better story than that.'

'I don't know,' said Weaver. 'Could you tell him I'm a painter?'

'No, he'd want to see you, might come bombing down to the place to "encourage" you,' Hazel said. 'Maybe I could tell him you're a writer, a struggling writer. He'd probably give you peace then, and the damned place for nothing—if he still has it, of course.'

'Where is it exactly?'

'Templehead.'

'I know the place,' Weaver said.

Once, years ago, he had driven Muriel and Gordon there for an outing. Gordon, four or five at the time, had paddled on the edge of the breakers which swept the crescent of muddy sand on the inner curve of the headland. He remembered a handful of cottages and a manor house and some farms, all close to the main highway, and thought of the track taking off around the point, a track which he had no inclination to follow. It sounded promising: too promising. He did not set much store by it, would not be disappointed if it turned out a dud. Still, he had to try.

Hazel rolled the strip of silverfoil around her pinkie like a folk-ring. The gold wedding band still circled her left knuckle and her fingers were grimy like those of a child who has been playing in the dirt.

'Don,' she said, 'you've got to tell me why you want it?'

'I want to lie low for a time,' he said.

'After . . . you . . . ?'

'No,' he said. 'Now. I want to think it all out.'

'Why not a hotel?'

'I want to be in a place where there are no other people.'

'Just you and me?'

'No.'

'Why not?' she said. 'I thought I was in it too.'

'I need you in the city,' he said.

'For what?'

'To keep in touch,' he said.

'With whom?' she said, alarm evident in her voice.

'With Greerson,' Weaver lied. 'I think they'll jump.'

'You mean O'Hara and Bremner?'

213

'Yeah,' Weaver answered. 'I think they'll jump now and I want you to tip off Greerson. He can pick up the ropes and grab them. I . . . I can't do it.'

'Then why don't you simply tell him about Doyle and we can go back to Spain?'

'I don't trust Greerson,' Weaver said. 'No, this is the way to do it.'

'You mean, you're afraid to kill them?'

'Yeah.'

'I think you're lying to me.'

'Will you contact McAllister?'

'Yes,' she said. 'If that's what you want me to do.'

'That's what I want you to do.'

'Just don't lie to me,' she said.

'All right.'

'Don't tell me anything, if you won't tell me the truth.'

'And you'll stay in the city?'

'Yes.'

'It won't be for long,' he said.

'Then what?'

'We'll leave here for good.'

'Spain?'

'If you like,' Weaver said.

'Will that be far enough?' she said. 'Far enough from Templehead?'

He looked at her steadily. 'I hope so,' he said.

'But you'll make no promises.'

'No,' Weaver said. 'No promises.'

A shotgun, man-sized, was bolted over the main street above the window of the sporting goods store. From his seat behind the wheel, Weaver could see a corner of the deep window, the stocks of other rifles, the elegant butts of salmon rods, deer stalkers in dull green tweed hanging in the collars of ulster capes, jade rubber thigh-boots, canvas and leather cartridge bags, a crowded window to keep him interested while he waited for the girl. He could see her too in the red phone booth under the clock outside the drapery. The main street of the market town was thronged now; it was the lunch hour and the small businesses had let out their staffs. The shops were

214

crowded. The smells and sights and sounds of the burgh did nothing for Weaver; he had never been a provincial in that sense of the word. Only the city was in his blood and the city, Glasgow, was as different from this county town as a Basque fishing village was from Madrid. He could see Hazel quite clearly, her back to the two women who waited impatiently to use the public kiosk after her. She gesticulated, smiled, crinkled her eyes, going through a whole coy performance, as if this McAllister could see her as well as hear her voice. What had happened to the paintings the man had made of her? Had he had sufficient talent to catch some of that beauty and get it down on his paper or his canvas? Had he painted her nude? McAllister was nothing but her stooge, and she was his stooge. All he wanted was the cottage. He was too tired to feel much in the way of excitement; the weariness in him made him unduly fatalistic. The fact that she was smiling and nodding into the receiver meant nothing. He watched her put the instrument back on its cradle and push out of the box. She came quickly across the pavement and got into the car.

'You've got it,' she said.

'No strings?'

'Marriage has mellowed McAllister,' the girl said. 'I think he regrets not having slept with me, and wants to make amends.'

'You want to?'

'No,' she said. 'Not when I've got you.'

'Tell me about the cottage?'

'He's having it renovated,' she said, 'but work won't start until Easter. You can have it, with his compliments, until then. I told him you're a writer, the next James Joyce.'

'When can I take possession?'

'Any time,' the girl said.

'Good,' said Weaver. 'We'll go down and look it over this afternoon.'

'To see if it suits your purpose?'

'Yeah.'

'Whatever that purpose might be.'

'Look, Hazel . . .'

'Don't,' she said. 'It would only be another lie.'

215

'No.'

'You're going to kill them there, aren't you?'

He pulled out the ashtray and tapped his cigarette ash into it. 'Yeah,' he said. 'And I don't want you around while I do it. I don't want anyone around.'

'And afterwards?'

'I want you with me then.'

'But maybe I won't want you.'

'You have a week,' he said, 'to make up your mind.'

'I don't need a week, I'll be here, Weaver,' she said. 'I'll be ready.'

'I . . . hoped you'd say that.'

She put her face down in her hands, bent over, the bronze hair falling across her, veiling her. 'Oh, God! Why can't it just be us?'

'Because I've lived too long,' Weaver said.

SIX

The black week ended and another began, and still Bremner could not shake off the insidious anxiety which was in him. He had scrounged round the office for a long haul, a trip south, but even the Ousbys could not give him what they did not have, and this week's work had been confined to short contracts around the city and the central belt. He resisted the pubs with difficulty, but resist them he did, preferring the safe dark of cinemas and the company he found casually in truckers' snack-bars. He kept away from O'Hara, afraid of the hatred which smouldered close to the surface of his own character, an inversion of friendship. Polished by a toll of chapel bells and baptised with stale fat, Sunday came upon him slowly. By early afternoon the dismal emptiness of the day drove him out of the flat and, because he had no place else to go, across the river into the reaches of industrial Renfrewshire. He fetched up at a tenement in Paisley, climbed the stairs and rang the bell. The name-plate gave him back his own name: Kenneth Bremner.

Indifference had always been the keynote of Bremner's

relationship with his father. It should have driven them far apart years ago, but for some reason it hadn't. Even the man's drunken tempers, the strap raw across the boy's back, the studded boot in the rump, the shouting, had somehow not put too large a division between them. At this time Bremner's father needed his son the way a showman needs an audience, needed to exhibit the smugness of a singularly unattractive ageing widower who, in the winter of his days, has somehow trapped a singularly attractive woman and persuaded her to become his wife. On the stale side of fifty, old Bremner enjoyed the opportunity of flaunting his vigour in his son's face; a bull showing off to a bullock.

Minding his manners, Kenny sat through dinner, stilled the sarcasm on his tongue, was quiet, not himself. He was thinking of the graveyard by the Grahamshill boulevard and of the forlorn bubble of withered flowers on it and wondered that a living father and dead mother could invoke in him exactly the same degree of apathy. The new stepmother, Jeannie, was a big buxom woman in her mid-thirties. She had a bovine winsomeness and was not above lavishing her charms on the lad. She served rich foods, Italian pastas, rough red wine, mock-cream pastries, coffee with blobs of the same chemical floating on the top; Kenny thought it tasted like semen. For the hundredth time that year Bremner vowed that he would not come visiting again. The sight of his old man and the woman together, billing and cooing, made him uncomfortable; he repeated his vow that he would journey to Paisley no more, knowing in himself, however, that a Sabbath restlessness would stir in him eventually and he would come to this house in search of comfort, come not with hope but with fortitude.

When the pointless ordeal was over and fond farewells said, he caught an early train back to Glasgow. He went directly to a city bar and drank a single pint of lager, laden with lime-juice and ice-cubes. He had lost his taste for beer. Anyway, filial unrest was not something that could be flushed out of the system like kidney grit. After one pint, he left. Half an hour later, with red Italian vino and mild lager fermenting in his bloodstream, he poured himself off the bus at the end of Whitecable Lane and staggered towards the sanctuary of his own tiny but luxurious flat. Must be more careful, he told himself: forgot about the wine. He muttered the maxim to himself as he climbed the steps to the close, saying 'Careful: wine: careful.' His voice echoed from the walls. He liked the sound of it and crooned a bit, but the song did not come out jovial, more like a lament played on a plastic chanter. He was very aware of his surroundings, very clear in his mind.

The windows of the first landing were empty of glass. Framed in the void he could see the circular moon, frost-bitten and flat and worn, like a Kitchener medal. It was mounted on the chimneyheads of the abandoned tenements across the backs. He studied it for a while, leaning his elbows on the window ledge, tasting the cleaner air of the Sunday night, his mouth open. Humour diluted his melancholy; the old bugger was probably all right. These old guys had hard heads, come off stock with skulls used to whacks from clubs and billys. He hadn't even touched it, him—the club or the old man. All O'Hara's doing. Nearly a week and not a breath of trouble, of curious cops or newspaper clips. He breathed the cold down into his lungs and let it sober him a little. Must definitely and absolutely be careful about that bloody red vino next time he went to Paisley. He braced himself, stood up straight, walked up to the flat and let himself in. He was bloody glad to be home.

The closeness of the lobby walls gave him an immediate sense of security. Cheerfulness welled up in him. He danced a little bow-legged jig, revelling in privacy and the safety of ownership. Cocking his elbows he horn-piped through to the living room. No moon here: got the sun in the morning but no moon at night. The moon was a back-door caller, matey with rats and big black tom-cats in the disintegrating brick wash-houses. What he did have was the light of the lamp at the lane's end and the rumble of heavy traffic through his shelves. Tonight his shadow was raffish, and even his head had the roots of a neck to it. With the energy running through him like water through a mill-race, he danced to his shadow, danced until his heels became leaden and the TV set rattled and dishes and ornaments and utensils shook and his clothes on wire hangers in the corner swung to and fro like a ghostly chorus line. At last, minutes later, he dropped exhausted into the armchair by the Sunglow, scuffed off his shoes and tweaked the fire's switch with his toes.

The warmth of the heater soon made him sleepy. Walking on his knees across the hearth rug he made for the alcove behind the blanket. Behind the blanket was his sleeping sack, best Continental make, filled with down; a snug, sensual thing smelling pleasantly of his own body sweat. He slept in it, snuggled down on a feather mattress on top of a bedframe bolted to the walls. He wanted to lie down now, to feel the puffy folds of the sack close about him and the soft feather pillow sigh under his heavy head. He would lie with the blanket open and the glow of the fire out there in the room and he would sleep and waken and put the fire off and sleep again until morning, Monday, another week; a week away from the business with the old man, old Doyle. He reached for the blanket and tugged it open, then he craned back and dropped on to his heels.

The shape was black and smooth, black and smooth as the marble slab on the lair behind his mother's grave in the boneyard over the hill. It did not shine like mineral though, but absorbed light into it, the worm of orange from the fire, the spill of lamplight from the lane. For an instant it struck Bremner that his sleeping sack had germinated life of its own and was now rearing up before him, a ghastly over-blown pod. As the shape on the bed developed limbs and moved and became the shape of a man, Bremner's neck rose out of his hunch. He thought now that it was O'Hara; shouted out profanities. Even when pain angled and bored down into his skull and bounced into his teeth and tongue, he still thought it was O'Hara come to settle a score. The second blow was like a rubber arrow in him, and the third trailed a ribbon of black crêpe all the way from his crown down to the bones at the base of his spine. No longer able to put up a token defence, no longer able to hold himself upright, he swayed forward. It must have been like this for the old man—*was it the old man?*—with the reverberations of the oak club running through the old bones. A crosscurrent of time and space had trapped him, come for him, nailed

219

him. He remembered the expression on Doyle's face and unwittingly mimicked it, hoping to persuade the attacker that he too was due his share of luck and must be allowed to survive. Then that instant's thought was exploded too and he fell further, grabbed at the man's knees. Silken tubes filled with goose-down, they buckled under him, and he landed on the edge of the rug, and the floor swallowed him up.

It was fitting that the boy should be drunk. Though it had no mark on it, Weaver assiduously wiped the butt of the Luger. The boy had a head like mahogany. He had been obliged to bring the gun down four times, had just begun to wonder if life and consciousness were so freakishly linked in Bremner that the snapping of one would automatically mean snapping the other when the boy slumped to the floor. Weaver pocketed the Luger. It was close to eleven, almost dead on the hour. He felt as if he had been in that room for hours, but it hadn't been really long since he had knocked on the door and received no answer. Coming prepared, he had cleverly worked the celluloid strip into the old lock and sprung it neatly and without damage. It was fortunate that Bremner had been out: it was cleaner this way, more effective and more satisfying.

Lifting the unconscious boy he threw him unceremoniously on to the bed. His feet caught the blanket and a couple of loose brass hooks pattered to the floor. Weaver checked heart beat and pulse rate and found both strong. He stripped the boy and flung the cheap clothes aside and dressed the boy again from the woollens and tweeds he had previously selected from the crammed drawers of the dresser. He made sure that he fitted on a double issue of everything, from underclothing to sweaters. The tattered leather jerkin would not zip up over the swollen chest but he completed the bundling process with a scarf. He then fetched a hank of nylon rope, hacked off a suitable length, and bound Bremner's ankles and wrists. With another thong he laced wrists to ankles and tugged the connection tight, arching Bremner's spine, trussing him beyond all possibility of escape. From his pocket Weaver unfolded a hand-stitched canvas mask which fitted loosely over Bremner's head and fastened at the throat with an improvised draw-cord. Air vents at the nostrils would make sure that the victim did not smother before his time.

Weaver switched on a lamp and by its light made a hasty examination of his prisoner, checking the security of the knots and the snugness of the mask; then he switched off lamps and the Sunglow, moved in under Bremner and hoisted the boy across his shoulders. Lugging the load he went out of the room, closed both doors carefully, and descended to the lane.

The Jaguar was parked on a stretch of muddy ground behind the empty tenements. Opening the rear door, Weaver laid Bremner into the space below the level of the seat, tucked a blanket round him and cowled the boy's head with the flap. He slammed the door and locked it, hurried to the driver's side and slid in behind the wheel.

When he pulled the car off the hard mud, boxes of groceries and other provisions clinked and shifted in the boot and on the back seat, but the bundle in the rear well made no sound at all.

The night clerk put the call directly through to her room. The connection was not of the best. Even through the frying cackle of static, however, Hazel recognised Weaver's voice. As she had acquired some of his caution over the past week, her first question was tentative and unrevealing. He answered it and she knew for sure that it was him.

'Weaver,' she asked, impatiently. 'Is it done?'

'Yeah.'

The hand holding the receiver began to tremble and she lay back against the pillows, stretching the cord.

'How . . . how is he?'

'Still out,' said Weaver. 'He's all right.'

'Where are you now?'

'The call box in Templehead, near the road end.'

'The people in the farm may see you.'

'Let them,' said Weaver. 'They know I'm here: I gave them the yarn about being a writer and brushed them off.'

'What do you want me to do now?'

'Stay put,' said Weaver. 'Be in the room until noon and after eight at night, so I can reach you if I have to.'

'Very well,' she said. 'You . . . you won't hurt him, will you?'

'No,' said Weaver curtly. 'Listen, I'll call again tomorrow.'

'Don,' she said. 'Listen—wait—Don.'

The bleeping obliterated her question. Weaver had hung up.

Hazel replaced the receiver and lit a cigarette. She lay where she was, propped up on the bed. The room seemed empty without him, the emptiness in her too. A call from Weaver; though it had no warmth or tenderness, it was all that he could give her yet in place of love. In spite of her disgust and constant fear, she would be here when he called again: she would do as he told her to do. She would not, after all, quit now, or leave him, or let him down.

The thought of that broken-down, draughty cottage huddled under the brow of a cliff with rough grey sea for a doorstep did not increase her loneliness; indeed, she thought of it wistfully. Even without luxury, without comfort, she wished that she was there now, with him.

What Weaver really intended to do with Bremner she did not fully understand. The shadow play of possibilities chilled her. She hugged the quilt around her shoulders and stabbed out the cigarette. Loyalty was a novelty; love, too, was a lovely sort of loyalty; but it made her a part of the thing he intended to do and she did not know how the accomplishment of that act would affect her feelings towards him. She was afraid not only of losing him but of losing her feelings towards him, deeper and truer than anything she had ever felt for anyone before. She did not understand why it should be so. Perhaps they were of the same order as the feelings which had compelled Weaver to return to the city, to answer the old man's summons. Now the old man was dead, wrapped like a turkey in the bathtub, and Weaver was down there lost in the bleak Ayrshire landscape orchestrating his revenge.

The weeping was stuffy in her nasal passages, like the beginnings of a cold. She did not try to staunch it. She turned on her side, wrapping the quilt tighter around her, and stared at the telephone under the cone of the night-lamp, waiting.

PART FOUR

ONE

Crabbing, Bremner managed four short paces to the left before the links locked tight and the clamps bit his ankles and halted all further progress in that direction. Counting aloud, he returned along the line. In his mind he stored a multitude of calculated facts and figures to help crowd out the terror which threatened, if given room, to reduce him to gibbering insanity. The full crossing totalled eight pinched steps, an attenuated arc limited at each end by the nab of the chain. The harness around chest and shoulders allowed more play than the anklets. Leaning on the harness, he groped out into the imprisoning darkness. His manacled wrists came short, fingers splayed, finding no solidity. He told himself that he was bloody lucky; if the tensions on the three root points had been exactly equal he would have been unable to stir at all. To Bremner, who had roved the roads of Britain sitting high in the cabin of a big pantechnicon, the bounty of eight curt steps now seemed like the epitome of freedom.

The movement itself was all he had. Though it yielded no information and little enough diversion, it kept the pilot light of his confidence alight. His senses were muffled by the rank-smelling, coarse fabric of the sack which shrouded his head and admitted only a minimum of air under the drawcord and through the nostril slits. Time and again he had struggled to hook his nails under the hood but the manacles were latched to yet another length of chain which passed between his thighs and choked off that particular movement as effectively as a straitjacket would have done. Cold sifted up from the floor; stone, flagstones maybe, or concrete. The chill crept up into his limbs and belly and his bladder ached with urine. As a counter to the burning fluid fullness below, his mouth was dry and yeasty with the thirst of his hangover and the taste of the unwashed sack canvas which, in his first bout of panic, he had gnawed with his teeth like a rat.

Backing up to his bonds he searched again for a tangible surface which would shape the physical lineaments of his dungeon. The men had been too clever; they had organised the harness so that he was blocked three paces to the rear. A bar or rod had been inserted into the draped chain; too clever for him all along the line. He did not consider himself the victim of sadists but only a prisoner. Really the trappings flattered his ingenuity; Christ, they must have supposed him to be a jelly-boned bloody mastermind to go to such lengths to hold him and thwart escape.

Hanging utterly still he listened until his ears seemed to ring with the strain; but he could not pick up audible, or at least identifiable sounds. Far off on the outer edge of his hearing was a faint regular pulsation, too regular to be traffic; a machine, perhaps a generator. Once, some hours ago, he had been frightened out of his wits by a loud squealing scream directly above him. It happened once, then was gone before he could collect himself and try to analyse it. Bremner was intelligent enough to believe that every horror, no matter how grotesque, has a basis in reason. Slowly, painfully, he dragged himself from the mental chaos of his first minutes of waking, had shaken off the awful inertia of being alive in a world without boundaries and without the reality of sensual experience. To save himself from total disintegration, he had quickly collated his meagre catalogue of memories, had gradually added tiny fragments of knowledge to it and had at last begun to make deductions and assumptions. Though he had no means of checking the validity of his theory, the rationality of it consoled him. The prime piece of logic, the star turn in his pantomime of deductive reasoning, was the realisation that if they merely wanted him dead they would not have gone to all this bother to keep him alive. The concept of imprisonment, of pain did not trouble him much; it was death he feared, really, deeply, hideously feared. The other things might be bad, unthinkably bad, but they would pass; only being dead would not pass. That state was permanent. They did not want him dead. He repeated the phrase and the reasons again and again until he fell softly into the trap of believing it not only to be his golden rule but the golden rule of those who had trapped him.

When the scream sounded again, a little more distant and a little less sharp, he barely flinched, falling forward on the harness, his head cocked under the hood—a yelping scream stripped away, failing. He closed his eyes, as if that would help, and listened intently. He grinned suddenly.

A gull.

A bloody seagull, that was all.

He had nothing to fear from a seagull.

Weaver said, 'Write a note; blank paper; no heading; no address; no signature, of course. Ready?'

Hazel said, 'Yes.'

'Copy it down.'

'I'll remember it.'

'All right,' Weaver said. 'Set down this—"Bremner is held".'

'Bremner is held.'

'"Templehead Cottage, Ayrshire".'

'You're not . . .'

'Repeat it.'

'"Bremner is held, Templehead Cottage, Ayrshire",' Hazel said. 'Is that all?'

'Yeah. Take the note to number eighteen, Radstock Road, in North Grahamshill. Use a street map if you're not sure where it is. Make sure you're not seen in the vicinity or at the house. Put the note through the letter box of the side house—that is number eighteen—then get to hell out of it.'

'When: now?'

'This evening, just after dark.'

'Don, he'll come . . .'

'Jesus, I know he'll come. I want him to come.'

'What will I do then?'

'Wait at the Coruna for me.'

'When will you be here?'

'Just as soon as . . . as it's over.'

'Call me,' Hazel said. 'Please, call me. I'll be ready. I'll be all packed and ready.'

'Do you remember the message?'

'Yes,' she said. 'Don, you will come for me, won't you?'

'When it's over,' he said, 'I'll come for you.'

'Greerson will know it's you.'

'Greerson's not important now.'

'I'm frightened,' the girl said. 'God, I'm frightened to death.'

'If you do what I ask tonight, then it'll be all over by morning.'

'Are you sure O'Hara . . . ?'

'He just can't afford to keep away.'

'I hope . . . No, I don't hope. I . . .'

'Hazel,' said Weaver, 'don't crack on me now.'

She braced herself and tossed her hair back, tilting her chin. Her father would have loved that Christian martyr pose, but Weaver could not see her.

'No, darling,' she said, and hung up before he could spoil it.

Marilyn Collins butted the gate with her rump and drew the pram full of washing after her on to the path. Radstock Road was filled with a cold darkness now and she was disappointed to detect no light behind the blinds of the upstairs house. She had eaten nothing since lunch time, except a cup of watery soup from the vending machine in the laundromat, and had hoped that Alex might be at home with the kettle on. Now, after she had draped the damp washing on the kitchen pulley, she would have to cook a meal for herself. She took the bag of laundry from the pram and dumped it on the steps, wheeled the pram to its place beside the hut at the back of the house, then returned and lugged the bag up to the front door. She opened the door with her key and let herself into the house. Grumbling, she flung the bag over her shoulder and climbed the long flight of interior stairs to the living room. Hardly had she had time to shuck off her burden than the doorbell whirred. Cursing, she flung the laundry into the kitchenette and clumped downstairs again.

The envelope lay plainly on the scarred square of linoleum. Though it was sealed it carried no address, only the name 'O'Hara' scripted across it. Marilyn picked it up and turned it curiously in her fingers, tempted to rip it open. She did not approve of Alex receiving strange letters. The doorbell rang once more. She tucked the envelope into her coat pocket.

She opened the door.

The bogey was admiring the stretch of unfertile earth between the houses. He had no discernible rank, a constable, and looked doughy, his young face balled into the space between the edges of his hard hat and rigid blue collar. In the palm of his hand he cradled a small notebook. Marilyn's heart bounded like a leveret in a sack.

'Marilyn Collins?' The bogey read from the book. He glanced at her, awaiting a reply.

The girl's brain reeled with possibilities. It was by no means the first time she had opened the door to discover a pair of big black boots on the doorstep.

'Aye.'

'Well, lass, I've brought you some sad news.'

Oh, Christ! Marilyn thought, Alex's done somebody: he's dead himself. Her mind shattered like a machine-gun, spitting out possibilities, all of them as fatal as bullets.

The bogey said, 'It's your granny, lass; she's passed on.' He uncovered his wrist watch and checked the accuracy of his statement. 'Passed to her rest an hour and ten minutes ago.'

'Jesus,' said Marilyn. 'Is that all?'

O'Hara signalled to the barman. The pint of heavy draught beer and the nip of whisky came up the bar and stopped at O'Hara's elbow. He lifted the pint pot and supped, filling his cheeks with the liquid. The bar was quiet; hardly more than a dozen men in it tonight. Bremner wasn't one of them. O'Hara had no valid reason to expect Bremner to be in the pub—Kenny wasn't much of a boozer these days—but the pub had once been a favourite rendezvous and he had come here on the off chance that he would find his mate and find a way to patch up the ill-feeling which last Monday's caper had incurred. He liked Kenny; Kenny was the only real mate he had ever had in his life. He preferred Kenny even to the girl. Now Kenny was scared though; Leadbetter wasn't the only one he had to fear. There had been fear and horror in Kenny's eyes when the old bugger went down and the blood started.

O'Hara planted his shoe on the rail, tilted his wrist and slid the beer into him. He glanced at the barman.

'Seen Bremner lately?'

'Who's that?'

'Kenny Bremner.'

'Naw, haven't seen him.'

The chop of darts sounded from the games alley but he could see the whole length of the alley in the mirror behind the bottles and Kenny wasn't there. The tables were empty. One man, big bellied and flushed, was listlessly lobbing darts at the worn board.

Though he could not define it, O'Hara wanted Bremner to walk through the swing doors and grin and bum a pint from him and give him all the old Wickerburn chat. He wanted to talk about the business of the old man, to get it all out and be rid of it and return the friendship to the point where it had been; not last week but last year, before Doyle and before Weaver. Covertly he watched the door, and supped his pint slowly.

The moment the girl entered he could tell that something was up. It was printed on her mouth like the headline in a newspaper. She came right up to him—this in the public, not even the bloody lounge—and kissed him with her mouth on his mouth.

'Get t'hell,' he said. 'You gone nuts?'

'Gran's dead,' Marilyn said.

'That's all I bloody need.'

'Come on home,' Marilyn said. 'We got things t'talk about.'

'What bloody things?'

He knew what she meant; her slyness sickened him. So the inevitable had at last occurred. The old cow had snuffed it and left the problem of the house. He had imagined that the old woman would always be there, not alive but not quite dead, stretched out under the pale hospital sheets. He had even visited her once, and badgered Marilyn to make a monthly trip up to the ward just to ascertain that the faint fluctuations of blood in the dried-up veins were still happening, so that his existence might bowl along undisturbed. Now there would be all the palaver of burial, and the bother of fighting for tenancy of the house. More than likely the bloody council would turf him and Marilyn out into the street. Marilyn was unmarried and not entitled to skip her place on the waiting list for council houses. He knew that she intended to use this change in circumstances as a tool to force him to marry her. If they were man and wife, legal and above board, then the council might tide the house over to him. He wouldn't find another place as cheap. For the cost of a marriage licence he could have himself a cheap head-quarters. The girl had already worked all this out. She was scheming to get him, to hook him. He was buggered if he would let anyone get him.

'Things,' the girl said. She mooned at him, and took his arm. He lifted the whisky nip and sank it, even as the bitch was tugging him towards the door.

'Okay,' he said. 'Okay.'

Jesus, the things they would do to nail a man of their own. He stopped thinking about Kenny and the old man, and applied his cerebral skills to matters more immediate and practical. He let the pudding-faced girl haul him out into the street to lead him back to the bed in the house. Like all bloody women she talked her best argument on her back, with her legs open.

Maybe he would tell her to frig herself, step over to Whitecable Lane and shift in with Kenny for a while. He fancied that. Kenny would not put him out. Kenny would stand by him in the end.

Aye: the idea of change appealed to him.

He patted the girl's hand consolingly and thought of how he could escape.

TWO

Now the wind had dispersed the dawn mist Weaver could see that frost patched the land around the cottage and the scrub country above. Untapped potato shaws in a strawed field were ruled out in oxalic white with the first melt of loam on the eastwards crusts. In the stone stable behind the cottage the air was as still and frozen as an ice-house. Even the daylight which seeped through a grid high on the sea-facing wall came clouded like breath. As he entered, a martin took off from the ledge with a rippling chirp of fright, the sound soon lost in the growl of breakers on the rocks. Sleep had settled into the folds of Bremner's muscles and his head lolled against the pull of the chains. Heels together, knees and thighs bent, his hands were flung to one side, like a golfer putting in a dream. His fingers were as mottled as a strip of ripe venison. Quietly Weaver placed the lavatory bucket on the floor and held up the invalid's dish like a cruse to lighten the darkness.

It was ten o'clock on Tuesday morning: it should have been over by now. He was beginning to be a little afraid of Bremner. The chore of keeping him alive without permitting even the slimmest chance of escape was a harrowing detail. He must not allow himself to succumb to pity, or come to know the boy, to have him emerge as a person in his own right. As long as he was trussed up and hooded, Bremner was only a cipher and Weaver could trick himself into indifference. If Hazel had done her work properly, O'Hara should have been here hours ago. All night long, alternating between a vantage point on the tor above the track and the warm cottage kitchen, Weaver had kept watch. But O'Hara did not come, and it was no longer possible to leave the boy hanging untended like a side of beef. Thirty hours without respite was almost too much. Even in this hive of odours the acrid stink of sweat already hinted at decay.

Steam wisped from the spout of the cup. Lifting the hood from the boy's mouth Weaver stuck the spout between the slack teeth and held it there while Bremner choked into wakefulness. No force was needed to make him sip the savoury mutton broth; he was greedy for the hot liquid and wasted no breath in screaming for answers as he had done the last feeding time. Saying nothing, Weaver fed the boy, then unlocked the manacles long enough to allow him to relieve himself into the pail. He did not permit himself to speculate on what Bremner might be thinking. Bremner must mean as little to him as Gordon and Doyle had done to Bremner. That was the valid equation; he could not at this stage question the usefulness of its application.

Weaver carried the empty soup dish across the stable and ducked under the harness rack. He checked the burner of the paraffin stove which he had installed in the middle of the night. The wick had charred and extinguished, and the tank was dry. If by some mischance Bremner was still here come nightfall he would be obliged to trim the wick and refill the tank to provide warmth for the dark hours. Weaver's quilted jacket was brand new and its silky outer covering hissed as he moved. The garment had served him well in the last twenty-four hours, protecting him from wind and from the draughts of the cottage kitchen and the graveyard chill of morning which came off the sea. He was not weary, was owned by a restless sort of energy. After it passed he sensed that he would slump into fatigue and in that slump he would certainly sleep—and while he slept O'Hara might show. Where the hell was O'Hara? What was holding him back? Guile, or cowardice, or indifference to Bremner's fate? Impulsively Weaver dropped the soup dish to a shelf and ducked again beneath the beam which held the rivets of the boy's shackles. He caught the sagging body and dragged it upright. Within the hood Bremner released a groan of resignation. Weaver fished keys from under the Luger in the pouch pocket of the jacket and fitted one to the stiff new padlock. He paused, inspecting the web of chains and straps and round iron staples, part of the history of this place, tethers from halters of cows or dray-horses or the savage unloved work-dogs of the shepherd-kind.

Knowing nothing of agriculture, Weaver could not tell if the pastures had ever been cudded or if rams had ever cropped the grasses of the cliff tops which hung like battlements above the cottage. He did not consider those trivial aspects when he had approved the place. What was important was that the nearest town was seven miles away round the curve of the bay, visible from Templehead only as a smudge of smoke and a glint of plant chimneys against sooty winter skies. The hamlet from which the peninsula took its name was nothing but a row of dilapidated fishers' shacks, all abandoned now. Only a single hunchbacked croft with a Post Office and tiny general store set into two sheds in its garden was occupied. In winter the store opened for an hour each day, serving a handful of farmers' wives from the inner headland. At the gate of the croft the metalled road abruptly terminated and a scant track took over. This track wended uphill a little and veered inland through a chasm in the ridge which came down at a right angle from the crest of the hill. It was the ridge, like the tail of a fossilised monster which screened the pastures of Templehead from the outside world. A mile of grazing and a narrow potato patch were cut off from the rocks and rough shingle shore, then the turn of the track for the cottage was screened again by a bristle of stunted thorn trees. On the first trip down Hazel had told Weaver something of the cottage's past. He listened to her only to be kind, to give her an excuse to blow off steam. Briefly they were like lovers seeking a hideaway, soulful romantics forsaking civilisation, like the McAllisters. After its life as a working croft the cottage had served as a home for a half-mad artist—before McAllister's term—then a paranoiac poet and finally as a refuge for a rich but eccentric vegan who, though he would not harm a gnat, had become so idealistic in his commune with nature that he had slowly fasted himself to death in his hermitage of rock and shrub and sea-shingle. All of these former occupants had left their mark upon the property; daubs of oil paint on the stable lintel; the likeness of a fish chipped into a stone in the silt of the yard; a scratched couplet on the privy door, the words punctuated now by lentils of wet rot. On an upper shelf in the pantry lay a bunch of herbs dried to odourless skeletons and, stuffed under sacking in the cambered bedroom, Weaver found a bird cage. Bent and warped, the door was still clipped tight to hold in the handful of mustard-coloured feathers which adhered to its mouldy base. McAllister had left his mark too; fresher paint stains, plastic vases, empty wine bottles and a clutter of creaky furniture. Weaver wondered what legacies he in his turn would leave; an inheritance of tales and tell-tale markings well suited to the nature of the place, haunting rumours and a whisper of unanswerable questions. Words were durable, though more susceptible to corruption than timber and slate and sandstone.

Lifting Bremner across his shoulders he carried the boy from the stable into the cottage, and set him down in an armchair by the fire.

Though Bremner was fully conscious, he was so stiff with fear as well as cold, that his gut was as hard as an oak slab and his legs as briar roots. With the heat of the fire on him, maybe Bremner anticipated torture by traditional methods. Weaver returned to the stable and brought back the padlocks. He removed the harness from the boy's body and the manacles from his wrists, linked the ankle-chain to the hob hook, then he slowly peeled off the hood.

Bremner's eyes were as sunken as a mole's. He blinked and squinted and turned his face from the flickering firelight. Outside the wind sliced through the thorn trees and rattled loose wires under the cottage eaves, drove the sonorous pumping of the surf into the building as if the walls had no more solidity than a crab shell. The rising wind tore off the gulls' screams like scrolls of living sound from the mass of the sea. In the flames Bremner's face was brutal with bewilderment and in the eyes, deep but constant, was a sudden vitality, an amused sort of cunning, as if he had already bested his adbuctor. The stubble beard all down his jaw was stained with soup.

'What's the intention?' Bremner asked.

Weaver gave him no answer, turning away to stand by the window, looking out. He was bone weary now and sickened by his own debility.

'That the sea out there?'

'Yeah.'

Now Bremner would be peering at the scudding sky, struggling to find himself a landmark with which to give this place a name.

'What d'you want with me?'

'The old man died,' Weaver said.

'What old man?'

'Doyle.'

'I never killed any old man.'

'And the boy, Weaver.'

'Just who the hell are you?'

Unlike Leadbetter, Bremner did not whine, did not cringe, showed no submissiveness, forming questions and denials out of the same stuff. Weaver watched the track as far as he could see it. It was unlikely that O'Hara would approach in broad daylight, but he knew so little about the man that he could not be sure. Just how would O'Hara come to this outlandish peninsula, with the sea on one side and the broken hillside on the other? Had Hazel failed him?

235

'Don't talk, Bremner.'

'You know me?'

'I know you.'

In a way he did know Bremner: he had known so many like him that he could not count them now, boys who had made one wrong decision in their lives and instantly regretted it. If you recognised the error swiftly enough it was still possible to revoke it, not to be proud about it, to let the choice lie and the years drift up like sand, until there was nothing to see, to feel. It would not be that way with O'Hara. O'Hara would never renege on his own guilt, leave it, abandon it. It wasn't Kenny Bremner's name which had come out of the tip of the pen in the old man's hand, but O'Hara's. An old man had died to tell him the truth, that one final struggling truth.

'I'm starved.'

Without moving more than his arm Weaver flipped open a plastic bin on the table top and plucked out a soggy bread roll. He tossed it underhand to the boy who caught it deftly in spite of the chains, and fell to gnawing on it like a wolfling on a spring lamb.

'I'm going t'be missed, y'know,' Bremner said. 'I got friends and work-mates, an' . . .'

'Will O'Hara miss you?'

Bremner's jaws stopped grinding. He leaned deliberately forward and spat the mess from his mouth into the fire. 'Fuck O'Hara.' Then his features closed up again and it wasn't like looking at a boy but at a man who has learned to contain his emotions in a capsule inside himself. Weaver remembered the polished little faces of the Spanish child-pimps, beguilingly inviting him to pay for instruction in all manner of sexual perversion. Their greed was the flower of necessity though, and he could not feel disgust without pity. They traded in terms which they did not truly understand, in acts which they could not yet perform. He had paid them money to leave him alone, but always there was another face and another hand and another mouth tempting and exhorting him, unfinished features and round eyes identical with the ones he had already bought off. How could he convince them that he was not of that stamp, that they had the wrong man? After that day the Spanish sun had never seemed quite so bright and he kept out of the cities and

236

the larger towns, hung close to his private white-walled villa above the beach where the children could not reach him.

Flames licked up over the lettering on the herring box which he had smashed for kindling. Bremner remained forward, warming himself, a fleck of the mush on the side of his mouth, his eyes smarting and watering with the light.

'You hear me?' Bremner said. 'Fuck O'Hara.'

Weaver walked across the kitchen and grabbed the boy's wrist, led the chain back and fastened it with a padlock to the window grid.

'I'm going out,' Weaver said. 'I won't be far away.'

Uncertainly Bremner watched him, bowed, inhibited but not immobilised by the chains. He was grinning again.

Weaver went along the cramped corridor to the front door. The wind struck into him as he walked to the beginnings of the track in the yard and set off towards the telephone box.

Bremner watched the man cross the yard and go out of sight. For an instant it looked as if the man was standing as still as a telegraph pole and it was the background which slipped past him. Even after the man had gone Bremner did not move, held rigid by indecision as much as by the network of chains. He studied the room, wondering if he had enough strength left to pull the hob hook from its stone. Flexing, he put a little easy pressure on the staple and on the grid, but he could not muster the determination to go on. Cloud had darkened the rocks now and the sea was like a school slate. Maybe this was some sort of testing period, a trial of his character. For all he could tell his future security might depend on what he did at this moment. Sense urged him to try to escape, but another part of him, more circumspect, advocated caution, meekness, cooperation. It did not occur to him to shout for help. The man was nobody's fool. He had contrived to lift him clean out of the city and bring him here, so he wouldn't be stupid enough to have him planted near other people. Though the man had talked of Doyle, of Gordon Weaver, and of O'Hara, Bremner could not yet figure out what exactly was required of him.

The house was on the west coast: he could tell.

His father had brought him down to the west coast resorts, not often, never for more than a day at a time, yet the Ayrshire coast was part of that part of childhood which he would not forget. He sat up at the windows of the compartment and watched the sea appear, rhyming off the the familiar and longed-for landmarks and wanted to be out there on the muddy sand with his feet in the breaking waves.

With food in his belly and the fire's warmth on him after a while he could fight sleep no longer. Dreaming of his father and his mother, his real mother, and the big soft-breasted woman in his father's house now, he dozed went deeper and had a momentary vision of O'Hara and the raised club and the beams of the truck in darkness of his own making. Then he went down too deep to remember anything or even dream.

'Of course I did.'

'When?'

'Last evening, about six o'clock; exactly as you told me to do,' Hazel said.

'You're sure you got the right house?'

'I'm positive. Number eighteen, at the side.'

'All right.'

'Perhaps he's scented trouble.'

'Maybe.'

'How is the other one?'

'Fine.'

'Don, do you want me to put another . . . ?'

'No,' he told her, sharply. 'I'll wait.'

'Won't the one you have be . . . be missed?'

'I doubt it.'

'Don, I really did do it right.'

'I'll call you again.'

'Yes.'

THREE

O'Hara tossed his jacket on to the couch and sagged down into the armchair. The girl did not come out of the kitchenette. He was glad of the respite. He was full of minor anxieties; about the house, about Marilyn, about putting an old woman into the ground tomorrow, and, most of all, he was worried because he had not been able to find Bremner. He needed Kenny, needed Kenny's help but it looked as if Kenny too had scabbed off and left him in the lurch. The flat in Whitecable Lane was locked, the windows dark. He had called up the Ousbys and found out from the chief that Bremner hadn't been around since Saturday morning and wasn't, as he had hoped, off on a haul south. The death of the old woman and Bremner's disappearance fused in his thinking, but he could not find a logic for this connection. Christ, he wished he was young again and stupid, free as a sparrow, living in his mother's house with a succession of generous uncles who were no more kin to him than he was to Marilyn. In those days nothing was expected of him and nothing was what he delivered. With the wheel of the truck in his hands and the rum roaring through him like an engine in his head he could have been hauling a slab over that early time. He could even feel the weight of the kid's body on the ground, acutely sensitive to the nature of the gesture as he pressed down the clutch pedal and engaged gear and tramped the throttle and let the truck spurt forward, dragging. The club too, a carved antique, was something with which he struck against the evil of living: the old man was part of all that he hated in life, and a person to whom the law would bow if he could only hang off the sauce long enough to scrape up the price of a bribe.

Marilyn was singing some daft bit of romantic rubbish as she brought him the pie. The plate was mounded with watery mash and a shingle of kelly-green peas. He had no appetite for food. The whisky he had downed on the way back from Kenny's house had stilted his hunger. The girl laid the plate on the table, came up behind him and rubbed his ear with her fingertips. Jesus! The tenderness was not fond or fey or innocent. He knew what she wanted.'

'Eat't, dear, before it gets cold.'

He did not even have to look round to realise that she had togged herself out in her best dress, the black middle-aged one with the silver threading around the collar. She was probably wearing the chestnut wig she had wasted good beer money on, and he could smell the cheap toilet water from the pint bottle on the shelf in the bedroom.

'What's all this in aid of?'

'All what, Alex?'

'The wife bit.'

Doyle was on the floor again, snakes of paint held in the air. Vividness in his eyes and ears and pungent smells in his nostrils and a great exultation of being in him. Down in the roots of his mind he could still feel the tremor of the truck going through him like worms through soft earth. He clamped on his senses and lay still at night in the bed with the girl, the girl curled against him like the dead thing he had made. He had created those two moments of life for himself out of death and he was not afraid of it now; the power of the doing would always be his because he had no fear left. From the old woman's passing he could suck no satisfaction: she had long since turned to mud and her dying was only dying. If he had to die like her he would fit himself for the travail with all the anger that was in him.

'Maybe I will be a wife,' the girl said.

Aye, he could marry her and live here for a while then up and leave her, but the notion not of leaving her but of going through all the trivial formalities beforehand bored him even in prospect and made crap of all the rest of it.

'We'll see,' he said.

'Worried about tomorrow?'

'What about tomorrow?'

'Going to the place?'

240

'Why should that worry me,' he asked. 'It's all taken care of.'

'Just as well she left that fifty quid with the lawyer to bury herself,' the girl said.

'Waste,' O'Hara said. 'I'd a buried her for nothin'.'

He transferred himself to the table and ate without hunger.

In the background the girl continued to sing.

Hazel was no giggling nitwit: she had done it correctly. He trusted her and did not now doubt her word. Still, that knowledge only made the delay less durable. It was as if he and not Bremner had become the bait. Head on his arms on the table, the Luger in his fist, he slept fitfully. The boy slept too.

Afternoon waned into evening and evening into night. When he wakened he came upright with a start, hearing the bellow of the wind in the chimney and the thunder of the surf, forceful, pushing. He got up stiffly and went to the fire and tossed driftwood on to the embers and returned to the table by the window and, sometimes sleeping but most often awake, sat out the rest of the night.

By daybreak on Thursday he knew that something had gone wrong, that he had misjudged O'Hara's tenacity and rashness or that in O'Hara he had found a young man with an old man's sagacity. Did O'Hara know that the long wait would affect him adversely? Was it O'Hara's intention to rub him down, wear him out, before he came? There was no danger of Bremner escaping. The notion had burned in the boy's head for a while but, Weaver thought, it had spluttered out like a flawed fuse now. When Bremner spoke to him he did not answer. He was afraid of what he would tell Bremner and of what Bremner might tell him in return. Justice was no longer involved, yet he was afraid that some sense of fairness in him still would compel him to give the boy the chance which had been taken away from Gordon and from the old man. He fed Bremner and waited, watched the track and waited, went out cautiously to the yard to pick up more fuel for the fire, and waited; then, though he knew for sure that it was futile, walked out to the tor above the chasm to keep a watch from there. When he got back from the high point above the track, Bremner was asleep again.

It was late afternoon before the boy stirred. Weaver watched him come awake, not suddenly as he himself came awake but gradually, like a mongrel on a sunny doorstep. Light flared in double measure, in the hearth and in the broken mirror of the cabinet by the door. It was wild out now and the gale tossed the thorn trees and laced the shore with spray. Cloud flew freely over the sunken horizon.

Bremner yawned and stretched his chest to the limit of his bindings.

Weaver said, '*Did* you kill him?'

He had no need to ask, no need for an answer. It was the curious sort of question which a solicitor might ask of his client after the verdict is given and the client already found guilty and committed.

'Bremner, did *you* kill him?'

He came out of the chair by the table at the window and threw himself across the kitchen. His hands found the boy's throat and the armchair rocked and cracked. The grin on the boy's mouth vanished like a crease smoothed out by a flat iron. It was that grin which had triggered Weaver; the smugness of innocence, an innocence to which this boy was not entitled and had not earned, the innocence of one to whom evil will always remain simple and who cannot be deeply touched by it because he has created his circumstances out of its heart. The mouth was kilted up in a smile which said that innocence was its own defence, like the mock leers of the child-pimps in the bright back streets of Barcelona or the cobbled alleys of Madrid; Bremner was a participator in a game he was not old enough to play properly. Leadbetter had been a coward and cowardice had been the very factor which set him so far apart from Weaver that he had been able to withdraw, let the boy go free. It wasn't so with Bremner. Bremner was the bystander, culpably innocent.

'Did you, Bremner, did you?'

He slashed his fist across that grinning mouth and the boy's fear blew up into anger and pain and all the righteous indignation of one who is entitled to worse treat-

242

ment than this. He cursed Weaver, rattled the links of the
chains, shouted; and Weaver, hatred going out of him
like blood spurting from a femoral artery, was suddenly
calm again. Even so he hit the boy a second time, coldly
not carelessly, knuckles striking into the bone so that
Bremner bled.

Now there could be no answers. He did not want
answers. Whether they had known what they were about
or what had given rise to their rage, whose hand had lifted
the rope which strangled the life from Gordon, the enigma
of what Gordon was doing there, were things which suddenly had no relevance. He was a man who had contrived
to shape an end to his particular destiny and who had
been broken in the attempt. Yes, he had bucked the city
and the women; for a time he had sunk himself in a role
more secure and comfortable than all the back kitchens
of all the tenements in the city, but the effort had broken
him, brought him by a long route to this. Gordon, and
that child that Gordon had been, were united into one
and he had come here to this lonely coast only to lay them
both in a ceremony of exorcism. All he needed to begin
was the priest of the cult; and the priest's name was
O'Hara. Down the road between cliff and sea O'Hara
would come, his shabby black vestments making him no
more than a shadow against the scrub, and O'Hara would
come straight and would not be afraid.

All Weaver needed to summon him here was patience.
In his trade surely he had learned patience above all
else. He tugged off his glove and licked the skin of his
knuckles. He dropped a clean handkerchief into Bremner's
lap.

'Wipe your mouth.'

Bremner lifted the cloth and dabbed at the wound
where his teeth had bitten through his lip.

'Listen,' the boy said, querulously. 'Listen . . . ?'

Weaver shook his head.

There was no more to say.

FOUR

The bus was empty. It shook and skidded over the broken cobbles around the periphery of the waste ground. Restlessly, O'Hara took in the scene. Soon the place would be barren no longer, and no longer recognisable. Already the foundation trenches of the highrise flats had gone down in the western sector, and the acres of shale and tamped ash over which he had bulled the truck would soon be squared off with fences. Builders' sheds and storage bays, drills and diggers, were already drawn up on the flanks, giving the land the air of an outpost, frontier village on the edges of the wilderness of Grahamshill. The freak would have a fine monument to mark the place of his death, a monument twenty stories high, ornamented with a thousand windows slanted to catch the glimmer of the sunsets over the Ridgeway.

Beneath his buttocks the seat reared and shook as if to loosen his casually morbid thoughts and shake them out through his mouth. The bus hurtled round the curve of Bankside Street and on up the foothills of the Ridgeway.

By his side the girl gripped the seat and stared straight ahead of her. As the hill steepened towards its summit the bus slowed a little, then the beginnings of the broad road began to carry them down into the outskirts of Baronwood and the stop by the gates of the crematorium.

Marilyn wore her overcoat and a knitted cap of dark blue wool, fit for solemn proceedings. O'Hara had donned a lilac shirt with a slim string tie clipped into the collar. He had neglected to shave, though, and his jaw was swarthy with a two-day growth. In spite of the wet, windswept weather he wore no overcoat, only a thin black jacket shiny at the elbows and collar. The girl was droning on, her voice rising insistently over the metallic clangour of the bus. He did not listen. It was enough to have donated his presence here today without having to give her his attention too. Even worry was a better mental

244

companion than the things she was mooing on about, gabbling about 'their future'. Soon, very soon, he would have reached a decision, but first he wanted a word with Kenny.

The cemetery was framed in the front window of the bus, then the vehicle dipped into the mansions which made up the prospect of Baronwood and the gravestones melted into the stone-coloured sky and only a few rich marble carvings of compassionate angels and virginal children remained vivid against the hill. The emptiness above the horizon was the same hue as the lawn, greenish-grey, like the sea under storm. O'Hara killed his cigarette with finger and thumb and propped the stub behind his ear. Quickly, angrily, Marilyn jerked it away and dropped it on the floor, not even breaking the stride of her monologue. O'Hara emerged from his private landscape long enough to snarl at her, but she would have none of it to-day.

'This's where we get off,' she said, primly.

Even as he preceded her down the pitching stairs her voice followed him. She was talking now about the old woman and about the house. The platform seemed to be poised out in space, pavements, trim gardens, iron gates racing the deck. The girl stood beside him, a little to the rear, one hand on his arm, the other in her pocket.

She took the letter from her pocket, held it briefly in her fingers and stared at it blankly.

The bus stopped.

O'Hara got off and turned.

'What's that?'

'Nothin'.'

She went past him and pranced towards the corner. Walking briskly now, O'Hara followed.

'In your friggin' pocket, what is it?'

'Don't know.'

He brought himself into step with her.

He did not know why the white envelope intrigued him, but her sudden slyness stimulated his interest. 'Give.'

'What?'

'That letter.'

'We're goin' t'be late.'

The knitted hat flaunted haughtily. He would have

245

grabbed her there and then if she had not evaded him by a neat side-step and ran towards the gates of the crematorium some fifty yards away. Her sudden flight was governed by fear of his irrationality and the taint of disrespect he would put on the ceremony in a place she regarded not with reverence so much as superstitious awe. O'Hara understood, but understanding did not temper his rage. He failed to catch up with her until he had crossed the line of the gates. Then, thinking herself safe in sanctuary, out of breath and rubicund with effort, she stopped to compose herself for the atmosphere of the chapel, leaned against the gold-painted scrolls and wondered just what she had been running for. At the top of the avenue of red gravel the door of the chapel was blocked with hired cars. She saw doors opening, stewards emerging, and glanced back for her man.

He caught her round the waist and dragged her to the verge.

'What's that letter?' he roared.

She had denied him. She should have known better. He slapped her cheeks. Already she was digging into her pocket to give him what he wanted. It meant nothing to her. He pushed her; she tripped and sprawled on to the grass. Staring along the ground past rearing towers of stone, she saw the chapel again and the black-garbed figures inclined towards her, startled and maybe afraid but too paralysed and shocked by the intrusion into the dignity of grief to offer assistance.

'Here, here, here,' she screamed.

She ripped her pocket and passed the envelope over her shoulder, and he took it.

She heard him tear it open, then silence, then the long hiss of his breath.

The wind scooped up her skirts and billowed them about her thighs.

'Where did y'get it?'

He kicked her, bent close.

'Through . . . through the letter box.'

'When?'

'I forget.'

'You forget,' he said. *'When, when?'*

'The night . . . the night the bogey came t'the house, when Gran died,' she sobbed. 'Monday night.'

'An' you didn't give it me.'

'M'granny just . . .'

'Jesus Christ!'

O'Hara's weight went away from her. She lay still as he hacked at her, feeling the pain, scalding her. Raindrops plopped and jerked the sapless grasses. She sobbed into them until a hand attached to an arm with a black linen diamond stitched to it reached down and touched her shoulder, then she got to her feet, adamant and independent, and staggered to the gates, yelling 'Alex.'

She'd lost a shoe. Coarse gravel pricked her sole. She stumbled and caught the gate and laced her fingers into the fretwork and pressed her brow to the big central medallion. Through a convenient curlicue in the metal she watched her man disappear, becoming smaller and smaller until he vanished over the crest of the hill, still running hard.

Sobbing, she turned to confront the startled onlookers who had lined up several yards away from her.

Across the gravel the letter rolled, a crumpled ball of pure white paper nosed by the wind. She picked it up, opened it and looked inside. Perhaps she expected some deadly object to drop into her palm, but the paper held nothing, only faint printed letters which she read. The message might have been in a foreign language. It had to do with bloody Kenny Bremner. Only for bloody Kenny Bremner would O'Hara run.

Her turgid self-pity changed into sparkling temper. She flung the paper from her and glared at the assembled mourners, as over the hill the hearse from the hospital, replete with her grandmother's corpse, slowly descended. Marilyn drew herself upright and buttoned her fury into the torn overcoat and snuffed it with the knitted hat.

When the cortège filed past, sedate and solemn, she followed it, limping all the way to the chapel door. Her gran and she went in side by side, the old lady in her coffin to the podium and Marilyn, alone, to the centre of the front row of pews.

When she got there, she wept, keening not for the old woman but for herself and the sudden revulsion of feeling

247

she had for her man. The outrage was too much even for her calloused sensibilities. He had done it this time, the madman, running off because Bremner called. From now on he could whistle for a roof over his head, hot food on the table and her comfy body to warm up his bed. She didn't give a bloody hoot if she never saw the mad bastard again.

Greerson stood in the corridor and listened. From the floors below he could hear the faint concatenation of hotel sounds, crockery and buzzers and muffled voices, but the corridor and the room behind the door were full of silence. He knocked on the panel, waited a while then knocked on the panel, waited a while then knocked again. The door came open. He hardly recognised the girl. It wasn't that she had shed any of her looks, but some ineffable quality had gone out of her, or was it that some quality had been added which had not been in her last time they met. She was less clean and neat, certainly, the cheek bones more pronounced, the make-up badly applied, and the shadows under her eyes were blue as bruises. She held the cigarette between finger and thumb and dragged on it even as she struggled to recognise him; then she gave a little grunt.

'I didn't expect you to come at once.'

Slipping into the room, he closed the door behind him. He glanced round, noting the disorder which, posh hotel or not, almost amounted to squalor. The place was foul with tobacco smoke and alcohol and in the bathroom he could see a light burning over the basin and knots of soft clothing on the floor. He did not expect Weaver to be around and, as usual, his judgement was sound.

'How are you, Hazel?'

'Awful.'

'Uh-huh!'

He had no hunger for her. Even the ungirded breasts under the thin sweater did not rouse him. It touched him, though, just a little, to realise that the Hazel Ferrier he had known had gone drifting into memory. That girl's body had been soft and sweet and had reacted to his cold assaults with a swarming sort of passion but it all might have happened to another man, as scant and lacking in

248

detail to him as evidence given by a minor witness in a case of no import.

'I'm glad you came,' she said. 'Really, I don't know what . . .'

Greerson tipped back his hat and put his hands in his pockets and sighed, not loudly but enough to let her know that his patience was not a well at which every frightened creature could come to drink at will. He wasn't here because of her, really. She had called him, urgently, but it was Weaver who had brought him here, the thought of what Weaver might have done. Anyway, McFadden was dunning him to substantiate his assertion that Weaver would be nailed, and Greerson hoped that the girl would give him just that kind of news.

'I can't stand this,' she said. 'Look, it's too . . .'

'Hazel, get a grip on yourself. Tell me what's happened.'

'I don't *know* what's happened?'

'He's . . . he's got one of them.'

'Killed him?'

'No, not yet.'

'Which one?'

'Bremner.'

'If he hasn't killed him, how do you mean, he's "got" him?'

'Held prisoner,' Hazel said. 'Ridiculous, isn't it, in this day and . . .'

'Where's he holding him?'

'In a cottage at Templehead.'

'North Ayrshire?'

'Yes.'

'I know the place,' said Greerson. 'Why has he taken Bremner?'

'As bait for O'Hara.'

'O'Hara?'

'Yes.'

So Weaver had been clever enough to find out about O'Hara. Greerson strived to calculate carefully, slowly, but his imagination accelerated his intellect and drove it too rapidly. A whirr of distress, not quite panic, sounded in him. This was more than he had bargained for. He had not counted on cunning, but on directness, urgency. O'Hara had been the time bomb in the briefcase, but the bomb had apparently turned out to be a dud. Suddenly he saw that the simplicity of his original scheme had not been a virtue after all; the looseness had been an error, a serious error. The cold-bloodedness of Weaver's tactic startled even Greerson.

'Does O'Hara know?'

'I delivered a note,' Hazel replied. 'It was wrong of me. I should have called you in then.'

'Look here, when did you deliver this . . . this note?'

'Monday evening.'

'Into O'Hara's hand?'

'Through the letter flap of his house.'

'And nothing's happened since?'

'No.'

'When did you last hear from Weaver?'

'Yesterday.'

'Directly from the cottage?'

'No, there's no line to the cottage: from a call box in the village.'

Greerson rocked on his heels, hands in pockets still. He did not look at the girl but at the carpet. 'What do you want me to do about it?'

'I don' know,' she said. 'You've *got* to do something. You're . . . you're . . . a cop.'

'Uh-huh!'

She was holding something back. He slid his attention up from the carpet to her face. She was seated on the edge of the unmade bed, huddled, her arms folded tightly across her belly as if she had cramp. Her features were contorted holding back what it was she wanted to tell him. He did not probe for it just yet. Damn bloody Weaver for taking the thing out of his bailiwick. He had not counted on it. It was just possible that Weaver had already slaughtered Bremner and O'Hara and was clean out of the country by this time. Weeks, months, might elapse before the bodies turned up. Greerson was well acquainted with the backgrounds of the lost sons of the city; no hue and cry need ever begin over their disappearance. They were, like Weaver himself, unloved, their comings and goings made vague by their waywardness and isolation. No one would take stock of them.

'How did he find O'Hara?'

250

'Leadbetter told him.'

'He saw Leadbetter? Is Leadbetter in the cottage too?'

'Weaver let him go.'

'Did he hurt him?'

'No,' the girl said. 'Terrorised him.'

Greerson laughed, and the sound took him by surprise. If innocence were bound to truth and honesty to justice then Weaver was working a different system from any he had encountered before. Behind the girl the light had dwindled and the glass was dark blue, saturated with the lamps of the river reaches and the streets of the city: dusk now and another whole day gone. The detective evaluated the variations of events which might have already taken place down on that deserted headland, weighed them carefully against what might happen in the future, his future. It could be that Weaver had killed and run, abandoning the girl. After all, she had served her purpose. Perhaps, though, there had been a slip-up. If Weaver or his victims were still alive the next few hours could be highly dangerous. His duty shift was over and he need not return home, could not return home and just sweep the girl and Weaver and the boys under the carpet.

'We'll go there,' Greerson said. Hazel looked up at him, eyes opaque, not trusting. 'We'd better. If we're in time we might be able to stop him. Is that what you want?'

She nodded, numb with her treachery.

'We'll leave separately. Meet me in ten minutes, no later, directly outside the staff entrance. You know it?'

She nodded again.

'I'm driving a Viva G.T.; you can't miss it. Ten minutes, Hazel.'

'I don't want to go there.'

'Good God, girl, I'm not going on my own. Come on, up with you. Hurry!'

Still she did not move, staring at him. He took her arm and lifted her from the bed.

'Hazel? What else?'

'No.'

'Hazel?'

'Yes,' she said firmly. 'We must go to Templehead and stop him if we can.'

251

'Hazel?'
But she had already gone into the bathroom to dress.

FIVE

It was raining hard now. The city wind was brisk and
constant. It chivvied the cowls of the chimneyheads and
sent them whirling furiously, drove flocks of landlocked
gulls to shelter on the pigeons' roosts up and down the
abandoned tenements of Whitecable Lane. The schools
were out and the first outriders of the rush hour had
already appeared in the district. O'Hara climbed the staircase. He was no longer afraid of what he would find. It
would not be Kenny.

The note was no prank. Kenny was not given to jokes
of that nature, especially at the present time. Leadbetter
was too scared ever to shake him with a note like that.
Only the old man could have done it. The old sot must
have had a harder head and more guts than he would
have thought possible to be back making smoke again so
soon. Smoke he would have now, all right, a houseful of
smoke, and fire to go with it. The note, though, was too
cryptic to carry a lie; if the old man wasn't lying then
Bremner had been taken and it was all part of a plan to
lure him out of the city to this place in Ayrshire. He had
a vague notion where Templehead was, a long spit of land
jutting out of the coast between resort towns. He could
not imagine exactly what they wanted with him,
but if they had Kenny and Kenny had cracked then
they would already have the truth. Then if they
had the truth, then they could only want his capitu-
lation, and he would not capitulate to freaks. He
would not surrender himself, not for any reason or to any
man born—even if it meant killing again. Christ, he would
blast his way through them the way road builders blast
through obstacles to forge tracks into open country. The
time lag was a real bastard, though. Four days or more

Kenny had been in their hands. Four days, thanks to that bitch of a girl. It might be better if Kenny was dead.

He rang the doorbell of Bremner's house, kicked and shouldered the wood until the lock splintered, then pushed inside. He walked into the kitchen and looked around. No snoop, he did not seek closely for clues. The immediate evidence of his eyes was enough. The working rig and boots were still in the bottom of the closet, the sleeping sack sprawled on the floor. The room held evidence of a struggle only the way a cave holds the echoes of a shout. He left the house again.

Then it was Walton Street and the smooth clean stairs up to the landing and the door of Doyle's flat, and even the heavy landing door did not deter him. He broke it down, disregarding the noise he made, and smashed the ornate glass of the inner door and stalked boldly into the hallway.

The pungent odour of chemicals had not quite evaporated but it was over-ridden now by another stronger odour which he could not make out. The house was dark but lattices of light from the doors and from other indefinable sources gave him enough definition. Though he had come forthrightly he knew by instinct that no gunner lay in wait to wipe him off. He wanted the old man, who would be hiding some place, hiding and shivering and afraid, if he was here at all. The wreckage in the parlour puzzled him, and the staleness of the bedrooms. Tangents opened in his brain like the spokes or an umbrella. Swinging the door briskly open he looked into the bathroom, saw the thing in the tub and gave out a rapid snickering groan.

The window was a plane painted with light. Frosted glass threw forth reflections like the colour of a TV screen, silvery-grey. The sheeting round the bundle propped against the taps had something of the same colour to it, phosphorescent, like a huge fish rotting under wraps. The smell was rife in the room; not the heated, feverish stench of corruption but a clammy thickness which made itself felt not only to the nose but to the other sense organs too, a dampness on the skin, almost visible, like a faint ectoplasm. A three-dimensional negative, a carving in alloy painted black, the thing in the bathtub did not move.

'Kenny!' O'Hara instantly sealed up his lips to close out the taste. He inched forward and stood by the side of the bundle, wholly enveloped in its aura. His hands were at his chest, pinched, the fingers nervously moving as if tolling a rosary on a chain round his neck.

A tasselled hem of eight or ten inches of scotch tape had uncurled from the region of the lower jaw. Putting out one hand, O'Hara gripped the tape. His elbow shook and his wrist was animated by a kind of dread. He furled it back and ticked loose an edge of the plastic, peeling the sheet away until a gout of blood, thick and black as molasses, dribbled out and his control snapped. He ripped at the covering, tore it, shredded it way from the face, then leaned forward, peering, thrusting. The old man's battered visage stared sightlessly back at him.

Released from the unexpected pain, he cursed the dead old man. He was no longer even revolted by the cadaver, raged at the mystery of it and at the cleverness of the operator who had thus arranged its secret display for his benefit. Still mouthing, he completed the round of the flat and left it too.

When he reached the street he lengthened his stride, walking very fast towards territory he knew and to a particular locale from which he would steal a car. He needed transport.

He had delayed long enough.

Blowing hard off the sea the wind was salt raw. It sought to weld the violence of the surf to rock and pasture, hill and tree, caught Weaver too in its indiscriminate fury and flailed him as it flailed all things living and dead. Even the lichen on the boulders against which he huddled to keep warm flaked under the impetus of the gale, peeling like paint crust where he laid his hand. Dusk had swept the distant arc of the bay and obliterated the metallic needles and the frieze of the town. Soon it would be too dark to keep watch at all; then he would withdraw once more to the hellish confinement of the cottage, and contain his rage and his pity throughout another interminable night.

The urge to kill Bremner out of hand tortured him now. Could he wrest life from the boy in lieu of penitence? If they were all here, every one of those men and women who had made him what he was, would they somehow conspire to reduce Bremner too to an image of their own disaffection. What was it now? No juryman's ritual but a calculated death, a private gallows, a firing squad of one. He was the one, the marksman, and he was responsible. But how would they tell him to act? Those who had lost nothing but their belief in law would give him thumbs up, but the others, the many, many others would show him the killing sign. He could not escape the finality of judgement, the judgement on him. At least the shreds of ambiguity would be gone, and Muriel and Doyle and Gordon, Hazel, Greerson, Fleming, maybe even Brown, would give him the last frantic nod, issue the decree and put his strength on test for the final time. Why must he bear their weaknesses in addition to his own?

God, if he had been O'Hara he would have come before now; would have rushed eagerly to it, not like a martyr but like a soldier who believes in the beauty of warfare and the hot glory in it. He could not survive another night in the cottage with the boy.

Against the cascade of branches on the shoulder of the road, side-lights showed, faintly yellow like feral eyes. They were far off as yet, beyond the croft. He set no stock by them; he had fancied lights before.

They swerved, travelling fast, and came on fast up the track, rushing, writing erratically against the darkness. Once more they swerved and he could, he thought, see the glint of the fender between; then they stopped, pointing in a slant at the sky. He made out the figure by the bonnet and knew it was O'Hara.

Weaver rolled away from the boulder, slid to the track beyond the pass and, running hard into the wind, struck back towards the cottage where Bremner lay asleep.

An ugly dwarf in a fisherman's sweater came to the back door of the post office, inclined out of the light and watched. O'Hara paused, waiting, but the man did not challenge him. He leaned on the gate and called out, 'Where's the cottage?'

'That way.' The dwarf pointed with his whole arm to the north-west, along the line of the coast.

'Thanks.'

He did not have enough control of himself now to be cautious, yet he had held himself beyond the vibrations of the light. He had known that it would be that cottage; the map in the locker of the stolen Rover showed it, a little rectangle neatly isolated along the wriggle of the coastline. He set off along the track in the darkness.

A narrow opening in the rocks brought him up short. He hung back from it, peering up at the tops of the boulders and into the scrub country above. The gale flicked at his hair and bellied out the breast of his jacket. It tugged at the heavy section of angle-iron which he had filched from the Rover's boot, tugged at it as if to disarm him. The roar of the breakers and the flurry of the trees swallowed his breath and he clung to the fence-post to anchor himself, waiting. Finding no alternative, after a minute, he trotted up the little summit between the high rocks, eyes raised to the paler patch of sky above in expectation of an ambush. Hugging the inside of the track he sidled clear of the chasm and emerged on to the fringe of the pasture. A sodden glimmer of light was on it still and away at the end of the plain, the cottage stood behind trees. Strangely, the buildings did not merge into the heavy darkness of the hill but caught some of that sourceless glimmer on gable walls and on the slope of the roofs. O'Hara glanced over his shoulder. Behind him, low set but visible, was a fragment of moon, fretted by the driving piles of scud. By its light he planned his approach.

Leaping a ditch he took to the fields, striking off across the stubble, aiming at the scrub under the protection of the cliff. Crows rose from late feeding in the furrows, heavy winged, croaking, then resettled in his wake. Their sudden raucous croaking made him sweat. Crouching low, he passed quickly down the nether end of the field until the tilled earth gave way, without benefit of fencing, to a tangle of birch and alder. As sure-footed as a poacher bred to night stalking, O'Hara swung left and picked his way towards the rear of the cottage buildings, less hurried now, shifting with as little sound as possible through the cover.

The reek of the farmstead had long since been ousted by salt-rot and vegetable dampness. It reminded O'Hara of the smell of backcourt wash-houses and the steep of

256

clothes in the cauldron. Slithering down from the embankment he dropped silently to broken flagstones behind the sheddings. Wind thrummed and whinnied in the orifices of corroded masonry, the sound deeper and more deliberate than the thrashing of the trees. He went down the side of the wall to the first door and laid his forefinger into the latch. The door squawked. He inclined himself into the darkness, squinting, the angle-piece greasy in his fist, the door like a shield across his body. As his eyes adjusted to the musty gloom he saw that the interior was empty. A crazy excitement was in him now and he fought to hold himself in stealth, to be furtive. He closed and latched the door again and darted five or six yards further along the wall to the next door, swung it gingerly open too. Beams and empty tackle, a drapery of chains signified nothing to him. As far as he was concerned the place was inhabited only by the ammoniac memory of horses or cattle. He pushed on once more, to the cottage itself.

A kitchen window, bug-stained, opaque with brine and dirt, was just clear enough to release the glow of a lamp or candle in the room at the forefront of the house. O'Hara groped for the latch and triggered it but the door would not give and he did not dare force it. He wanted to force it, though, to give vent to the destructive power which was strong in him. The impulses were injudicious, suicidal, came up from his gut and hung him tight. He made an effort to restrain his impetuosity a little longer.

Skirting the north-westerly gable he came to the front of the building. The sea was loud now and the surf on the shingle formed a pale mobile line in the middle distance. The car was unmistakable, a big Jaguar, a Mark 10; O'Hara's lingering doubts dissolved. He studied the car carefully to make sure it did not contain a sniper, then crept up to the single window and stood on the very edge of the rug of light which it cast into the yard. Stooping, he crouched under the sill and came up slowly, flicking his gaze into the room.

A fire flared high in the iron grate, creating warmth and a fall of light more diffuse but stronger than the plume of the oil lamp's wick. The funnel of the lamp was close to him. It nestled in the window recess like a beacon put out in memory of more hospitable times, a welcome to travel-

257

lers or the menfolk home from the fields. Before the fire
was a high-backed chair. A person was seated in the armchair, the fold of a blanket, the creasing of the leather
suggesting that the person was sound asleep. O'Hara
reckoned it might be Kenny; he was not so certain, however, that he responded immediately. He was nervous now,
but not afraid, keen. His fingertips brushed the icy surface
of the glass. The shadow of his hand projected out upon
the stones behind him. Worming his nails under the frame
he coaxed the window from its runnel and eased it up an
inch or two. It grated and squeaked slightly but he went
on steadily until the gap was six inches or more and the
wind found it, scooped through, billowed the tattered
curtains and winnowed the lamp-wick. Smoke bloomed
fatly from the funnel and obscured his view of the room.

Something inside O'Hara burst. He bellowed out Bremner's name and heaved the window frame high and flung
one leg over the sill. He swung the angle-iron before him
like a scythe to ward off anyone who might be lurking
there, then the voice said, clearly, 'Wait.'

Already in the act of lifting his body into the room,
O'Hara flung his head round. His shadow on the stones
was massive now, consuming all the light, mingled and
blotted up by the shadow of the man. Unprotected,
trapped, O'Hara did not move. Even in the darkness he
realised that the man had a gun in his fist.

'I knew you would come, O'Hara.'

O'Hara screamed, 'Where's Kenny? I've come for
Kenny.'

The boom of the gun was warped and thinned out by
the wind; even so it was loud enough to deafen him. He
fell backward into the yard.

The shot stunned Weaver. He had not intended to squeeze
the trigger and supposed that, after all, he had killed
O'Hara outright. He snapped his finger away from the
Luger as if by that belated action he could undo what
damage he had already done: then he heard the shattering
of the glass and the tinkle of the chips tumbling to the
paving and saw light flood out from the window space and
the swaying shape of the young man, and was grateful for
the bounty which chance had again bestowed on him.

258

O'Hara's scarred cheek was high-lighted, the iron bar magnified for a brief moment; O'Hara was back on his feet and coming at him hard. Clenching the Luger by the stock, Weaver raised the gun again and backed up two paces. Shoulders flung forward in the exaggerated pose of a sprinter coming out of the blocks, O'Hara halted.

'I come for Kenny.'

'You've got to take me first,' Weaver said. 'Come on.'

Ponderously O'Hara lifted the angle-iron, hefting it to a level with his face, but out, like a torch, a brand, but he did not come on again.

'Or do you only take on kids and old men?' Weaver said.

'Bastard.' The word was caressingly soft.

Weaver could see nothing of O'Hara's face, only the claw around the bar, the hand which had knotted the ropes around Gordon's wrists, the hand which had lifted the club and brought it down on Doyle's defenceless head.

'I'm Gordon Weaver's . . .'

'Kenny dead?'

Weaver shook his head.

'You don't give a damn who I am, do you, O'Hara?'

'Is Kenny dead?'

Weaver changed his position. He shifted from the packed gravel to the flagstones again. It had all been for nothing; all the planning and the elaborate schemes had been so much waste. Christ, he could have taken O'Hara in any dark alley in Wickerburn or North Grahamshill for all the difference it would have made. Remorse, the catharsis of fear, were not his to demand. He had no right to speak to this man; the thing between them was physical. O'Hara, perhaps, was an embodiment of the devil in himself, the little carping demon, yelling now to cohabit with its soul-mate in the gut of the boy. This had nothing to do with Gordon. Now he saw it. Now he saw that he had long ago killed Gordon in his heart and had assumed that he had been dead to the boy even as the boy was dead to him. All that was really left to him was the exercising of his skill, that talent which had matured into the image he had built out of unreality and the illusion of luck. He held the Luger casually, quite relaxed.

O'Hara zoned him, crouched, his weight in the springs of his calves and his thighs, wary of taunts and the invitation to carry the attack. Weaver slipped on down the flank of the Jaguar, wide of it, stepping backward, pushed by O'Hara's unrelenting advance, yet leading him. He kept retreating, gingerly, until the thorn trees' desiccated ranks would let him retreat no further. A pale flit of moonlight showed him where O'Hara was. He prayer that the young man would have the wit to understand. Cocking the Luger, he snatched the trigger and let the bullet wing off into the roaring wind above the cottage.

O'Hara dropped, huddled close to the Jaguar's tyre.

Weaver pumped out another round.

It was so easy to fire the automatic. It would be so easy to kill with it, to drill the cranium, to perforate the lungs, to open a mortal wound in the belly. As he had intended, the bullet ricocheted wildly off the slates. Scuttling and perhaps afraid at last, O'Hara reached up and jerked the handle of the door of the Mark 10. To confirm it, Weaver fired a third time. Recoiling a little, he looked up and saw O'Hara behind the wheel.

The beams of the headlamps cut the darkness and pinned him like a fish on the tines of a trident. He turned his back on the car and ran.

He ran down the path to the track and through an open gate at the merging of field and garden, ran on over the borders of the potato shaws. The gale was dense here, filled with spume and debris plucked up from the shore. The Jaguar rolled out of the gate, fifty yards behind him. He ran faster, too fast for a man of his age, yet heart and lungs might have been rigorously exercised just to stand the strain of this moment. He felt no labouring, no strain in them. His goal lay ahead on the crests of the swollen, nervous storm-sea. He felt intoxicated, swallowing air in long sobbing draughts, running even harder now, his head flung back, running with a free flowing stride, limbs in rhythm, no hurting in his mind or his body. Oblivious to what he had engineered and what this final part of it really signified, he ran as if the wind had plucked him up and carried him seaward like a stalk of straw or a gull's feather or an empty shell.

All about him the lanterns of the car bobbed, illuminating the tussocks or the verge or the whale-black rocks, drumming the sound of the engine over him so that he could feel it even through that matted mass of other turbulent sounds.

Reaching the drainage ditch, he hopped over it, tripped on a grass snare, stumbled and fell heavily on his belly, driving the air from his lungs. On the track the car fled past him, rammed to a halt and reversed, whining. Just as he got to his feet, the long snout went past again. He reeled on to the scored ledges of the shore. The Jaguar pitched over the verge and obligingly rippled out a carpet of light all the way to the surf. He went on down it, digging his heels into the loose shingle, struggling now, close to his limit, off the land into the sea.

Slick tongues of surf lashed his thighs and pounded his back and he stopped, bracing himself against the waves, pushing his buttocks into them, holding himself upright. The beams narrowed on him, the engine snarled and the big sleek shape of the car flew at him along rails of light. The cold fluid strength of the sea and the power of the gale held him and the light bathed him in a liquid glow, like guilt. The prow struck him in the groin. He flung up his arms and barked with astonishment, and the car came on and gored him clean, lifting him from the leaves of water. His chest and head smashed down upon the bonnet and his torso was broken over the grill.

The car dipped into the shallows, stopped, reversed abruptly, shedding Weaver's body like so much ballast. He slipped and slithered back and the breaking wave swallowed him. A long strident blast on the Jaguar's horn followed him into torrential darkness and the last flutter of life before he drowned.

SIX

Milling up shingle and great cartwheels of spray, the Jaguar bogged down and bedded axle-deep a yard back from the sea's edge. With the door gaping and the engine

261

throbbing, O'Hara abandoned it. He was sweating heavily, a little drunk with the power and the triumph of the chase. He leaned on the car, looking out over the headlamps to the waves. There was no sign of the man's body, no sign at all. O'Hara was not curious. Kenny would be able to explain who he had been and what it all meant and together they would devise some plan to thwart the snoops and buzzards who would sooner or later descend on this deserted beach and try to place the blame. He pushed himself away and swarmed up the beach and over the rocks, back to the cottage.

The stranger had been a freak too, a weakling without the skill to fire properly, to wound him or kill him. The shots had been pure panic reactions, and yet they reminded him of the kid's reactions to the rope, and the last run had a quality about it which he could not at that moment define. He was more afraid of the barren coastline and the broken-down cottage now that he had been before. Was it possible that there were others? He didn't think so. Only Kenny. He trotted across the yard and climbed through the open window into the living room, calling out to Kenny that he had finally arrived.

The winged chair was empty.

Only a huddle of blankets covered it. O'Hara lifted them, bewildered, and looked beneath them as if he thought that Kenny might be hiding out. In pique he kicked the chair across the room. He yanked open the cupboard by the fire then, shouting loudly, wended through the cottage's rooms and cubbies in search of Bremner. He did not find him.

He tried the outbuildings and the yards, bawling Bremner's name, full of spleen, cheated. He traversed the litter of sheddings and returned at last to the broken window of the living room. The fever was dwindling in him and a weakness crept up in its stead. He slumped against the wall, his arms spread to embrace the frame, the empty room, fire-lit, against his chest, the wind pressing on him. Sweat cooled stiffly across his skin and his gut heaved. He kept his head down, gathering himself, then, after a minute, broke away once more from the cottage, fell back into the yard and wheeled out on to the track.

He jogged loose at first, contained, then increased his

pace trotting then running as hard as the man had done along the same rough line, leaping the ditch, scrambling over the rocks to the shingle. The last of his control was gone. He ran frantically, fearfully, over the pebble beach towards the Jaguar by the water's edge.

Hazel gripped Greerson's arm. 'There.'

'O'Hara.'

'Yes,' she said. 'O'Hara. He got here before us after all.'

Greerson cut the lights and drifted the Viva up past the cottage yard and along the track after the boy's flying shape.

'Weaver,' Hazel said.

'Best worry about O'Hara first,' Greerson said.

He stopped and peered from the windscreen, using the faint slant of moonlight to follow the running man. The man, the boy, O'Hara, seemed oblivious to their arrival, like a person stunned by shock or driven by unmitigated arrogance.

The Viva jarred over the ruts of the track, and the wind sucked the sounds away and dispersed them over the cliff-top. Hazel glanced behind her and, with a kind of longing, saw the lighted window of the cottage warm in the partial darkness.

'Look,' Greerson told her. 'Down there: what is it?'

On the beach the Jaguar was almost swamped by the flood-tide, the waves lashing over the grill, flecking the headlamps with foam.

'Weaver's car,' she said.

Quickly Greerson climbed from the Viva. Hazel, though, clung to the car, reluctant to step out into the wind, into the dreadful discoveries which waited for her there. She watched the detective grab at his hat, pick his way cautiously over the edge of the track and mount the rocks. He stood motionless for a moment, then went down out of sight. Immediately a frantic longing welled up in her. She could not see Weaver, could not find him there in the rushing darkness. Reaching forward she switched on the Viva's lights but even in the dim fork of their spots she could not make out the meaning of what was happening there on the beach below.

She quit the shelter of the car and, drawn up, trailed

Greerson over the rocks to the shingle spit. The wind stung her, made her eyes water but she did not blink against it. All the tiny muscles were frozen and she could not look away. No more could she retreat. Her feet probed for holds in the shifting surface, her legs prompted her forward towards the white sea rime and the tableau built at the back of the big car. She would have gone on down and made herself part of it, if Greerson's arm had not barred her, caught her by the waist. She craned over it, seeing what it was that drew her and what it meant.

In the slivers of light from the boot of the car, it was all quite clear. O'Hara knelt on the pebbles, knees buried deep, little hasty mounds of stones and piles of scraped sand around him, the rubber of the sunken tyre exposed. Ropes were still coupled to the axle-tree, snaked out of sight under the sill, but O'Hara had found what he came here to find, held it in his arms, across his belly. Bremner's head was thrown back and the neck stretched, both oddly elongated, his battered skull cradled in the hollow of O'Hara's thighs, mouth open and the tongue curled up like a small soft animal in its lair. By that grotesque expression it appeared that he had died laughing, tickled by some strange private joke which only he was wily enough to understand.

Greerson imposed his will on her as he might have restrained a dog, not speaking, holding her back with his arm. She could not go on now, anyway, not even to the man who knelt on the shingle or to the thing which had floated up out of the dark sea into the full flush of the lamps. Thrust forth for inspection by the tidal drift, it had the slackness of a straw effigy, hollow-limbed and lifeless.

'Weaver?' Greerson asked.

'Yes.' she nodded. 'Yes.'

Now she would never learn the truth, if the sacrifice had been made out of vanity not love, out of hopeless resignation. Now she would be denied contact with that source of merciless power which for a time she had been foolish enough to confuse with strength.

She did not wait to watch Greerson lug the body from the waves or hear him mutter formal warnings to what was left alive of the man with the livid scar by his mouth and weeping eyes. Angrily she shook herself free of his restraint and turned away, walked with the wind at her back over the beach and over the rocks on to the track, walking still towards the light in the window of the cottage where no one lived.

EPILOGUE

He did not know why he had come to this place. It was reached without conscious decision, because it was quiet and his footsteps sounded firm on the old sunken cobbles. But when he came to it he knew where he was and what odd quirk of recollection had guided his aimless wandering to this particular spot.

The rope was frayed, the tyre bald, the tree branch denuded and the elm itself sick and mottled and unsafe; yet it seemed to him just as it had been then, only a step over the low wall of the deserted mansion. The tyre cast oval shadows across the grassland and the earth under it was worn into a brick-red patch, down over the place where his father had stood. He had perched in the hoop of the tyre, smelling it, gripping it tightly. The man had steadied him, hands on his waist, and asked him if he was ready and he said *yes*. The hands had lifted him up, giving security and momentum at one and the same time, and he had gone up laughing into the lavender sky and then come swooping down, like a swallow, seeing the woman below him looking up, and his father's hands had steadied him once more, and pushed. Even the woman seemed to have gone, though she was still his mother and the same, he supposed. It did not occur to him to step over the broken wall, to sit in the swing. It would be too small for him now, anyway; and the man wasn't around. Five years seemed like a long time; five years or more since the soft spring night when they had walked together up from Wickerburn to the heights of Ridgeway to breathe the scent of the grass and the flowers.

At first his mother told him that his father would come back; then she told him nothing, would not speak of it;

then she told him that his father would not come home; and, latterly, that he was dead. Though she screamed it at him many times, still he did not believe her. Now she was kind to him and anxious for him to accept the new father, Brand. He couldn't do it; he hated Brand and he might even have learned to hate his mother too if the ingrained habits had not been in him. Brand laughed too, shouting laughter at him; but it was unreal, not meant. His own father did not laugh much and when he did it was short and sharp in his throat, but it was real. His father had laughed that night on the Ridgeway, here, as he had gone higher and higher into the smoke-blue sky. His mother had called out to him and his father's hands had been tight about him and he could hear that laughter and see the way his father had been, tall and neat and confident and full of laughter. When he stepped back from the wall the angles of the shadows changed, intersected like the petals of a black flower in the breeze. But there was no breeze tonight. The air was cold and still and the city behind him was like an ocean shrouded in mist. He knew it was late and that he should begin the long journey home but he liked it here and did not want to go. He liked it here in the quiet tree-lined street, alone; better than the club, better than home too now.

When they had told him exactly what Fleming was he did not believe them, but he had lately come to understand and knew that it was true. The novelty of understanding things, many things, held him to old haunts and uncomfortable runs. Since they had told him what Fleming planned to do to him, he had learned much from the sounds in the bedroom, guttural laughter and muttered words, demands. Maybe his mother's smothered giggling, like a girl, a child, was the worst of all sounds. So familiar but ill-considered phrases had finally acquired meaning for him and he understood what they meant about Fleming and how it was possible. Image overlaid image in his mind, like the ellipses of the shadows of the tyre hung from its threadbare rope on the tree in the empty garden. How it was when Brand had taken her from the table at the end of the evening meal and they had gone together out of the kitchen: then the meat had stuck in his gullet and he had spat it on to his plate and gone out into the lobby to

leave. Down in the depths of the lobby the open door and
the tilt of the wardrobe mirror had shown him the new
thing too, the man's massive nakedness and the smear of
flesh that was his mother over the chair by the electric fire.
He closed his eyes and went out, knowing that the house
was not his house any longer but Brand's. It cost him
effort to go back there, but he had no other place to go
and could not loosen the caring that was in him, either,
half selfish. What Brand had shown, maybe intentionally,
had ten names he knew of and purposes he could not com-
prehend, but he did not think it was a thing to boast about
or covet. When he thought of what manhood was, he
thought of the shape of his father's hands and the fit of
them around his ribs or shaped around his own small fist;
and the other thing was irreconcilable. There was nobody
he could ask to explain it to him. They had killed his trust
in Fleming and even his grandfather was unapproachable,
most of the time.

His grandfather was an old man behind a haze; what he
hoped for he never got—only money; a shilling or a florin
pressed into his palm. Only lately had he come to realise
that he embarrassed the old man who, with more words
sunk in him than in all the books on the shelves of his
shop, could find none mild enough and safe enough with
which to make communication. How could the old man
even hear him? Sweet and vague with whisky from the
bottles with the two dogs on the labels, Grandpa Doyle
would not tell him the things he most wanted to know,
about his father and how his father was not dead. If he
asked, the old man would only have grinned at him and
winked and offered him ginger pop out of a dirty glass
and chocolate from a drawer in the table and the usual
silver coin. Maybe if he pushed, the old man would frown
over his glasses and growl, 'Best to forget it, lad. Best to
forget it.' And he would shout, 'Forget what?', and the
old man's milky indifference might turn to anger and
there would no longer even be the minor consolations of
chocolate and florin pieces.

They imagined that they were protecting him, but he
sensed now that they were only protecting themselves. He
could not capitulate yet, had not learned that knack. He
had to push on through the humiliations of trying to ask,

trying to find out, without giving offence. So he would sit in the musty kitchen in which the only clean smell was the smell of the whisky and struggle to frame the questions innocently, and would watch the old man fading away even as his mother was fading away and know that soon he would be relieved of the hopelessness of trying, of mouthing things of no importance. The most urgent need of all was to discover what made them afraid, what it was that they withdrew from, so that he too might learn a defence against it, young. Perhaps he was learning it, how to close the door, to shutter himself within the small and utterly private room he had inside his brain and which he would not now open to anyone. Only the sound of the soft dry sharp laughter entered because he could not yet blot it out.

As he dropped downhill from the Ridgeway and set off across the waste ground towards the lights, the sound seemed to come to him. Once he was back in the Wickerburn it would go away and he would forget the feelings that the sight of the swing had given him. He walked steadily but without haste across the deserted lot. The circle of threadbare rubber receded behind him as if he had stepped out of it, like out of a tunnel or a hole in an invisible wall. Distances were around him again and the faint dunning of traffic came from beyond the houses. The Wickerburn was a long way off, but he wasn't tired. The centre of the plain was dark like a lake of oil, thinned and watered round the edges by street lamps and lights cast through the houses. The truck was beyond the darkness, clearly visible, gaunt and isolated like abandoned junk or a civic monument.

The truck had no meaning for him. He hardly noticed it, went on his own undeviating course towards the standard nearest on the bordering road. Then the men were visible too. He took them for workmen on a late shift. He had no business with them nor they with him.

He walked on.

His exercises in the study of consequences had not progressed far enough for him to recognise danger. His thinking was still a little fuddled by the swings of memory. Hands in pockets, he strolled on. Only when he looked up and saw the young man planted before him did a glimmer of recognition cross his mind. He felt he had seen the face before but he could not put a name to it. The young man was squat, burly, and drunk.

He was, even now, indifferent.

He took another pace forward, stepping to one side, and the man stepped out too like a shadow. A first twinge of apprehension touched him deep down. If he could think of a name to put to the face the man might tell him what he wanted with him. He waited with the mild despair of one who has waited too long and too often for explanations which never came. Close to the young man now, he could smell the stale sweetness of beer. He stopped, waiting to be told. He had done nothing wrong and therefore was not afraid of punishment.

Then the lights hit him and dazzled him. He heard another voice shouting out. They wanted his attention, wanted him to recognise them even in drink, but they were still blurred and vague, and he could not. The truck was roaring loudly and the voices were closer, shouting and full of fury and hatred. He sighed at their mockery of authority and shook his head and took a last step forward.

The blow stunned him; one chop, hard and unexpected. Pain went squirming through his head and he could no longer think straight. He had nothing of value that they could want from him. Arms drawn back, their bodies rubbed against him, rough and heavy as the flanks of cattle. He breathed in the sour cloud of beer, sour not sweet now, and the mouth was close to his mouth; then he was struck from behind again. The sky seemed to brighten to the hue of lavender silk and the ash pack beneath his knees to blow and billow like a sea wave. Not quite enveloped in darkness yet he clung to them, hung between them as they dragged him along. The voices muttered, sly and adamant, and he heard the echo of a guttural laugh, then he gave up trying to think and did not struggle against the hands. The hands pinned him, nailed his wrists and shoulders, hooked into his hair. His head snapped back. For an instant he was jerked out of despair. He seized the chance to call out once, call out aloud.

'Daddy,' he shouted. 'Da . . .'

And then they put the rope around his mouth and pulled it tight.

McBAIN
A MATTHEW HOPE MYSTERY

SNOW WHITE AND ROSE RED
by ED McBAIN

Sarah Whittaker, said her attorney, was nuttier than a fruitcake. When Matthew Hope visited her in the institution he was half-expecting some shaven-headed basket case in a uniform that looked like mattress ticking.

Instead Sarah Whittaker was wearing a wheat-coloured linen suit and a saffron silk blouse open at the throat. She had a generous mouth and eyes as green as the Amazon jungle and Matthew Hope fell in love with her on the spot.

'So why are you here?' he asked. 'Ah,' she said, and started to tell him a story. And it certainly wasn't the kind of tale a mother would read to her children at bedtime . . .

0 7221 5726 6   CRIME   £2.95

A CLASSIC CRIME THRILLER . . .

THE SENTRIES

ED McBAIN

Jason Trench had had it up to here with the way
those Commies were giving his country the
runaround. If the politicos weren't going to get
up off their fat butts and do something then he sure
as hell would. He wanted action *now*.

Jason wasn't just some patriotic fruitcake who'd
seen one too many John Wayne movies. Jason
had a plan. He had forty-two loyal men behind him
and they were even crazier than he was. He didn't
need speeches or slogans.

He had guns. And he used them . . .

0 7221 5762 2   CRIME   £2.95

Also by Ed McBain in Sphere Books:
JACK AND THE BEANSTALK
SNOW WHITE AND ROSE RED

FICTION

CYCLOPS	Clive Cussler	£3.50☐
THE SEVENTH SECRET	Irving Wallace	£2.95☐
CARIBBEE	Thomas Hoover	£3.50☐
THE GLORY GAME	Janet Dailey	£3.50☐
NIGHT WARRIORS	Graham Masterton	£2.95☐

FILM & TV TIE-IN

INTIMATE CONTACT	Jacqueline Osborne	£2.50☐
BEST OF BRITISH	Maurice Sellar	£8.95☐
SEX WITH PAULA YATES	Paula Yates	£2.95☐
RAW DEAL	Walter Wager	£2.50☐
INSIDE STORY	Jack Ramsay	£2.50☐

NON-FICTION

A TASTE OF LIFE	Julie Stafford	£3.50☐
HOLLYWOOD A' GO-GO	Andrew Yule	£3.50☐
THE OXFORD CHILDREN'S THESAURUS		£3.95☐
THE MAUL AND THE PEAR TREE	T.A. Critchley & P.D. James	£3.50☐
WHITEHALL: TRAGEDY AND FARCE	Clive Ponting	£4.95☐

Cash sales form:

All Sphere books are available at your local bookshop or newsagent, or can be ordered direct from the publisher. Just tick the titles you want and fill in the form below.

_____

Name_____

Address_____

_____

Write to Sphere Books, Cash Sales Department, P.O. Box 11, Falmouth, Cornwall TR10 9EN

Please enclose a cheque or postal order to the value price plus: UK: 60p for the first book, 25p for the second book and 15p for each additional book ordered to a maximum charge of £1.90.

OVERSEAS & EIRE: £1.25 for the first book, 75p for the second book and 28p for each subsequent title ordered.

BFPO: 60p for the first book, 25p for the second book plus 15p per copy for the next 7 books, thereafter 9p per book.

Sphere Books reserve the right to show new retail prices on covers which may differ from those previously advertised in the text elsewhere, and to increase postal rates in accordance with the P.O.